I'd call Buxton a ghost town but that would make it sound so much livlier than it is. There are two fish and chip shops. Dolphins is shut today. The other one, The Friery, ofers something called 'Chinese chicken curry and chips'. I suppose that's globalisation for you. I chose to take my chances elsewhere.

The whole town feels damp. Buxdon smells a bit like the dungeon at Warwick castle, with an added overtone of exhaust fumes. It's the kind of place you might expect to find a Wimpy, except that I couldn't. The Market Square is dominated by a looming car park on one side, and on the other side by a block of offices the colour of an oily puddle. I thought any moment I was going to wake up in a cold sweat and discover I was Prince Charles. There were a couple of empty White Lightning bottles and chip trays lying around the war memorial.

D09933399

Paul Vlitos was born in 1979. Having lived and taught in Japan for several years, Paul can confirm that the Sunday feeling really is an international phenomenon. His previous novel, *Welcome to the Working Week*, is also available is Orion paperback.

By Paul Vlitos

Welcome to the Working Week
Every Day is Like Sunday

Every Day is Like Sunday

Paul Vlitos

An Orion paperback

First published in Great Britain in 2008
by Orion
This paperback edition published in 2009
by Orion Books Ltd,
Orion House, 5 Upper St Martin's Lane,
London WC2H 9EA

An Hachette UK company

10 9 8 7 6 5 4 3 2 1

Copyright © Paul Vlitos 2008

The right of Paul Vlitos to be identified as the author
of this work has been asserted by him in accordance
with the Copyright, Designs and Patents Act 1988.

All rights reserved. No part of this publication may be
reproduced, stored in a retrieval system, or transmitted,
in any form or by any means, electronic, mechanical,
photocopying, recording or otherwise, without the
prior permission of the copyright owner.

All the characters in this book are fictitious,
and any resemblance to actual persons, living
or dead, is purely coincidental.

A CIP catalogue record for this book
is available from the British Library.

ISBN 978-0-7528-8459-2

Printed and bound in Great Britain by CPI Mackays, Chatham, Kent.

The Orion Publishing Group's policy is to use papers that
are natural, renewable and recyclable products and
made from wood grown in sustainable forests. The logging
and manufacturing processes are expected to conform to
the environmental regulations of the country of origin.

www.orionbooks.co.uk

Acknowledgements

I'd like to thank the following people for their advice and encouragement during the writing of this book: Katy Vlitos, my parents, Cara Jennings, Oliver Seares, Louise Joy, Alex von Tunzelmann, David McAllister, Julia Jordan, Florence Gibbs, Dorothea Gibbs, Tim Robey, Claire Sargent, Sarah Deane, Pete Ewing, Mark Farley, Kate Montero, Rupert Taylor, Alex Smith, Jennifer Smith, Ella Smith, Lucy Daniel and Binx.

For their kindness, generosity and friendship I would also like to thank Professor Eiichi Hara, Miki Iwata, Peter Robinson, Ornella Robinson, Mattie and Giulia Robinson, Wataru Fukushi, Chikako Saito, Machiko Fujita, Akiko Nanbu, Kazuhiko Saigusa, Stephanie Assmann, Satoshi Ogihara, Denis Devienne, Daniela Lupsa, Rory Rosszell, Isabelle Giraudou, Peter Connell, Thomas Schaefer, Marion Hegemann, Cecilia Silva, Sumio Yamada, Dave Taylor and my students and colleagues at Tohoku University.

Very special thanks also to my agent Gráinne Fox, and to Genevieve Pegg, Jon Wood, Jade Chandler, Angela McMahon and the team at Orion Books.

Prologue

It didn't look so bad from the train. They passed trees, hedgerows, a cow ruminating in the corner of a field. The announcer recited the familiar litany of stations: Elmsfield, Little Chipping, Buxdon ...

For a moment Matt felt an impulse to get off at Buxdon, to wander over to the school and see if any of the old gang were still about. He stifled the urge without much difficulty as they drew into town. Buxdon station, as ever, looked not only closed but quarantined. The shutters were down on the jauntily grim sandwich shop, the platform deserted. The remains of a bike were chained, de-wheeled and seatless, to the railings.

It was ten years since Matt had last been along this line. Another country, the 1990s. What did people do there? Apart from being quite impressed with e-mailing, listening to drum 'n' bass and thinking Howard Marks was cool. There was an inexplicable lime-green shirt in Matt's cupboard at home that he was pretty sure was never going to come back into fashion. Mercifully he didn't think he'd ever worn it to teach in.

Why had he taken the job at Buxdon in the first place? As the train pulled away, Matt tried and failed to recall. He remembered explaining his reasons to Caroline, and he'd certainly convinced himself they were logical. Presumably Buxdon had seemed like the least bad option at the time. Certainly better than more substitute-teaching in London, or going back to Japan for another year of TEFL. Back then, twenty-six had seemed a little old for temping. Besides, he'd needed some space and time to work on his book.

Caroline had remained sceptical, and with some justification. Matt had tried to win her over by pointing out that, like most so-called public schools, Buxdon was in fact a registered charity. The headmaster reminded the boys of this during the first assembly of each school year, and told them to mention it if ever anyone was giving them 'bother' about being the beneficiaries of elitism. This still ranked as some of the worst advice Matt had ever heard. Caroline's final words as he left for Buxdon were: 'Give my regards to The Man.'

It had been a strange sort of year.

Part One:
Michaelmas

August

Well, here I am. I'm writing this in my new room in something called Mercers' Lodge, looking out from the window over a lawn of grey mud. Beyond that there's a tree of some description. It's rather peaceful here, now the cement mixer has stopped and the builders have gone off for their lunch.

I've got a bed, a wardrobe, and a little desk with a standard-lamp. I must remember to buy a bulb in town. And some pillows. The room itself is pretty cosy. The wardrobe doors pop open when you sit on the bed, but there's room to open a newspaper if you put one elbow out the window. You could even have a friend in for coffee, if one of you doesn't mind squatting under the desk. There's also an armchair you have to climb over to get to the window. It looks like someone died in it. The general vibe is old folk's home meets hall of residence. Someone has tried and failed to give the place a welcoming feel by sticking some flowers in a vase. They look to have been there since about 1982. A very small and very ugly oil painting of some hedges and a stile lends the room a hint of depressing B&B. So this is my new home.

I'll unpack in a minute, but first I want to work out what this stain is over the door. It's been produced by rising damp or leakage of some kind, clearly, but what is it? At first I took it for a sinister bearded face, but now I'm coming round to the

5

opinion it's a map of Greenland. You'll have to check it out and see what you think when you come down.

God knows who had this room before me, but they've sure left some peculiar books behind: *On War* by Carl von Clausewitz, *101 Classic Love Poems For Today*, and a copy of *Little Dorrit* with a bookmark three pages into the introduction. I can only assume my predecessor was a lovesick Dickensian with a taste for nineteenth-century military strategy. Or someone with a worrying approach to seduction and a sideline interest in sentimental Victorian novels. The evenings are going to fly past with that lot to keep me company.

As for the rest of the house ... There's a bath at the end of the corridor which is full of rugby balls. I mean the bath is full of rugby balls, not the corridor. The corridor is full of laundry bags. The rugby balls are covered in mud, as is the bath, the taps, and the door handle. There's a mouthguard on the edge of the sink. So far these are the only definite signs of habitation I've encountered.

The natives don't seem too friendly. I went to make a cup of tea in the kitchen and I could hear feet scurrying and doors slamming all over the house. I went to the loo and there was a stampede to get out the front door. However, contact has been established. There was a note pushed under my door saying the toaster is broken and would we all please chip in to get a new one.

Which reminds me, I'm pretty peckish. I passed the kitchens already, but the new caterers aren't moving in until the start of next week. I'm going to explore the town and scavenge for provisions, and I'll finish this later.

It's later, and I'm absolutely ravenous. There's some graffiti under the railway bridge announcing that 'Buxdon Sux'. I'm inclined to agree. Slightly more worryingly, the piece of graffiti next to that simply declares 'Granny Love'. I'm not sure whether to find this touching or disturbing. Maybe it's a person. The only person I saw out and about was an old man waiting outside Totes the bookmakers with a three-legged dog. He looked miserable and the dog didn't seem too thrilled with life either.

I'd call Buxdon a ghost town but that would make it sound so much livelier than it is. There are two fish and chip shops. Dolphins is shut today. The other one, The Friery, offers something called 'Chinese chicken curry and chips'. I suppose that's globalisation for you. I chose to take my chances elsewhere.

The whole town feels damp. Buxdon smells a bit like the dungeon at Warwick Castle, with an added overtone of exhaust fumes. It's the kind of place you might expect to find a Wimpy, except that I couldn't. The Market Square is dominated by a looming car park on one side, and on the other side by a block of offices the colour of an oily puddle. I thought any moment I was going to wake up in a cold sweat and discover I was Prince Charles. There were a couple of empty White Lightning bottles and chip trays lying around the war memorial.

Chopstix at the top of the High Street is either being renovated or had a very rowdy weekend. Further along, A Taste of the Raj offers 'the authentic flavours of the Subcontinent without leaving Buxdon', which wouldn't have been the angle I'd have played up. I didn't fancy the Buxdon Tea Shoppe, and from the looks of it neither did anyone else under seventy. It has a giant teddy-bear dressed as a Beefeater outside. Someone's stolen its hat. I toyed with the idea of buying three quid's worth of pick 'n' mix and a Woolworths cola, but decided it might look a bit unprofessional if anyone saw me.

When I got back to the school I managed to locate the tuck shop, which is next to the Sixth Form centre. The Sixth Form centre was apparently designed in the 1970s by someone with the ambition but not the vision or talent to build student unions. It's a testament to the impressive workability, compressive strength and ugliness of concrete. The building lets out a low hum when the wind blows, which I'm not sure was intentional. As for the tuck shop itself, it's a portacabin with wired-over windows. It's for boys only, and they seemed sceptical when I insisted I was the new English teacher. You know the look someone gives you when they're trying to size up if you're a kiddie-fiddler or a harmless buffoon? Neither did I, until today.

My stomach had started to digest its own lining by that time and the queue was enormous. Some piggy bastard was buying 100 penny sweets with 100 pennies. I left my sandwich and stalked out when penny number fifty-seven turned out to be Scottish and there was a heated debate over whether or not it was legal tender. He's outside my window now, throwing sweets into the mud and shouting 'Scramble!', while a crowd of First Years fight each other for them.

To help you picture the place: The Old Building is the one that looks like Gormenghast; The New Building looks like a photocopier. Mercers' Lodge, where they've put me, reminds me of one of those photos in the paper with the caption: 'Neighbours never suspected what went on behind closed curtains ...' There's a shared kitchen and a living room with a TV, video and selection of highly-flammable-looking sofas and armchairs. Orange curtains in both rooms complete the scene. When you put the heaters on, the place fills rapidly with the smell of hot dust.

Oh God, Caroline, I miss you so much already. Good luck with your preparations for the big presentation next week. It was kind of Rychard to offer to help you. I hope you can come down here some weekend soon; I know I've really been selling the place. For all my grumbles, I do think this is going to be a good place to work on the book. At least, there don't seem to be many distractions. As they said about the Overlook Hotel ...

All my love,
Yours hungrily,
Matt xxx

P.S. Bugger it, I'm going to steal some toast from downstairs.
I'm sure no one will mind.
P.P.S. I forgot the toaster's broken. I'll have to steal some bread.
Is it a crime if a man steals a piece of bread to feed himself? A
chorus of a hundred impeccably grubby urchins says not.
P.P.P.S. My neighbour is in. I'd ask him if he has any bread
to lend, but he seems to be suffering from some acute internal
malady at the moment. I suspect he doesn't know this room is
inhabited. I hope he either improves or dies rapidly.
P.P.P.P.S. Take good care of yourself. Did I mention I miss you
more than I can write?
P.P.P.P.P.S. I shall be sure to pass your regards on to 'The
Man'. To be honest, so far Buxdon has struck me as a
somewhat unconvincing bastion of privilege. I'm so far yet to
see anyone eating a roast swan with a silver fork or making a
younger boy warm his toilet seat. No doubt it's simply a matter
of time.

Friday, 30th August. I thought for a moment I'd left this journal at Caroline's. That might have been awkward. Although
it would have been a little out of character for her to show
too much interest in something I've written. I sent her a good
long letter yesterday. Hopefully I hit the right note of affection mixed with self-pity. She probably won't be able to feel
sorry for me and still be angry at the same time. I was going
to add that this interlude apart might even bring us closer
together, then I realised I haven't quite figured out how that
would work yet.

There was a letter waiting for me when I arrived.
Unfortunately it wasn't the note I was expecting from Mr
Garnett – my predecessor – explaining what I'm supposed

to be teaching this term and perhaps why he decided to leave so suddenly. It was from the headmaster – Edmund Josephus Perse, MA (Oxon). He'd have greeted me in person but he's been in Malaysia promoting the school to prospective parents and won't be back until this afternoon. He wants to welcome me to Buxdon and remind me that it's the first Boarder's Chapel of term tonight. He mentions that I should wear my gown. Of all the things I forgot to pack … Moreover, *Josephus*? Caroline did warn me this was going to be weird, but I thought at least they'd ease me in a little first. I've just got to think of myself as an anthropological observer. You can find something interesting without approving of it. Anyway, it's a bit rich Caroline being so bolshy about all this. Of the two of us, mine was not the school with the Sixth Form paddock and the school polo team.

I spent most of this morning running around Buxdon trying to rent, buy or steal a gown, all to no avail. I don't know what I was expecting. I described what I was looking for to someone in the clothes shop and they asked if it was for a fancy-dress party. This was after I had clarified that by gown I meant a robe, not actually a dress.

Perhaps I underestimated the liveliness of Buxdon in my letter to Caroline. There's a town punk, who sits and drinks cider on the steps of the war memorial in a 'Sid Lives' jacket. He demanded to know what I thought I was staring at, which raises the possibility he's unaware that he has the words 'Swindon Town FC' tattooed on his forehead. It's a big forehead. I didn't think he'd be the obvious person to ask about gowns.

The headmaster adds in his letter that he greatly looks forward to discussing my year teaching English in Japan with me, and informs me there is an annual soiree in February for scholars and their parents, featuring an informal lecture given by one of the staff. Last year Mr Brimscombe gave a very well-received talk on 'The Local History and Folklore of

Buxdon.' The Head hopes I'll accept the honour this year – he says that something along the lines of 'First Impressions of Japan' or 'Japanese Society: Tradition and Change' would be appropriate. I don't expect I have much choice in the matter. Well, it'll be another chance to give the gown an airing, if I've managed to acquire one by then.

I'm also supposed to be coaching some of the scholarship boys for their Oxford and Cambridge interviews. 'No doubt this will be a rewarding and interesting experience,' the headmaster opines. I need to prepare a reading list for them by the start of term. I shall definitely play this up with Caroline. Just me and the plucky underdogs, making our way in this crazy world on our wits and ambition. The other way of thinking of it would be that they've stuck me in charge of the Geek Squad.

The letter ends by noting that 'due to Mr Garnett's unexpected and precipitate departure, you will be required to teach the courses he has planned for this year. Mr Garnett should have left a detailed set of instructions for you, detailing your classes and other duties for this term.' Yes, he should have. But he hasn't.

On the plus side, there's a start-of-term dinner after chapel, if I can hold out on bread and biscuits until then. I'm still famished. I should have asked Mum to send me a tuck box.

Saturday, 31st August. Boarders' Chapel last night: my first opportunity to observe a collection of Buxdon boys en masse. They look no more unprepossessing, surly and morose than one would expect. A fair smattering of pimpleheads, growth-spurt giants, grubby homunculi, dandruff cases, jaw-danglers, pop-eyed gogglers, junior geriatrics, roly-polies, jug-heads, bean-poles, foetus-faces, midges and oddbods. But only in about the same percentage as in the average minor public school, Tory cabinet or outsider-unfriendly village downwind of a nuclear power plant. And looks aren't everything, as no doubt some of these freaks have been told more than once by well-meaning adults.

Fortunately the headmaster had a spare robe, and we walked over to chapel together. On the way I asked whether I should call him Edmund, or Mr Perse, or perhaps Ed ... 'Headmaster will be fine,' he reassured me.

I meant to tell the Head I still haven't located the letter from my predecessor explaining what I'm meant to be teaching tomorrow (as well as where, when and to whom), but I didn't get the chance. First he was telling me that there's been a complaint about food going missing in Mercer's Lodge, and asking whether I'd had anything disappear. It took me a moment or two to realise he was probably referring to the two slices of bread I liberated from the kitchen the other day. Hopefully they'll blame the builders.

After that he was asking whether I'd had a chance to learn the school song. It hadn't been my top priority actually. It's OK, I thought, I'll just do church-singing: keep my head down, mumble along, and pick up the tune if any from the person next to me. That plan was scuppered when we got to the chapel and none of the other staff had turned up apart from the chaplain. As the headmaster and I filed in, in a procession of two, it became clear that we wouldn't be sitting in the pews or discreetly at the back. Instead, were stuck up in a sort of wooden box or pen at the front. We had a great view of the congregation. They also had a great view of us. According to the service sheet we weren't due to sing the school song ('Buxdon, Advance!') until the end. I wasn't too worried. If things went badly I figured I could pretend to have dropped something and go down after it, not to re-emerge until Buxdon had finished advancing.

Before the song we got a morale-booster from the Head. 'What is it that makes a Buxdon boy?' he asked. Slugs and snails and puppy-dogs' tails, at a guess.

'I was in the Far East recently, and someone asked me:

"What are parents paying for when they send their sons to this school?" It was a good question.' No shit at seven grand a year, plus meals, uniform and trips.

'What is it that a Buxdon education provides?' I was all ears. 'I could have mentioned our excellent facilities, or our first-class staff, or our proud history. But I did not. Those are only the setting for what we provide. What Buxdon truly offers, to everyone who passes through its hallowed portals, is ... *it*.' I may have invented the bit about the hallowed portals. I'd previously thought Buxdon was all about not having girls around and getting good A-level results. Turns out it thinks it's a finishing school for idiots. 'You cannot buy *it*. You can only buy the trappings of *it*,' the Head burbled gnomically. I'd have focused on the facilities and the proud history, if I were him.

'And now, we will join together in the school song.'

Is it his wild hair? His singing voice? His crazed eyes? His tweed jacket? Something about the Head really reminds me of Christopher Lee in *The Wicker Man*. Perhaps it's his ability to deliver 24-carat bullshit straight-faced. Whatever *it* is, he's full of it.

The tune of the school song started off as a mixture of 'Oh God, Our Help in Ages Past' and 'Praise my Soul the King of Heaven'. The Headmaster bellowed it out with his eyes closed. The mumbly church-singing approach was employed by most of the boys. I think I managed to fake my way through the first verse at about the same time and in the same key as everybody else:

Let friendship shine forth 'til the end of our days,
And *something or other* in ev-e-ry way,
'Til *somethingty something* we'll not quit the fray,
Never shirking *something*, and valiant al-ways.

Then, for no possible reason I can think of, and somewhat to my surprise and alarm, the second verse lurched abruptly into a pretty fair facsimile of The Marching Song of the Fascisti:

Advance, Buxdon, Advance!
Faith my shield and Hope my lance,
Advance, Buxdon, Advance!

By this point the headmaster seemed hard-pressed to prevent himself advancing up and down the aisle swinging his arms. I was merely trying look serious and keep my mouth moving more or less in time with the words. Rather than filling the chapel with peals of mocking laughter and fleeing into the night. Or invading Abyssinia. With rising curiosity I awaited the arrival of verse three. What form would the setting take this time? Stately Waltz? Lively Mazurka? Free-jazz freak-out?

Without explanation the third verse went back to the original tune, which wrong-footed me again. The whole thing was either written by a lunatic or by an acute musical satirist who has tragically failed to achieve the reputation he deserves. I suspect the former.

At dinner, the headmaster helped me to some of Buxdon's own wine, produced as it turns out entirely in the United Kingdom. 'I do think there's a lot of rot talked about French wines,' he informed me, pouring out a glass of what looked and smelled exactly like ear wax dissolved in nail polish remover. Or what I assume that would look and smell like. 'What do you think?' The first reply that came to mind was an expression of polite surprise that they'd found a way of fermenting mushrooms. Dinner itself was colourless beef from an animal that that had died of advanced old age, with a side of warmish carrots scooped up from a high-street pavement on a Sunday morning.

*

I phoned Caroline afterwards to tell her about my evening. She's spending the weekend preparing her presentation for work on Friday with the aid of her boss, Bloody Rychard. Caroline still refuses to recognise that Rychard is: a) an aging wine-bar Lothario with a face like a sheep-killing dog, and b) desperately trying to get his nasty hands on her.

Apart from anything else, why can't or doesn't he spell his own name properly? Is there some family tradition involved or is it pure affectation? Rychard strikes me as the kind of person who never gets caught out by a tricky bra. He can probably undo them with his teeth. I doubt he's ever fallen out of bed and landed on his own erection either. I expect he's thrilled I've moved here. Rychard took a hamper with him when he went over the other night. Is that professional? Surely there are guidelines about that sort of thing. I know what you're doing, Rychard, with your hamper of seduction. 'Here's a little bottle of Moët … some paté and crackers … and, oh, how did that get in there? It's a big bottle of massage oil …' Stop it. That almost certainly won't have happened. But I think it's fair to say Caroline wasn't thrilled about me leaving London … and she hasn't even seen Buxdon yet.

My neighbour emerged from his room this morning looking like Lazarus out from the tomb. I was waiting for the shower, and he was suitably discomfited to learn that my room is occupied. As well he might be, since for the past two days he's been subjecting me through the wall to an intimate acquaintance with his disordered digestive system. After groaning out of both ends all yesterday, punctuated only by frequent dashes down the corridor, I heard him about midnight begging God for release, and adding a subsequent plea that 'A Taste of the Raj' on Buxdon High Street be subjected to an almighty smiting. He was asleep most of yesterday, snoring like a coffee grinder. It was like being trapped in an episode of *Men Behaving Badly*. He still looked very peaky this morning, although better than the translucent bag of skin I was expecting.

'Barry Taylor, rugby and maths,' he said, extending a large, pale and clammy paw. 'By the way, I've got something for you.' This proved to be an envelope.

'I hope I haven't been disturbing you,' Taylor added. 'I'm afraid spicy food doesn't seem to agree with me. I'm half the man I was Wednesday lunchtime.'

I didn't hear a thing, I assured him. He seems like a decent bloke, despite his racist stomach. The envelope he gave me was simply addressed 'To My Replacement', and had my timetable in, as well as a letter from the mysterious Mr Garnett. It was less helpful than I had hoped.

What the hell am I doing here? Oh yes, I remember: I need a job to earn money to buy clothes, food, CDs, and so on. Bloody capitalism. Working in a boys-only, fee-paying school is hardly the quickest way to get the system to crumble, either. I am the system. Fuck me.

September

To My Replacement,

Welcome to Buxdon. I expect you can figure out what to do
with most of the classes I've stuck you with. There were some
course plans at one stage, but I'm afraid that the cleaners mis-
took them for a couple of bar mats someone had scribbled on,
and binned them. I set *Little Dorrit* for second-set GCSE. It'll be
right over their heads, but I've always wondered how it ends.
I'm afraid you have First World War Poetry with both the
Third Year sets. I ran out of inspiration and we had the books
lying around. In my experience the idea that teenage boys
find the poetry of World War One interesting is a sentimental
myth. Try to avoid using the phrases 'and they were no older
than you are now', or, 'It was the war to end all wars – or so
they thought.' You might also think it would be a fun exercise
for them to imagine themselves in the trenches and to write a
fictional diary. This is a common mistake. However, I did give
young Tipton extra marks last year for dunking his exercise
book repeatedly in a puddle for 'authenticity' and ending his
piece with the unforgettable line: 'I think I'll just pop me head
over the top and see if anyone wants a game of football,' followed by a spattering of real blood across two pages. If it had
been his own blood I would have given him a commendation.

You're probably also stuck with my General Studies set. If
you can figure out how I intended to fill two hours a week on
the subject 'Theories of Art and Society 1815-1974', then you're
doing better than I am. The dates, by the way, were carefully
selected. I was going to begin with the battle of Waterloo and

end with the Abba song 'Waterloo'. Anyway, no one keeps General Studies up for A Level, and if you are lucky then no one will sign up for this at all. That was certainly the intention.

If you can stick your colleagues, the boys should be no trouble. The headmaster is very particular about the staff knowing everyone's names. It may help if you give the boys nicknames, at least in your own head: 'Stretch', 'Boggle', 'The Cave-Troll', 'The Lady Dowager', 'Bucketface', that sort of thing. To save time and effort I suggest categorising your students according to the simplest terms, the most convenient definitions: brain, athlete, basket case, princess or criminal. I've given you a list of some of your more notable Sixth Formers to get you started:

Bagley – Nickname: 'Wild Man of the Woods'. Possibly raised by wolves. I'm not convinced he can talk. It's worth checking now and again to make sure he's breathing.

Chivers – Nickname: 'The Plasterer'. Good lad, plays a lot of rugby. You will know him by the fact he is never off crutches or without at least one limb in a cast.

Ellis – Nickname: 'Will O' The Wisp'. I have taught this boy for a year and yet have no memory of him at all. My rule of thumb is: if there is a grey mass you can't quite put a name or shape to, it's probably Ellis.

Hallbrick – Nickname: 'Flower'. Looks and sounds like a lady vicar. V. wet. If he was any wetter he'd have to be brought to school in a sponge. His father is Head of Music, and makes Hallbrick Jr look like Genghis Khan.

Iles – Nickname: 'The Lurking Horror'. Great hair. Shame about the boy attached, who is an annoying little sod. Has a habit of materialising out of darkened stairwells and trying to start conversations about the relationship between Music and Painting, or The Novel and Society. He crawled out onto the chapel leads to spend the night under the stars last term and ended up spending a

week in the san suffering from exposure. On no account
agree to read his poetry.

Monk – Nickname: 'The Bloody Monk'. Prone to nosebleeds. Otherwise contributes little in class.

Norrington Major – Nickname: 'The Catatonic Kid'.
Clearly in his mid-thirties. Why he chooses to
impersonate a rather dull seventeen-year-old we can
only speculate. I spent several classes under the firm
impression he was the man from OFSTED. Can sleep
with his eyes open. Not worth waking unless he starts
screaming.

Tipton – Worth cultivating. His parents are loaded and he
can score you some excellent draw. I hold him personally responsible for the burst of inspiration that led to
'Theories of Art and Society 1812-1974'.

Unman –

Wittering –

Zigo –

I made these last three up. They still contribute a fuck of a lot
more in class than Bagley or Norrington.

Also, this may sound funny, but it's worth learning the school
song before the start of term. You'll see why. One more thing:
it would be a very bad career strategy to fall in love with Lucy
Salmon.

Best of luck,
Garnett

P.S. If they offer you a choice of sports to supervise, choose
fives or fencing. At least then you'll be inside.

Sunday, 1st September. Re-read the letter from Garnett in
preparation for my first classes of term tomorrow. I'm not

sure how useful his advice is going to be, but I can't wait to meet this Lucy Salmon.

I found a copy of the school newsletter in the staffroom, which afforded me some baffled amusement. I'm particularly fond of the part about what Old Buxdonians are up to:

- The first of what it is hoped will be many joint Hog Roast/Discos for OBs and Old Girls of St Margaret's was a great success in June. Jeremy Wilt (1992) won 'best costume' for his uncanny impersonation of Henry VIII. Congratulations Jeremy. Music for the diners was provided by the Fat Cats Blues Band.
- The City Lunch was a success again this year, from what those present can recall. Some twenty OBs were in attendance at the Bankside restaurant including City Lunch veterans Chris Nutworth (1977), Andy Hackett (1980), Justin Le Fay, Gareth Tucker, Simon Edgworth (all 1986), Miles Longside (1992) and a fresh crop of recent leavers.
- Calling all 1960s Leavers! Peter Harding (1968) would like to hear from you. He would particularly like to get in touch with other former members of 'Equinox', and wonders if any of the rest of you still play your instruments. Perhaps a reunion is on the cards?

I hope no one minds me clipping that out. It did have a coffee ring on it.

I doubt anyone is looking forward to the start of term less than me. As they told us back in teacher training, the first day is when you have to make your decision: will you be liked, feared or respected? I think I'd settle for any of those three. I also suspect you get the same advice when you arrive in prison. Buxdon can't be as bad as the last couple of places I've taught, anyway. For one thing, you don't have to lock yourself in and out of the classroom at the start and end of each class.

Then again, if there weren't benefits, they wouldn't call it selling out.

I really hope the kids like me tomorrow. Perhaps I should give out sweets. No, that didn't work when I was at school and it won't work now. It's the balance between affection and dread in the pupils that's so vital to achieve early. Maybe I should give half of them sweets and half of them detentions.

Monday, 2nd September. The introductory class for the Third Years went OK today once I'd found the right classroom. You'd think that room thirteen would be between rooms twelve and fourteen, rather than on another corridor and floor entirely, but I'm reassured that's a common misapprehension. Some little stinker advised me to go back to the lobby and take the lift up to the seventh floor. I probably should have guessed that there isn't a lift. There isn't a seventh floor either. The Main Building seems composed entirely of identical gloomy corridors, but I'm getting the hang of navigating the place. By following the smell of the kitchens you can tell you're heading west. I passed the headmaster three times and tried to look insouciant.

It would have been helpful if at some point during teacher training they'd mentioned how to write on a rolling whiteboard. It kept scrolling down as I was trying to write my name up for the class. I started writing at shoulder-height and finished practically on my knees. I doubt I've achieved much in the way of liking, fear or respect, but at least no one threw a chair at me or deliberately jostled me in the corridor.

The Third Years are about thirteen, which means that, in the usual way of boys that age, half of them look about ten and the other half look about forty. One guy hardly fits under his desk and spent the whole class alternately stroking his incipient moustache and ineffectually tugging his trouser legs down. He's also going bald. Two thirds of the class have come up through the Lower School and probably know a lot more about how things work at Buxdon than I do. The kids who've just arrived from their prep schools tend to have briefcases and a look of glazed terror. I expect both will disappear after a couple of weeks.

Tuesday, 3rd September. Over lunch today the Head let slip that he wrote the words and music for 'Buxdon, Advance!' himself. I should've known.

I went to see my head of department in the afternoon to pass on my reading list for the Oxbridge candidates. Dr Cumnor is an amiable chap who sports a hairpiece so unconvincing I initially took it for a petite fuzzy hat. His nickname among the boys is Davy Crockett, which puzzled me until I saw what was on his head. Please God let me get a good nickname. I do wish my surname rhymed with something other than retch or letch. Although that still doesn't explain why at school everyone called my brother 'Big Frank' and called me 'Milksop'. I think it would have stung less if Frank hadn't come up with my nickname and popularised it himself.

Whatever the kids here call me will at least be better than 'Mister Goblin', which is something. Hopefully I've left that particular nickname far behind me.

Wednesday, 4th September. The General Studies class has been cancelled, having attracted only one taker. Unfortunately this means that Bagley (the wolf-boy) is now taking English instead. Bagley spent the class this morning eating pages out of his exercise book. Or rather, chewing them up and using them as ammunition, because during lunch I was having a cheese sandwich in my classroom and bits of semi-digested papier maché started falling off the light bulb. I'll keep an eye on him next time – I was distracted today because one of the boys had a terrible nosebleed and was forced to dash out of the room. 'Keep your head back,' I advised him, just before he ran straight into the doorframe. I'll keep a bucket of sawdust handy in future.

I met Lucy Salmon at last. She teaches religious studies, is quite pretty and seems pleasant. Put it this way: on our first meeting she displayed only limited signs of being a freak. On the other hand, I found it unsettling that within five minutes of our having met each other Lucy had revealed she was having an affair with a man called Charlie. After our little chat I knew quite a lot about Charlie – certainly more than his wife does, and possibly more than his GP. But hey, this is the 90s. Why wouldn't you tell a complete stranger the intimate details of your adulterous love life? Charlie sounds like quite a guy. I was worried Lucy would expect an equal brace of confidences in return, perhaps something about my earliest sexual experiences or my potty training, but this wasn't required. I didn't get anywhere trying to find out why my predecessor left so suddenly, either.

As for the staffroom, it has dark brown carpets that seem to be made of corduroy, with a remarkable capacity for building up and delivering static electric shocks. I have a pigeon-hole in there, which still says Ian Garnett on it. There's also a communal kettle that with much moaning manages to get water semi-warm. The atmosphere they've gone for seems to be shabby gentleman's club of the early 1950s: leather armchairs, overflowing ashtrays, and gilt-framed paintings of headmasters past. I'm an especial fan of Harold Graves (HM 1933–7), who looks like a mix between Julius Caesar and a tortoise. The staffroom curtains are the colour of old smoke. For some reason there was a man in lycra shorts doing press-ups in the corner.

Later I made the rookie error of mentioning Lucy's mild attractiveness on the phone to Caroline. Damn, I'm going to regret that. Caroline's lovely, but she does get touchy about that sort of thing. Even down the phone I could tell she had her unamused Victoria face on. I was forced to backtrack frantically in the face of an immediate barrage of suspicion. Did I say pretty? I meant moon-faced and spaghetti-haired. Sorry, Lucy, needs must when the Devil drives. I think Caroline's suspicions were soothed. For the moment.

Friday, 6th September. Buxdon wine with dinner again last night. The red this time: scabs dissolved in vinegar. The main course was roast crow with a side of sautéed oak apple.

I rang Caroline again, to wish her luck with her presentation. Rychard answered the phone and claimed to be 'just checking everything over for tomorrow'. I'll bet he bloody was. He then had the audacity to invite me to my own girlfriend's celebratory drinks at some bar after work. He gave me directions to get there, which I see I have transcribed as: 'Green Park tube station, turn left, turn right, blah blah blah fuck off Rychard.' The rest I appear to have written in Sanskrit. I bit my tongue and asked if Caroline was about and if I could possibly speak to her – as opposed to asking what the fuck Rychard thought he was playing at and if he fancied a kick in the mouth.

Caroline accused me of being tipsy. I denied it, but looking at the evidence this morning, she was probably right. While on the phone I produced a pretty good sketch of Bloody Rychard being eaten by bears, and wrote the words 'Paper Shoes', which for some reason I have underlined three times.

Monday, 9th September. Back to Buxdon on the last train yesterday. Not as exciting as that sounds, since the last train leaves Paddington at 4:30 on a Sunday. What a flaming disaster of a weekend.

I found the bar on Friday, after first having been wildly misdirected by everyone from the doorman at the Ritz (very affable once reassured I didn't want to get into the Ritz) to an insistently helpful homeless chap whose knowledge of snazzy central London bars proved to be shaky. I gave him a quid for directing me up a long dark alley with a puddle of piss at the end of it. For a long while I gave up even expecting to find the place, and wandered around pretending to be Peter Ackroyd exploring London's hidden byways and lost thoroughfares. When I did finally locate Bar Cartouche – announced by the smallest conceivable sign in an illegible font – the bouncer wouldn't let me in because I wasn't wearing 'proper shoes'. We discussed semantics a little, then he told me to sod off.

At this point a woman with a clipboard and a head like a brick in a baseball cap emerged, and I told her I was with Caroline Appleby or perhaps the Rychard Dyer party. No, there was no Matthew Bletch on the list. No, she wouldn't check her clipboard again, she had already looked once and I wasn't on it. The woman said this in a voice that implied she had been more than indulgent towards me despite my improper footwear and I should probably watch it if I didn't want to be wearing the pavement as a hat. She wouldn't let me in to tell Caroline I was there, but she could pass a message on. I assumed she had misused 'could' to mean 'would', but as time passed it turned out she hadn't.

It started to rain, of course, so I took shelter in the minicab office opposite. Rychard and Caroline emerged from the bar at nearly midnight. I dashed out and explained what had happened, probably looking and sounding more like the Ancient Mariner than I realised at the time. Rychard gave the door staff an impressive ticking-off which in no way removed my suspicion that my name was never on the guest list in the first place. He and Caroline also claimed not to have got a message. How Rychard got in wearing tasselled loafers and no bloody socks I don't know.

When we (Caroline and I) got home and into bed I pointed out how much Bloody Rychard looks like Michael Portillo. Caroline would much prefer it if I didn't insist on calling him Bloody Rychard. I would prefer it if the misspelled creep didn't insist on limpeting onto my girlfriend, but there you go. I had just raised the possibility that Rychard had deliberately not wanted me to be at the bar, when Caroline interrupted me. 'You don't get it, do you? This was supposed to be my evening, to celebrate my presentation. Instead you somehow managed to make it all about you.' Yes, that's exactly what I did. Belatedly, I said I was glad it went well and got a turned back in reply.

The next morning, as I was rustling up some tea and toast and generally running around making up for myself, it transpired that B. Rychard had arranged brunch for two at his club to discuss further how the presentation went. Caroline explained that Rychard belongs to a private members' club, in case I was under the impression they'd be getting together to paint lead figurines or build a model railway.

This left me to spend the rest of Saturday morning making awkward conversation with Caroline's new flatmate, Sig (short for Sigourney, rather than Sigmund). Things got off to a flyer when I speculated that the flat must be great during the carnival. 'It's wonderful,' she agreed, 'having people of all creeds, colours and nationalities coming together to take a slash on my doorstep.' I suggested we watch Saturday morning TV, and Sig gave me a look like I'd proposed kidnapping an infant. I put the television on when she had gone off for what turned out to be an impressively long shower. I know it's Sig's flat and everything, but that really was a shower and a half. It's possible, of course, that she was just avoiding me. I tried to take a shower later, but there was no hot water left. Most of it seemed to be on the bathroom floor. Things went steadily downhill from there. I attempted to ingratiate myself by doing all the washing up, and managed to take the glaze off Sig's wok. I kept scrubbing but it failed to reappear.

My pièce de résistance was deciding I'd be safely out of harm's way if I popped onto the balcony for a sneaky smoke. Sig seemed puzzled by quite how I managed to lock myself out. To be honest, so am I. She also seemed surprised when I appeared directly outside her bedroom window waving a fag around and shouting 'Sig! Sig!' Sig looked like she was weighing up whether to call the police. In short, by the end of the morning I'd managed to convince Sig once and for all that her flatmate's boyfriend is a total fuckwit. Maybe that's an exaggeration. She probably just thinks I'm a twat.

Caroline got back about two, full of bruschetta and the wonders of Bloody Rychard. We wandered around the market in the afternoon. As usual, it was pretty close to my personal idea of hell. A man who may or may not have been Terence Trent D'Arby trod on my foot, and I was almost run over by a woman pushing a giant pram. Then we played 'How many idiots can you fit into a boutique?' for a while. I waited for Caroline to try on a dress and watched a shop assistant with an experimental haircut try and fail to work the till. A sixty-year-old man in tiny leather trousers was attempting to key a number into his very small mobile phone without taking his sunglasses off. Eventually he got through and gave someone a piece of his mind in high-volume Italian. There was also a woman with a small ugly white dog or perhaps albino bat in her handbag, a man with blood-coloured hair, a woman dressed for no obvious reason as a farmer from the future, and a young couple having an impressively lengthy and impassioned conversation about socks.

On the way back to the flat we took a shortcut through the scary estate and some kids kicked a half-flat football at me. Despite there being a notice that specifically prohibits ball games. They also called me a munzie, which I doubt was a compliment. I tried to focus on how much cuter they'd be dressed as Victorian urchins. A suggestion I may pass on to the council or tourist board, although Caroline described the idea as semi-fascistic. The tourists would like it.

Caroline and I had a not-as-depressing-as-it-could-have-been-which-isn't-saying-much talk about our relationship. I pointed out that no one can say I haven't paid my dues: I've worked in an office ('As a student,' Caroline added); I've stacked shelves in a supermarket ('As a student,' Caroline repeated); I've worked on a building site ('For one summer, as a ...' Yes, I get your point, C). We went through the whole thing all over again, about how I needed money and time to finish my book, and about how it would only be for a year at the most. I reminded her that during the War couples would often be separated for years. She queried the parallel between my situation and the struggle against global totalitarianism. But she hasn't heard 'Buxdon, Advance!' yet.

Caroline asked how I'd got on with Sig, and I said quite well on the whole. Fortunately Sig had gone out when we got back, and to my relief she had neglected to change the locks and deposit all Caroline's possessions out on the street. In the evening we ordered pizza and watched a video. Sig reappeared at about eleven and wanted to know what had happened to her wok. One small mercy: Rychard didn't turn up disguised as the pizza delivery boy or strumming a lute under the balcony.

When I got back to Buxdon I found Lucy Salmon in my kitchen, telling Barry about her weekend with Charlie. Personally, I could quickly get tired of hearing about Charlie's many virtues. He gives Lucy a quivering feeling inside. Is she sure it isn't just the beginnings of dysentery? Just hearing about Charlie was starting to give me a certain queasy sensation.

After Lucy left, Barry asked me what I thought of her. One thing's for sure: I'm definitely not falling in love with her. Lucy says things like, 'Well, you know what I'm like' when you've only met her twice. What Lucy's like, for the record, is 'terribly' insecure. This struck me, probably unfairly, as something that people who actually are terribly insecure tend not to point out to people they don't know. I mentioned this to Barry and he put on his thinking face. 'So you don't like her?' It's not that, exactly ... I just could have lived my entire life quite happily without being told that Charlie's manhood resembles Ross Kemp wearing a pink polo-neck. I feel slightly violated just knowing that. Then again, I'm not exactly in a position at the moment to get too picky about who I hang out with. That Barry Taylor is one of the few adults I know who puts on a special face when they're thinking rather bears this out.

Tuesday, 10th September. Knobbled by the headmaster and dragged into his office for a quick chat about my sports supervision duties for the term. Garnett was quite a big rower and I fear I may prove a disappointment on the secondary activities front. I volunteered to help out with Charity Club, which according to the newsletter I read the other day is 'keenly supported, especially in the Sixth Form' and 'gives boys a chance to interact with the local community'. Unfortunately, it's been temporarily suspended. I got the impression not all the recipients were as grateful or deserving as they might have been.

The Head offered me the choice of supervising fives or Archery Club, and I chose fives, which should at least be warm, dry and sedentary. There's also less chance of getting hit with an arrow. I should probably find out what the rules are.

Wednesday, 11th September. I'd just finished photocopying the Oxbridge candidates' reading lists when Dr Cumnor pointed out an unfortunate typo. Professor Stanley Button's book is in fact entitled *The Solitary* Voice: *Twentieth-Century Poetry and Readers.*

There was a note in the post this morning from my estranged brother Frank. The elder of my two estranged brothers. In full the note read:

Hello, Milksop,
How are you?
It's cold here.
Frank

Based on the fact Frank lives in the Alps, I think I could have deduced the third line for myself. Frank still has the ingenuous and for that reason extra-disturbing handwriting of a small child, madman, or small mad child. What can this mysterious epistle portend? Knowing Frank, it's nothing good. I wish he wouldn't call me Milksop.

Thursday, 12th September. Drat and double drat. The headmaster didn't see fit to mention yesterday that Fives Society meets on Saturday afternoons. Why it does that, fuck only knows. Caroline is going to hit the roof when she finds out. Luckily she's busy with reports this weekend. Bloody Rychard has entrusted her with them specially, which is apparently a good thing. I await the inevitable news that he's invited Caroline to work on them in his boudoir, while he plies her with funny-coloured booze in entertainingly-shaped bottles and puts on Sade and a velvet smoking jacket. He'll probably tell her he's going to slip into something more comfortable and emerge from the bathroom in nothing but his contact lenses.

I've so far kept schtum about my new weekend duties. I'll get out of them before next week even if it means getting one of the Archery Club to shoot me through the foot.

Young Sam Tipton finally deigned to make an appearance in class today, almost a fortnight into term. He was precisely two weeks and twelve minutes late, but he didn't let it bother him. He's bronzed from head to toe, having spent the last month in the Cayman Islands with his parents. I went pointedly silent as he came in. I stayed silent as he waited for someone to shift out of the seat he wanted, dug a torn scrap of paper, a pen, and a pager out of his bag and arranged them carefully on his desk. Finally it came to his attention that the class had come to a complete halt to watch this little performance. 'Oh carry on, don't mind me,' he announced. Surely I imagined him accompanying this with a princely twirl of the hand. You'd better watch it, sunshine, or I'll be down on you like a ton of bricks. Nope – I definitely can't pull that line off.

Actually Tipton's not bad at English. He made a few decent points today, which is more than Bagley (the feral child) has managed in a fortnight.

It took me a whole double period to notice Ellis was absent.

Sunday, 15th September. I feel terrible. Barry Taylor invited me out for a drink or two last night and we made it an evening to forget. We invited Lucy Salmon but she was off in a Travelodge somewhere with Charlie. And Mr Kemp too, I imagine. Although on balance I'd really rather not.

I feel like death warmed up. My eyes are like two lychees, my tongue was used to spring-clean a dungeon while I was asleep, and my face has a haggard, haunted look that would go well on the cover of a Dostoevsky novel. Perhaps *The Idiot*. It was a night of gradually escalating errors of judgement culminating in one massive final mistake before bedtime. My breath is like something that would come out of a vent on the ocean floor.

After dinner in school (grilled mole with lightly-tossed bat droppings) Barry showed me the bright lights of Buxdon. Buxdon has two pubs, which tradition divides one each between the staff and the Sixth Formers. The Sixth Form place is supposedly a bit trendy. I presume after seeing 'our' place this means it possesses such innovations as light, air and customers. I promise never to complain about old-fashioned pubs being changed into trendy aluminium-tabled gastro bars ever again.

'Now that's the smell of pub,' Barry announced as we

ducked through the medieval-hermit-sized door of The Albion. I tried unsuccessfully to gauge the precise level of satirical intent in this statement. 'Pub', according to Barry, is a delicately-layered combination of stale smoke, fresh smoke, despair, and wet dog. The offending animal was lying in front of the fire, and didn't move all evening. If it was dead I wouldn't be at all surprised. It started smouldering at one point. Barry had assured me in advance that the landlord of The Albion is 'a local character'. This translated as 'a tedious misanthrope'. His wacky eccentricity manifests itself by barring people at random, not playing music, not serving food, being comfortably the drunkest person in the establishment (not statistically difficult since there were only four people in there), and sounding off at full volume on such topics as what he'd do with the Palestinians if he was in charge and why South Africa is going down the pan. It was like having one of those fillings that starts picking up talk radio. How I longed for a pounding juke box or lively hen party. At least I found out where Catweazle's beard got to.

I got off on a bad foot by ordering a lager. After a lot of grumbling and some rooting around under the bar, a very dusty bottle of Stella appeared. I evidently should have gone for a half of what looked like river water, as Barry did. He went up to get a round in later and he and the landlord enjoyed a great deal of witty banter on this precise topic. The banter mostly consisted of saying the word 'lager' in high ladylike voices and staring at me.

After that I switched to Minerva's Owl (the river-water drink). Its immediate effects include not being able to feel your toes, the unsettling sensation of a ghostly finger forcing itself insistently down your throat, and a head that feels like it's been stuffed with wire wool. But its other effect was to make The Albion relatively bearable, and as a result I drank a considerable amount of it. Stupidly I was trying to keep up with Barry, who has a head like a medicine ball and is about six-and-a-half-feet tall, as well as probably half that wide. His hands are like a gorilla's feet. Physically, he's built along the same lines as my estranged brother Frank, although Barry has an impressive mane of blond locks like a surfing instructor, and lacks Frank's air of primitive malice and low cunning. Having supped not wisely but too well (my first miscalculation, or series of them) I did something which I'll no doubt regret.

When we got back to Mercers' Lodge we listened to some music on the CD player in the kitchen. Barry gave me my choice of CDs. He owns two: *Rock Anthems! Volume One* and *Rock Anthems! Volume Two*. Both CDs have a picture of an exploding planet on them, I suppose to demonstrate the power of anthemic rock. I believe it came as a double CD set, although he's lost the case. The world did not explode at any point during the evening, although I might have been getting off relatively lightly if it had.

Pretty much immediately Barry and I got onto the subject of our most humiliating secrets. As one does. Yeah, small talk is for wimps. I can only say in my defence that I'm fairly definite it wasn't me who raised the subject. Barry confessed that there's one thing he's always wanted to do before he dies. 'Just once,' he told me, 'I'd like to punch a carp in the mouth. You know, really smack it one in the mush.' I'm not sure why. He added that it wouldn't be cruel, because carp have no feeling in their faces. 'I wouldn't want to hurt it. I'd just like to see its look of surprise.' He also claims there's a Van Morrison song about punching a carp, although he couldn't remember what it's called. By this point I was wishing we'd stuck to a safe blokey topic like breasts or fantasy football.

Barry asked what my deepest, darkest secret is. My next move should have been to make something up. I should have pretended I have a silly middle name or that I've always wanted to kick a kangaroo when it's not looking. I should have just told him about the time Mum caught me in church taking

33

money out of the collection bag. Even better I could have just changed the subject entirely and tried to find out why Ian Garnett left Buxdon so suddenly. And left his books. But at that precise moment my brain was refusing to cooperate, so I confessed to him that in Japan I earned myself the nickname Mister Goblin.

Why did I tell him that, I wonder? Was it camaraderie? Loneliness? Male solidarity? Being pissed? A little bit of all four, probably. But mostly it must be that I'm a five-star fool. Maybe I just despise myself in previously unsuspected ways that a couple of glasses of Minerva's Owl let off the leash. Of course, once I'd told him the nickname, I had to tell him the whole story. If anything, that's even worse than the nickname itself. I even admitted that I still have the costume in a cupboard at home. What was I thinking? If I'm that hell-bent on convincing people I'm a loser, I should just go the whole hog and tattoo 'Swindon Town FC' on my forehead. On a related note, Barry's talked to the old man with the three-legged dog once or twice, and informs me the dog is called Tripod.

This morning I must track Barry down and have a word with him. I could say I made it up to sound cool. No, that won't work. I'll explain that I find what I told him exquisitely embarrassing and I'd prefer it if he didn't tell anyone. I'm sure he'd understand if I explain the position sensitively and sincerely. Or I could Super Glue his mouth shut. He can't have got far if he feels anywhere near as wretched as me.

Right. First step: get out of bed. Then I must get out of this room. Which seems, incidentally, to be shrinking. I think the walls are closing in.

Despair. Still, at least we got a new toaster this week.

Monday, 16th September. I reckon I've worked out what kind of person would go to the school office to report the theft of two slices of bread. I was having a mug of coffee in the kitchen this morning when Peter Wyndham walked in. I know he teaches French, but was it really necessary for him to say *'Bonjour'*? I'd also question the necessity of dressing like a provincial French teenager and driving a Citroën 2CV.

'I have a mug just like that,' Wyndham observed.

Yes, he does, and I was drinking out of it. Luckily I'm not aware of having any diseases communicable by mug. Wyndham looked at the drying-rack, opened his locker to bring out a cafetière, then looked back at the mug again.

'I don't mind you using my mug,' he lied, 'but how am I supposed to have a cup of coffee?'

I should note that there were three perfectly serviceable mugs sitting on the sideboard. I looked significantly at them; he looked significantly at me. Gradually it dawned on me that he was waiting for me to pour my coffee away.

After fifteen minutes faffing about with the cafetière, Wyndham produced a cup of coffee he could have drunk out of a thimble. He made me smell it. I'm bloody glad I stole his bread. Wyndham has the kind of beard someone would have if they were playing a marine biologist in a bad horror movie. He was also wearing sandals. In autumn.

Wyndham also told me he 'wouldn't drink instant coffee if someone was holding a gun to his head'. I'm tempted to put that to the test.

Tuesday, 17th September. Oxbridge preparatory session today with Iles, Hallbrick and Bagley (!), among others. That Iles is a cocky little bastard. He gave us a fifteen-minute critique of *Portrait of a Lady* before admitting he'd only read the introduction. Even after that he corrected me on its publication history. He tried to catch me after class – I suspect to give me some of his poems to read – but I managed to dodge him. For now.

Bagley would be OK if he ever spoke and didn't smell like swamp gas. Hallbrick, quite apart from his extremely irritating voice, mannerisms and face, makes Fotherington-Thomas look like B.A. Barracus. How they ever expect to fit in at Oxford or Cambridge I can't imagine.

Wednesday, 18th September. Caroline asked me what my problem is with Bloody Rychard. She asserts that there's nothing wrong with dressing nicely, taking care of your body and knowing about PEPs and ISAs. I would query Caroline's definition of 'dressing nicely'. Rychard dresses like something out of *L'Uomo Vogue*. He's the kind of person who thinks his watch needs to make an impression. He could also do with toning down the aftershave, which comes off him in wafts that could blind a beagle. He smells like a rapey eurowaiter. Oh, and I suspect he's trying to steal my girl. Other than that, I don't have a problem with him.

Caroline's agreed to come down to Buxdon this weekend. I should probably try to find out what PEPs and ISAs are.

Thursday, 19th September. Decided to buy some kitchenware of my own before Caroline gets here. The first place I tried was the school office, which has a wide range of Buxdon-related tat available at discount prices to members of staff. There are Buxdon mugs, Buxdon ties, Buxdon tie-clips, Buxdon cufflinks, Buxdon scarves and Buxdon jerseys. All are in the school colours of pink, yellow and silver. That's my Christmas presents sorted for this year. I found the prospect of drinking every morning from a mug that says 'Buxdon Forever' on it too painful to contemplate.

Friday, 20th September. I've read up on the rules of fives, ready for tomorrow. What a seamless combination of arcane complexity and pointless stupidity.

Sunday, 22nd September. The sleeping arrangements at Buxdon were a bit cramped with Caroline here. I don't think my bed is even a single. Not that anything bigger would fit in the room. It's a choice between waking up in the middle of the night with your back against the freezing wall or waking up with a bump on the floor. Sleep, not to mention anything more lively, was pretty much out of the question. I did have a crack at it, though. Ah, nothing says seduction like a cold tentative hand creeping about under a shared single duvet. Caroline doesn't feel that my room is very private. She has a point. The other day I could hear Barry Taylor through the wall clipping his toenails.

Caroline and I decided that the stain over the door is a run-over kitten.

Caroline arrived at Buxdon on Saturday just as I was in the middle of a frantic search for the caretaker with the keys to the fives courts. We eventually tracked him down having a smoke behind the Sixth Form Centre.

It seems fair to speculate that Fives Society doesn't attract the cream of the school's athletes. I suspect fives isn't much of a spectator sport at the best of times, and watching weirdly shaped boys throwing a ball at a weirdly shaped wall rapidly lost its appeal.

As we were lugging the equipment back to the gym, we bumped into Lucy Salmon coming back from town and she offered to show us the sights of Buxdon School, which didn't take long. She and Caroline seemed to get on quite well, which was a relief. We encountered young Sam Tipton admiring the graffiti on the noticeboards in the Old School lobby and he came over to introduce himself. '*Enchanté*,' he murmured to Caroline, and went so far as to bow and brush her hand with his lips. 'What a remarkable scent you're wearing. May I be so bold as to ask what it is?' Sig's biological hand soap, as it turned out.

After that Lucy showed us round the staffroom, the library and the school well. As we were walking back to Mercer's Lodge I had the uncomfortable feeling we were being watched.

Turning around I caught a glimpse of three pale little faces squashed up against one of the windows. 'They don't see many attractive females around here,' Lucy explained. I was a bit surprised that Lucy was around at the weekend but the mystery was soon cleared up. One of Charlie's kids has got the mumps. 'So I'm stuck here at the idiot factory.'

In the evening Caroline turned down the offer of a trip to the worst pub in the world (downside: the landlord is a ranting racist; upside: it has a dog). I strongly advised against eating in the refectory and we had dinner in the kitchen. Caroline didn't seem to find the plastic tableware I got in Buxdon the other day as fun as I expected. 'It's like having a picnic!' I enthused. 'Yes,' she repeated more slowly, 'it's like having a picnic.' We had hot dogs and a nice bottle of red. I'd spelled out 'I love you' on the side of the plate in alphabites. Caroline asked if we were having any vegetables, which reminded me I'd forgotten to get the ketchup out. 'Well, if passion doesn't keep us together, rickets will,' she observed.

We watched TV in the lounge for the rest of the night. I've come to the conclusion that the lounge smells like a mix of church hall and youth hostel. There was something on Five about people who've had accidents with kitchen appliances. Barry Taylor came in and said hello. He told us an intriguing story about once peering into a toaster to see if his snack was done and ending up with a smouldering Pop-Tart stuck to his forehead. I'm not sure whether Barry was aware just how self-deprecating he was being.

I asked Caroline what her first impressions of the place were. She said it seemed all right, pulling a face like someone had just run over her foot. And she hasn't even been into the town yet.

Monday, 23rd September. Iles cornered me after class and gave me some of his poems to read. I would have escaped out of the window but we were on the second floor. I said I felt very honoured. Honoured? I should get a medal. There's a whole folder full of them. Who knows? They may be quite good. I guess what happens now is that they turn out to be brilliant, I pass them off as my own, and I get the hell out of here. Roll on the secluded château and the midget chauffeur.

I think Caroline is a hit at Buxdon. I've spent the day being followed around by gangs of boys asking if she is my girlfriend, whether I kiss her, and (on one occasion) whether we are 'doing it'. Actually, Barry Taylor asked much the same questions.

Tuesday, 24th September. Over dinner tonight the Head asked how I felt I was settling in. 'I like to think we're one big family here.' So were the Mansons.

Halfway through one of my classes this morning I was distracted by the appearance of Barry Taylor's grinning face bobbing around outside the window. I ignored him for as long as I could, but he didn't show any inclination to move on, so eventually I went to the back of the class, opened the window and asked him what he wanted.

Barry: Hi.
Me (to the class): Keep reading *quietly*, and if you finish that section read it again. (To Barry): What is it, Mr Taylor?
Barry: I was just wondering what you've got drawn on the board there.
Me: Bishop's Mitre. We're doing *Murder in the Cathedral*.
Barry: Are you sure? Because from back here it looks like an enormous ...
Me (having looked): Christ, you're right.

Further confirmation that Barry's mind works in exactly the same way as that of a teenage boy. No wonder the kids in the back row were sniggering away. Still, that's another piece of classroom advice they could have helpfully mentioned in teacher training.

Wednesday, 25th September. Caroline revealed tonight that Sig's hobbies include trampolining, in the living room, in her underwear. I agreed it does sound odd, but added that I'd have to see her in action before I come to any further conclusions. Caroline assured me that was unlikely to happen. She also got a bit shirty when I demanded a more detailed description. Caroline has to work again this weekend, so I won't get the chance to find out more until next weekend at least. She has, however, agreed to try out something with Sig on Sunday afternoon called Reggaerobics. I suppose it was only a matter of time before someone combined the world's most boring activity with the world's most tedious music. Caroline accused me of never wanting to try anything new. Not strictly true, as I pointed out. She doesn't think colourful plastic cutlery counts as adventurous.

Nor was Caroline particularly sympathetic about my having told Barry that I once had the nickname Mister Goblin. And how I earned it. She asked if I was going to put it in my book, and I replied with the hollowest of laughs. If I'm that sensitive about people finding out about it, she suggested, I shouldn't have told literally the first person I met. She suggested that if I don't like it at Buxdon I should move back to London and do substitute-teaching again. After all, she says, I can't let one classroom mugging haunt me for the rest of my career. I could even apply to teach in a girl's school. Yeah, being mugged in class by a twelve-year-old girl is going to be so much less humiliating than being mugged by a twelve-year-old boy. I know they were only safety scissors, but they looked really sharp when they were being poked at me.

Caroline sent me a letter today. I wonder what's in it. Something erotic, I hope.

Thursday, 26th September. I've read Iles's verse, and the plan isn't going to work. It's dreadful. One of the poems compares love to an octopus, and includes the memorable line: 'We all have flaws/ You have fangs, scales and claws.' Which suggests both that a) he isn't really in love, and b) he's never seen an octopus. It's called 'The Octopus'.

I still haven't got to the bottom of why my predecessor left so suddenly. Although the fact that he read Iles's poetry may help explain it.

Friday, 27th September. My First Staff Meeting. The worst name for a children's book ever?

The headmaster announced a successful start to the Auditorium and Drama Lab Fund. He reminded staff that profits from this academic year's June Ball will be put towards the project, and that tickets are available at a discount rate for staff and Old Buxdonians. He also suggested that each department comes up with their own fundraising suggestions. Dr Morris set the ball rolling by suggesting a sponsored fancy-dress party, which met with a notably muted response. I was slightly too far away to kick him under the table.

Emily Browning, the chemistry teacher, mentioned several teething problems with the new science block, including some windows that don't open, some windows that don't close, the absence of sufficient bench space, and inadequate ventilation in the chemistry laboratories. The headmaster agreed that these problems should be thoroughly investigated and raised with the company responsible, Tipton Construction. He added that full details of the budgets and accounting for the project would be made available shortly to all the members of staff and parents who had expressed an interest in seeing them. Lionel Brimscombe raised the issue of the leaks in the library roof, which threaten to endanger some of the stock. He also asked for the Walking Club noticeboard to be given a glass case, due to the continuing problem with notices being defaced. Brimscombe is Head of History and the author of *Historic Walks in Buxdon, Elmsfield and Little Chipping* (1996), *A Short History of St Agnes' Church, Buxdon* (1994) and *What Kind of Pebble is This?* (for younger readers, 1993). All are published by the Perpendicular Press and are available in considerable numbers from the school office, local churches and the Buxdon Tea Shoppe. Brimscombe himself could win a Lord Longford lookalike contest. I wonder if he has a literary agent he could put me in touch with.

Other notables at the meeting included:

Mr John Beale – Physics. He also runs the Electronics Club. Excellent facial hair. He affects the kind of moustache that led the Charge of the Light Brigade. I think he may be looking after it for Lord Lucan. Beale's stock has been low in the staffroom since he advised the school to buy Betamax in the 1980s.

Miss Emily Browning – Chemistry. Flawless safety record, without a single accident in her labs since 1968. Spirit undimmed by thirty years of having to field questions regarding the possibility of formulating recreational drugs using school equipment.

Mr Matthew Bletch – Beloved alike by boys and staff, this latest addition to the staff is a pearl among men and the shining prince of the Buxdon School English Department. Author of *Every Day is Like Sendai: Twelve Months in Northern Japan* (unpublished, unfinished, title may be revised).

Mrs O. Digby – The school secretary. What does the O stand for? Nobody knows, but I bet it's not Orgazma, whatever Barry Taylor claims. That isn't even a real name.

Mr Tom Downing – Classics, cross country and rowing. All great men have their tragic flaws. Tom Downing's is to wander around the school premises in a pair of lycra running shorts. He has a poster in his office with the caption 'Be the best. Be a rower'. Despite being a reasonably nice guy, Downing has the intensely annoying habit of telling you things. I know that doesn't sound too bad …

Mr Rudolph Fane – The oldest living science teacher currently in captivity. Every year Fane insists on holding his 'handling mercury' class to get First Years interested in science, despite an annual series of regrettable incidents. Since approximately 1993 he's been puzzled by the shouts of 'Call him Mr Raider, call him Mr Wrong/ Call him Mr Fane' that follow him around the school.

Dr Andrew Hallbrick – Head of Music and father to Hallbrick of the Upper Sixth. Possessor of the world's weediest handshake. It's like a cherub farting in your palm. Appears to share a hairdresser with Simon Rattle.

Dr Malcolm Koch – Clearly a seventeen-year-old boy. Why he chooses to impersonate a rather dull thirty-something German teacher is a mystery. At some point someone should have taken him aside and mentioned that there might be advantages to a career which doesn't require you to go through every day being referred to as Herr Koch. Although even the dullest day in the staffroom is usually enlivened at some point by someone coming in and announcing, 'There's a boy outside looking for Koch.'

Mr Johnno McPhee – General sports dogsbody. Lives in Mercers' Lodge, which is why my bath is always full of rugby balls. Owner and trainer of the world's most ludicrous goatee. Has two T-shirts. One says 'Just Doing It', and has a picture of a couple making love in the curve of the Nike swoosh. The other says 'Mad Dog

Surf Wax'. Wears shorts all year round. Apparently unafraid of being seen as a cultural stereotype. Either Australian or a New Zealander, and I expect he gets quite cross if you get it wrong.

Dr Paul Morris – Drama and theatre studies. Apparently you can be a doctor of theatre studies. *O temporae, o mores.* They are building him a brand-new auditorium and drama lab, if you can believe it. His 1993 production of *Lord of the Flies* ended with the police being called in.

Miss Lucy Salmon – Religious studies. The darling of the Buxdon School Common Room. And doesn't she just know it.

Mr Barry Taylor – Lifetime ambition: to punch a carp in the mouth. When not pursuing this dream, Taylor supervises firsts rugby. He also teaches maths to some of the middle-school Morlock sets. Hopefully he doesn't teach geometry. Yesterday I heard him on Upper Field telling three 'lads' to 'pair up and form a square'.

Mr William Trotter – Head of Geography. He has his own boarding house, Trotter's, which reliably comes last in all school competitions. It also has some discipline problems. Last term a boy was kept imprisoned in his locker for three days before anyone heard his cries for help. Mr Trotter has an excellent selection of knitwear, including several knitted ties.

Mrs Edwina Trotter – Teaches Russian and, apparently, knits.

Mr Peter Wyndham – The bloke who I suspect went to the authorities regarding the Great Buxdon Bread Robbery. Also a French teacher, which explains but doesn't excuse why he reads *Le Monde* every morning while eating a croissant and drinking real coffee from a doll's-house cup. I bet he wears tight luminous Speedos and does European sevens. He annoys Dr

Fane by referring to his classroom as a 'language lab', as if three tape-recorders and a video of *Café des Rêves* makes him Marie Curie. I have similar reservations about the drama 'lab'.

It was agreed that I could swap Fives Society for Running Club. It's important to distinguish the Running Club from the Cross Country Team. The Cross Country Team meets on a Sunday and gets their kicks by dashing along through fields, lanes and hedgerows with no regard for life, limb or private property. The teacher in charge has to keep up and disentangle boys from barbed wire, guard dogs and angry farmers. Running Club involves a jog around the local park and is the minimal-legal-requirement sports option for geeks, idlers, the obese and boys on the after-school drama option. It will be a nice chance to see most of my Sixth Form English set in a less formal setting. My supervising duties seem largely to consist of taking a register, having a brisk but brief walk, and keeping hold of people's inhalers. The Running Club meets on Thursdays after school.

A non-erotic letter from Caroline arrived this morning. I'll compose a non-erotic reply over the weekend.

October

Mercers' Lodge
Buxdon School
Buxdon

Dear Caroline,

Thanks for your letter. It was really encouraging and supportive. To answer your questions:

– No, Miss Salmon isn't going to be my 'fancy lady'. While perfectly friendly, she remains a self-absorbed drama queen with a head so swollen the Montgolfier Brothers could stick a basket under it. She also teaches religious studies.

– No, I wasn't going to show your letter to everyone to prove I really have a girlfriend.

– No, I didn't move to Buxdon in order to letch on 'isolated floozies' and 'prettyboy Sixth Formers'. I moved here to have some peace and quiet to finish my book without having to go out every Friday night with Bloody Rychard.

– No, I don't think the atmosphere here is making me overly sweary and laddish.

– No, I haven't demanded 'kinky sex letters'. A list of querulous questions will do fine.

– By the way, I'm not a teacher; I'm a man who teaches.

– And yes, if this experiment *is* going to be like 'Prague all over again', then I agree we should forget it.

But I sincerely hope it won't be.
Love,
Matt

P.S. I quote: 'I wonder if this hotel used to be a hospital or a morgue?'

P.P.S. I don't think you ever gave Prague a chance. And yes, I do think the Kafka museum was romantic. And I definitely was not staring at those prostitutes.

P.P.P.S. Of course it was cold. I never 'misled you', I just assumed a basic level of common sense.

P.P.P.P.S. I'd better leave it there, because now I'm really starting to sound like a teacher.

P.P.P.P.P.S. But if you leave all the map reading to me, then I find it rather churlish to complain about us repeatedly getting lost. I think I did OK. Especially since it turned out I was consulting a map of Budapest. No wonder we never found the castle.

P.P.P.P.P.P.S. I do love you, by the way x x x

Tuesday, 1st October. Lionel Brimscombe is right: they really do need to put a glass front on the Walking Club noticeboard. The graffiti itself has now been graffitied, so that all the notices now read 'Winking Club'. He'll have a heart attack when he sees it. Although to be honest Brimscombe looks like he could have a heart attack tying up his shoelaces or getting out of a chair anyway.

There's a pay phone in the main corridor in the Old Building and a board to write messages on, which gives the boys an opportunity to display what a recent OFSTED report referred to as the school's 'highly developed culture of mutual respect and encouragement'. I quote:

– Message for G. Wilson (Fourth Year): Your mum rang to say you left your lunch at home today and she will be driving it in. Please meet her at the front gate at one fifteen.
– Message for G. Wilson (Fourth Year): Your mum has arrived with your lunch. In a fork-lift truck. You need to cut down on your pork life, mate. P.S. GET SOME EXERCISE.

47

Someone called M. Lau's parents are sorry to hear about the food and hopes he is keeping warm, and allegedly Hallbrick's mum rang to tell Chivers that he was great last night and to bring the pig mask again on Thursday.

The notice announcing the School Sponsored Walk has already been vandalised too.

Today I attempted to disabuse my Oxbridge set of some of the more common misconceptions about the interview process, and to dispel a few myths. It's possible that when they go in there'll be a brick on the table and the interviewer will ask them to throw it through a window to see how they respond. But it's much more likely they'll be asked to close-read a bit of prose or poetry and have a chat about their hobbies and interests. If there is a brick on the table, the trick is to open the window first. And not get trapped in a cupboard on the way out. None of the boys looked too blown away by any of this. I told them in future they didn't need to wear their scholar's gowns to our sessions.

Iles stayed behind afterwards to ask me whether I'd had a chance to read his poetry yet, and what I thought of it. He then mentioned that the poems he gave me were the only neat versions, which gave me a momentary pang when I realised I had mopped up some spilled tea on Saturday morning with the sole extant copy of 'The Octopus'. Well, said I, it's very hard to judge poetry, isn't it? It's all very subjective. Brilliant. I expect Immanuel Kant is spinning in his grave somewhere. To avoid hurting one boy's feelings I've undermined the basis of my entire professional career as a teacher of English literature. To my horror Iles announced he was writing more poems, and would let me read them in due course.

Wednesday, 2nd October. I won't be seeing Caroline this weekend, because she's going to the Bloody Isle of Wight for a training weekend with Rychard. She says he's a well-respected figure in the industry, who has a lot of help to give and advice to pass on, and who has taken a personal interest in her career. I said he was a letchy old swine in a black leather tie and slip-on loafers who has taken a personal interest in what she looks like naked. I pointed out that I spend all day making Rychards, so I do have some insight into how they operate. The long and the short of it is that she's still going to the Isle of Wight with Rychard and now she's in a huff with me. Nice work, Bletch. The boy plays another dazzler.

Ended up reading von Clausewitz this evening, in search of helpful stratagems for getting Rychard off the scene. What advice has the wily Prussian for me? 'Between the moment of the first assembling of military forces, and that of the solution arrived at when strategy has brought the army to the decisive point, there is in most cases a long interval; it is the same between one decisive catastrophe and another.' That sounds about right. 'Camp should never be pitched with its rear close to a river, morass, or deep valley'. Possibly less helpful.

There was a piece in the *Guardian* today about the unfair advantage certain schools give their students in the Oxbridge interview process by means of intensive preparation and expert coaching. Clearly the article was not written by someone who witnessed my badly prepared and disastrously un-expert coaching session with the scholars yesterday. The article did have a point, though. For one thing, where else but Buxdon would a kid like Bagley be encouraged to apply to read Classics at Magdalen? I thought I'd misjudged him, actually, because he spent the whole hour scribbling feverishly in his notebook. It was only at the end I realised he'd been drawing a robot.

Thursday, 3rd October. First meeting of the euphemistically named 'Running' Club this afternoon. We have three boys all nicknamed Fatty, one of whom is the aforementioned G. Wilson and two of whom did the whole circuit holding hands.

Not that there's anything wrong with that, but it does tend to slow them down. Unfortunately for the boys it was raining. Even more unfortunately, Tom Downing had one of his rowing squads running around the park at the same time as us, but in the opposite direction. Some of those collisions didn't look accidental.

Friday, 4th October. Called Caroline at work to wish her good luck on the Isle of Wight. She asked what I was up to over the weekend, and I mentioned that Barry Taylor and Johnno McPhee have invited me out to The Albion for a pint this evening. I suspect she doesn't feel she's missing out on much, although I mentioned the impressive range of local brews and the dog. I wonder which of his two T-shirts Johnno will be wearing.

Saturday, 5th October. I called Caroline from the staffroom at about eleven. They were about to go kayaking, and it's been raining non-stop since they arrived. Caroline accused me of sounding hopeful when I asked whether kayaking wasn't potentially very dangerous. She refused to say 'I love you', because people from work were there. I was reduced to begging, and she finally gave me a quick little 'I love you' that could have passed for a sneeze, then hung up. Sam Tipton, who came in to look for Mr Downing while I was on the phone, gave me a look of withering contempt. I informed the brassy youth that the staffroom's out of bounds to boys. 'That's OK,' he replied, 'I'm not "boys". If you see Downing about, tell him I've got something for him.' I think on the basis of Garnett's letter I can guess what.

I took it easy on the treacherous local firewater at The Albion last night, not wanting the evening to end up like last time. I ordered a half of Old Father Thames, or some such disgusting swill, and joined in the mockery of Johnno's Fosters. Actually

I was quite envious of him, particularly when I got to the bottom of my glass and discovered some kind of tidal sediment. I switched to Hangman's Daughter after that. In retrospect I regret this decision, as it's given me a savage hangover without actually getting me anywhere near drunk. Johnno was wearing the T-shirt that says 'Just Doing It'.

As he sank the glasses of Minerva's Owl, Barry Taylor was dropping increasingly leaden hints about what I told him the other day. I was thinking of dropping a snidey allusion to sucker-punching a carp into the conversation, but the opportunity didn't arise. Eventually Barry just announced: 'It's your round, Mister Goblin.' Fortunately I don't think Johnno managed to make very much of it.

Sunday, 6th October. Johnno may not know what it means, but that hasn't stopped him making 'Mister Goblin' my new nickname. I walked in on him in the bathroom today (not bathing, but getting the mud off thirty pairs of rugby boots) and he said something along the lines of: 'Aargh, me guts are crook after last night, cobber. How you doing, Mister Goblin?' Rak off, sport. That's how I'm doing.

On a more upbeat note, Caroline is back home safe and apparently sound. Bloody Rychard had a nasty slip during the trust exercise when they all had to fall back into a colleague's arms. I say 'slip', rather than accident. He landed on his coccyx and ended the weekend early in a huff. On the ferry back he found he had left one of his cufflinks in the hotel, and insisted they turn around and go back. The captain was having none of it and there was a huge row, but alas they didn't just throw him in the brig with a long hose on him. As it happens, Caroline overheard him on the phone to the hotel, and the cufflink turned out not to be in his room. They finally found it on the bedside table in the room that had belonged to the work experience girl.

*

Monday, 7th October. The Trotters brought their baby into the staffroom today. In a breathtakingly obsequious gesture they've named it Edmund, after the headmaster. It was wearing tiny knitted bootees and a little handmade jumper with a picture of a sunflower on the tummy. Over the sunflower there was writing that read 'Cute Baby Alert'. This would have been sweet if it hadn't been a total lie. Some babies are cute, others aren't. This one is gruesome. It has eyes like greedy buttons.

I was having coffee with Lucy Salmon when Mrs Trotter carried it over.

'Lucy, do you want to hold Munchkin?'

Lucy visibly shuddered.

'What is it?' she asked suspiciously.

'It's a boy.'

'Oh I see,' said Lucy, going up a notch in my estimation, 'It's some kind of baby.'

The confusion was quite understandable. It could pass for the Samiad.

What did you do today, Matthew? I satirised a baby. How will I top that, I wonder? Direct a blind man into oncoming traffic? Let down the tyres on someone's shopmobility vehicle? Loosen the screws on someone's callipers?

Tuesday, 8th October. I got stuck with Tom Downing and his lycra shorts at lunch, perhaps in karmic repercussion for being so snotty yesterday. God, he's a know-all. I offered to pass the salt, and he told me that in olden times salt was used to stop meat from going rotten. Yes, but would you like some to put on your chips? It's not so much that Downing tells you things (although that is presuming and tiresome) so much as that he tells you things all the time that you either don't care about or already know or both. He even tells you things if it's perfectly clear that you already know them. Perhaps Downing thinks he's being charmingly donnish. After all, he studied at

Cambridge, which is a well-respected university in the east of England. In actuality it not only makes him sound like an idiot, it makes him sound like an idiot who's talking down to you. I suppose getting into the habit of telling people things and giving them advice is something of an occupational hazard if you're a teacher, like cobbler's thumb or coal-miner's stoop. It's still really annoying, though.

I asked Downing if young Tipton managed to track him down on Saturday, and he suddenly went cagey. Presumably he couldn't think of any advice to give me about buying dope off one of the Sixth Form.

'Buying dope' indeed. I sound like someone's grandfather. One of the things I hadn't anticipated about becoming a teacher is how instantly decrepit it would make me feel. One of the Third Years asked me the other day how I felt when The Beatles broke up. Well, I was one at the time, so I don't recall taking it too badly. I think the kid was taking the mickey. I hope he was, anyway. Perhaps he thought I'd go off into a patchouli-scented reverie and forget to give them homework. Even my hip references are out of date. I casually dropped a reference to The Fall into a class on Blake the other day and everyone looked at me like I'd started babbling away in Assyrian. Christ, I dropped a reference to *The Fall* into a class on *Blake*. Is there anything more embarrassing than a hip teacher? Yes, since you ask, a teacher trying to be hip and missing by a mile. I might as well have been comparing Wordsworth to Bob Dylan. Or Shelley to The Cure. Sometimes I make *myself* cringe. People probably don't even use the expression 'hip' any more.

Wednesday, 9th October. I spoke to Caroline about weekend plans this evening. She and Sig have arranged a picnic on Saturday afternoon with Sig's PhD supervisor and boyfriend, who it turns out are the same person. Caroline has also invited Morgan Hartley, her childhood chum and human megaphone for the world's poshest voice. His voice is so posh I literally only understand about one word in every three he says. I don't imagine I'm missing much. When he speaks I have an almost instinctive reaction to reach for my forelock.

I'll also have to put up with Morgan and Caroline talking endlessly about people I've never met and never want to. Most of them sound like fancy drinks or legal firms: Squiffy Bolley, Tink Weevil, Arthur Braces, Hugo Duff-Barnet, Bohemond Crouchback, Alicia Power, Jaques Gadzookis, Woggy Hops, Henry Hamlet (really), Peveril House, Bartlett Bartlett, etc., etc. I guess if you're called Morgan Hartley it doesn't do to start getting fussy about that sort of thing. Or if you're Matthew Bletch, for that matter. I may be wrong about some of the names. As already mentioned, I find Morgan about sixty-six per cent incomprehensible. It's possible that Jaques Gadzookis merely works for the firm of Bartlett & Bartlett and lives in Peveril House. Then there's the apparently endless stream of Emilys and Jameses, some or all of whom I have met, but can never keep straight. Still, at least we're not getting Bloody Rychard.

I asked Caroline to pass on my best wishes to Rychard and his bruised coccyx. What a pain in the arse. I asked Caroline to do me a favour and have an excuse ready in case he asks her to rub ointment on it.

I bet Tink Weevil goes like a train. If Tink Weevil is a plummy girl, not a crop parasite or a banking house. But Arthur Braces sounds like a music-hall turn.

OK, so I made up Hugo Duff-Barnet.

Thursday, 10th October. Nothing of note happened today, except that Chivers hobbled into third period English on crutches. Rugby injury? No, freak Frisbee accident on Mercers' Field.

Friday, 11th October. I was faced with an unforeseen problem when I tried to take the Third Year kids' homework in today. It was the big balding kid with the moustache-smudge, one of the boys who've just come up from prep school. He shambled up at the end of the lesson. 'I do have my essay, sir, but I'm afraid I can't give it to you.' I asked why not. He held up his briefcase. Someone had surreptitiously changed his combination during the lesson. He couldn't imagine how they'd guessed the original combination.

'Was it 007 007?'

'Yes, Sir.'

Well, it would hardly have taken a mastermind to work that out. Fortunately I know a trick to open briefcases. The essay was inside, along with some neatly packed sandwiches, a copy of *White Dwarf* magazine and a rather chunky calculator.

'How did you know how to do that, Sir?'

Well, for the same reasons I know how to get chewing gum out of hair and how to unpick a tie that someone's tugged on until the knot's the size of a peanut. The same reason also I can never stand at a urinal without the lingering paranoia that someone might be about to run up behind me and give me a hearty push into it. I gently suggested it might be time to exchange that briefcase for a canvas bag with the names of his favourite bands written on it.

I've prepared an ingenious stratagem to get Peter Wyndham back for branding me a bread thief. I bought a sugar-sprinkled croissant from the Buxdon Tea Shoppe at mid-morning break, and before I go away I'm going to leave it out temptingly on the table in the kitchen. My bag is packed and I'm off to the big city. The snare is baited, and now I just have to wait for Wyndham to put his greedy claw into it ...

Saturday, 12th October. I met Sig's boyfriend Anton last night. Manfriend, really, since he must be pushing fifty. He opened the door of the flat when I arrived and my first impression was of two enormous melancholy eyes staring out of a pale corpsy face. Anton physically recoiled at the sight of me. If he'd been wearing a cape he would have drawn it around himself and hissed. There are many things I'd change about myself if I could, but at least I don't look like The Cryptkeeper. On the other hand, Anton's someone who seems unlikely to lock himself on a balcony. If he did he could probably just crawl down the wall head downwards.

Anton followed me upstairs, where Sig had two bowls of watery gruel waiting. As we passed the television he gave it a very disapproving look which he didn't bother to disguise. He probably has a very small TV hidden in a pretend drinks cabinet.

He and Sig spent the evening watching a film in black-and-white and Polish, and Caroline and I joined them. We missed the beginning, and as we came in a corpse-laden trolley was wheeled over a blank landscape by a man wearing a harlequin outfit. 'I think I've seen this,' I wisecracked. 'Isn't Joey from *Friends* in it?' Apparently not. I'd got it confused with *Ed*, the film where Matt le Blanc forms a baseball team with a chimpanzee. Anton left halfway through, explaining that his wife expected him back to tuck the kids in. I bet they get great bedtime stories. I gave Caroline a look at this point that Sig must have registered, because after Anton had slunk into the night she explained that although he and his wife are separated he sleeps in the basement. That must be convenient. I restrained myself from asking whether he sleeps in a coffin or hanging from the ceiling by his feet.

'Anton's really such a sweet man,' Sig added, 'but he's a little bit shy. He's a profoundly serious person.'

He definitely takes himself profoundly seriously. That film had fewer laughs than the Old Testament. As for 'shy', it wouldn't have been the word I'd have chosen. Kids are shy; and small woodland creatures. Anton in contrast is someone who does absolutely nothing to make you like him. Either he conserves his energy by only talking to people he wants to talk to about things he wants to talk about, or he's just a rude prick. I've never met anyone who seems so consciously to radiate the fact that he is not suffering your foolishness gladly. That he's also Sig's PhD supervisor makes the relationship even more of an excellent idea.

We didn't bother with the rest of the film. I'm fairly sure it was going to end with everyone getting plague. By the time Sig told me she plans to ask Anton's wife to be internal examiner on her PhD, I felt like I was stuck in a 70s art-house film anyway. All we were missing was someone wearing classical robes and the mask of tragedy to emerge from the kitchen every so often and denounce our bourgeois complacency.

I hope Sig doesn't ask Anton to move in. Caroline and I would never be able to watch *Hollyoaks* in peace again.

Sig and Caroline have gone out to the market to get provisions for the picnic, and I'm having a shower and getting ready. Despite Caroline's assurances, I'm not convinced that Sig likes me very much. She spent most of this morning asking leading questions about who washed up her wok the other week. She's also lent Caroline a book by Dr Hart Adams PhD with the unfortunate title *Is Your Relationship a Floater?* I think I'd have more confidence in Dr Hart Adams PhD's advice if the sequel wasn't called *The Power of One: Learning to be Single*. Dr Hart Adams PhD is also the author of *When Love Curdles Make Yoghurt*, *Alone is Not a Four-Letter Word*, and *Excuse Me, That's My Orgasm You're Having*, all of which Sig has on her shelves. Strangely enough this doesn't immediately make me assume that she is a totally sorted person. She also has a book entitled *What Your Doctor Doesn't Know About Preventing Cancer*. I suspect that what your doctor doesn't know about preventing cancer is most likely bullshit, but I haven't mentioned this to Sig. No sign of her trampoline so far.

*

Sunday, 13th October. Caroline, Sig, Shouty Morgan, Creepy Anton and I had a rather chilly picnic in the park yesterday. I discovered that Anton has met my estranged brother at a SECS conference. My younger estranged brother, Dominic, rather than my elder estranged brother Frank. SECS is the Society for Eighteenth Century Studies, a fact that could helpfully have been dropped into the conversation a lot earlier.

Morgan is the same as ever, from what I could gather. His love life is still reassuringly shambolic. He told us he'd been on a blind date the other day and the woman stole his wallet. He doesn't think he'll be seeing her again, but he'll wait and see if she rings. It could have been worse. She could have stolen his phone.

Caroline then regaled the company with the tale of how for our first date we went on a picnic, and how we missed each other and spent hours wandering around the park. She claims that I told her to meet me at the corner of Round Pond. As I pointed out, her version of events is disputed. Caroline most likely simply misheard or misunderstood the instructions. I didn't realise at the time that this mix-up would be a massive clunky symbol for our subsequent relationship.

Caroline also let me know that my habit of referring to Frank and Dominic as my estranged brothers is an annoying affectation.

On the train from Paddington the woman sitting behind me phoned everyone she'd ever met to tell them about her weekend, in exactly the same words, over and over. Then we started going under bridges and she kept getting cut off and having to phone back. It got quite irritating after a while.

When I got back to Buxdon I found a note waiting for me from Mrs O. Digby. There have been complaints about food being left lying around in the kitchen. Keeping shared areas in a tidy and sanitary condition is a matter not only of mutual respect, but of health and safety. Zounds, hoisted on my own pâtisserie. That's £2.10 I won't see again. I think I can guess who reported me, too.

Monday 14th October. Thank God it's half-term. Caroline wanted me to stay up in London for longer, but I've got a bloody great pile of marking to do, including the first crop of GCSE essays on *Little Dorrit* and a foot-high pile of Third Year essays on *Wuthering Heights*. I'll get the marking out of the way sharpish, then hopefully have a day or so clear to work on my own writing. Well, that's the plan anyway. So far today I have woken up, lain in bed for three hours listening to Radio 4 and thought about having a shower. I'll get up when *Money Box* comes on.

I may also try to knock off the final two hundred pages of *Little Dorrit* itself, which I'm still slogging my way through, dry-eyed and stony-faced. The trick is to keep motivated. Five pages earns a cup of coffee, ten pages earns a cigarette.

Tuesday, 15th October. There was a big parcel from my estranged brother Frank in the post this morning – short on postage to my not very great surprise. When opened, it contained a pair of ski boots, a tiroler hat and a T-shirt reading 'Beer Me Up, Scotty'. No note. Cheers, Frank. What on earth am I supposed to do with these? Go skiing presumably. While looking a prat.

I marked three or four *Little Dorrit* essays. Only forty left to go.

Wednesday, 16th October. I think I'm going to have to have a word with Dr Cumnor about one of the Third Year essays. Most of the efforts were pretty heart-rending, but this one really does make little baby Jesus weep. I ran off a photocopy, because it really does need to be savoured whole for the full effect. In its entirety it runs:

My name is Marcus Lau. I am a boarder at Buxdon School in Trotter's House. It is a good place to live and I have made many friends from all over the world. Sometimes I play soccer with younger boys from Hong Kong, Singapore and Malaysia. We are allowed to watch television between 8 and 9. Light's Out is ten o'clock but often I can't get to sleep and I miss home. The food is not good. My favourite restaurant is Chopstix in Market Square. I have been there twelve times. On Sunday Mr Brimscombe takes us for a long walk and tells us about the history of Buxdon but sometimes it is cold and raining. I enjoy wuthering heights and I look forward to learning about it more with you.

I expect Dr Cumnor will agree with me that while this essay is adequate as far as it goes, it doesn't really answer the question: 'To what extent is Nelly Dean a reliable narrator?'

I rounded off the evening by spending four hours in the lounge with Johnno McPhee and Barry Taylor, watching videos of the rowers at Henley this summer. It wasn't a great night, but it was a damn sight better than marking essays. I can literally feel the remains of my youth dribbling away. I keep expecting to find a little puddle of it on the floor.

Later on, Barry Taylor and I had a difference of opinion over which is the best song on *The White Album*. Extraordinarily he claims it's 'Ob-La-Di Ob-La-Da', and then insisted we listen to it. Twice. Nope, it's still rubbish. I was still fuming when I spoke to Caroline, who told me to calm down and that I should have compromised for diplomacy's sake. What's the point of compromising with someone who's empirically, provably wrong? The best song on *The White Album* is clearly 'Martha My Dear'. Even if it is about Paul McCartney's dog. What do I care? I hate The Beatles anyway, as the latter part of this evening vividly reminded me. 'Why Don't We Do It In The Road?' Because you'll get run over, you silly hippy twats.

*

Thursday, 17th October. Great! Caroline's coming down to-morrow night. I need to change my bedding, and pick a few of the most prominent dust fairies off the carpet. I couldn't find the hoover so I shuffled up and down the room in big socks instead. It kind of worked. Certainly the floor's no grubbier than before. I bought some scented candles as well. According to Dr Hart Adams PhD that should help set 'the mood'.

I tried and failed to find somewhere to stow the box Frank sent me. I tried under the bed, but it didn't fit, so I've covered it with a bit of tie-dyed cloth I requisitioned from Lucy Salmon and now it serves as a low bedside table. I was hoping to be able to stick the box up in the attic, but it was locked and bolted and Mrs O. Digby claimed not to have the key. I also had a poke around the top floors of the Old Building to see if there was room in the attics over there, with even less success. There definitely is an attic that runs the whole length of the building, because you can see the windows. But the only door leading up there that I could find was not only locked, but nailed shut and painted over. It also has an out-of-bounds notice on it. That's rather mysterious. I'll keep my ears open for ominous thumps and rattling chains. Perhaps there's a really young-looking portrait of Rudolph Fane up there having a whale of a time.

Now I must mark, mark like the wind, and get the remaining essays out of the way. I'm fully caffeinated and ready to go. Sod it, after the first ten essays you're basically marking the handwriting anyway.

Friday, 18th October. Finally finished the marking, but signally failed to get any real work done on my book this half-term. After three hours today searching for the *mots justes* to describe the night sky over Matsushima Bay, I found myself faced with a piece of paper on which I have written the words 'sort of purple'. I couldn't decide between 'purple' or 'purplish'. However, I've arranged for Caroline and I to tag along with the Walking Club on Sunday, so I should get the chance to ask Lionel Brimscombe about literary agents. On second thoughts, maybe 'purplish' was better. I should also make sure I've got the spellings of 'cumulonimbus' and 'fluorescent' correct.

Monday, 21st October. My legs are absolutely knackered. I'm surprised they haven't dropped off in the night. Caroline and I went for an excursion yesterday with Lionel Brimscombe's Walking Club, and climbed every church tower within a ten-mile radius of Buxdon. If I'd had to look at one more rood screen, lancet window, flying buttress or Quadrifoil spandrel my eyes would have popped. I had a dream about brass rubbing.

As it turns out, all the effort was in vain. Brimscombe isn't only his own agent, he's his own editor, typist, proofreader, cover designer and publisher. He also looks like he could drop dead at any moment. He's got the complexion of a professional darts player. I've heard people described as a heart attack waiting to happen, but Brimscombe looks like a heart attack in the process of happening. We were climbing the tower at St Agnes' and he stopped for what I thought was a stroke but turned out to be a breather. We did get some lovely views of Buxdon from the top. It's like a poor man's Didcot.

Poor Marcus Lau was there as well, and I had a chat with him about his essay. He says he misses home a lot. I'm not surprised – Trotter's boarding house is like a borstal. They barricaded Trotter in his own office with a table-tennis table the other day and went on the rampage. Bagley was sitting on the floor with a metal bin on his head and the others were taking turns to whack it with a pool cue. And people say the kids these days don't know how to make their own fun. Luckily the Head was showing some prospective parents round the school and managed to restore order and let Trotter out.

Caroline says I'll have to do a bit better than scented candles. It seems the perfumed atmosphere was less reminiscent of an exotic harem than it was of the guests' loo at her Auntie Lydia's. Which we've previously established is not a place Caroline particularly wants to have sex.

Tuesday, 22nd October. Caroline had a teary phone call from her sister tonight. Lulu thinks she's cocked up the bar exam again. Well, all the fluffy mascots and lucky knickers in Christendom won't help if you don't do any revision. I do sometimes wonder whether Lulu is cut out for the Law. Perhaps someone should suggest to Lulu that being a barrister is not all shagging in the office, sharing a cool house and listening to Sneaker Pimps. We've been invited to go down and see Caroline's parents in three weeks' time, so if Lulu's there I may mention it then. I reminded Caroline that Thursday night is the Fundraising Halloween Fancy-Dress party, but she has some stuff to catch up with in London. I don't think I can get out of it and I still haven't thought of a costume yet. Cunning Dr Trotter volunteered to show a video in his boarding house for boys whose parents objected to the pagan nature of the festivities.

I also reminded Caroline that it's my birthday coming up ... She hadn't forgotten.

Wednesday, 30th October. Into Buxdon today to look for a Halloween costume. Barry Taylor suggested I go as a goblin, which I didn't find particularly helpful. Also I don't have time to ask Mum to send me the outfit. Barry has decided to wrap himself in a sheet and go as a Roman. I'm not sure what's Halloweeny about that idea but it does sound terrifying.

Thursday, 31st October. Barry Taylor informs me that there'll be an Interschools Running Competition at the end of term.

By then I'll no doubt have transformed my pet bunch of so-called 'losers' into a team bursting with confidence and camaraderie. It'll have to be a hell of a long montage, though. As we were drifting around the park today the First VIII ran past, with Tom Downing cycling along behind them holding a megaphone: 'Do you want to be like those losers? Where's Second Place?' 'Nowhere!' 'I can't hear you!' That's probably because you're shouting Nazi platitudes through a megaphone, you tool.

The headmaster used today's staff meeting as an opportunity to express his dismay and disappointment at the recent incident which resulted in the toilets in the Sixth Form centre being temporarily placed out of bounds and one member of the cleaning staff being given a week's compassionate leave. He promised that the incident would be thoroughly investigated and the culprit reprimanded with the greatest severity. He asked all staff to remain vigilant and to report any rumours regarding possible suspects to him immediately.

Barry Taylor suggested that this kind of thing is just natural teenage high spirits. Yes, or the type of behaviour more commonly associated with depressed chimps in an over-crowded zoo. Poor Mrs Tarawicz the cleaning lady left her mop and bucket temporarily unattended, and when she came back someone had availed themselves of the bucket in an unorthodox and truly disgusting manner. As the headmaster described the outrage. He meant they'd taken a dump in it. Whoever it was had also written a message on the mirror: 'The Beast of Buxdon strikes.' Fortunately the message was written in Tippex. Mrs Tarawicz has been given the rest of the week to recover.

The headmaster was asking what kind of mind would even conceive of doing something like that. I'm more interested in what they were thinking as they did it. I can't decide whether it's more disturbing if it was a premeditated protest or a spurof-the-moment impulse, unwisely indulged. What's that I can just make out in the distance? Ah yes, the very final outskirts of decency. The Head says he hasn't been this shocked by an incident at Buxdon since the football-stickers-for-sexual-favours scandal of 1986. 'No civilised society can tolerate this kind of behaviour.' He's right. We're probably weeks away from machine guns on the chapel roof. I think a truly civilised society would also have some stern words to say about Tom Downing's running shorts.

The Head told us he was very tempted to cancel the Halloween Party tonight. Disappointingly he's decided not to.

November

Sunday, 3rd November. The Halloween festivities on Thursday night were appropriately ghastly. There was a horrible 'hop' in the Sixth Form centre after dinner. It was actually called 'The Horrible Hop'. I can't believe they charged us £5 each to get in.

Emilia Bartlett came as a witch, and didn't seem to approve of my mad scientist costume i.e. a lab coat out of lost property spattered with fake blood. Lab safety is nothing to joke about. Johnno McPhee was Young Einstein, and spent most of the night explaining the cinematic career of Yahoo Serious to those too slow to escape. Rudolph Fane provided further evidence for the general rule that there's absolutely nothing sexy about a man dressed as a naughty vicar. Ah, Buxdon. You don't have to be mad to work here, but it helps if you're a bit of a twat.

Dr Morris, whose drama lab the whole thing was in aid of, was the inevitable person who took the costume thing way too seriously. I suppose dressing up and pratting about is part of his job, after all. Morris came as the Elephant Man and spent the night lurching around with a pillow case on his head and breathing heavily. I'm always suspicious of people who choose a fancy-dress costume that doesn't let them drink. Morris won the costume prize, and started punching the air and shouting, 'Third year in a row!' The First Year who came as Piggy from *Lord of the Flies* only got runner-up, and left in tears. Possibly because he hadn't come in costume, or perhaps it was the sight of a grown man with a pillow case on his head waving a walking stick at him and shouting, 'In your face,

Piggy.' Peter Wyndham turned up with an enormous facial wound. Unfortunately this proved to be fake. Lucy Salmon was an allegedly sexy cat.

Lucy was hitting the Buxdon wine pretty heavily, and she rounded the evening off by snogging Barry Taylor. He's still audibly humming with smugness about it, despite the fact that she followed the snog by: a) throwing up in the car park; b) bursting into tears; c) throwing up again and refusing to come out of the disabled toilets.

After that, Barry Taylor disappeared for a bit, then re-appeared with his toga dripping wet. He accidentally fell in the pond – or so he claims.

The Tipton parents made an appearance as well: Mr and Mrs Charles Tipton 'of Tipton Construction', the crack team that built the new science block. Mr Tipton made rather a scene by claiming to be able to do that trick where you pull the tablecloth off a table without disturbing the punch bowl, glasses and floral arrangement. It turns out he can't, although he had several attempts at it. He then announced that he was driving a group of parents home in a minibus.

According to Barry, Lucy Salmon has a long and very energetic tongue, which is a piece of knowledge I could have lived without. It's like having a curious little goldfish in your mouth, I'm told. I very much wish I hadn't been.

Caroline dropped a hint on the phone tonight about what I'm getting for my birthday. She mentioned that she's been out shopping for underwear. For me or her, I wonder? Also, Caroline unveiled the theory that my loathing for Rychard is actually … repressed sexual attraction. Well, it couldn't just be genuine loathing, could it? What could there possibly be to loathe about a man who shamelessly angles himself at my girlfriend, probably wears a leopard-skin thong, and wanders around closely pursued by the ghosts of a hundred dead civets? I don't feel threatened by him either. I just hate him. I expect he listens to the Lighthouse Family, reading *GQ*, with his feet up on a glass coffee table. I wouldn't be surprised if he's seriously wondered whether he could carry off a cravat.

I didn't say all this to Caroline, of course. Because if I say that I hate Rychard, it proves I love him. Obviously. I was a bit too cunning to fall for that one. I said I'd seriously consider the possibility I fancy him. In fact, of course, the only thing I'm seriously considering is the most elaborate way to fuck him. Stick that in your pipe and smoke it, Dr Hart Adams PhD.

Fuck him up. I meant to write 'fuck him up'.

Monday, 4th November. Dr Cumnor took me aside in the staffroom and reminded me that we have a poet visiting the school next week. I tried not to look too blank when Cumnor told me the name. Apparently he's on the GCSE syllabus and everything. But then so are Simon cocking Armitage and Carol Anne sodding Duffy. I'm supposed to get some questions together for after the reading.

I hot-footed it over to the library and took out everything they have by Kevin Williams. He's written three volumes of poetry, *Current Address Unknown*, *Everybody Works at the BBC* and *Jumpers for Goal Posts*, and a sodding play: *Who Do You Think You Are, Benny Wilson?* It might be helpful to have a chat with Kevin Williams and find out who his agent is. Or even better if he knows who Simon Armitage's agent is.

Later on I finally got the chance to sit down with Cumnor and discuss Marcus Lau and his essay. Dr Cumnor read it and chuckled. 'Oh, this is very good, yes. Do you mind if I have a copy?' He dabbed his eyes with his tie. If anything's going to be done about this I guess I'll have to do it myself.

Caroline's parents have invited us down to spend the weekend with them. I've turned down their last three invitations, so I really do owe them a visit. Great, a birthday on my best behaviour.

*

Tuesday, 5th November. It was the school fireworks display tonight, so we all trooped out to the top field to stand in the drizzle and watch Tom Downing fail to make a Catherine Wheel go off. Lucy Salmon was notable by her absence, and Barry Taylor took the opportunity to confess to me that he's really fancied her for months. That explains a lot, not least why I keep catching him palely loitering around the religious studies department. Lucy hasn't talked to him since Thursday night, which doesn't strike me as terribly encouraging. Nor does the fact that she followed their kiss with a bout of weepy vomiting. He asked me what I thought he should do. Frankly, anyone turning to me for love-life advice is nine-tenths doomed already. 'How can I compete with a bloke like Charlie?' Barry asked. 'Lucy wouldn't notice me if I was leaping around in a big gold hat,' he added, miserably. I reassured him that she most certainly would. I'm not sure she'd fancy him, but she'd certainly notice him. I suggested perhaps he make some effort to find out what her interests are. He said 'religious studies', but I'm not convinced there's that much romantic mileage there.

Fortunately they examined the Guy before they burned it, since: a) it was wearing most of Hallbrick Jr's wardrobe; and b) the head was entirely composed of bangers. And not just joke-shop bangers, those continental ones designed to give rooks a heart attack. The involvement of the Beast of Buxdon is suspected. Mostly because around the Guy's neck was a sign reading 'The Beast Strikes Again'.

Who is this mysterious Beast of Buxdon? I have my suspects – about seven hundred boys and about twenty-five teaching and admin staff. Although, on reflection, it's unlikely to be young Hallbrick.

Wednesday, 6th November. Iles wants to prepare a folder of his poetry to show Kevin Williams when he comes to visit the school. Lucky old Kevin Williams. Fortunately Iles didn't seem too fussed about my reading any of his latest work. There seems to me a certain arrogance in describing your current work as 'Juvenilia'.

I still haven't managed to read any of Kevin Williams' poetry. Hopefully I'll get the chance of a quick skim at the Applebys' this weekend. I spoke to Mum, who took the news I wouldn't be home for my birthday surprisingly well. She seemed more interested in whether I'd spoken to Frank or Dom recently. No, I haven't. That's kind of the point of being estranged from them. She wishes I wouldn't say that – it's not that it upsets her, it's just it sounds so affected. I reassured her, as I did Caroline the other day, that my feelings about Frank and Dom are in no way affected. My present is in the post.

Thursday, 7th November. I spoke to Lucy Salmon today, who claims to have absolutely no memory of last Thursday night.

Still haven't come up with a plan to help Marcus Lau. He looked absolutely miserable in class today. The big balding kid with the moustache didn't look much happier. He's written the name of his favourite bands in Tippex on the side of his briefcase. Strangely enough lugging a briefcase around with 'AC/DC' on one side and 'Status Quo' on the other doesn't seem to have done much for his popularity.

Sunday, 10th November. Down to the Garden of England to see Caroline's parents. As ever, a weekend with the Applebys was a refreshing plunge into the world of the bizarre.

Caroline's father, Henry, picked us up from the station. I have a new theory regarding him: that at some stage he got so posh he came out the other side. To all intents and purposes he's now indistinguishable from a tramp, except that he drives a Land Rover. After about two minutes of his driving I stopped even trying to listen to what he was saying, and concentrated on hanging on to the dashboard and not weeping in terror. According to Caroline, apparently I nodded in approval when Henry asked if teaching was 'a bit of a cop-out profession', then shook my head when he asked if I had any longer-term goals. From the way he said it I doubt he even really considers teaching a proper profession. At least not in the same way as the Army, the Church or the Law.

There was a long story, apparently involving an otter, a townie and a bridle path, which ended with him closing his eyes in mirth and actually rocking back and forth with wheezy hilarity, which Caroline joined in with. I made some appreciative noises, and would have thrown myself into the occasion with more abandon if I hadn't thought that at least one of us should keep their eyes on the road.

Henry took us to the 'new restaurant in town', which is a McDonald's. He pottered about the place examining everything with the wide-eyed wonder of a child or a curious Martian. He didn't want to cause a scene, so he sent me back to the counter to mention quietly to the staff that they'd forgotten to give us any cutlery. Another of my theories about Henry was proved when the same mayonnaise stain on his chest was clearly in evidence throughout the weekend.

From talking to Henry you'd assume that he was a tiresome minor character from a Thomas Hardy novel, rather than a city lawyer on early retirement. Thank God he didn't retire to the seaside, or he'd probably be hopping around on a peg-leg, puffing on a corncob pipe and affecting a Cap'n Birdseye beard. And he'd insist on telling you stories about Mermaids and smugglers. He asked me, over our burgers, why Whitehall never listens to countryfolk. I mumbled something about it being a shame. I suspect it's something to do with the fact they're constantly telling incomprehensible anecdotes about otters and bridle paths. Henry then embarked on a long story about their neighbour getting his foot caught in a badger trap and having to wait two hours for an ambulance. As good a summary as any, I think, of why I don't ever want to live in the country. 'You urbanites,' he said, with a sweep of the arm that took in only me, 'think badgers are cute. Well they're a ruddy pest. Nasty bastards, too. He'll take your face off, a badger, soon as sniffle.' Well, then, I shall endeavour to live where badgers are not.

On the topic of sniffling, I had dosed myself up with heroic quantities of antihistamines before arriving, so unlike last time I didn't immediately start sneezing my guts out at Chez Appleby's distinctive combination of dust and dog hair. I managed not to flinch at the amorous attentions of the various blind, bald, stinking dogs that peeled themselves off the carpets at Caroline's arrival. Her favourite, Moldy, has an enormous chancre on its forehead, which no one in the family finds as disturbing as I do. You have to take your shoes off in the porch, with the result that you spend all your time carefully picking your way around the house avoiding various hair-covered dog eggs everywhere.

Caroline's brother Toby was away on manoeuvres, or night training, or something, but his girlfriend Hannah was there, helping out in the kitchen. It's amazing to me the amount of time, effort and attention the Applebys put into feeding themselves. The day begins with Margery Appleby producing a vast cooked breakfast, then asking you what you want for lunch. All plans are arranged around the need to buy, prepare, cook and clean up the day's three vast meat feasts. You literally can't leave the house without being informed of when the next feeding time is, and no one can drive into the village without being ordered to pick up shallots, or a goose, or a bag of trotters.

In the brief intervals when the Applebys aren't eating, they're discussing food. I made the mistake, early on, of agreeing fairly non-committally with Margery's suggestion that pheasant would be nice for Sunday lunch. I mean, why wouldn't it be? For the rest of the time I was there I was condemned to the role of eccentric spokesperson for year-round fowl-eating. Throughout our afternoon walk I was subjected to an amused but rigorous interrogation on the subject from Henry, Hannah and Lulu. 'How small is the smallest bird worth eating?' Henry asked me at one point. 'I'm sure you disagree, but in my opinion when it gets down to anything smaller than a poussin, the game isn't worth the candle.' I agreed, but Hannah demanded where I stood on the question of quail. I think it was a trick question. Which is bigger, a quail or a poussin? Then, with a mad sparkle in her eye, Lulu asked if I would eat a sparrow. Not raw. I'm not sure but I suspect she would.

How is it that no one else seems to have noticed the evident fact that Caroline's sister is off her rocker? Only counterpointed by the enormous eccentricity of the other Applebys can she pass as a sane member of society. For one thing, she sleepwalks nude. Last time I visited the Applebys, I could hear Lulu wandering around the house all night and as a result spent the early morning hours lying awake in terror with a hugely-swollen bladder. And, it must be confessed, a naggingly persistent erection.

Caroline warned me on the train down that Lulu hasn't told her parents yet that she thinks she's failed the bar exam. Yes, that's the brilliant logical mind and sound grasp of detail that will take Lulu all the way to the top. I don't suppose she's even considered that her story will fall to pieces once it becomes apparent that she is not in fact a practising lawyer. I suspect Margery isn't rushing out to buy a new hat just yet, anyway.

Unfortunately the antihistamines I'd taken combined badly with the industrial-strength gins and tonics that Margery gave us before dinner. I crashed out almost immediately after dessert, which took the form of frozen blackberries 'prepared' by Lulu. Caroline and I had separate rooms, and Moldy (or Pongo, or Limpy, or Mr Slobber, or Squits, or one of the other decaying canines I'm expected to dote on) had been sleeping on my bed. As a result I woke up with hugely swollen itching eyes and a streaming nose. About nine a.m. Margery came up with a plate of sausages and offered me an 'eye-opener'. This proved to be a huge gin and tonic. Another kick in the liver. It's always gin o'clock at the Applebys'.

There was no question of getting away before lunch today, not least as it was the pheasant that I had apparently demanded for my birthday and was so excited about. It was a little dry, but I managed to get through it. I baulked at 'thirds', though. Baulk? I almost boked. Which I'll make a note of as a title for my future autobiography. I could already hear my chair creaking under me when the lights went off and a giant cake was brought in.

We went out in the early afternoon to try to waddle off our lunch. I was glad I checked the Wellingtons Margery offered me, because there was the fattest spider I've ever seen living in one of them. He looked like the plump and prosperous chief burgher of Spidertown. I tipped him out and off he ran, but he couldn't fit under the door. I think he eventually went out the cat flap. I borrowed an umbrella too and was less than thrilled when I opened it to be showered in desiccated insects and mouse droppings. I'm definitely never living in the country.

I hate spiders. About as much as I hate badgers, and almost as much as I hate stories about badgers.

Lulu gave us a lift for the train, and we left as the discussion of what to have for dinner was starting up. We swung by the butcher's on the way to the station, and she purchased most of a cow. The butcher's has a sign outside that reads: 'Pleased to Meet You, Meat to Please You.' Which sounds like a terrible chat-up line. Certainly Caroline didn't go for it when I tried it out later.

I feel like I've got gravy coming out of my ears. Stick an apple in my mouth and I'm done.

So what did I get for my birthday? Apart from indigestion. Caroline gave me pants. Tiny pants. Mum gave me a giant silver pen. Although much too heavy for everyday use, it will come in very handy if I'm attacked by a werewolf.

In all that birthday excitement, I almost forgot that I'm in charge of Boarders' Film Club this evening. I've spent the past forty-five minutes going through the English department's video collection, trying to find something suitable. This has proved to be harder than it sounds. They've got: *The Charge of the Light Brigade*, *Biggles*, *Breaker Morant*, *Zulu*, *Zulu Dawn*, *39 Days in Peking*, seven documentaries about Captain Scott, *Kim*, *A Passage to India*, *The Malta Story*, and three versions of *The White Feathers*. Who the hell chose all these? Gordon of Khartoum? I finally dug out a copy of *Howards End*. After all, what twelve- to eighteen-year-old-boy doesn't love a good Merchant-Ivory? It came down to either that or *Brief Encounter*, and I didn't want to end up weeping everywhere.

Monday, 11th November. Still stuffed. Will I ever be hungry again? I can physically feel the outline of my stomach inside me. Now I know what being a larder would feel like.

There was an astonishing turnout for the film last night. Even Bagley was there, which suggests a previously unsuspected sensitivity on his part. Or perhaps Sunday evenings at Buxdon are just really boring.

Caroline rang about eight o'clock, a bit perturbed by a conversation she'd just had with Sig. Caroline had gone into the kitchen to put the kettle on and Sig asked her to guess what she'd found in the communal bins that morning. A load of rubbish? Some bin-liners? Body parts? Cauliflower leaves. What surprised Caroline more is that Sig took them out of the bin, has washed them off, and is now seriously proposing to eat them. 'How can people be so wasteful?' asks the woman whose showers use enough water to float a battleship.

Tuesday, 12th November. I realised just now that I've some-how managed to leave the collected works of Kevin Williams on a bedside table at the Applebys'. I rang them up to say thanks for the lovely weekend and to ask if they could pos-sibly send the books on. Unfortunately I only managed to get through to Lulu. Inasmuch as one ever really gets through to Lulu. It seemed rude to ask a 23-year-old woman whether there was a grown-up there I could speak to. They definitely found the books, and she thinks that they sent them off to me yesterday. But then Lulu also thinks that it's acceptable to publicly French kiss a dog. Even if they have enormous growths on their foreheads. She informed us over dinner on Saturday that she is seriously thinking of 'chucking the Law in' and going into business breeding ostriches (which led to a long interrogation as to my opinion of the edibility of vari-ous ostrich products). Lulu warned me that one of the books was 'slightly chewed'. I imagine by Pongo, Dribbles or Mr Incontinent, but she may well have chewed it herself.

Wednesday, 13th November. No sign of the books. Dr Cumnor asked how the questions I'm meant to be preparing are com-ing along. So far I have one: 'Does a poem have to rhyme?' I really hope he just replies: 'Yes, next question.' But he prob-ably won't. I suppose in a pinch I could ask where he gets his ideas from.

I took my birthday pants for a test drive today. Not only are they tiny, they're very badly designed. The fly involved a kind of elaborate and oddly placed pouch arrangement, which left me groping around at the urinal in the Main Building for about two minutes before I was lined up for action. I thought for a moment my watch strap had got stuck. The kid next to me looked very nervous, not surprisingly since I was doing a

good impression of either an automolesting pederast or someone who'd temporarily misplaced the world's tiniest penis. So
thanks again, Caroline. I'm thinking of composing a stinging
letter to the retailer.

Thursday, 14th November. Still no sign of a package from the
Applebys. I asked Caroline if she wanted to come down for
the dinner afterwards but she didn't sound terribly interested.
She's going to the NFT with Sig and the sulky cadaver. I promised to come down on Saturday. Sig's having a dinner party
in the evening with her friends, Anya, Beatrix, Francesco,
Mathilde, Jesus and Rolph. I expressed some amusement
that Sig has a friend called Jesus – although I bet being called
Rolph isn't a barrel of laughs either. It's pronounced 'Hey
Zeus', Caroline corrected me, before reminding me that we've
all got a friend called Jesus. I wonder if Sig's friend has heard
that one before.

I was passing the phone in the Old Building lobby today
when it rang. Someone called Sketch asked for Sam Tipton,
and I explained I hadn't seen him around. I was asked to
pass the message on that Sketch will be in the multi storey
at five tomorrow. I said I'd write it on the board, but Sketch
thought it would be better if I told young Tipton personally.
Seems reasonable enough. I'm sure there are plenty of things
someone with no car might be doing in a multi storey car
park other than buying drugs. Perhaps they're going to do
some graffiti or urinate in a stairwell.

Friday, 15th November. Went to collect Kevin Williams from
the station before lunch. I had a final check in the Lodge before
I set off, but there was still no sign of the books. Fortunately,
Williams didn't talk about his work on the way to school, and
was more interested in whether he could get his fee in cash
and complaining about the British Rail sandwiches. I got to

carry the huge bag of his books he'd brought to sign and flog after the reading.

We had lunch in the refectory: I'll be able to mention to Mr Appleby next time I see him that pigeon really isn't worth the bother. Iles kept the conversation flowing with a stream of embarrassing flattery. He asked at one point whether 'this is the hand that wrote *Who Do You Think You Are, Benny Wilson?*' Fortunately he refrained from asking to kiss said hand. Tom Downing asked Williams whether he was worried that in the age of word processing and e-mail communication, his correspondence and early drafts would be lost to future generations. It turns out he prints everything off and keeps it. Thank God for that. Monk had a nosebleed halfway through dessert.

I was surprised by the turnout of boys at lunch, but the mystery was solved when the headmaster brought out the Buxdon port after we'd finished eating. He measured us out a dose each, with the care and frugality of someone dispensing cough medicine. It wasn't bad, although somewhat gritty.

The talk went off OK. Kevin Williams started by asking what a poet is. People are always surprised when they hear he's a poet, because, and I quote: 'You probably think of a poet as someone who wanders around in pointy shoes going "la-di-da-di-da".' Actually Williams looked more or less exactly what I expected a poet to: leather jacket with an elasticated waist, tapered stonewash jeans, roll-up-stained fingers, blue-ish teeth and receded hairline. The jacket had a patch on the shoulder rubbed bare from lugging a bag of books around. He was, I should note, wearing quite pointy shoes.

Williams also reassured us that you don't have to speak in a posh accent to be a writer, which suggests he had sadly misjudged his audience. After the reading we had time for some questions, and Williams revealed:

– He does a first draft in pen, then types it up.

– He is immensely flattered to be the youngest poet on the A-Level syllabus, but he doesn't think about it when he's writing. Which raises the mildly disturbing question of when he does think about it. He did manage to mention it three times in a one-hour talk.

– Asked where he gets his ideas from, he replied that mostly he just steals them. Often from the unpublished manuscripts that young poets give him. When he really needs to come up with something original he closes the curtains, lines up three buckets by the side of the writing table, handcuffs himself to his typewriter, and shoots speed into his eyeball.

– He didn't really say that. He says all his best poems are dictated to him by a moon-man who sends him coded messages in the shipping forecast.

– He didn't say that either. He actually said that inspiration can strike at any time, so he always carries a notebook. Just this morning a haiku came to him on the train.

There's £250 well earned, Kevin Williams. I wish I was on the national curriculum. He probably sits around all day eating money sandwiches and scratching his back with a diamond-studded back scratcher.

Over dinner we got onto the subject of our *Desert Island Discs*. I have the horrible feeling Kevin Williams had given his selections some serious thought. He'd chosen: a Beatles song; an old music-hall tune that reminds him of his mother; a classical piece that he listens to while writing; an aria; a song by a band that he played hooky from school to see play at the Free Trade Hall in 1977; a song that reminds him of all those cold afternoons in the stands at Maine Road; Beethoven's Ode to Joy and a recent rap song. He wasn't specific; he just said 'a recent rap song'. He hadn't heard most of mine, and promised to check them out. He actually used the phrase 'check them out'. If Kevin Williams was stuck on a desert island, his one book would be *Ulysses*, because he could reread it endlessly. Could he. Could he really.

Barry Taylor and I came close to a row over his insistence that 'Dreadlock Holiday' is the best song Bob Marley ever wrote. I also had to explain to him that the songs don't actually have to have a tropical island vibe. Iles said obsequiously that his book would be something by Kevin Williams.

I did ask about literary agents and Williams promised to pass on some of my work to people he knows in publishing. I hope he meant like agents and editors and stuff. I was mildly flattered, although he said he'd do the same for Iles, who then produced something about half as long again as *The Lord of the Rings*. I noticed that he's gone through and done a little copyright sign and his name after each poem.

Since he has previously shown very little interest in contemporary poetry, I suspect Barry's attendance at the dinner was something to do with trying to impress Lucy Salmon. Unfortunately, she didn't show up. After dinner, he took me aside to mention that that he had seen her meeting young Tipton in town several times outside school hours, and asked whether I thought they were having an affair. I suspect not.

Sunday, 17th November. It was Sig's dinner party last night. I think the kindest way to put it would be to say that it wasn't my kind of thing. At all. Before dinner Francesco brought a classical guitar and serenaded us with the melancholy ballads of his homeland. He had a bit of a lump in his throat towards the end. Unfortunately Jesus couldn't make it. Goodness knows what Anton made of it all.

Beatrix goes into schools and gives talks on traditional music. She says you can really see the kids' eyes light up. Unfortunately someone broke into her side-car on Wednesday and stole all her instruments. They even took her hurdy gurdy.

'What kind of person would steal a hurdy gurdy?' asked Beatrix, not unreasonably.

'I'm sure whoever took it really needed it,' said Rolph, and Beatrix agreed. I've got the feeling that wouldn't be my reaction. Not that I really know how it would feel to have someone half-inch my flageolet. I expect the police are on the lookout for someone in a cap and bells. Or particoloured jerkin.

I put my foot in it later when I asked Mathilde what she did. She told me she was training to be a missionary, and I chuckled appreciatively. No one else did. Apparently she was being serious. Luckily she and Rolph got into a conversation about AIDS and the moment was smoothed over. I'm aware that people do train to be missionaries, and I'm sure it's very admirable. Just like I'm sure there are professional puppeteers, trampolinists and I suppose Reggaerobics instructors. It's just that I've never met one before.

Looking on the positive side, all Sig's friends are such interesting people with interesting lives. They've all got things like genuine interests and hobbies and passions. Mathilde can do the Sermon on the Mount in pidgin (again, not supposed to be funny); Rolph studied mime at Jacques Lecoq in Paris; and Anya makes curtains. I just wish I found it possible to like them.

Francesco's ponytail had my fingers twitching for a pair of shears all evening. I don't think Anton enjoyed himself much either. From the facial expression he was wearing throughout the meal, he either found the company and conversation exquisitely painful or he was sitting on a pin.

The food was good, though.

'What are these wonderful greens?' asked Anya. Sig explained they were cauliflower leaves. Fortunately for politeness' sake, I'd already finished mine.

Over coffee, Sig was telling us about how she and Anton got together. She has twenty-five qualities she looks for in a partner, every one a deal breaker. Her criteria include: political commitment, an interest in art, passionate about opera, preferably vegetarian, sexual confidence, non-smoker, serious, ambitious, talented in one or more fields, open minded about astrology, well groomed, tidy, energetic, and not afraid to express their opinions even if other people disagree with them. It's a shame Handsome Mr Hitler's off the market. I think Sig probably means liberal political commitment. Twenty-five criteria and you end up with Anton. He was actually sitting there throughout this little encomium, smiling faintly.

Caroline says she only has one criterion: she only fancies people six feet tall or over. Caroline has nothing against short men, it's just their 'creepy little hands' that weird her out. It's probably a bit late now to tell her I exaggerated my height when we first started going out. I mustn't ever let her discover I'm only five foot eleven.

Caroline's out at the moment at Reggaerobics with Sig and Anya who makes curtains. They invited me along too, but on balance I decided against. I was just about to kick back with the *Sunday Times* when I noticed that Caroline has left her diary out ...

It's locked. Furthermore, it turns out that action movies make picking a lock with a hairclip look much easier than it is in reality. Next time I come to stay I'll have to remember to pack a hack-saw. No, that would probably be taking things a bit far. I'll probably just have a cup of a tea and a flick through the paper instead.

Worryingly, I also found Caroline's copy of *Is Your Relationship a Floater?* in her room. She's filled in the Sensitivity Quiz at the end of Chapter Three and according to Dr Hart Adams PhD, I'm emotionally on Pluto. Great. I guess that means I have to put in some 'personal work' before I'm even on Mars. My emotional peers are Frosty the Snowman and Dustin Hoffman in *Rain Man*. That Dr Hart Adams PhD thinks he knows it all, but he's very much mistaken if he thinks I'm going to take love-life advice from a bloke in a jaunty bow tie.

I wonder if it lights up and spins around when he makes a particularly pertinent insight.

Although now I think of it, the fact that I think forcing entry to my girlfriend's diary using a hacksaw is the best way to find out what's going on in her head suggests he may have a point. Hacksaw? What is Buxdon doing to me? Jesus. I can't be autistic, though – I'm crap at maths. There's something to cling to.

Monday, 18th November. I missed a scandal at Buxdon this weekend. Dr Trotter took some of his boarding house on an excursion to a local wildlife park, and managed to almost lose a boy. It seems the back doors of the minibus were unlocked, and Marcus Lau (author of the most moving answer ever to the question 'Is Nelly Dean a Reliable Narrator?') made a bolt for it. It was a shame that he chose to do so as they were driving through the lion enclosure. Fortunately the lions had just been fed, and Johnno managed to catch him before he scaled the fence. Apparently he runs at quite a lick, because Johnno McPhee was limping when he got back, and has spent yesterday afternoon in the lounge at Mercer's Lodge, groaning while Barry Taylor applies ice to his knee.

The school has agreed not to pursue disciplinary measures, as long as Marcus Lau doesn't mention the incident to his parents. Trotter is thoroughly in the doghouse, not least because baboons tore the windshield wipers off the minibus. I'm not sure that anyone else noticed that half the Sixth Formers came back drunk, although I'm sure whoever has to clean up the Old Building toilets this morning will. The entire lower corridor smells of cider and Malibu.

Tuesday, 19th November. The parcel from the Applebys finally arrived. I didn't know they still sold third-class stamps. It's amazing it reached me at all, thanks to Henry Appleby's astonishingly illegible handwriting. It looks like it's addressed to Matthew Botch, Meercat Loose, Brixton Squirrel. No post-code. Someone has circled the word 'squirrel' and written 'prison?' with an arrow. *Jumpers for Goal Posts* is missing its cover, and has a paw print on page nineteen.

We've been warned that a reporter from the tabloids has been approaching pupils from Buxdon to enquire if they know anything about the school trip at the weekend. He's been escorted from school property twice already. The headmaster is throwing a fit about it. He reminded us at assembly that confidentiality and loyalty are paramount virtues at Buxdon, and that there is the serious possibility if this matter receives any more publicity that future trips will have to be postponed or cancelled.

Wednesday, 20th November. Crisis meeting with Barry Taylor over weak tea and lardy cake in the Buxdon Tea Shoppe. It's about as bad as you would expect something called a Tea Shoppe to be, if not slightly worse. The owner is a wizened little geezer in a green suit that would look better on a snooker table. He spent the entire time we were there flirting with a pair of septuagenarians and complaining about young people and their manners. I can't imagine they see that many young people in the Buxdon Tea Shoppe. Perhaps he was talking about us.

Barry has been stalking Lucy Salmon for weeks to try to find out what she's interested in. I don't remember those being my exact instructions. He's found out:

– She buys food at the Co-op;
– She has her hair cut and coloured at From Hair to Eternity on Market Street;
– She occasionally has a sneaky smoke, either sitting in her car or on a bench in Abbey Meadows;
– She doesn't like being followed around.

*

Dangerous Liaisons this ain't. God knows why he thinks I'm the person to ask for relationship advice. The implication was that since I'm not interested in rowing, rugby or football, I must have some special insight into feminine psychology. What do I think he should do? Um, lots of eye contact? Try not to be a dick in front of her? He should probably stop sneaking around after her, too. At that point the owner announced that it was time for the Buxdon Tea Shoppe to close for the evening. He swept up around us furiously as we drank the last of our coffees. It was 4:46 by my watch.

In return for my advice I made Barry promise not to tell anyone else about my nickname. 'Even Peter Wyndham?' he asked, and looked mildly guilty. Fortunately none of them know the full story, or so I assume on the basis that I can walk around Buxdon without everyone pointing and giggling.

I didn't manage to get Barry to spill the beans yet on why Garnett left, but he did let slip that Garnett was having a thing of some kind with Lucy. I don't fully get the Lucy Salmon phenomenon. She's quite cute, at least in comparison to Emilia Bartlett or Lionel Brimscombe. But the bloke who runs the Tea Shoppe is quite cute in comparison to either of those two, and he looks like a bad glove puppet of John Major. In comparison to Lionel Brimscombe, with his twitchy eye, mauve complexion and fondness for Norman arches, the landlord at The Albion is something of a catch. It must be that the somewhat claustrophobic and almost all-male atmosphere of Buxdon has produced some kind of mass sexual hysteria. The only female competition of a similar age is the woman who works in the kitchen, walks like a man, and has a tattoo of a quad bike on her not-inconsiderable left bicep. And she got three Valentine's last February. Lucy Salmon got 116. That's probably more than Princess Diana, and only one of them is an averagely attractive religious studies teacher.

*

85

Thursday, 21st November. It was drizzling, so I showed the Running Club *Chariots of Fire*, hoping to get them inspired for the Interschools Running Competition. Well, that back-fired. Three boys came up afterwards and told me they won't run if the meet is on a Sunday. I knew I should have showed them *Ed*. On reflection, the prospect of a baseball team with a chimpanzee in it winning the World Series is about as likely as Team Bletch covering themselves in glory next month.

About halfway through the film Tom Downing and the cross country team appeared, huffing past the window in the mist, and treated us to a variety of unfriendly gestures and hoots of mockery. Which reminds me: Barry Taylor told me yesterday that he's invited Lucy Salmon to watch the cross country team compete three times, but she keeps turning him down. For some reason watching a bunch of boys scrambling through damp hedges egged on by a grown man in skin-tight shorts has so far failed to appeal.

I've told Caroline that I'll be staying in Buxdon this week-end to work on my book. I asked her what she thinks of the latest title, *Far East Far Out: The Stranger Side of Japan*. She circumspectly hinted it could probably do with another trip to the drawing board. When asked if she had any ideas she suggested *I Was Mister Goblin*. I suspect she might be a bit annoyed that I can't make it up to see her. She has stuff on of her own, though: Rychard's applying to change branches and move to Edinburgh, and Caroline is helping him with the application. I told her to make it a good one, because I genuinely hopes he gets it. And what Edinburgh really needs is another strutting English Sloane.

Friday, 22nd November. I had a chat with Marcus Lau during mid-morning break. I suggested that if he finds Buxdon lonely he might want to join in with more after-school activities. He could join Art Club – that seems to be what every other lonesome misfit does. He volunteered for Running Club, which wouldn't have been my choice as a fast-track to social acceptance, or indeed to anywhere. But he sure is speedy. Johnno McPhee is still smarting from the revelation that he himself runs 'like he's wearing clown shoes'. Not my words, the words of the regional news team, who last night showed CCTV footage of Johnno's dash through the lion enclosure as the evening's lighthearted closing story. Actually they showed the footage twice, once in slow motion. The bit when Johnno slips in the lion poo is a particular highlight for me.

We were all called in for a meeting at lunchtime, and the hunt is on for whoever sold the details of the story to the *Sun*. I thought 'Lions Reject Posh Dinner' was quite a clever headline. Their cartoonist caught the matter with his usual wit and insight, with his picture of one lion saying to another as Marcus dashes past: 'Nah, Mate, don't bother. You'll only feel hungry again in half an hour.' The headmaster seemed particularly annoyed by the fact the article got the school fees wrong.

My estranged brother Dominic rang after work, to see if I knew why Frank has sent him a large box full of total rubbish, with insufficient postage. Dominic had to get his girlfriend Karla to drive him to the depot to pick it up. Dominic? Girlfriend? Karla? He dropped that little nugget into the conversation as if it was the most natural thing in the world. She's another academic. They probably fell in love when their hands brushed as they both reached for the same copy of *The Proceedings of the Henry James Society*. I expect they hold hands in the British Library café and share in-jokes about *The Golden Bowl*. They probably lie in bed and read Dryden to each other, chuckling like idiots.

Dom is still on the outs with Frank: 'Does he think he can buy my respect and affection?' Frank will need to try harder if he does, because he sent Dominic a selection of novelty hats, a bunch of *FHM*s and *Loaded*s and a pewter tankard with 'Pissed on the Piste, Val D'Isère 1993' on it. Frank Bletch is thirty-two. Is it a cry for help? If so he should have paid the full delivery charge. I expect he's been evicted again.

Dom was going on about Frank's imperturbable moral self-ishness. I agree with Dom that Frank is amoral and selfish, but it's not that I think he's a bad person. Well, I do think Frank is a bad person ... but mostly I just think he's something of a tit.

Caroline asked how Dominic and I can be estranged if we talk on the phone perfectly amicably. I conceded that I do talk to him, but added that all the time I'm shouting abuse at him in my head. I don't expect Caroline has that problem with her sister. I imagine that when Lulu is talking she's secretly think-ing things like: 'Who invented shoes? Was it a man called Mr Shoe?' and 'Why aren't there any green mammals?' In fact the second of those is a perfectly reasonable question.

Saturday, 23rd November. Worked on the book all afternoon and evening. It's still neither finished nor very good, but I did get through a lot of coffee.

Sunday, 24th November. Tom Downing is really starting to get on my wick. Not only was he lounging around my kitchen doing stretches while I was trying to eat my corn flakes, but he also repeatedly addressed me as Mister Goblin.

I decided on a quiet night in, as I was in no mood to watch *Zulu* with the boarders. About eleven o'clock Barry Taylor came past my window singing 'Men of Harlech'.

Monday 25th November. Barry Taylor has started reading the *Guardian*. As the staffroom only takes one copy, this means that Lucy and I are reduced to the *New Statesman* or *Rowing Weekly*. The headmaster has cancelled the staffroom subscription to the *Sun* after their article this morning, 'They Call Him Dr Doom', showed him in his gown, looking insane, chasing their reporter. They also mentioned a 'forty-five minute rant' at the last Headmasters' Conference ('Other delegates wondered whether he had been drinking') and referred to his 'jamborees around South East Asia at the parents' expense'. The article is factually incorrect, though. We call him 'Mr Doom, MA (Oxon)'.

I did tell Barry to try to establish some mutual interests with Lucy. But I think forcing himself to laugh out loud at *Pass Notes* is taking things a bit far.

Tuesday, 26th November. Buxdon is almost pleasant early in the morning, bathed in the rosy glow of dawn and exuding a sense of calm contentment. The flag was flapping gently on its pole and the dew was on Upper Field. The only noise was the clatter from the kitchen as the breakfast preparations began. Mrs Tarawicz was having a reflective fag outside the Old Building, with her mop and bucket by her side. Mr Downing ran past with a bunch of boys, steaming gently in the early chill. One of them spat and only just missed my shoe.

Wednesday, 27th November. Caroline rang to say she doesn't think she'll be able to come down this weekend because Sig's broken up with Anton. Although it sounds from Sig's reaction rather like it was the other way round.

I'm seriously starting to worry about my relationship with Caroline. We slowly seem to be turning into penpals. I don't think von Clausewitz's advice is proving very helpful. To be fair, he wasn't writing a guide to late twentieth-century dating. You probably wouldn't get far on the battlefields of nineteenth-century Europe with a copy of *Is Your Relationship a Floater?* by Dr Hart Adams PhD either.

Thursday, 28th November. Marcus Lau showed up for Running

Club today. Wow that kid is fast. The problem is stopping him. Dr Trotter bumped into him halfway to Buxdon, running for dear life and apparently heading for the bus depot. Showing *Chariots of Fire* has really backfired. Now half the team did the whole course in slow motion, whistling Vangelis. I hope they were deliberately running in slow motion.

Friday, 29th November. Over lunch Downing told me mockingly that he saw one of my Running Club boys being overtaken yesterday by an old person with a three-legged dog. He said it was a chunky kid in glasses, which doesn't narrow it down much.

Buxdon is turning out to be a fairly productive place to write after all. I managed 250 words this evening. Then I sat down and worked out that at this rate I'll be finished by 2006. Japan probably will have fallen into the sea by then.

I did however make very good use of my birthday present from Mum to write a stern letter to a well-known retail chain regarding my birthday present from Caroline.

Saturday, 30th November.

All work and no play makes Matt a dull boy
All work and no play makes Matt a dull boy
All work and no play makes Matt a dull boy
All work and no play makes Matt a dull boy
All work and no play makes Matt a dull boy
All work and no play makes Matt a dull boy
All work and no play makes Matt a dull boy
All work and no play makes Matt a dull boy
All work and no play makes Matt a dull boy
All work and no play makes Matt a dull boy
All work and no play makes Matt a dull boy
All work and no play makes Matt a dull boy
All work and no play makes Matt a dull boy

All work and no play makes Matt a dull boy
All work and no play makes Matt a dull boy
All work and no play makes Matt a dull boy
All work and no play makes Matt a dull boy
All work and no play makes Matt a dull boy
All work and no play makes Matt a dull boy
All work and no play makes Matt a dull boy

December

Dear High-Street Hosier,

I was recently given a selection of your pants for my birthday by a beloved relative. I can't tell you how long I have sought a snug pair of pants ideally designed for my own unique body shape. For as long as I can remember I have been ashamed and embarrassed by the fact that my 'gentleman's companion' emerges from a point unorthodoxly high on my torso and proceeds horizontally for a bit, before abruptly changing direction by ninety degrees and aiming itself straight up for daylight. You can imagine how much ribbing I get from the other guys on the Rowing Team. How painful it is to hear the crowd on the bank shouting 'Come on, Oddcock' and 'I think there's a problem with his rudder.' By 'rudder', as I'm sure you have gathered, they are referring to my peculiar manservant.

As you can imagine, in so-called 'normal' underwear a trip to the urinal has been a dreaded and potentially mortifying experience. However, the cloud this cast over my work and social life has now been lifted, by your remarkable range of elasticated boxer briefs (in four colours, no less). It is as if your designer had me in mind all along. With the ease of access and absence of social embarrassment that these remarkable creations have given me, a trip to the urinal is no longer a gruelling trial, but something to which I have even begun to look forward.

It is of course possible that this remarkable design is not in fact the product of a plan to tailor your products solely to me, but is rather evidence of a basic lack of anatomical knowledge

on the part of your designer. I hope this is not the case, but if
it is, please have them consult the attached drawing, which
should set them straight on a few things.

Keep up the good work, and I look forward eagerly to your
reply!

Yours sincerely,
Tom Downing
Buxdon School,
Buxdon.

Sunday, 1st December. Got the details of Sig's break-up with
Anton. He refused to give her a reference for a funding application. Apparently he sees a conflict of interest there. Anton
also mentioned that he doesn't consider Sig a 'truly serious'
person. She and Caroline spent Friday night in a Bacchante-
style rampage around the All Bar Ones of west London,
and last night settled in for a night on the couch with some
chocolates and a bottle of Sambuca. An ill-advised combination, as they soon discovered. The trampolining afterwards
was definitely a mistake.

Sig was having a shower when I called, but when she comes
out she has told Caroline that they're going to have a proper
talk about her and Anton. As Caroline pointed out, this raises
the question of what they've been doing for the past half-
week. Sig has declared that she needs to have a long think and
perhaps reformulate her criteria. Could she not just get drunk
and go around to Anton's house in the middle of the night to
shout abuse at him like any normal human being?

Rychard sent his application for the Edinburgh job off on
Friday. I said I'd definitely be keeping my fingers crossed for
him.

Monday, 2nd December. Dr Trotter is in hot water again, as
several parents have now filed formal complaints about the

video he showed the boys who didn't attend the Halloween party. In retrospect Trotter concedes that he should have made sure exactly what *Trainspotting* is about. It had a powerful effect on Marcus Lau, although I'm not sure he quite got it:

This film is a very funny comedy. It was a bit like *Mr Bean*. My favourite bit was when the man swam in a toilet. He was the same man who falls asleep everywhere. One time he even fell asleep in a taxi cab!

That's certainly an original take on a film about the desperate adventures of a gang of heroin addicts. As an answer to the question 'How sympathetic a character is Mr Lockwood?', however, it's a non-starter. *Trainspotting*'s depiction of Edinburgh as a city with a dark underbelly of violence and crime does, however, make me even keener for Rychard to move there. That probably makes me a bad person.

Tuesday, 3rd December. The search for the *Sun*'s inside man, woman or boy at Buxdon continues. I'm keeping my ears open for someone who speaks in very short sentences and uses bold to emphasise their points. Please God let it be a disgruntled Mrs O. Digby. At least the *Sun* haven't heard about the exploits of the Beast. Yet.

Mrs O. Digby still doesn't seem to have quite got used to the fact that I work here. Each time she sees me in the staffroom she does a little double take then looks at me suspiciously like I've snuck in to steal the biscuits. That's better than Rudolph Fane, though, who after almost a whole term is still calling me 'Garnett'.

Talked to Lucy Salmon over lunch, who's glad that Barry Taylor doesn't seem to be following her around any more but is a trifle disturbed by his new habit of relentlessly eyeballing her. I told her I'd have a quiet word.

*

Wednesday, 4th December. Sig's been throwing herself into her work, which I expect is a good thing. According to Caroline, she's managed to bash out half a PhD chapter since Sunday night, fuelled almost solely by Turkish coffee and roll-ups. She's told Caroline that we can read it when she's finished. I'm flattered, but on the other hand reading someone's PhD dissertation is generally about as much fun as being hit around the head with it. Sig's up to three showers a day. How long before her toes begin to web? I know what to get her for Christmas: one of those waterproof notepads scuba divers use.

Barry was in the lounge this evening, and I asked how things are going. He said the eye contact campaign seemed to be paying off. He's thinks Lucy has started noticing him a little more. That's unarguable. However, I mentioned that glaring in through the windows when she's teaching probably crosses a few boundaries. It also might be worth his blinking now and again.

Thursday, 5th December. The Interschools Running Competition is two weeks from today. I reminded everyone to make sure they have all the right gear. G. Wilson was running today in black school shoes, his vest, and the largest pair of tracksuit bottoms we could find in lost property. Off to London after school tomorrow.

Friday, 6th December. A final session with my Oxbridge candidates before their interviews next week. Hallbrick looked like he was about to start crying, but then Hallbrick always looks like he's about to start crying. The only one who didn't seem nervous was Bagley. Perhaps because most of his attention was focused on surreptitiously eating the sweets he had in his jacket pocket. I reminded them that they're all scholarship boys and they should just go and give it their best shot.

Anyway, it's not as if getting into Oxford or Cambridge is the be-all and end-all of life. Iles gave me a highly sceptical look as I was saying this. I just hope he doesn't start reading the interviewers his poems.

Saturday, 7th December. Terrible night's sleep. There was a party going on at the place around the corner Caroline reckons is a crack den, and Sig was banging around all hours arguing on the phone with Anton and making coffee to fuel the final push on her PhD chapter. After a bout of furious trampolining at about three in the morning, she had a shower and went to bed. I snatched about two hours' uneasy kip before the street-cleaning vans started trundling past.

For reasons I appear to have missed, we had brunch with Sig and Shouty Morgan. Morgan's big news is that Alicia Power and Woggy Hops have got engaged. Whoever the hell they are. 'It'll all end in tears,' Sig balefully observed. I think she's milking it a bit now:

> *Morgan*: You're looking great at the moment, Sig. What's your secret?
> *Sig*: I'm incredibly miserable. The only thing I've eaten since Thursday is a scotch egg and some hummus.

Sig asked what Woggy was like, and Morgan explained that he's a terribly nice lad when he's sober.

> *Sig*: What happens when he's drunk?
> *Morgan*: He climbs.

I hope Alicia knows better than to arrange the engagement party in the vicinity of any scaffolding, statuary, obelisks, cranes or cathedrals with gothic façades. To my disappointment, Morgan doesn't think Alicia will be double-barrelling her surname.

I'm still not convinced that that place around the corner from Caroline's is a crack den, but when we walked past this morning there was a fully-grown man sleeping in a pram in the front garden.

Sunday, 8th December. Caroline and Sig are currently having yet another serious chat, and I've retired to Caroline's room to read Sig's chapter, which she finished at four this morning. It's pretty good so far.

Sig told Caroline and me last night that she thinks she needs new criteria and has to re-examine her entire attitude towards relationships. Yes, either that or she could just get a hobby. We also learned that for some mysterious reason, Anton shaves his chest every other morning. Which explains why Sig has stubble rash over two thirds of her body. I thought it was eczema. Sig had no proper answer for why Anton would do that in the first place. Surely any amount of body hair is preferable to nipples with five o'clock shadow?

I assured Caroline there's no way I would ever shave my chest. It would only grow back even bushier and I'd have to walk around looking like Cousin Itt.

Monday, 9th December. I finished Sig's chapter before I left London. It seems to me to be well written, closely argued and flawlessly spelled. As far as I can tell it makes a genuine contribution to knowledge in the area, or at least pretends to fairly convincingly. 'Cheers,' she said. 'And did you notice? The first letter of the first word in each sentence in the first paragraph spells out "Anton is an arse".'

Back in Buxdon now. Amazing how much smoother my English class went without Iles there to interject every five minutes and Bagley to slow the whole thing down by not having his book, by having the wrong book, by not having a pen or by chewing the end off his pen. Ah, the average kids. My people. The kids who can answer questions put to them but don't feel the need to ask any of their own. Not here to show

97

off or to draw attention to themselves, just here to keep their heads down and get through the time somehow.

Tuesday, 10th December. I had a note in my pigeon-hole from Tipton's parents this morning, with an invitation to a party on 22 December. It's white-tie, no less. I don't even really know what that means. I can't wait to see the house. In an episode that has since passed into Buxdon legend, the boy Tipton once came in late to one of Dr Fane's classes and left the lab door open. Fane asked if he'd been dragged up in a barn, and raised the usual semi-obligatory titter. Tipton looked Rudolph over in either confusion or disdain, depending on who's telling the story, before replying: 'Yes, sir, I was … but it did cost half a million pounds to convert.' Maybe if I play my cards right the Tiptons will offer to adopt me

I'm not quite sure why I was deemed worthy of an invitation. Perhaps I made a really good impression on the Tiptons at the Horrible Hop. However, Lucy Salmon and Tom Downing are also going, which suggests the Tiptons have simply invited all the people who take their son for A Level. Barry Taylor is practically evaporating with jealousy. Downing says the Mayor of Buxdon will probably be there. 'I hope he wears his chain,' Barry snarled.

Wednesday, 11th December. Spoke to Caroline and agreed to come up to London again. I mentioned that I seem to be spending more time in London than she has in Buxdon. She claims it evens out because time in Buxdon passes so much more slowly. She also says we never do anything exciting any more. I suggested a trip to the Sir John Soanes Museum, which turned out not to be the kind of thing she had in mind at all.

Thursday, 12th December. The final Running Club session before the big day. Morale is surprisingly high. G. Wilson even told me he's been in training. Although he was eating a Cornish pasty at the time. Marcus Lau made a moving speech about how no one is a loser unless they believe they're a loser, and we all carried him around on our shoulders for a bit, cheering. When we got back to the changing rooms we discovered someone had borrowed or stolen Ellis's underwear.

Friday, 13th December. End of term next week! I reminded the Sixth Formers that their coursework folders have to be in by next Friday. Groans all round.

Saturday, 14th December. Caroline has decided we're going out clubbing tonight. We are the dance generation, after all. Generation E. I hope I don't wig out and think I can fly. Relax Matthew, you're not on *Hollyoaks*. I wish she'd let me know about this in advance. I probably could have got a discount from young Tipton. We'll most likely end up buying dodgy pills off some Thatcher-spawned teenager and end up as embarrassing grainy photos under the word 'tragedy' on the front cover of the *Observer*. Either that or we'll dance for hours then come home to mate like beasts in the tooth-grinding dawn, not knowing whose erogenous zones and elbows are whose.

Sunday, 15th December. Or we could end up standing in a queue for five hours, before getting to the front and being told it was one in one out. Ministry of Sound, my giddy arse. We would have had more fun standing outside the Ministry of Agriculture and Rural Affairs, and at least then I would have had something to talk about next time I see Caroline's father. Christ, I would have had more fun talking to Henry, even if he did insist as usual on mithering on endlessly about sheep dip or DEFRA. The gurning mooncalf behind us in the queue blagged four fags off me, each time asking us if we were having a good night. Yes, I was having it all right. I couldn't have been having it larger if I'd been lining up for my weekly potato ration in Stalin's Russia.

I tried to keep the mood with Caroline lighthearted and romantic. 'Is it raining? I hadn't noticed.' I bloody had, though. I refused to let her find a phone and give Rychard a call to see if he could get us into his club. Luckily about quarter past twelve someone stood on a broken glass in strappy sandals and her friends had to take her to A&E, so Caroline, I and the Lord of the Dance got in. It was shit. Four quid fifty for a vodka and tonic? I feel like I've been mugged by a building. Although muggers usually just go about their business of parting you from your cash without insisting you pretend you're having a good time and wave your arms about like a wanker while they do it. We did all the latest dances: we screwed in the invisible light bulb, played imaginary chess with giant pieces, and I even spent half an hour miming folding clothes and packing them into a large suitcase. There wasn't a single moment when I wouldn't rather have been in a hot bath with a crossword. If I ran a soul-sapping superclub I'd charge people to leave. I might write a letter of complaint and send it to the editors of *The Times* and *Mixmag*.

There were no black cabs when we'd eventually managed to retrieve our coats and leave, so we paid some random madman £25 to drive us home in a blue Vauxhall Astra with one hubcap missing and a flickering headlight. Caroline had to give him directions to Oxford Street. On the way home we listened to literally the worst pirate radio station I've ever heard.

'I think I definitely felt something for a bit,' Caroline was claiming unconvincingly. 'Did you get anything?'

Yes, Caroline. Clicky fingers, a mild tummy ache and an overarching sense of paranoia which then opened out majestically into an almost mystical sense we'd been ripped off. As Frank would no doubt point out, pills aren't like they used to be. I wonder if they let you secede from the chemical generation. This week I'm going to find out who first proposed the Criminal Justice Bill and send them a warm message of congratulation. And people say the Tories have never done anything for this country. When the last frayed strand of the symbolic rope bridge is finally severed, with the Pigs on one side and a lone crusty on the other giving them the finger, I know which side I'll be on. The side with running water, truncheons and electricity bills.

To add insult to injury, we had lunch today with Rychard. No word yet on his Edinburgh application, but he's off to the Maldives for Christmas. Loser. I couldn't resist asking if his family didn't want him. That was a mistake, because it gave him the opportunity to boast that he's flying his mum out as a treat. And his old granny. He gave Caroline her present, which I have my fingers crossed is a huge box with a tiny present inside. I suppose I should be grateful Rychard's not offering to fly her off to the tropics. I must arrange another getaway with Caroline soon, this time to somewhere less cold, dank and depressing. Although we had a good laugh at the Kafka Museum.

Rychard then invited me to his New Year's Eve party. I said I thought I might be coming down with something, and wasn't sure I would be well enough to go. I really should've saved that excuse for slightly closer to the event.

I mentioned the Tipton party and Rychard offered to lend me his white tie, etc. Don't try to outflank me with niceness, mate. I don't think Rychard needed to add that the trousers might be a bit big, either. 'I'm not being funny,' he said, 'It's just that I'm six foot ...'

Caroline reminded me again that I'm welcome to share an Appleby Christmas with her, but I said I really ought to go and spend a few days with my brothers. Still, it would be worth putting up with Toby and Lulu just to see what the Applebys eat on Christmas Day. Probably a boar. With a turkey inside, and inside that a chicken. And then inside that a poussin, then a quail (or vice versa). Caroline was trying to guess what I'm giving her for Christmas. To be honest, so am I.

I got the train back in the afternoon, chalky mouthed and chemically depressed. My fingers ache from all the clicking.

Monday, 16th December. Iles, Hallbrick and Bagley have all had their Oxbridge interviews. Iles seems confident, Hallbrick less so, and God only knows what Bagley is thinking. Hopefully he refrained from eating paper or running around on all fours during the proceedings.

As I was getting rid of my lunch tray I spotted Bagley sitting with two First Years. I take it he doesn't think much of the school catering, because he'd constructed an unsettling little figure out of his lunch. It had a doughnut head, salad hair, potato feet, and forks for arms. He was walking it up and down the table, insisting everyone shake hands with it. The First Years looked terrified, and I don't blame them. Neither of them had cutlery. 'Mr Bletch! Come and let me introduce you to someone. I call him the lunch monster.' I can't wait to read Bagley's coursework folder.

I'd been having lunch with Dr Cumnor and Dr Paul Morris of the drama department, discussing next term's Sixth Form theatre trip. Neither of them thought *Starlight Express* or *The Mousetrap* was a good idea. Apparently there's going to be a *Lear* at the Hackney Empire that they want to see. I've seen it already, though, so I know how it ends. Which is still more than I can say for *Little Dorrit*. I bet *Lear* won't have anyone on roller skates, either. Paul Morris eats his jelly with a knife and fork, an affectation almost as difficult to perform as it is annoying.

Tuesday, 17th December. Sad news from Caroline. The vet has told the Applebys that Mr Snuffles has a growth in his sinuses. They're going to have to take him back in a few weeks to have it operated on. I guess we know why he's so very snuffly now.

Caroline accused me of never showing fondness for any of her dogs, and I had to explain how men sometimes have trouble expressing our affection in words. Or actions. Caroline thinks it's cruel to keep dogs in the city. Yet another excellent reason for us to live in London. 'You can never truly tame a dog,' I observed philosophically. Turns out that's wolves. And killer whales. Clue's in the name, really. According to Barry Taylor, dolphins are vicious bastards as well, but I'm inclined to take this with a pinch of salt. Not least because he's also under the impression that there's a northern town called Lanchester.

Popped into town today to pick up Caroline's Christmas present and some wrapping paper. After that I picked up the starting pistol for Thursday's Running Meet from the school armoury, and was given a long interrogation by the prefect with the wonky eye who's in charge of it. Why he got the job I don't know, although clearly no one else on the staff has seen *If...* The prefect's name, it transpires, is Richard Darling. As he himself added, 'They call me "Dead-Eye Dick" Darling.' I guess that's because he's a good shot, although it wouldn't be the nickname I would have chosen if I was him. I wondered whether he was going to make me raise my hand and swear an oath, but I just had to sign for it. He warned me that a starting pistol isn't a toy. No, but it's not actually a proper gun either. As I was leaving one of my First-Year inductees came in to collect the CCF bayonets. As we were waiting he turned to me and whispered: 'Is Dead-Eye giving you the usual old ball ache, Sir?' I don't think I inspire the respect here that's due my position. I checked whether the school armoury includes landmines. It doesn't. Pity, since that would be one of the few ways of giving Team Bletch the edge they'll need to win on Thursday.

Wednesday, 18th December. The Head summoned us all to the staffroom today to discuss a most regrettable incident. The Beast of Buxdon has made his presence felt again. When Tom Downing came back from rowing practice this afternoon someone had crapped in one of his teaching shoes. The headmaster went nuts, as indeed did Downing. Although he would have been more impressively furious if he hadn't been hopping on one foot at the time. The Head demanded to know what kind of savage craps in someone's shoe. Well, it definitely wasn't me. I wish I'd thought of it, though. Downing received thirty pairs of free underwear in the post the other day and was over the moon.

I still haven't heard anything from Kevin Williams about the sample chapters I gave him. Maybe he's a really slow reader. Having said that I haven't made much headway with *Current Address Unknown* and I promised I'd let him know what I thought of it. I must get out of Buxdon. I want light. I want air. I want beauty, and art, and intelligent conversation. But most of all, I don't want anyone crapping in my shoe.

The weather forecast for tomorrow's Running Meet is dreadful, but I suppose I should at least put in an appearance. Based on the speed of most of the Running Club, I can probably send them off at the start, wait for Marcus Lau to complete the circuit and congratulate him, then head off for a three-course lunch before returning at dusk to cheer the rest over the finish line.

Thursday, 19th December. Well, we lost. Not only did we lose, we got a worse time than the other schools' second and third teams as well. And our own Juniors. 'I guess we really are losers,' one of our team observed. Behind steamed-up glasses, tears and rain mingled on his chubby cheeks. I'm afraid so, son.

All in all the day was a bit of a disaster, although I did finally discover why Garnett left. Peter Wyndham obviously hasn't heard about the code of silence surrounding the incident in question. I got the full story from him this evening in the kitchen while he was making a cup of posh coffee. He's not such a bad bloke – he even gave me some of his coffee when it was finally done. I've started blinking again now, after a three-hour hiatus. My heart was beating like a hummingbird's wing.

The story is this: As I already knew, Garnett was having a semi-secret thing with Lucy. They got together at Open Day last year, which suggests Open Day at Buxdon is a little different from how I remember it from my schooldays. Perhaps they had a romantic little dinner at the French department café, and held hands as they watched the Combined Cadet Force drill. Things must have been getting pretty hot and heavy, because over the Easter Holidays he lent her a copy of *Howards End* on video, with the warning that there was 'something pretty special' at the end. Yes, a man getting killed by a falling bookcase.

Lucy didn't get around to watching it, but during the summer term decided to show it to some of her GCSE students as a treat during one of their revision periods. Amazingly she was able to tear herself away from the gripping drama and went off to make a cup of tea or something, leaving the film running. While she was out the film ended, but the video didn't. As the boys were reflecting on the struggle between Art and Commerce, or whatever, Mr Garnett popped up on screen. And when I say 'popped up', I mean it.

It appears he'd used the Rowing Club camcorder to record a moving and romantic declaration of affection for Miss Salmon. Which he had, in some moment of madness, decided to deliver in his Y-fronts. While smacking his own bottom suggestively. And prancing. I'm told he makes whinnying noises and claims to be 'Your Sex Pony'. While galloping on the spot with imaginary reins in his hands. At one point he hops up on the very desk at which I am writing this. With both his hands on one coyly raised knee and a bollock hanging out, he says, 'This is where we first made love, do you remember?' Pretty unforgettable, I'd imagine.

So the story goes, Miss Salmon came back in and managed to hit pause just as the Y-fronts were coming down to reveal the world's hairiest arse. Wyndham has heard it compared to one of ZZ Top peering out of a cave.

If nothing else, this explains the turnout for Boarders' Film Club the other Sunday. Actually, pirhouetting around in one's underwear and mooning people seems to me a fairly sensible reaction to the cinematic oeuvre of Merchant and Ivory. But it does seem rather beside the point for Garnett's letter to me to have warned me not to fall for Lucy Salmon. Perhaps he should have added the clarifying suggestion not to film myself pounding flat-handed on my own buttocks and shouting 'the human bongos'. Only 'connect', indeed. At least if I get really sick of it here I now know a sure-fire if humiliating way to break my contract.

I spent most of the remainder of the evening scrubbing my desk with bleach.

Friday, 20th December. Last day of term today. I collected the coursework folders from the Sixth Formers and let them watch a video. Enthusiasm turned to disappointment when I offered them a choice of BBC Shakespeares.

About halfway through the video I realised that at some point in all the excitement yesterday, I managed to misplace the school starting pistol. I think I may have left it in the pavilion, where I was sheltering from the sleet. It wasn't there just now when I checked, though. I checked Lost Property, but no one had handed it in. Oh well, it's the end of term. I expect it will turn up. I can always get a new one over the holidays. How much damage can someone do with a starting pistol, anyway?

It's the Tiptons' party tonight. A parcel from Rychard arrived for me earlier in the week, with the white-tie get-up inside. It is bloody big. I look like I've shrunk in the wash. I'll probably be the only person there with turn-ups on my dress trousers, and certainly the only one with turn-ups held up with Buxdon English department staples. I've just bathed in Old Spice and cut my toe nails, and now I'm going to make a fifth attempt on this bow tie. The jacket fits just right, if I was planning to wear a huge jumper underneath it.

Saturday, 21st December. I didn't have any trouble finding the Tiptons' house. The taxi driver just followed the stream of Peugeots and Beamers up to the huge illuminated house on top of the hill. Mr Tipton was greeting guests in the hall dressed as Santa. He complimented me on the fit of my suit. It was quite hot with two T-shirts underneath.

The young folks were having their own side-party in the summer house. The summer house is bigger and better furnished than Mercers' Lodge. It even has a telephone, which the boy Tipton was using to order more drinks from the main house. Occasionally, scantily clad teenagers would emerge to run across the lawn howling and laughing.

It was an amazing party. There were even waiters and waitresses going around with trays of drinks. I didn't know any of the people milling about in the entrance hall, but I found Lucy Salmon in the kitchen. She was agreeing with Mrs Tipton that Sam has a real affinity for religious studies. A few minutes later I saw him and Gordon dragging a begging and wriggling Norrington Major towards the swimming pool. Norrington Minor was following with his brother's shoes, shouting, 'Don't forget to throw these in too.' It was snowing.

Mrs Tipton fixed me a gin and tonic that made my sinuses ache. She asked whether Lucy and I were a couple, and kept trying to get Lucy to say that I was handsome. It was a bit embarrassing, to be honest, but Lucy managed to get out of it by admiring various watercolours around the kitchen. They turned out to be by Mrs Tipton. 'They're of our place in Tuscany. I'd love you to see it.' Mrs Tipton invited us both to stay with them there over the summer. I asked if I could bring my girlfriend, and Mrs Tipton asked whether Lucy wasn't my girlfriend. I guess being rich means never having to listen to what anyone says. I don't think Lucy needed to make such a show of having hysterics about the idea. The message obviously finally sank in, because Mrs Tipton spent the rest of the evening introducing me as the man who taught Sam English and was here without my girlfriend. I didn't attract much interest, particularly as my bow tie kept coming undone. Finally Lucy helped me fix it, but we hastily separated as Mrs Tipton hove into view wielding half a hedge's worth of mistletoe.

I spoke to a man who manages a bank for about forty-five minutes, largely about the routes by which we both got to the party. I did my best to come across as a man of the world. Although I did keep accidentally picking up his glass from the mantelpiece and drinking from it, and asked the question, 'Much money in banks?' I managed to lose an entire lit cigarette at that point as well. One moment it was there, the next it was gone. I seem to have missed a brilliant career as a conjurer. I also asked him if it's true that working in a bank is just like any other office, except that the paper's more expensive. Apparently it's a myth.

Me: Have you ever been tempted to …
Him: Rob my own bank? No, I haven't. That was what you were going to ask, wasn't it?

I spotted a waiter going past with a tray of glasses and made an impulsive lunge for another gin and tonic. I thought it a bit strange that there was lipstick on the rim and most of the ice was melted, but I didn't want to kick up a fuss. The waiter gave a polite cough. 'Perhaps sir would like to wait for a clean glass. I can bring you one if you'd like … after I've finished collecting the empties.'

After that I retreated to the hall to get some fresh air. I spoke to a man in a snazzy waistcoat for about twenty minutes before it dawned on me that I had no idea who the son he was talking about was, although I clearly teach him. Anyway, this chap is a classics don at Oxford, and was talking about how he'd enrolled said mystery boy in French conversation classes at the age of five, and taught him Latin himself from the age of six. He started quoting Virgil or something at me and for a moment I thought I had lost the ability to understand English. Turns out the kid is Bagley.

I rescued Lucy from a conversation with Tom Downing, and we got onto the topic of her and Barry Taylor. I have to say, things don't look too hopeful for him. For one thing, she's still seeing Charlie. For another, she doesn't think she and Barry have anything in common. I tried to be encouraging, although I don't think I helped much by saying she should give it a go 'and not care whatever anyone else might think'.

Towards the end of the evening Mr Tipton invited me outside for a cigar. I told him how much I was enjoying the party, and what a lovely house and wife he has. 'Do you want to know the secret of my success?' he asked me. Very much so. 'Hard work and a lot of bullshit,' he confided. We talked about Tuscany for a bit, and he asked if I'd had a chance to look at young Tipton's coursework folder. I haven't yet. I hope it's good. It's going to be pretty embarrassing sitting around the pool in Tuscany if Tipton's failed his A level.

Sunday, 22nd December. Frank's back for Christmas. Thanks, Santa. Mum had a phone call from Heathrow about two hours ago asking if anyone could pick him up. So, the last of the brainless international playboys is back on his native soil.

The abominable ski instructor is at home now. He's sleeping in my bedroom – without my permission – because Mum has turned his room into a storage space. There's a big hint there for you, Frank. At this very moment he's probably tucked up in my bed, wondering what's in the fridge or blowing his nose on my sheets. I e-mailed him earlier. I know an e-mail isn't the nicest way to welcome Frank home, but it wasn't intended to be.

From:	**mbletch@buxdon.org.uk**
Date:	**Sunday, 22 December 14:35**
To:	**frankbletch69@hotmail.com**
Subject:	**RE: Welcome Home**

Dear Frank,

I've rung a couple of times, but you were in the bath. I see from your e-mail address that you've either started knocking two years off your age or you're even more of an irredeemable tool than I had previously imagined. Thanks for the box, by the way. You paid insufficient postage on it. Don't worry, I'm looking after your treasures for you. You can pick them up at any time. Better still, I'll send them to you. Mum mentioned on the phone that it's Christmas next week, so I suppose we will see each other then. Did you mention it to her? Dom and I were planning just to keep quiet about it and hope she forgot about Christmas this year. In fact, if you could just take December out of the calendar in the kitchen and put in two Novembers, that would be great.

Sorry to hear you lost your job, although I have no doubt that you deserved to. What terrible cock-up did you make? Or should I just ask who the girl was this time? Dad would be so proud.

Have you got any plans for the future? I think that perhaps by January you should have moved out of the bath. If you're looking for work, I think your bike is still in the shed, and I'm sure the newsagent would be glad to have you back.

Welcome home, by the way.

Lots of love
Matt

P.S. Don't touch my stuff.

From:	**frankbletch69@hotmail.com**
Date:	**Sunday, 22 December 15:52**
To:	**mbletch@buxdon.org.uk**
Subject:	**RE: RE: Welcome Home**

Hi Milksop,

Sorry to miss your calls. I'm out of the bath now, and I
was very hurt by your previous message. Matthew, you're
my brother and I love you. Why does it always have to be so
hard with us? I know you have a lot of anger towards me, but
we're both grown men now, and as you see, I no longer need
to demonstrate my affection towards you with merciless verbal
mockery and the occasional affectionate drubbing.

In answer to your question, I wasn't fired for sexual
misdemeanours this time. I hope to have put that period of my
life behind me. I now realise how shallow and meaningless all
those years of mind-boggling drug-fuelled international sex
with young, beautiful and charming eurogirls were. Actually,
at the last place I worked I was having a fling – another
mindless, frantic fling – with a young Slovenian cleaner. But it
became so much more than just amazing sex when I discovered
the discriminatory terms on which she and her compatriots
were being employed. I was outraged, and for the first time I
felt genuine passion, the passion of being swept up in a cause
bigger than myself. I organised a strike, and confronted the
manager. Unfortunately I was immediately fired without notice
or back-pay, but I hope that the fire we lit that cold November

night, protesting in the snow, will be harder to extinguish than my little 'career' was.

Your loving brother
Frank

From:	mbletch@buxdon.org.uk
Date:	Sunday, 22 December 16:17
To:	frankbletch69@hotmail.com
Subject:	RE: RE: RE: Welcome Home

Really?

From:	frankbletch69@hotmail.com
Date:	Sunday, 22 December 17:32
To:	mbletch@buxdon.org.uk
Subject:	RE: RE: RE: RE: Welcome Home

Fuck no. I got caught with my cock in the cookie jar again. I merely wanted to give you, for a few short hours, a sense of what it might feel like to respect your older brother.

I'd appreciate it if you wouldn't disillusion Mum.

By the way, I'm working on paying you and Dominic back the postage on those boxes. For real.

Frank

P.S. I wouldn't hold your breath, though.
P.P.S. I'm touching your stuff. And there's nothing you can do to stop me.

Monday, 23rd December. I wonder exactly how much DNA I share with Frank and whether I can have it surgically removed. Frank Bletch: the unacceptable face of European Union. If the Queen knew what he was getting up to she'd ask for his passport back. I shall print off those e-mails and keep them, just in case Caroline or Mum ever ask me again why I refer to Frank as my estranged brother.

Mum says she's looking forward to seeing me tomorrow, although she doesn't know yet where I'm going to sleep. In my own bed in my own room would be the obvious solution, but there's no way I'm sharing a duvet with Frank.

Weird event of the day: A pair of Japanese girls appeared on the grounds about mid-morning and were having the builders take pictures of them in front of the school. Perhaps they were under the misapprehension that it's The Good Mixer. I went to have a chat with them, and quickly remembered how little Japanese I actually speak. I can hold a conversation, but that conversation does have to revolve around directions to the train station. I agreed to have my picture taken with them. Obviously, they did that V-sign thing with their fingers. So did I, just for old time's sake. To my relief neither started laughing, pointing and calling me Mister Goblin.

Tuesday, 24th December. I got home about lunchtime, walked through the front door, and instantly reverted to being fifteen years old. I've had a squabble with Frank already about the bedroom arrangements. I kept my dignity, arguing calmly and logically why I should sleep in my own bed. Frank pulled faces and told Mum I punched him when she wasn't looking. I'm sleeping on a camp bed in my own bedroom, unless I can fill Frank with enough food and booze that he falls asleep on the living-room couch.

I tried to phone Caroline, but Frank came and stood right next to the phone. He asked if I knew where his air rifle had got to. It's probably in 'Frank's room', as Mum still refers to what is now a storage space. Caroline is totally excited about the Christmas present I sent her, and was trying to guess what it is. Unfortunately all her guesses were way better than the actual present. She asked if I was going to get presents for Toby and Lulu. Jesus, I wasn't even sure I was going to get presents for Dom and Frank until I knew I'd be seeing them. Not that it's a problem – I've got my sample chapters with me on disk, and I can just print Toby and Lulu off copies. I'm having second thoughts about the latest title: *Twenty-Five Temples Not Worth The Bother*.

Mum's very excited about Dom bringing his girlfriend to-night. His 'new American girlfriend' is how she refers to her, as if Dom has a long list of previous girlfriends of differing nationalities. 'She does know you can drink the tap water, doesn't she?' I expect so, since she's lived in England for the last five years. Frank reckons she'll definitely be obese. He's still referring to Dominic as 'big bad Dom', a joke that lost any semblance of relevance or humour at least four years ago. I don't think Frank even remembers why it used to be a joke. Caroline doesn't know how lucky she is to have been spared my family. Frank's presently sitting in my room with his air rifle and the lights out, waiting for carol singers. Next year I'm celebrating Kwanzaa, on my own.

Wednesday, 25th December. Bloody Christmas. Despite my best efforts I didn't manage to get Frank to pass out on the couch, although he was looking a bit green around the gills during the Midnight Service. He got up to go to the bathroom four times during the night, before eventually throwing up in my bed. The whole room smells of marzipan and brandy, which I now regret encouraging him to indulge in all evening. At five o'clock this morning he got up again, managed to kick the leg of the camp bed and folded me up inside it.

Karla's not obese. Neither is her name Karly, Kylie or Kayleigh, a fact Frank seems unable to grasp.

Uncle Jeremy and Aunty Maureen should be arriving for lunch shortly. This was met by universal groans, and I made it clear there's absolutely no way I'm going to be the one who gets stuck talking to Uncle Jeremy and has to hear every single detail of the drive over from Northampton. He once spent twenty minutes telling me what he keeps in his glove compartment. Mum got a bit teary and told us they're the only family she's got. Actually, they're Dad's relatives, a point Dom made and which led to Mum locking herself in the pantry for the last two hours, weeping. Frank is talking to her, although when I last went past he seemed mostly to be trying to persuade her to slip him a pizza under the door.

I phoned Caroline just now to wish her season's greetings and interrupted the Applebys eating.

Later: Frank fell asleep after lunch, and I can see him as I write this. It would serve him right if I let him sleep through the Queen's speech.

I expected Frank's face in repose to be strangely innocent, reminding me of happy childhood days. But he has the same expression of dopy malignancy unconscious as he does when he is supposedly conscious. He made us all cards with his own fair hand, which would have been a sweet gesture if he was eight years old. Mine just said 'Merry Xmas' in scrawled letters on the outside of a folded sheet of A4. Inside it said: 'Matthew. You are my brother. HA HA HA. Frank.'

I just rang Caroline again to say thanks for my present. It was a watch, which was extremely generous, but also made the present I got her look a bit shabby. The Applebys were still eating. Bloody Rychard's present turned out to be a hamper from Fortnum and Mason's. I expect the stuff inside was from Fortnum and Mason's too.

Caroline sounded a bit pissed off about something. Or perhaps just very, very full. She made the astonishing suggestion that I introduce her to my brothers by inviting them to Rychard's party. I explained that would be a very, very bad idea. Part of the deal with us being estranged brothers is that we don't invite each other to parties, unless someone's died or got married. Caroline claimed to like her present, although not completely convincingly.

Mum gave me a hat. A kind of small pork pie hat which makes me look like the drummer in a Madness tribute band. Frank said the nose-hair trimmers I got him will come in handy, and threatened to try them out on Dom at the dinner table. Dom and Karla appeared mildly thrilled to get my sample chapters. Frank said he hadn't had time to get me a present, but he'd let me keep the box he sent me.

Frank gave Dom one of my records, and gave Mum a Hoover. Karla looked like she was going to say something pointed about housework and equality when Mum opened it, but Dom helped her to more nut roast. Mum gave me a book about Japan, and I gave her some bath oils or something like that which was on the shelf at Crabtree and Evelyn nearest the door. She appeared pleased.

Uncle Jeremy's sole contribution to the conversation was to interject: 'No cracker for you, Dom! You've already pulled one!' God knows how many Christmasses he's been saving that up for. Fortunately I don't think Karla got it. The joke would also have worked better if we'd actually had any crackers. Mum spent about thirty minutes apologising that we didn't. Auntie Maureen appears to be under heavy sedation – and if I was married to Uncle Jeremy and his spiv's moustache, I would be too. He must Brylcreem it. Imagine having breakfast with that every morning of your life. Imagine it coming for you under the duvet.

Karla asked me earlier what I got Caroline for Christmas. An unlockable diary and a copy of my sample chapters. 'That's one way of finding out what she really thinks of it,' Karla noted. I hadn't realised I was that transparent.

Dom announced over the dishes that he and Karla will probably spend Christmas at her folks' place next year, and Mum got a bit emotional again.

*

Thursday, 26th December. I got up early to watch Frank asleep again. He really is a hell of a guy. Even sleeping he is twice the man I'll ever be. He snores like Thor the Thunder God. I feel really guilty about not inviting him to the party. It's only 'cos I'm afraid he will nick Caroline off me, just like he nicked that other bird when I was fifteen whose name he probably can't even currently recall. What is his secret? He's a slob, he dresses like a gamekeeper and he's never had a proper job. The only book I have ever seen him reading involves the adventures of a duckling and is OK if you drop it in the bath. I am so sensitive and lovely. My skin is soft and smooth and I pretend to be interested in what women say to me. Look at my pretty little hands. I could model ladies' gloves. Also, Mum loves Frank so much more than me. She let him move home, and she wouldn't let me or Dom. God, I wish I was him. I'm so pathetic. I have kept all my school reports in my desk, with all my clippings from the School Magazine. I can't even think of a decent place to hide my diary, even though I had all that time when Frank was asleep yesterday.

When he wakes up I think I'll invite Frank to the party on New Year's Eve.

I haven't written in this diary yet today. Lizzie. The first and last girl I ever brought to the house was called Lizzie. She went on one date with Frank and her family moved to Aberystwyth.

I need to find a better hiding place for this diary. I thought it would be safe behind the books on the shelf in the lounge, but Frank either figured it out counter-intuitively or had lost the remote control again.

Unfortunately I let my guard down earlier and had a bath. I leaped out, dripping, as soon as the phone rang, but it was too late. Frank was talking to Caroline and as I slithered soapily down the stairs I could hear him telling her that we've talked about New Year's and he was looking forward to finally meeting her. He turned to me with an evil grin as he was talking, and started wiggling his tongue around.

I do worry about Frank. I know my diet isn't great, but it's the third day I've been home and I'm yet to see Frank eat anything that isn't orange.

Mum and I had a long conversation regarding the possibility that Frank's adopted. 'I'm afraid not,' she sighed, wistfully. I suggested it might not be too late to put him up for it.

We ran out of booze this evening, and the off-licence around the corner was closed. Karla observed that in New York they serve drinks all night. Frank pointed out that this wasn't much use to us, and for once I was inclined to agree with him. By this point I was ready to put her on a plane to go and pick some up for us. Her presence has inspired Dom to try to get everyone to play party games, apparently under the impression that's what a real family does. This is largely why we ran out of booze. Charades went quickly downhill as we started to sober up. We spent about forty-five minutes trying to guess Karla's fourteen-word book. It turned out to be *The Intellectuals and the Masses: Pride and Prejudice Among the Literary Intelligentsia, 1880–1939*. She did 'intellectuals' by pointing at herself and Dom, and 'masses' by pointing at Frank. Mum guessed *Beauty and the Beast*. Finally Dom got it, with a bit of cheating, and spent ten minutes flapping around the room coughing. It was clearly *The Wings of the Dove*, but by that point I had lost all interest. Also, I wanted to see how long he would keep it up. Frank just kept shouting 'My Brother is a Twat.' It's not clear whether he thinks there's a book of that title. Frank did *The Lion, the Witch and the Wardrobe*, then claimed he couldn't think of any other books. Karla told him he could do a film, so he did. I didn't realise they made a *Police Academy VI*.

He's in the kitchen now, trying to get drunk on brandy butter.

*

Friday, 27th December. Frank and I took a stroll to the news-
agents this morning. The woman behind the counter asked
when Frank was coming back to work for them. He introduced me to his latest discovery: King's Lager. It only costs
80p a can, and I found out why soon enough. It saves time
by already smelling like tramp sweat. 'Ah, the lager of Kings,'
Frank rhapsodised.

Dom and Karla announced they had to leave, and escaped
shortly after lunch.

According to the paper today Britain is in the grip of Lad
Culture. Our heroes are David Baddiel and Frank Skinner,
our films are *The Italian Job* and *Trainspotting*, and our pin-
ups are Denise Van Outen and Jo Guest. I was telling Mum I
felt that was an offensively reductive stereotype when Frank
wandered through the living room in an England shirt, whistling 'Three Lions' and sipping on a King's lager. You see that
stereotype, Frank? That's you, that is.

Saturday, 28th December. This morning I found the cigarette
I lost at the Tiptons' party. It was in the roll-up of Rychard's
trouser-bottoms, along with two olives and half a pretzel.
There is a sizeable burn about halfway up the shin of the
trousers, which I have entirely failed to conceal with Tippex.

I moved into Dom's bedroom last night. He and Karla have
both left their copies of my sample chapters behind.

Frank is dropping heavy hints about coming to Rychard's
party on New Year's Eve.

Sunday, 29th December. I got an e-mail today from Mrs Tipton,
reminding me about Tuscany and saying that Caroline and I
would be very welcome in July. The Tiptons will be away,
but we can get the key from Mrs Frattini next door, and her
husband should make sure the pool's been cleaned for our
arrival. The picturesque local peasantry will apparently insist

on bringing us eggs and fresh fruit every day. We'll be there for some kind of local festival in the village, too. I couldn't tell from the note whether that means a jazz band in the village square or everyone getting together to throw a donkey off a tower, but I guess we'll find out soon enough.

Monday, 30th December. Sad news from Buxdon. Lionel Brimscombe had a heart attack yesterday, and died before the ambulance came. He was staying with his sister in Wolvercote at the time, and she found him in the bath. The funeral is going to be in the school chapel.

Tuesday, 31st December. I tried to sneak away early, but Frank woke up. He'd put a pile of books outside my room, which I knocked down the stairs. He tells me he has already got the address of the party from Caroline, so there's no point trying to sneak off. I can only hope the world ends before eight p.m. this evening. In fact, that's probably more likely than Frank getting through this party without embarrassing me, himself, and Western Civilisation. He brought me a cup of tea in my room, put his hand on my shoulder, and looked deep into my eyes.

'Hey, Matt, just think of it this way,' he said. 'You don't much like this Rychard bloke anyway.'

Hopefully Frank will protect me if Rychard cuts up rough about the trousers. Caroline's not going to be too impressed either. I could pretend to be deep in grief. Great idea, because that's what everyone wants at their New Year's Eve party: a mourner. Maybe if I fold the trousers right when I give them back to Rychard he won't notice.

There was a load of tomato ketchup at the bottom of the tea. I realised while drinking it that I'm genuinely looking forward to getting back to Buxdon.

Part Two:
Lent

January

Sunday, 5 January, 1997
Mercers' Lodge
Buxdon School
Buxdon

Dear Caroline,

I hope your cold is a little better. The funeral this morning was very moving. The CCF gave a twelve-air-gun-salute and Brimscombe's sister gave a speech about how much his twenty years at Buxdon had meant to him. Twenty years at Buxdon. I expect they'll name a boathouse after him. There've been arguments all week, actually, because the headmaster suggested that the collection should go towards the Auditorium and Drama Lab Fund, but Brimscombe's sister said he would have much rather the money went towards fixing the leak in the library roof. They're attaching the Lionel Brimscombe Memorial Tarpaulin tomorrow.

Please tell Rychard thanks again for being so good about the burn in the trousers. I'm so embarrassed. Thinking about it, I'm not entirely sure it was my cigarette. Perhaps someone else dropped it.

The first sight that greeted me on my return to Buxdon was Marcus Lau making a spirited dash in the direction of the bus station. I know the feeling. He'd almost made the gate when he collided with Mr Hallbrick.

The builders finished clearing the ground for the new drama building over the holidays. They've cut down my tree, which makes the view even bleaker than usual. The old tuck shop is gone, although there's a new one being set up next to the Sixth Form centre. Incidentally, *The Old Tuck Shop is Gone* would be a potential title for an autobiography, I think. Not mine, though. Mine already has a title lined up: *My Brother's Zoo Keeper*.

Love,
Matt

P.S. About the party: Caroline, I'm sorry. I'm so very, very sorry.

Monday, 6 January. Oh, the bastard. Oh, the rotten stinking unspeakable rat bastard. Frank was the hit of the party.

We finally found Rychard's flat after wandering through the icy winds of Docklands for about an hour. Frank was drinking all that time, so when we'd been buzzed in and were going up in the lift, I realised: a) he was completely smashed, and b) all he had left to give the host was a single can of King's Lager. He was wearing a Hawaiian shirt with two buttons missing, jeans with no knees and shoes with no laces. What happened to the laces? Perhaps the police took them away.

Rychard and Caroline introduced themselves, and Frank asked if there was anything to eat. He handed me the can of King's, opened my bag, and presented Rychard with the bottle of Dom Pérignon that I'd brought. Rychard then took the single lager from me, with a quizzical look. I tried to take him aside to explain about the trousers, but realised that I no longer had direct visual contact with Frank. He was in the kitchen. Not only that but he was going through the fridge. He took out a packet of smoked salmon, opened it, sniffed it, took a bite, then chucked it back in. Sig came up to confront him, and demanded to know whether he would do that to stuff in his own fridge. Frank straightened up and stared at her, perplexed. He asked where she got her hair done. She asked if he liked it. He offered to 'get' the guy who did it.

I took Caroline aside at that point to explain the situation. She went off to mention to Rychard that it might be a good idea to lock the balcony. Preferably with Frank on it.

When I got back into the kitchen Sig and Frank were laughing and talking, and she asked me where I have been hiding Frank all this time. In a cold, damp cellar, I replied. Frank then pretended to look hurt and whispered something to her. I heard the word 'jealousy' mentioned. I decided to leave him to it. And that's practically the last time I talked to him all night. The party was absolutely rammed by this point, so I decided just to hope that whatever carnage Frank wrought was mistaken for the work of a large group of drunk people.

I wandered into the lounge, looking for Caroline, when Rychard decided to leap off the coffee table and get me in a playful headlock. We toppled over, scattering cans and people in all directions. I was just about to punch him in the kidneys, when I saw he was just mucking around. I still would have jokily punched him in the kidneys, but I couldn't get either arm free. Eventually I let him get off me and sit up. He'd discovered his trousers are ruined. He discovered this because Frank told him. Frank had then tried to pour oil on troubled waters by suggesting that if Rychard painted his shin then the hole was hardly noticeable. Rychard wanted to know if I had been planning to tell him about the hole any time. Of course I had, I assured him. Perish the thought that Rychard might turn up at a fancy party with a little peep-hole in his trousers. I decided I might as well admit that some idiot got red wine on his shirt, as well. Technically true, even if I was that idiot. Rychard asked if I was enjoying myself. Yeah, the whole thing was a fucking hoot. I still have a carpet burn on my scalp. I asked where Caroline was, and Rychard told me she was out on the balcony. I didn't fall for that old trick.

About forty minutes later a blue and shivery Caroline came

in and asked if I hadn't got the message she was waiting for me. She wanted to have a serious conversation with me. No problem. We had about seven minutes until midnight, after all. Caroline told me that Sig is very vulnerable right now, and asked if I could take Frank to one side, explain the situation and ask him to go easy. I said I'd certainly ask him, if I could find him. It didn't turn out to be that hard. At that very moment a bunch of people started chanting 'Frank! Frank! Frank!' and he emerged through the door of Rychard's bedroom. *Through* the door. First a foot emerged in a shower of splinters, then an arm, then finally the rest of Frank, with one arm around Sig and a Marlborough school tie bandanna-fashion around his head. Frank didn't even go to Marlborough. Rychard seemed to find it as hilarious as anyone. I wish I'd known he had such a laissez faire attitude to his possessions. I would have brought a fire-axe and chopped his bed up.

I eventually managed to separate Frank from his new crowd of admirers, and drag him into the bathroom to talk about Sig. He seemed to be listening carefully and taking in what I had to say. Then he put his arm around me. 'Milksop, I hear what you're saying, but it might be a bit late for that now ...' I feel like I brought a dog to the party and it peed on the carpet. And everyone still preferred the dog to me.

There's a picture of Rychard in his bathroom in which he looks exactly like Michael Portillo. I thought at first it was him and Michael Portillo, then realised I wasn't focusing too well. Rychard also has a glass-fronted and backlit case to display all his aftershaves. Or at least he did, until I tried to open it and pulled it off the wall. Frank seems to have endless licence to behave like a recently defrosted caveman. When he smashes something up it's funny and charming, and everyone cheers. When I accidentally break something a bit I get taken aside by Caroline and asked if I think I need to deal with my underlying hostility issues. She also informs me I'm quite a nasty drunk, news I greeted by sneering majestically and moodily rolling my eyes. I no doubt came across like Heathcliff, Byron or a total wally. Despite what romantic fiction would have one believe, she didn't find this particularly attractive. I don't suppose it's much consolation that I'm not terribly nice sober.

I did get the chance to have a poke around Rychard's flat a little. The guy has more shoes than Beau Brummell. To my surprise and annoyance his CD collection is both extensive and sophisticated. Although he does have the second Tin Machine album. It's hardly a severed head in the freezer, though, is it?

Tuesday, 7th January. The school is interviewing for a new member of the history department this week. To my utter disbelief, they've made Barry Taylor a housemaster. Three people, including me, thought it was the headmaster's New Year's joke, and laughed out loud. It's utterly inexplicable to me. If I had known they were searching for the worst possible candidate, I might have put myself forward. This is a guy who refers to everyone in the Lower School as 'Stumpy'. To their faces. He's a friend and all, and I'm pleased for him, but you would have thought we could have found a better candidate to put in charge of the intellectual and emotional development of eighty teenage boys than Barry Taylor. Barry 'There's a lot of mathematics in rugby, actually' Taylor. And vice versa: I saw his end-of-term tests, and there wasn't a single question that wasn't along the lines of 'Barry has scored a try and is attempting a conversion. If he gets it, how many points will the French need to score in order to win?'

Barry moved into Brimscombe's (as everyone is still calling it, much to his annoyance) this morning. I helped him carry some boxes up to his room. He's got the whole top floor of the house to himself. There's still a few things Brimscombe had left lying around – some unmarked essays, several decades' worth of walking guides to Europe, a tiroler hat, a few other books Brimscombe's sister didn't have room for (called things like

A Tramp in the Pyrenees and *In the Footsteps of Charlemagne*), a load of diaries and an alpenstock. There's also a big box of unsold copies of *Historic Walks in Buxdon, Elmsfield and Little Chipping*.

We tracked down Mrs O. Digby and asked whether it might be possible to stow some of it in the Old Building attic. 'There is no attic in the Old Building,' we were told. Yes there is, I insisted. You can see the attic windows from her office. 'It's out of bounds.' She doesn't have a key and we wouldn't be allowed up there even if she did. I was quite keen to investigate the mystery further, but Barry's more interested in finding out what Mrs Digby's O stands for. He suggested anonymously calling the school office. 'Hi, is that Olive?' 'Can I talk to Ophelia please?'

I've been given Brimscombe's old tutor group. No, I'm not sure that's a terribly good idea either. Still, it's only one hour a week. I don't quite know what I'm supposed to do with U6Bletch but I think I'm meant to give them personal, academic and career advice. And take a register.

We heard about the Oxbridge interview results. Hallbrick got a conditional offer, Iles got rejected. I was slightly surprised about that, actually. I was even more surprised to hear that Bagley has got an unconditional offer to read classics at Oxford. Except that in fact I wasn't surprised at all. I wonder who interviewed him. His dad?

Wednesday, 8th January. Spoke to Caroline. I'm still in her bad books. Rychard wasn't at all convinced by my story that I saw someone in his kitchen confessing to having smashed his bathroom cabinet. He claims not to have seen anyone at the party with an artificial hand and curly red hair. I knew I should just have blamed Frank.

I asked Caroline what she'd thought of Frank. 'I didn't expect him to be so dishy.' Exactly what I wanted to hear.

According to Sig, Frank is actually really sensitive and shy. They had a long talk about Dad, and Frank cried. Caroline asked why I never open up like that. Because I'm not a mad scheming liar? I bet Frank didn't mention that at Dad's wake he was trying to cop off with people by telling them Dad used to touch him inappropriately and beat him with a coat hanger. Mum was very upset.

Why has everyone else missed the blatant fact that Frank is a cross between Walter Mitty and Attila the Hun? He may, deep down, have a sensitive layer. But it's way deeper than anyone has ever excavated. What Sig fails to realise is that she has cut through a layer of rough gravel to find a very thin layer of mixed emotion and horseshit. Then under that there is another near-impenetrable layer of emotional granite, then under that there are a load of bodies, then under that there is volcanic lava, then under that there is a weird country full of dinosaurs and men with spears, then somewhere, very, very much further than anyone has gone or would care to go, there is some kind of emotional core to Frank. Possibly a crying child with an ice cream cone but no ice cream, but more probably just a very small version of the exterior Frank.

Richard 'Dead-Eye Dick' Darling was glowering at me all through lunch today. He tried to catch me as I was getting rid of my tray, presumably to ask me ask me what happened to that starting pistol, but I managed to avoid him by ducking through the kitchens. The tattooed dinner lady looked up from stirring a vat of unidentified vegetable matter to call me Mister Goblin. I didn't say anything. She's really not someone I want to mess with.

Thursday, 9th January. I was coming out of an indescribably tedious double period on *Of Mice and Men* when I almost walked straight into Miranda Bell from uni. To my surprise she actually remembered me. I was beginning to wonder whether I'd cracked and this was some sort of hallucination, except I doubt my psyche would let me hallucinate anything so pleasant. She still looks amazing. She was there to interview for the job in the history department. She was asking about Buxdon and I tried not to be too discouraging. We actually had lunch together, in the Buxdon Tea Shoppe, and I prepped her on the headmaster's idiosyncrasies so she could shine in the interview.

We were reminiscing about the great times on G floor, and the time she broke up with that guy Guy, and he got upset and kept setting off the fire alarms. And the time she had an essay crisis and I stayed up all night making her cups of tea. And the time Guy thought I fancied her, and tried to crawl in my window at two in the morning with a Stanley knife. The last I heard Miranda was engaged to some Argentinian playboy, but things didn't work out with José in the end. I asked if it was a case of 'No way, José' and then really wished I hadn't. It's always nice to see old friends and remind yourself that you're exactly as gauche as you ever were.

Friday, 10th January. First meeting of my tutor group this morning. I told them not to be discouraged if their mocks hadn't gone as well as they hoped, because there are still a few months until the A levels, and took a register. That left me with fifty-five minutes of tutor group left to fill and nothing much left to say. I took the register really slowly, too, to fill time. Suffice it to say, when I asked if anyone had any personal, professional or academic problems they wanted to air, I was met with blank, incredulous faces. Thank God for that at least. Luckily I'd had three cups of coffee as breakfast, and so managed to keep gabbling for the allotted time without repetition or hesitation. Ah, the *Just a Minute* approach to classroom management. And I have to do this every week? I'll either start giving them presentations to do or I'll just bring a board game next week.

Dr Morris reminded me that next Friday is the Sixth Form theatre trip to see *King Lear*. There's definitely no roller skating in it, and I already know who done it. I hope the bar isn't too expensive. I offered to stay there all night to make sure none of the boys are buying alcohol. Morris doesn't think this will be necessary. I'm up in London this weekend as well. I did ask Caroline if she wanted to come to the play but she thinks she'll give it a miss.

Sunday, 12th January. I'd previously thought Caroline's New Year's resolution was to give up smoking, but this weekend has proved me wrong. From the available evidence her resolution was to give up *buying* cigarettes, and scab them all off me instead. And then complain that I've been encouraging her to smoke.

Sig was asking about Frank. I was as discouraging as I could be within the bounds of politeness, which in the long run will prove the less emotionally damaging option. She's rung Frank a few times, but he's been in the bath. She asked me if I thought he was avoiding her, and I told her he does exactly the same thing to me. Which, thinking about it, wasn't really an answer. They definitely have something in common, even if it's only unusually protracted personal cleanliness routines.

Caroline wasn't sure if she remembered Miranda. 'Wasn't she that drop-dead annoying Sloaney girl who was always getting essay extensions and who never gave people the right change in the union bar?' I daresay Caroline was thinking of somebody else.

No word from Caroline about what she thinks of the book. I didn't get the chance to spend any alone time with her diary. She did, however, seem genuinely enthused about our trip to Tuscany. Mustn't forget her dog Sniffles is having his operation on Tuesday. I should have got him a card.

*

Monday, 13th January. I took the coursework folders with me to mark on the train back to Buxdon. It was only as we were passing through Little Chipping that I got to Sam Tipton's. It contains nothing but four sheets of blank notepaper headed 'Tipton Construction'. No, I exaggerate. There's one page torn out of an exercise book, with 'To What Extent is Nelly Dean' written on it in biro. On a positive note, there are no grammatical or spelling errors so far.

Tuesday, 14th January. I phoned to send Sniffles my best wishes for his operation, and asked Caroline to have Lulu kiss him for me. 'Actually, his name is Mr Snuffles,' Caroline told me huffily, and accused me of not really caring about him. The response to that depends on how strongly you emphasise the words 'really' and 'caring'. For the purposes of my relationship with Caroline, I care a lot. If Mr Snivels doesn't wake up from the sedation I'll be very sad-faced and would even go so far as attending a funeral. I might even stretch to a wreath with Bonios and squeaky toys on it. Not that I'm one hundred per cent certain I could pick Snuffles out of a line-up alongside Sodden-Nose, Lord Rottenguts, Archduke Oddballs and Old Sleepy.

  The thought occurs to me that in the several times I've been to stay with Caroline's parents, I've never seen Old Sleepy move. I'm not entirely sure that the Applebys haven't had him stuffed and not mentioned it to Caroline or Lulu. I have more or less the same question about her brother Toby. I wouldn't say that to Toby, though. He might shoot me. Or even worse, try to befriend me. We'd end up spending weekends in a tent on Dartmoor, sharing a Kendal Mint Cake and rationing our loo roll.

Wednesday, 15th January. I had a talk with Tipton today, and asked why his coursework folder has no coursework in it. 'Doesn't it?' he asked insinuatingly, 'That's surprising.' I told him he had a week's grace to get some work together, and if he needed any help to come and ask me.

I spoke to Lucy Salmon about it, and she said Tipton's coursework essay on 'Just War' was one of the best pieces she'd ever read. She also mentioned that easyJet has some really good offers on flights to Tuscany at the moment.

I started reading the book Mum got me for Christmas. I don't suppose it was an intentional dig that the author's two years younger than me and that his book is on exactly the same topic. *Gaijin Blues* by William Further. Thankfully the book is atrocious. Someone has persuaded Further to dress up as a sumo wrestler on the cover. He looks like a prize plonker, and his book confirms it. He might as well just have called it *You Don't Have to be a Racist to Hate Japan, But It Helps!* If you don't speak or read Japanese and loathe neon lights, karaoke, crowds, nude public bathing, fast trains, sumo, flower arranging, elaborate cuisine, idiosyncratic English, bamboo, bonsai trees, dried squid snacks, bowing, self-heating toilet seats, castles, eating with chopsticks, urban sprawl, kimonos, kneeling, exchanging business cards, temples, fish, rice and Japanese people, then chances are you'll have a fairly unhappy time in Japan. I see the bastard's actually had two books published – the other one is *Further Around the East*. I wonder what brilliant observations he dishes out in that? Vietnam: 'A beautiful country putting behind it a legacy of colonialism and war.' Singapore: 'Very clean and orderly.' China: 'Loads of Chinese people, many of them on bikes.' Hong Kong: 'What a lot of skyscrapers.'

Thursday, 16th January. I was sitting with Lucy at lunch when Barry Taylor came over and sat down. He was asking Lucy if she wanted to come and see his new house room, but she didn't go for it. 'I've already seen around Brimscombe's,' she said, before remembering she had some urgent class preparation to do.

'Joke's on her. I've put loads of new posters up and we're getting a dartboard next week.'

'Oh, by the way,' Barry added, 'who was that attractive woman you were having lunch with in the Buxdon Tea Shoppe the other day?' I explained it was an old friend, and we were talking about professional matters.

'Better not let Caroline find out.'

Why would Caroline care? I was just having lunch with an old pal. Although now I think about it I don't think I did mention the lunch part to Caroline. It was strange having lunch with Miranda. She seems to cast a balmy radiance everywhere she goes. Even the grumpy bloke in the Buxdon Tea Shoppe was fairly polite. He fetched new butter for the table and everything.

'Balmy radiance'? Probably best not to use that exact form of words to Caroline. Keep it together, Bletch. You'll start gibbering on about 'geometrical cheekbones' and 'limpid eyes' next.

Friday, 17th January. The tutor group went slightly better today. No one had any pressing moral, philosophical, personal or political issues they desperately wanted discussed but I've developed the theory that if I coffee up enough beforehand and just keep talking very fast, then hopefully no one will notice what a tremendous waste of time the whole thing is. I've also discovered that if I leave the register in the staffroom, that knocks another ten minutes off the hour. I found this out by accident this morning, but I'll probably start doing it deliberately in future. I can probably push it up to fifteen if I stop to tie my shoelaces really slowly on the way.

Saturday, 18th January. If not the best production of *King Lear* I've seen, last night's was certainly the funniest. It was a special school's preview. The preview was supposed to be special, not the schools. Special it certainly was, but I hope it improves before they invite the critics.

It was certainly a brave move to do the storm scene naked in front of a house of schoolchildren. And teachers. Dr Morris turned to me, rubbing his hands, and said quite audibly 'Brrr. It seems to be a mite chilly out on the heath tonight.' Otherwise it was all in 1920s dress. Lear's crown was an MCC cap. I could have found out why if I'd wanted to spend £5.50 on a programme.

The part when Lear announces his Fool's been beaten got the biggest cheer of the night. God, that guy was annoying. Some kid from another school sitting in the row behind us started answering all his rhetorical questions by calling out the words 'Prithee, nuncle, shut the fuck up.' Dr Morris turned around to have a word, but this kid was massive. He observed that if he'd beaten the Fool, he would have stayed down. I believed him, too.

I guess the actor playing Lear had been in *Casualty* or something, because as he cradled the dead Cordelia, people started calling out: 'Get me that defibrillator!' and 'We're losing her, dammit. We're going to have to go in.' I felt mildly sorry for the cast, although my sympathy rapidly dissipated when it became apparent that the play was going to end with a period dance. I started to wish it was my own vile jellies that had been gouged out when Goneril and Regan came on dressed as flappers and were made to do that dance with the hands on the knees. Alas, they didn't do it to the sound of 'Tragedy' by the Bee Gees. I knew we should've gone to *Starlight Express*.

I went on directly to Caroline's, which at least saved me the trip back to Buxdon in the minibus with Iles saying things like: 'It's funny, isn't it, Sir, the way that *the Fool* is really the only one who's *wise*.' A point that got rather lost in this performance, I felt.

*

Sunday, 19th January. Caroline and I went out for an eye-wateringly expensive brunch. We could hardly get into the restaurant for oversized baby-transports. The phenomenon of the posh fried breakfast still eludes me. Wow, it's on a square plate and there's a sprig of parsley on my scrambled eggs. Here's my wallet, take what you want. I paid £1.50 extra for a black pudding barely an inch in diameter. Who came up with the idea that what the world has been waiting for all these years is a dainty black pudding? A black pudding that ounce for ounce was more expensive than caviar. Steak, Sir? No, waiter, today I believe I'll be having the magic beans.

I think I recognised our waiter from *King Lear*.

After that we had a walk in the park. Caroline hasn't got around to reading my book yet, but she says she's looking forward to it. She reminded me that it's Toby's birthday coming up soon, and to make a note of it in my diary. It's a journal, actually. Another excursion into the wacky world of the Applebys. This time I'll remember not to eat for a few days beforehand.

Caroline's been online looking at flights to Tuscany.

I got back to Buxdon in the late afternoon. Great news! Miranda got the job.

Monday, 20th January. I took Iles aside after class to have a word about his university options. It strikes me that now is rather a bad time for the class to start studying *Jude the Obscure*, perhaps the only major tragedy in the Western Canon to revolve around an Oxbridge rejection.

Iles got a polite rejection letter from a literary agent last week, with an attached note of encouragement from Kevin Williams. Where's my polite rejection letter? Is it possible my sample chapters are actually worse than Iles's poetry?

It seems I forgot to mention to my tutor group that today is Home Clothes Day. Or to give it its Buxdon name, 'Mufti Day'. All proceeds are of course going to the Auditorium and

Drama Lab Fund. Tipton and Chivers had been tipped off, but the others were among the tiny handful of embarrassed kids walking around school in their uniforms. The balding growth-spurty Third Year with the incipient moustache turned up in his school shoes, black socks and Bermuda shorts. He was carrying his briefcase too. He had an argument with the Headmaster because he insisted on only paying £2.50 rather than the full fiver.

I can guess where the other £2.50 went, on the basis that he was handing out sweets in the lobby all through lunch break. I took him aside to remind him that real friends you can't buy with sweets. 'I know that, Sir, but you can bribe people not to attach test-tube clamps to the back of your jacket and flick ink on you.' I tried to get a pack of Polos off him, but he'd run out.

Tuesday, 21st January. Spoke to Caroline, who's coming down for the weekend. Mr Snuffles seems to be recovering from his operation. I refrained from asking how he smells.

I finally got some feedback from Caroline about my sample chapters: 'Are you going to publish this under your own name?' In retrospect, I think that's most telling critical response I have yet received. Largely because it's the only critical response I've yet received. I spent the evening trying to think of pseudonyms. I must ask Caroline what she thinks of 'Jasper Darke'. I'm thinking about an 'e' on the end of the 'Jasper' as well. I'm rather fond of 'Hew Atlee McBotch', which is almost an anagram of Matthew Bletch. 'Wet Thom Belch, MA' could also work, and calling myself 'Guy Gin' is a definite possibility.

I suppose a more fruitful use of my time might be to try to finish the damn thing. I should have it done over the next couple of weeks.

Wednesday, 22nd January. Still no coursework from Tipton.

I'll have a word with Dr Cumnor about the situation. Unfortunately he's down with a cold at the moment. Tipton himself was nowhere to be seen in today's class. I suppose I should prepare Caroline for the fact that we might not be going to Tuscany after all.

It's not just the ethical aspect of the situation that's bothering me, it's also the practical question of whether I can actually face writing 2,500 words each on the role of symbolism in *The Go-Between*, how comedy is generated in *The Importance of Being Earnest*, and whether Lear is more sinned against than sinning. I want to do the right thing. But then I also want to see Caroline in a bikini next to that swimming pool in Tuscany. It's not that my moral compass is skewed. I consulted it, but I really don't think 'North' is the answer to my dilemma. I need guidance. I wonder if *The Moral Maze* takes requests.

Thursday, 23rd January. I had lunch with Lucy Salmon and Miranda Bell. Miranda and I are initials buddies! I didn't point this out, except in my own increasingly banal interior monologue. They seemed to be hitting it off. Barry Taylor tried to muscle in on the conversation, but Lucy remembered something very important she had left on the photocopier. About a second later Miranda said something like, 'Oh, yes, the *photocopier*, I too have an urgent thing to photocopy,' and made her escape. So I ended up hearing about Barry's miserable Christmas in Hull. After a while I switched off and started counting my peas. I didn't think Barry would be the most sensible person to ask for advice regarding my Tipton dilemma.

Friday, 24th January. I spoke to Dr Cumnor today. He's had a meeting with the Tiptons, and assures me that the coursework folder 'misunderstanding' has been satisfactorily resolved.

There was a note in my pigeon-hole from Mrs Tipton.

Unfortunately they are having some refurbishment done on the place in Tuscany over the holidays and it wouldn't be very comfortable for Caroline and me to stay. She's sure I understand.

Saturday, 25th January. Rather awkward encounter with Miranda in town today. It seems I hadn't mentioned to Caroline that Miranda got the job, and hadn't mentioned to Miranda that I'm still going out with Caroline. Miranda didn't help matters by getting Caroline's name wrong, although they had three seminars together at uni, and then asking, 'Have you changed your hair? I liked it so much before.' Miranda's having a house-warming party next week, to which we're both invited. 'Wonderful,' Caroline commented afterwards. 'Another chance to see all those people I spent so much time avoiding at college. Miranda can bring the twats, I'll bring the flame thrower.'

We had a walk down by the canal later. Caroline thought she spotted a kingfisher, but it turned out to be a crisp packet. Then we encountered some charming local rascals throwing broken bricks at a duck. Caroline gave them a stern telling off in a headmistressy voice, which I found not unarousing.

I had a poke through Caroline's bag when she was having a shower, but there was no sign of her new diary.

Sunday, 26th January. Miranda came round this morning to ask if we could help her move a few things into her new flat. Caroline didn't seem thrilled. 'A few things' proved to be a sofa, three rugs, several boxes, a massive TV and a fridge. The fridge was entirely covered with pictures of Miranda and her mates: Johnno doing a yard of ale, Guy on a jet ski, Tiggy wearing angel wings, several rugby lads dressed as women, and Miranda herself looking sunburned.

While we were unpacking, Caroline found what she thinks is her yoga ball, the one that went missing in Fresher's Week.

'Oh that?' said Miranda, 'Guy found it somewhere and gave it to me.' Caroline looked like she was biting her tongue quite hard. To my alarm, Guy is going to be at the party next week. 'He's such a laugh,' Miranda said. Yes, if there's a fire alarm to be set off at two in the morning or a traffic cone to be put on a statue, Guy's your man. Come the revolution, Guy, come the revolution …

Caroline and I had a sandwich at the station, and I caught up on the rest of her news from the week. She wanted to know what Frank thinks about Sig, but as I told her it's impossible to tell what Frank thinks about anything. Or if he does. He might be sitting by the phone, wanting to call but nervous of making a fool of himself. He might be deliberately playing it cool. He might be eating hot dogs in brine straight from the tin with a broken plastic fork. Sig had a meeting with Anton this week, and they ended up having a blazing row about *The Structure of Complex Words*. Not an argument she's likely to have with Frank if they hook up, I'd wager.

Lulu rang Caroline on Thursday, very upset. She'd been watching a nature documentary, and found out that an ostrich can easily break someone's arm. So can a chicken, if you swing it right. Lulu seems to think this is the major drawback in her great scheme to set up an ostrich farm. It's a drawback, definitely, but hardly the first and foremost. Terrifyingly, Lulu has had a serious talk with Mr Appleby and if she can put some business plans together he'll think about lending her some money. The fact that someone would even consider just giving Lulu money to start an ostrich farm is possibly the single most devastating single critique of late capitalism I've ever encountered. Thank God the job of putting together a proper business plan is almost certainly beyond Lulu. I don't think she's even considered yet how she's going to persuade the ostriches to transform themselves into food.

Rychard's up in Edinburgh this weekend for the job interview. He told Caroline that he'll be turning on all his charm. Lord help them. He's confident, anyway. 'I should walk it, unless I get one of those feminists on the panel,' he told Caroline. She asked what he meant by that, and pointed out that she considers herself a feminist. He didn't look fazed at all. 'You know what I mean, one of those *real* feminists.' Apparently he thought that was a compliment. I'm rather torn now between wanting him to get the job and wanting the interview to be a humiliating disaster. On the one hand it would be nice to think there's more to success in this world than boundless and misplaced self-confidence, a giant watch and a selection of cool shoes. But on the other hand anything that gets Rychard out of my life can only be a good thing. It's just a shame Edinburgh's not further away. Do they not have a branch in the Faroe Islands?

I explained to Caroline it looks like Tuscany isn't going to happen, and why. She said she's proud of me for doing the right thing. It was easy, actually. I just thought to myself: 'What would Tony Blair do?' Not really. As I do in most situations I thought 'What would Frank do?' and did the exact opposite. Caroline's already asked for time off at the start of April, so I said to leave it in my hands and I'd sort something out. 'Are you sure?' Yes, Caroline, I really don't think booking a holiday is beyond me.

Monday, 27th January. The revolution failed to arrive this morning, yet again. After school I went over to Miranda's to lend her a hand with her curtains.

Tuesday, 28th January. Caroline was hugely unimpressed when I told her how I spent yesterday evening. What, she wondered, would Miranda ask me to do next? 'Check her guttering?' 'Fiddle with her fuse box?' 'Move her bed around a bit?' Do I detect the hand of the green-eyed monster?

Caroline also mentioned that she finds my attitude towards Lulu patronising. What's so amusing about her sister? Well, for one thing, Lulu thinks appropriate dress for a Sunday walk in the country includes high heels and a mini skirt. For another, she never fails to draw your attention to animals in a state of arousal and to comment on the phenomenon in some detail. Dogs, horses, bulls, anything. She is a connoisseur of the bestial erection. If it bothers her, perhaps she should try refraining from kissing dogs, sleepwalking nude and climbing over stiles in a mini skirt. And perhaps the clincher: She's afraid of the colour blue, because it's such an 'angry colour'. Only certain shades of blue, Caroline said defensively.

Wednesday, 29th January. I went through Marcus Lau's latest essay today. I think our defeat at the Interschools Running Competition hit him pretty hard, because he's submitted a 3,000 word piece about how sometimes defeat can be as positive an experience as victory, and relating this to how hard he has worked to make friends at Buxdon and contribute to the school. The essay is at best, however, an oblique approach to the question: 'Discuss the theme of friendship in *The Royal Hunt of the Sun.*' Still, I guess failing the Third Year can be as positive an experience as passing it.

Thursday, 30th January. Went into town today to try to find Caroline's brother Toby a birthday present. I soon realised this was an almost impossible task. I'd give him book tokens, but it might look like I'm taking the mickey. He never finished *Bravo Two Zero.* In the end I settled on a Buxdon mug and a copy of my sample chapters.

I have, in contrast, come up with a brilliant plan regarding Marcus Lau. I've decided to change the questions to fit his answers as closely as possible. As of now his set texts are *The Loneliness of the Long-Distance Runner, Nicholas Nickleby* and *Decline and Fall.* I've given him high marks for his initial essay on Nelly Dean, which is now a response to the question: 'Imagine you are a pupil at Dotheboys Hall, writing a letter home to your parents.' I had to change some of the names, of course.

Friday, 31st January. Went over to Miranda's yesterday after work to help her lay some carpet. Caroline isn't thrilled I'm going to Miranda's house-warming tomorrow night. She's also insisting I get her yoga ball back. I said I'd see what I could do, and she told me she'll be very disappointed if I fail. 'Go, my pretty, bring me the yoga ball of Miranda Bell.' The word 'fail' suggests to me this may be some kind of test.

I haven't got around to looking into holidays yet. There's plenty of time. I was going to investigate possible options on-line on the library computers, but instead got involved in an electronic exchange with Frank, which I think justifies being printed off and preserved in full for posterity.

From:	**frankbletch69@hotmail.com**
Date:	**Friday, 31 January 11:45**
To:	**mbletch@buxdon.org.uk**
Subject:	**RE: ????!!!!????**

Hi Matt,

Hope your New Year is going well so far. Nice weather we're having, I had a great time at the party, give my love to Caroline, did Sig say anything complimentary about me?

Enough of this small talk.

About half an hour ago I was going through your cupboards, looking for anything I could eat or sell, and I came across something that rather surprised me. I imagine you can probably guess what it was. I'm just wondering why I found what can only be described as a latex pixie costume hanging in your wardrobe. With matching pointy hat and winged rubber boots. I've been wracking my brains, but I can't come up with any explanation that doesn't make me want to laugh, weep or both at once. Is there something you haven't been telling Mum? Do you have a hidden identity as a costumed crime fighter? By night does Matthew Bletch, mild-mannered English teacher, become Rubber Hood, the waterproof avenger? Do you have a sidekick called Gimp-Boy?

Your loving, but bemused, brother,

Frank

P.S. Why is it pink? Luminous pink.

From:	mbletch@buxdon.org.uk
Date:	Friday, 31 January 17:15
To:	frankbletch69@hotmail.com
Subject:	RE: RE: ????!!!!????

Frank, I've told you to stay out of my stuff ... I don't suppose you'd believe I've been moonlighting in Santa's workshop. The other elves were picking on me so I decided to make my own way in the world ... Probably not.

Let me assure you that there's a perfectly logical explanation and that it's really not something I want to go into with you. And can it with the false expressions of concern.

To put the matter very briefly: When I was in Tokyo I was getting short of cash and an opportunity presented itself to make a bit extra. It's not something I'm proud of or want people to know about, but I did it and I'm not ashamed.

Satisfied? Can we leave it there? I'm pretty sure it's not what you're thinking.

By the way, if you're looking for a job, as you have repeatedly assured Mum, the best place to find one is not at the back of my wardrobe. Narnia isn't really back there, either. Sorry to disillusion you.

If, on the other hand, you've been trying to root out my old grumble mags, you're out of luck. I threw them away years ago. Try behind Dom's radiator.

Matt

From: frankbletch69@hotmail.com
Date: Friday, 31 January 15:35
To: mbletch@buxdon.org.uk
Subject: RE: RE: RE: ????!!!!????

Hell no, I'm not satisfied. Tell me, Matt, or I start breaking your records. And lay off with the snidey 'get a job, get somewhere to live' stuff. I'm a free spirit, Matt. You can't just put me on little tracks and expect me to run back and forth like a tank engine, just to please you. Besides, Mum likes having me around to help out around the house.

Frank

P.S. Don't patronise me, Milksop. I'm a lout, not a moron. We have separate unions.

From: mbletch@buxdon.org.uk
Date: Friday, 31 January 15:55
To: frankbletch69@hotmail.com
Subject: RE: RE: RE: RE: ????!!!!????

Dear Frank,

While I'm sure Mum is happy to have you around for a while, I hardly think reminding her to turn your jeans inside-out before she washes them and giving her a Hoover for Christmas constitutes 'helping out around the house'. Neither do I think that suggesting you find paid employment makes me some kind of fat controller.

OK, the story is this. And promise me it goes no further …

At the beginning of my second year in Japan, when I was living in Tokyo, I had a pupil whose Dad worked for a TV company. I was living off rice cakes and little cans of coffee and sharing a flat the size of a cupboard with three Australians at the time. And the opportunity arose for me to make a few yen by appearing on TV. There's this programme on NHK late at night called *Let's Talk in English*. And they sometimes have native speakers on who give advice about pronunciation and idiomatic usage. So I thought it would look good on my CV and possibly be interesting at the same time. Do my bit for cross-cultural understanding.

Is that enough information for you?

Matt

From:	frankbletch69@hotmail.com
Date:	Friday, 31 January 18:01
To:	mbletch@buxdon.org.uk
Subject:	RE: RE: RE: RE: RE: ????!!!!????

Thanks, but that doesn't really answer my original question, which is why you have the merriest man in Sherwood's clubbing outfit in your closet ...

From:	mbletch@buxdon.org.uk
Date:	Friday, 31 January 18:12
To:	frankbletch69@hotmail.com
Subject:	RE: RE: RE: RE: RE: RE: ????!!!!????

What I hadn't gathered was that the producers didn't want me for my language skills and cultural insights. They wanted me to dress up in a silly costume and sing songs about the alphabet. Some capering was also contractually obliged. By the time I realised this, of course, I'd already put stamp to paper. The programme had these kind of dramatic interludes, during which I would occasionally appear in a puff of smoke to dispense language advice. I also had a wand that could roll back time. The character was called 'Mister Goblin'. I even had a snappy catchphrase: 'Ya-ya-koshi-ya', which I'm reliably assured means 'It's so confusing!!!!' I'd usually say it at the end of a scene, while the camera zoomed in and out on my grimacing face. Needless to say, the episode isn't going to be in my book, I haven't got it on my CV, and I don't think Mum needs to know about it either.

As for the wand, I lost it one sake-sodden night in Roppongi. I think it was stolen by someone who claimed to be a yakuza boss but who I suspect was in fact a steamed-bun delivery driver. He called himself Steve, on the tenuous basis he looked like Steve McQueen. Needless to add, he didn't. If anything, he looked more like Miriam Margoyles. It's a very long story, also not in the book. I have no idea why the costume needed to be pink.

Believe me, the money was good. Foolishly I frittered most of it on gimmicky plastic crapola and hypnotic arcade machines, but I did at least earn my airfare home. I acquired something of a cult following actually. There was some talk of making a plastic figure of me. I even once got chased across a Temple precinct in Northern Tokyo by a gang of schoolgirls, although it's possible they'd mistaken me for Jude Law.

Frank, on a serious note, I think we need to sit down and have a proper talk at some point. If you have to call me by a nickname at parties, I'd prefer it if the nickname wasn't 'Milksop'. Why not call me 'El Tigre', like Dad used to?

From:	frankbletch69@hotmail.com
Date:	Friday, 31 January 18:15
To:	mbletch@buxdon.org.uk
Subject:	RE: RE: RE: RE: RE: RE: RE: ????!!!!????

Dear Matt,

I have no memory of Dad ever calling anyone 'El Tigre', least of all you. I've checked with Mum and she seemed to have some vague recollection of Dad maybe saying it once, ironically. But for the record, Mum then added: 'But didn't Dad just call him "Milksop" like everyone else?'

Best regards,

Frank

February

Sunday, 2nd February. Miranda's so nice. It's a double shame therefore that her friends are such a collection of ass-hats. What a shower of hambones. What a feast of fools. What a fiesta of fuckwits.

I'd expected more people from uni to be there, but it was almost all people Miranda knew from school. They were all men too, which added to the generally unsettling atmosphere. They didn't really mingle with the Buxdon lot, who spent the evening squeezed into the kitchen. Occasionally someone would go out and attempt to be sociable, only to return scowling about two minutes later. Essentially it was just a room of rugby types glowering at each other while Miranda flitted around and tried to get them to interact. What a magnificent array of chins. The kind of chins that built the British Empire.

The one person at the party from uni was Guy, who was lurking around in the corridor outside the kitchen like a hungry ghost all night. He didn't seem to remember me from Halls, despite the aforementioned incident when he appeared on my windowsill with a Stanley knife clenched in his teeth. He's working in the City now, but he's not really enjoying it. I expect that's why they pay him an obscene amount of money. I told him I'm a teacher and he said something like: 'You won't believe it, mate, but sometimes I actually envy people like you. I sometimes wish I'd gone into something like that. The problem is it gets so much harder to change once you're used to making real money.'

After that I briefly found myself stuck with some clown

called Roland Rawlinson. We were standing by the drinks table with beers in our hands and he introduced himself with the words: 'Drinking, eh? It's great, isn't it.' Well it makes people like Roland Rawlinson a lot more tolerable, any road. He's not actually a clown – he's an investment broker. Although he could have been a professional competitive cyclist if he'd wanted. 'You cudda been a contender?' I ad-libbed. His thighs were as thick as my torso. He shook his head sternly. 'I could have been a winner.' Sadly though, Roland, you're not.

Miranda made me dance with her for a bit, to the sounds of Ricky Martin. I was uncomfortably aware of everyone else in the living room staring at me with unconcealed malice. Tom Downing tried to cut in, despite the fact he dances like someone at a Party Conference. He has two moves. The first is like a man on a running machine on lowest setting, trying to hail a series of buses. The second is like someone repeatedly coming to brink of throwing themselves down their stairs and then bottling it. He was trying to hit on Miranda all evening, which was excruciating even to witness. It was like watching a slug repeatedly throwing itself on salt. Downing found a couple of Yakults in the fridge and asked Miranda what they were. 'Oh, you've found my beauty batteries,' she sort-of explained. 'You don't need any of those,' he said. He managed to say it without puking, although I almost did. What a cheesemonger.

Lucy seemed a little cross not to be getting her usual share of attention, although she and Miranda have decided that they're new best buddies. They kept sneaking off together. 'What do you think they're up to?' Barry Taylor kept asking me. 'Probably talking about you, mate.' 'Really?' No, not really. Despite the fact that they spent almost the whole night in the same five foot by five foot space, I think Lucy successfully avoided talking to Barry at all. That's a trick I wish she'd teach me.

*

I think Miranda's thoroughly sweet. I'm sure Caroline would agree if she'd only give her a chance. It must be hard for Miranda to make female friends, being so attractive. I expect it brings out a lot of envy and malice. She almost admitted as much, actually. The irony is that if you give her a chance you find out that's she's incredibly kind and intelligent, as well. She was very complimentary about Caroline. I think they'll probably get to be really good friends in time. That would be nice. Miranda and I have agreed to play squash at some point soon. Caroline will be pleased to hear that I'm getting a hobby at last – or at least another hobby. Caroline still insists that reading books and reading newspapers don't count as two separate activities.

I find it almost impossible to imagine what it must be like to be Miranda. What does the world look like, when you're seeing it over heart-stopping cheekbones? She must think it's full of people falling off ladders and accidentally stepping into manholes, and just generally being pleasant to you for no apparent reason. I expect it's easy to be a nice person if people are continually letting you off your bus fare and giving you an extra bun and asking if you're a model. Talking to Miranda makes me feel like something pale, hunched and malicious that lives under a mountain in German folklore. I also feel thoroughly wretched for having stolen her yoga ball.

Monday, 3rd February. The headmaster has reminded me that I'm supposed to be giving this talk about Japan to the scholars and their parents next week.

'Perhaps you can tell us all how you got the nickname "Mister Goblin",' he added.

Perhaps I should ask Mum to send me the costume. Perhaps I should have a long talk with Barry Taylor.

Tuesday, 4th February. Miranda and I are booked to play squash tomorrow She was asking around the staffroom today to see if anyone had seen what happened to her yoga ball at the party. I'll probably let her win a few games out of guilt.

Wednesday, 5th February. Someone needs to take Tom Downing aside for a quiet word and tell him exactly how many people you need to play a game of squash. When I got there he was showing Miranda how to warm up, a procedure that according to Tom Downing involves bending down a lot. No one needs to see a man in lycra leaning over that far.

Not only that, but for the next half an hour he sat at the back, giving Miranda advice and me grief. 'Why does he call you Mister Goblin?' she asked. Because he's a dick, that's why. Then, to my utter horror, Downing got on court and started showing Miranda how she should be holding her racket. I couldn't believe it. Talk about every cheap, tawdry move in the book. Miranda gave me a look like 'I suppose we have to humour this joker,' and played a few rounds with him while I sat at the back of the court. Her problem is that she's too nice. I was glad to see she thrashed him.

Thursday, 6th February. Dom rang tonight to tell me he has a book coming out with the Parnassus Press. Get off my schtick, Dominic. It's his long-awaited study of aberrant masculinities. A scholarly monograph, rather than a memoir of life growing up with Frank. There's going to be a book launch party at his department in June. The department's laying on the booze, and he advises us not to get our expectations up.

Actually, I'm glad for Dom. Glad and bubbling with jealousy. Anyhow, it's nice to see the Flaubert of the funding-application form branching out into other genres.

In contrast, I failed to make much headway on the Japan talk. Decided to have an early night and get up to start work on the talk before school tomorrow.

Friday, 7th February. I should have known that plan was never going to work. My alarm went off at five thirty and I spent the next hour lying in bed with the words 'He leaped out of bed and into a flurry of activity' going around and around in my head. I've looked back through my manuscript for suitable bits to read out, without much success. I don't suppose I'll get much done at the Applebys' over the weekend, either.

Bagley came up and asked if he could talk to me about something after my tutor group meeting. I congratulated him on his Oxbridge success and asked whether there was some aspect of student life he was anxious about. There isn't, because he's decided he isn't going to go to university. He'd always been really into horses and he's got an apprenticeship lined up as a stable hand. I told him that's great and he can defer college for a year. 'You sound just like my dad. I'm not going to defer anything, because I'm not going to university. I don't want to be around students, I want to be around horses.' He must feel strongly about it, because for Bagley that was quite a flight of oratory. I think that's the longest continuous speech act he's attempted since I've met him. Fair enough, he's got a passion and he's taking practical steps to follow it. Possibly he's not the one who should be asking me for careers advice. I said it sounded like he had things all planned out. University isn't for everyone. Although I wouldn't want to be there when Bagley tells Iles he's turning Oxford down. I told him sometimes you have to follow your heart.

On which note, I'm off to see Caroline.

Sunday, 9th February. Lunch with the Applebys yesterday was little chickens personally spatchcocked by Lulu. I suppose they could have been quail or poussin or something. I say spatchcocked, but usually that involves putting the spatchcocks through the chicken diagonally. These were, more accurately, crucified chickens, which I personally found a little unsettling. Lulu seemed to be having such fun doing it that I didn't want to say anything. Toby appeared pleased to get a copy of my sample chapters for his birthday, although I have to admit he'd be no one's first choice of *Late Review* panellist. 'Is it going to be this big when it's published?' No, you chucklehead, I very much doubt it's going to be on A4. He seemed relieved. 'Because books are usually much smaller than this.' I then had to reassure him the published version won't be 'harder to read', because they'll probably change the pagination and typefaces, rather than just photocopying it half-size and dropping it off at Waterstone's. I probably should have added that the final version is likely to be professionally bound as well. Lulu seemed worried about something, perhaps the possibility that they'll give it a blue cover. Although it may just have been the fact she had three little crucified chickens on her plate.

When bedtime finally arrived I folded back the covers to find an enormous spider squatting in the middle of the mattress. It looked very comfortable. I gave it several seconds to run away. It eyed me beadily and waited for me to do the same. It was like something out of *National Geographic*. I'd never previously considered that there might be a sensible reason why the Applebys have Napoleonic-era sabers hanging in every bedroom. That bastard would have chewed up a *Radio Times* and spat it out again.

We all went to church this morning. There was an awkward moment on the way out. Mrs Appleby has obviously never had explained to her the difference between a 'twit' and a 'twat', and as she was shaking hands with the vicar she said something along the lines of: 'I heard about the mix-up at the PCC, you silly twat.' The vicar looked like he thought that was a bit strong. Although he was probably just sending up a quick one and steeling himself for one of Henry Appleby's bone-crushing handshakes. I wouldn't want to be the one who explains the twit/twat difference to Margery. The woman terrifies me. She wouldn't have put a spider in my bed, would she? A two-flush spider, at that. It reappeared around the

U-bend the first time looking like I'd just managed to really piss it off. I had the plunger poised, spear-fisherman-fashion, in case it tried anything.

Caroline wants me to get to the bottom of my fear of spiders. She was asking if I think it's something symbolic to do with anxieties in my childhood. I think it is to do with childhood fears, but there's nothing symbolic about it. It's more to do with every time we went to a pet shop Frank dragging me sobbing towards the spider cases and threatening to feed me to a tarantula. I'd be sobbing, not Frank. He'd be chuckling.

Mum told the story again at Christmas of how Frank used to try to push me away from the breast and would stomp and storm around whenever she was giving me any attention. Ha ha, the lighter side of the fratricidal impulse. I've long since given up anyone expecting anyone to notice that he still does the exact same thing to this day. Symbolically, of course.

Caroline is now not one hundred per cent sure that it is her yoga ball after all. Nor can she satisfactorily explain what you're meant to do with a yoga ball in the first place. I wish she could have mentioned that before I surreptitiously bounced it out of a first-floor toilet window and carried it all the way to London on the train.

Monday, 10th February. One more week to get through before half-term.

Tom Downing cornered me in the corridor today. I wondered for a minute if he was going to demand my lunch money. 'Listen, Bletch, you've got your own toy soldiers to fiddle with. Don't try to stop me playing with mine.' Don't get gnomic with me, Downing. 'I could make life around here very unpleasant for you if I chose to.' Trust me, mate, you already do.

I should have said that at the time, rather than saying 'I

hope you're enjoying your pants' not quite loud enough for him to hear.

After a frustrating hour in Woolworths, I finally managed to find a suitable Valentine's Day card to send Caroline. It was surprisingly difficult to find a card that hit a suitable compromise between puky sentimentality and the kind of language that under most circumstances would be considered a threat of sexual assault.

Peter Wyndham was disdainfully browsing the racks at the same time. He commented that in France they take sex and sensuality seriously, whereas British people find it funny and embarrassing. I did feel a bit of cultural cringe, until I remembered you can say the same thing about Johnny Hallyday.

Tuesday, 11th February. I'm having major doubts about the card I sent Caroline for Friday. Spoke to her tonight and she wants to know what I have planned for the weekend. Spent the evening desperately flicking through *Time Out* and trying to find something romantic yet inexpensive.

I went over to see Barry Taylor after school and found Lucy Salmon in his room, in tears. Charlie has cancelled the romantic weekend in Weybridge they've been planning for weeks. Barry was being as consoling as he could: 'Really, Weybridge isn't all that. Once you've been to the Brooklands Museum and had a cream tea, there's really not that much to do.' Somehow I don't feel that was what Lucy was really upset about. I made my excuses and said I had to get on with writing my talk for Thursday.

I have a first paragraph for the talk now. I've timed myself, and it takes about a minute to deliver. It asks the age-old question: 'What is Japan?' before suggesting that: 'One answer is that it is a country made up of around 6,800 islands, the five largest being Honshu, Hokkaido, Kyushu, Shikoku and Okinawa. Another

155

is that it is a land of some 127 million people, a unique people among the most ethnically homogenous in the world. A third answer is that Japan is one of the world's most prosperous economies, a centre for global banking and technology with one of the highest standards of living in the world. In this talk I want to examine another way of looking at this unique culture, this mixture of East and West, of dazzling modernity and ancient tradition. For me, Japan is primarily a state of mind.' Bloody hell, I've accidentally written a merciless satire on myself. And I had to look up the name of the fifth island. It would be nice before the talk to come up with an opening that doesn't make me want to punch myself repeatedly in the side of the head.

Wednesday, 12th February. Miranda mentioned today that she's worried she won't get any Valentine's Cards. I've been wondering, should I ...? No, that would be a really bad idea. But no one would know ... I'd know. I'd have to live with myself. I've read *Far From the Madding Crowd* – nothing good ever comes from that sort of thing. And my luck I'd probably do something stupid like sending it to Caroline, or signing my name on it, or just telling Caroline with a big goofy grin on my face.

Anyway I saw Tom Downing coming back from town earlier with something large and rectangular under one arm, so I imagine Miranda will be getting at least one card.

I spoke to Frank on the phone. He's not only sent Sig a Valentine's card, but he made it himself. How romantic. How cheap. I expect it will just be a piece of A4 paper folded in half with 'Dear Sig, I am your Valentine. HA HA HA' written on it. I don't expect she'll have much difficulty guessing who it's from.

Getting ready for the final push on my talk for tomorrow. I'll bear Mum's public speaking advice in mind: 'If you're nervous, try to imagine everyone sitting there naked.' I suspect, however, that she never saw the Buxdon scholars and their parents. They're a pretty scary-looking bunch when they're wearing their clothes.

Thursday, 13th February. Finally finished preparing my talk at two this morning. It seemed to go down OK. No one heckled, anyway. For the first ten minutes I was saying what I had thought Japan would be like, then for the next ten minutes I pointed out some ways in which my expectations were off mark. The rest of the time I filled up with reflections on funny bits of English I saw and heard, a bit of history I cribbed from the back of *Let's Go,* and a few anecdotes to show I don't take myself that seriously. I threw in a few interesting facts, such as that Japan has one vending machine for every twenty people, and that the average Japanese businessman bows five thousand times a year. I did puncture one common misconception about the country during the question session by saying that I had never seen a single vending machine selling schoolgirls' knickers. Mr Hallbrick looked very disappointed. I added that I hadn't been looking particularly hard. I decided not to tell the Mister Goblin story, for reasons that are presumably obvious.

One thing I regret is my answer to the question: 'What did you like most about Japan?' I should have mentioned the kindness of my colleagues and the people I met, or the food, or the temples, or the cities' general cleanliness, politeness and order. Indeed almost any aspect of Japan's fascinating society, history and culture I could have mentioned would have been better than: 'They let you smoke in McDonald's.' Fortunately people thought I was joking.

There was Buxdon wine afterwards. The headmaster got a bit tipsy and started doing songs from *The Mikado.* Mr Bagley took me to one side: 'What the hell have you been telling my son?' He's considering suing. The headmaster isn't too pleased with me either. I explained to him later that I'd been under the impression Buxdon tried to encourage each boy to develop personally as well as academically and to discover their interests for themselves, rather than just an impersonal boy-polishing machine designed to get its pupils into good universities. Perse slapped me on the back with mock ami-ability. 'Good one, Bletch,' he guffawed. 'How did you come up with that?' It was in the prospectus. Both Bagley and the Head asked me to have another word with Bagley junior and this time strongly advise him not to follow his heart.

I've booked a romantic Valentine's surprise for Caroline and me tomorrow. It's half-term so we'll finally have the chance to spend some real quality time together. Valentine's Day? Hell, Matthew Bletch takes a Valentine's Week. I'd better eat up all my greens tomorrow.

Friday, 14th February. On a romantic note, one of my tutees consulted me about a personal problem in the tutorial meet-ing today. It was a bit uncomfortable, actually. Monk told me he really fancies a girl, has sent her a card, and was asking what he should do about it next. The others had various suggestions, none of them particularly constructive. I said he should find out how she feels and if she likes him, muster up the courage to ask her out. Perhaps he could invite her to the cinema, or the June Ball. 'Wow, that's really helpful, Sir,' he said. Then he asked what line I would use to ask out someone I fancied. I said it's usually better just to say the first thing that comes into your head. Wouldn't it be a lovely world if that were true.

I didn't mention that in Caroline's case I saw her in a coffee shop, recognised her from uni, and noticed she was reading *The Alchemist* by Paulo Coelho. Fortunately there was a free seat next to her, so I moved in. I thought she might recognise me, but she didn't seem to. After panicking for a while about whether she was ignoring me or was just engrossed in read-ing, I leaned over and said: 'I've read that. Rubbish, isn't it.' Probably with a little more thought I could have come up with something better than that. It took me three lattes to build up the nerve to talk to her, so I was a tad jittery. Turned out she'd thought I was a bit of a freak at college, and she actually had been ignoring me. But it all worked out in the end, and it's a mildly amusing story now. Although deep down I suspect she still thinks I'm a bit of a freak. I was so right about *The Alchemist*, though.

Miranda needn't have worried. She got fifty-three cards. She was asking whether Caroline doesn't like her, and I hedged a bit. I think it's safe to say that she wasn't among the throng who sent her a Valentine's card. Miranda seems to get along well with Lucy Salmon, though. Miranda's been giving her advice about what to do about Charlie, and described her to me earlier as her 'new best friend'. No word on what Miranda thinks about Tom Downing. He's been giving me evil looks all week.

Lucy was down to twenty-seven cards this year. Which is still twenty-seven more than I got. I rang Caroline before school to tell her I love her and complain, and she said she'd be giving me my card when I come down. But then I'll know it's from her. 'Well, who do you want to pretend it's from?'

I wish I'd signed mine now. I asked Caroline how many cards she got, and she said only one, of course. So I pretended as if it wasn't from me and got faux jealous and demanded that she describe it. She said it was about a foot tall and had a pair of teddies cuddling on the front. She claims to really like it. The postman had to ring the doorbell to give it to her, and told Caroline someone must really think she's great. He's right. There's only one problem. That's not my card.

Saturday, 15th February. What kind of freak would send a

Valentine's card like this? And to my girlfriend, at that. Caroline's put it on top of the telly, from whence it's been mocking me all morning. There's no message inside, just a bear holding a balloon with 'Bear my Valentine' on it. What does that even mean? More importantly, who saw that and thought it was precisely the romantic message they wanted conveyed to my girlfriend? I'm screwed if Caroline ever asks me why I chose it. The one thing I do know for certain is that whoever chose and sent this card was an utter fool. What troubles me acutely is that Caroline thinks I am that fool. Rychard. It was definitely Bloody Rychard.

There's no sign of my actual card.

To add insult to injury, my Valentine's surprise was a total damp squib. I'd booked us two tickets to see a special showing of *Breakfast at Tiffany's* at the NFT, assuming it would put us both in a romantic mood and we could have dinner afterwards. I thought Caroline would be pleased, because she used to have the poster on her wall at college. Boy, was I wrong. Turns out she's never actually seen *Breakfast at Tiffany's*. Unlike the poster, the film has Mickey Rooney playing a comical Japanese person, turning in a performance that would look unnuanced in a piece of wartime propaganda. About the point George Peppard out of *The A-Team* turns up onscreen I felt Caroline's hand moving along my thigh in the gloom. She was reaching for the programme. Her lips brushed my ear. 'How long is this film?' she whispered. 115 minutes, apparently. It seemed much longer than that. After almost an hour and a half of wriggling, sighing and shuffling her feet, Caroline put her head on my shoulder and had a forty-minute nap. She woke up a little before the end and groaned when she realised where she was. 'What are they doing?' 'They've spent the last ten minutes looking for a cat. A cat called "Cat".' 'Do you know what I wish? I wish this film was longer and more whimsical.'

When we got out, the restaurant I'd planned on us going to

was closed and we wandered around for a bit before finally getting some food in an All Bar One. I think we could have had more fun actually looking for a cat in the rain.

My misery is complete.

Sunday, 16th February. Did I think my misery was complete? I was wrong. My misery was previously only partly complete. Now my misery is complete. It's just like *King Lear*.

This morning I was waiting, as usual, for the shower and Frank came out. Nude but for a facecloth, which wasn't on his face. No one should have to see that before breakfast. This week has really made me rethink the pros and cons of having eyes. I asked Frank what he would have done if it had been Caroline waiting and he just tossed his shoulders. When I brought Caroline her breakfast she said I was looking a bit shell-shocked.

To top that off I was having a cup of tea later on and Sig came out of the lounge with a tetrapak in one hand and a soggy hunk of bread in the other. 'Milk? Sop?' she asked. Hilarious. What rib-cracking antic will she and Frank come up with next? Throwing a big rubber spider at me?

Caroline says she understands it must be unsettling for me, having my brother around. It's not having my brother around that unsettles me, so much as that brother being Frank, and Frank being almost entirely naked. On the plus side Frank and Sig spend most of their time in her room, with the door closed. On the negative side, I can still hear them. Even in bed with Caroline and with *I'm Sorry, I Haven't a Clue* at top volume. I never thought I'd actually start to miss Anton. The noises emerging from Sig's room a few minutes ago sounded something like a rubber dinghy being attacked by a bear.

Oddly enough, that's not the worst thing about this. The worst thing is that Frank is, by and large, acting like a human being. I actually saw him ingest a vegetable at lunchtime, with every appearance of pleasure. Mum'll be glad that someone's finally found a way to get Frank to finish all his vegetables. I shudder to think what it is, though. He was making small talk with Caroline and Sig, and didn't have his elbows on the table or chew with his mouth hanging open, and not once did he wipe his hands on the tablecloth or break wind. Which means that he can impersonate a human being when he wants to, but for all these years he just couldn't be bothered. He did the dishes. He not only did the dishes, he offered to do the dishes. With warm water and washing-up liquid and a dish cloth. My mind reels at the perfidy of it.

I even heard him telling Sig that he'd really like to try tofu. He won't be able to keep it up. He'll crack. He'll wig out in *Planet Organic* and start screaming for a pork pie. They'll be forced to intravenously inject him with a Peperami. It's a bit of an animal. The anus and lips and whatever they can power-hose off the spine, mostly.

I don't know which, if any, of Sig's criteria Frank supposedly meets. I asked Caroline and she replied that he 'is really sexy'. Aaargh. Exactly what I wanted to hear on a full stomach. Sexy? I've seen him blow his nose on a sock. And then put that same sock on and wear it for the rest of the day.

Monday, 17th February. Frank's still at the flat, as am I. Neither of us is particularly thrilled about this. Between Frank and Sig you can never get in the bathroom. Sig was meant to go to the library this morning and Frank was supposed to go home, but in the end they went ice skating instead.

I found the card that I sent Caroline under her bed. I'm not really surprised that Caroline preferred the other one. Mine isn't even a proper Valentine's Day card, with innuendoes and slush. It's a still life of some limp-looking flowers and has 'From a mystery admirer' written in it. It's the kind of Valentine's Card your gran sends you when you're eleven. Frank's card for Sig was a big red piece of paper with 'I want to bite your bum' written on it in Magic Marker. A little crude, perhaps, but it seems to have got the message across.

Shouty Morgan rang in the early evening to see if Caroline wanted to go to the opera tonight. With him, he clarified. Morgan bought two tickets because he had a date lined up, but she was forced to cancel due to having been sectioned. It's remarkable what some girls will do to get out of a date with him. Caroline suggested he take Lulu instead, who's up in town housesitting for Caroline's aunt. I wonder how far they'll be into the first act before she discovers she'd lost her handbag or remembers she's left a bath running?

Tuesday, 18th February. Frank's still here. I'm glad he's so comfortable in his skin, but it would be nice if Frank put all his clothes on occasionally. When I came back from picking up some supplies for dinner he was sitting in the sofa in boxers which were gaping wildly and distractingly in all directions, and talking on the phone. After about half an hour of chatting and laughing with whoever was at the other end of the line, he told me it was Mum and she wanted to say hello. Then he sat there all through our conversation, watching *Newsround*.

Caroline got home from work and asked what I've been up to. I told her: an hour of writing, some shopping, spoke to Mum. Looking back, I'm surprised that took all day too. Did I look in the *Times Educational Supplement* to see if they had any teaching jobs in London? No. Did I get in touch with any of my friends in town? No, they'll all be working and I don't really like them. Did I go to the travel agents and look into holidays for us? No. Did I put the Hoover round in her room? God, I've got to leave some things to do tomorrow.

I did, however, come up with the perfect plan to pay Rychard back for his Valentine's sneakiness. I've put a little surprise for him in the post … Bear this Valentine, jackass. Revenge with a first-class stamp.

*

Wednesday, 19th February. Will Frank ever go? Doesn't he have shelves to put up or jeans to wash? Caroline had a quiet word with Sig about it. 'Do you mind? Is he in the way?' No, not exactly, Caroline told her. It's just that when Frank is here, he's very much here. You can hear him all hours, bumping into the door frames and belching when no one else is in the room. He's also left big soggy footprints on the hall carpet. It was either Frank or Bigfoot.

I wrote in the morning then spent the afternoon wandering around Central London trying to find a replacement starting pistol. I finally found one in a rather sinister Army and Navy shop on the fringes of Soho. They had one left, on a dusty shelf between a stack of bongs and a glass case full of World War Two medallions. Well, I had already tried Argos and got some very strange reactions. I asked the guy behind the Army and Navy shop counter whether it was actually legal to sell medals. He replied it was simply a display case, then asked if I was interested in Nazi daggers at all. No, not particularly. I think I would have been more perturbed by that question if I hadn't been busy wondering what kind of Army and Navy shop sells poppers.

Thursday, 20th February. The Rychard plan worked a treat. He had an absolute fit, it seems. He spent the whole day phoning around old girlfriends and freaking out, before finally working out it was a brilliant prank. Caroline asked me what kind of sick madman would even think of something like that. Sick madman ... or perhaps genius. An out-of-season Father's Day card from an imaginary child. I spent ages writing it, left-handed. Don't mess with the Bletch, Rychard, because the Bletch don't mess.

I took the starting pistol out of its box earlier and made sure it looks more or less like the one I lost. I think it will pass muster. Frank reckons I should file the serial number off.

Caroline and I went out with Lulu for dinner and heard about Lulu's date with Morgan. Apparently he didn't stop talking about Caroline all through the performance. The volume he speaks that must have been fun for the closest twenty rows or so. Lulu doesn't think they'll be going out again, which is a shame because in some ways they're perfectly suited. When they got to their seats they found that Lulu had forgotten her glasses and Morgan had left his briefcase on the tube.

There's nothing left in the fridge. Absolutely nothing. Not only has all my shopping from the other day been devoured, but even the sinister-looking marmalade that's been there since before I first started going out with Caroline has vanished. When we got back from dinner I found Frank thoughtfully sucking on a bit of ice he'd prized out of the freezer compartment.

Friday, 21st February. Frank and Sig are gone. At last I can have my bran flakes without consciously having to ignore whatever bits of Frank's anatomy have snuck out at any given moment. But I can't believe they're going to Amsterdam. They've only been together about a fortnight. The last time Caroline and I went away was that godawful trip to Prague. A beautiful, historic city, but not one known for the attractiveness of its industrial outer suburbs. It was kind of perversely impressive that I even managed to find us a hotel that far from the centre. It certainly wasn't in the *Rough Guide*.

I'd almost managed to block that hotel out of my mind. It looked like a disused TB sanatorium. You had to tell the old fellow at the front desk when you wanted to use the shower, and he'd shuffle along the corridor and put the light bulb in for you. Then he'd wait outside until you were finished. The most positive spin I could put on it was to call the whole experience 'Kafkaesque'.

*

With Frank and Sig away, I've warned Caroline to prepare for an erotic onslaught of previously unimaginable intensity. She's in the shower getting ready now. Come to think of it, she has been in the shower for a really long time. Perhaps she's going to come out in a negligée, drenched in perfume. Perhaps she's crawled out the window.

Saturday, 22nd February. The erotic onslaught was conducted with all the success of the British Expeditionary Force at Dunkirk. It encountered stronger than expected resistance and was forced to retreat in disarray. I was lucky not to have to escape in a commandeered rowing boat.

Things started badly, when Caroline returned to the boudoir in a Snoopy T-shirt, and asked, in a husky voice, whether I thought the chicken at dinner had been quite done. Not an erotic husky voice, an invalid's husky voice. It wasn't an erotic Snoopy T-shirt either. The suggestive mood lighting I'd carefully arranged caused Caroline to bark her shin on the bedside table then stub her toe on the wardrobe.

As Caroline got into bed she told me Rychard's really upset about the card. It's really shaken him up that someone could have such malice towards him. The whole prank was so sick. 'What kind of twisted freak could even come up with something like that, let alone think it was funny? How could anyone be so savagely lacking in empathy?' The really sad part was that when he opened the card apparently he looked really pleased for a moment.

I intuited from this line of discussion that Caroline was more or less out of the erotic mood. I put a dressing gown on and fetched a glass of water, then we cuddled for a bit.

'So this is the ravishing I was promised. No, it's too late now.'

Sunday, 23rd February. I told Caroline that Lucy Salmon and Miranda seem to be getting on well. She raised an eyebrow.

What? 'She'll soon see. She'll be best mates with Miranda for about a month, tops, before they have some kind of dramatic falling out. Then we'll all have to hear all about how hurt and baffled she is that Lucy doesn't like her any more and how it's probably because Lucy is so insecure. When it's closer to the truth that Lucy has just worked out how draining, tiresome, ultimately unrewarding and possibly threatening to your mental health a friendship with Miranda is. I guarantee it. End of March at the very latest.' Nor, allegedly, is Miranda even that beautiful. I didn't think it would be diplomatic to enquire how someone 'looks prettier than she actually is.'

I can't avoid the feeling that in some ways I've frittered this half-term away. At least I've finally finished the first draft of my book. There's still some room for elaboration and rewriting though. I don't imagine that in the finished draft the final chapter will simply read 'And then I went home.' Caroline said she can't wait to read it, although it has to be said she didn't manage to sound totally convincing.

And then I went home. Or at least back to Buxdon.

Monday, 24th February. Went out for a drink last night with Barry Taylor. Barry was drinking Soldier's Cloak. I tried a pint of Grandfather's Chest, which tastes like Minerva's Owl with a twist of hawthorn berries. He'd invited Lucy, but she ducked out. Afterwards we went back to his palatial rooms for a nightcap. I started flicking through Brimscombe's diaries, which Barry still has lying around. God they're depressing. The entry for 12 November, 1987 reads:

It rained this morning. I ate porridge for breakfast, and received a letter from the couple I met last year at Innsbruck. Unfortunately their lovely daughter has been run over. I have decided to have an early night.

In its entirety, the entry for the first Saturday of his first term at Buxdon reads: 'I telephoned Mother, but she was out.'

In assembly this morning the headmaster regretfully announced that a number of complaints have been made about threatening, offensive and obscene Valentine's cards being received by both staff and pupils. The issue is being investigated and if necessary the sending of Valentine's cards will be strongly discouraged next year.

Miranda enlisted my help to find somewhere around the school to dump the various oversized teddies, plush hearts and stuffed cherubs she was given the other week. She'd already tried the Old Building attic and got the brush-off from Mrs O. Digby. We asked around the staffroom but no one seems to know when or why it was sealed off. Eventually we took most of the stuff down to the dump.

Miranda mentioned that she's getting a team together for the pub quiz at The Albion on Thursday, and asked me who she thought would be good to have on our team. I suppose we could also ask Johnno McPhee and Barry Taylor, for the sports answers. For once even the presence of Tom Downing might not be utterly surplus to requirements.

Tuesday, 25th February. Hallbrick has been made a prefect. I'm not quite sure how they settled on Hallbrick as a figure to inspire respect and admiration in the younger boys. He now has the official power to make people pick up litter and to give them lines if he catches them smoking. Whether he has the gravitas to enforce this is another question entirely. He's very excited about it, mostly because he's discovered, after careful consultation of the school records in the library, an olden days' statute that has never been revoked allowing prefects to grow a beard and keep a goat on top field. I suggested he takes the matter up with the headmaster.

*

Wednesday, 26th February. Gearing up now for the pub quiz tomorrow night. I'm covering literature and popular music, Barry Taylor sport, Miranda history, and Downing I guess everything else. How can we fail? There's always a question about the FA Cup, and in the other sections one or more of the answers is always, without fail, either 'Kid Creole and the Coconuts', 'Reg Dwight' or 'Joining the Common Market'. We're going to own this quiz.

I swung by the armoury at lunchtime to 'return' the starting pistol. Dead-Eye Dick Darling gave me a peculiar look as he ticked the pistol off on his checklist. I think he was looking at me.

'You're sure this is the same pistol you borrowed?'

'Yes. Of course it is.'

'It's just that I wasn't aware the school had any replica Lugers. And starting pistols tend not to have a fifty-five degree grip angle and a toggle-lock action.'

Thursday, 27th February. Hallbrick has had a chat with the headmaster, and he won't be keeping a goat on top field in the near future. Neither will he be allowed small ale with breakfast, to bear a sword around Buxdon or to keep a carriage and four.

I let my final class of the afternoon entertain themselves (technical term: a supervised study period) and prepared for the pub quiz. 'What year saw the sinking of the *Belgrano*, the birth of Prince William, and Captain Sensible's number one UK hit with "Happy Talk"?' 1982. 'What's the capital of Brunei?' Bandar Seri Begawan. 'Name the original line-up of The Soup Dragons.' Sean Dickson, Ross A. Sinclair, Ian Whitehall and Sushil K. Dade. Ian Whitehall was later replaced by Jim McCulloch. I hope they ask that. Not only is that the most profoundly useless piece of knowledge I possess, I'm beginning to wonder whether it's taking up part of my brain that might much more practically be used to remember something else.

Friday, 28th February. We didn't win the pub quiz. 'The Buxdon Irregulars', which was us, came next to last. We beat 'The Questionnnaires', but only I think because they were just three regulars who'd come in not realising it was quiz night and weren't taking things particularly seriously. The winners were a team called 'Pentangle', by a considerable margin. I developed the theory as the evening wore on that 'Pentangle' don't actually know or like each other, but that each is an expert in a specific area, and they come together to slightly ruin the atmosphere at pub quizzes throughout the local area. There's an old lady, a guy in denim with long thinning hair, a little guy in big glasses, a middle-aged guy who is almost perfectly spherical, and someone who looks about twelve. They don't talk much. In fact, for each round they pass the answer sheet to one member of the team, and the others wander off to the bar or the quiz machine. They only really come together as a unit to shush anyone who talks or laughs during the questions.

Things have been a bit tense today. Barry Taylor is still angrily insisting ping pong and darts aren't proper sports. We probably shouldn't have followed my plan of putting 'Daddy Haystacks' as the answer to every question, on the basis that that's always the answer to at least one sports question in any pub quiz. This proves to be factually incorrect.

The History Round gave me a fascinating glimpse into how the final test for *Theories of Art and Society* might have turned out in some parallel universe: 'In what year were the Oslo Peace Accords signed? In the same year Whitney Houston had a number one hit with "I Will Always Love You", and the television series *Cheers* ended.' Barry knew that one, but blotted his copy book by adding: 'But who were the Norwegians at war with?'

It's not like Tom Downing covered himself in glory either. I'm not going to say anything more about it, except to point out I said at the time I was sure he was wrong, and got out-voted. Apart from anything else, the question asked which two public roles Archbishop Makarios was best known for. Two roles. Winning the Eurovision Song Contest isn't even one role. But even had the question been: 'Which single achievement is Archbishop Makarios best known for?' it wouldn't have made a whit of difference. Downing's answer still would have been wrong, and no amount of asking to see the answer sheet would have made any difference. One of the answers to the actual question is right there in his title, for God's sake. Just writing 'Archbishop' would have got us one point, rather than the *nul points* we were actually awarded. Downing thought 'And Dr Alban isn't really a doctor' was such a smart comment at the time. No, but he is a qualified dentist.

Tom Downing got a text message this morning which con-sisted solely of the message '1991'. There goes his boastful claim that mobile phones will revolutionise the pub quiz as we know it.

I know one thing for sure. Even if I ever dare show my face in The Albion in future, I'm never again going to attempt drinking four pints of Soldier's Cloak in one sitting. It's not so much like getting drunk as getting flu really suddenly. I feel utterly pestilent.

So I got my Brontë sisters mixed up. It was a sneaky ques-tion. I don't think that's even on the same scale as confusing the President of the Republic of Cyprus from 1960 to 1977 with the singer who performed 'Ding-a-dong'. Who, by the way, was a woman. Which makes short work of Downing's claim it was the beards that confused him. Downing isn't very happy today, which partly explains why he wasn't 'singing a song that goes ding-a-dong'. Everyone else in the staffroom was, though.

I was confronted with another difficult question in today's tutor group meeting. Ellis wants to know why he has to go to chapel every week even though he doesn't believe in God. I didn't manage to come up with much of an answer. Just to be on the safe side? Because it's the school rules? Because everybody loves a sing-song? To be honest, although I didn't say this, I doubt his absence would be much remarked.

I took Bagley aside afterwards and we had another chat about his career plans: 'It's not that I want to be discouraging, but it's always worth having a fallback position. Why burn your boats?'

'I thought you said I should follow my dreams, Sir.'

'Yes, but what I'm saying is that you should follow them cautiously.'

It was as I was saying this I realised that's more or less exactly how I ended up at Buxdon. I don't know how I would have responded if he'd asked me when I first dreamed of being a teacher. Ignore my words, boy, just look at my face. These are the eyes of an animal with its leg caught in a trap.

I must write a covering letter and send some sample chapters out to agents this weekend. Otherwise I'm going to spend the rest of my life stuck in a staffroom with Barry Taylor, a man who thinks the capital of Mongolia is Ylang Ylang. I must also book that holiday. At the moment I'm being outromanced by Frank. And outwritten by Dom. And outargued by Bagley.

I telephoned Caroline, but she was out.

March

Matthew Bletch
Mercers' Lodge
Buxdon School
Buxdon

Aemilia Griffen
Griffen and Robsart Literary Agency
London NW10

Dear Ms Griffen,

Please find enclosed a synopsis and three sample chapters
of my memoir of a year spent living and teaching English
in Japan. I hope that the book combines wry insight into
the pleasures and frustrations of expat life with a sharp but
essentially affectionate portrait of contemporary Japan.

The sample chapters I am sending describe in a lighthearted
tone my initial struggles with the language, loneliness, and
cross-cultural misunderstandings – as well as a memorably
frustrating encounter with a recalcitrant Japanese cash
machine. The book is aimed at a wide audience, and should
appeal to anyone who has enjoyed the work of Bill Bryson and
Yukio Mishima.

I very much hope you will be interested in representing it
to publishers. You are currently the only agent looking at this
material. In fact, you are the first to have a peek – I hope you
enjoy it and would like to see more.

It's tentatively entitled *A Picnic at the War Shrine*.

Yours sincerely,

Matthew Bletch

Monday, 3rd March. I got stuck with supervising detention this afternoon. It only struck me about halfway through that I was getting exactly the same punishment as everyone else, except that I hadn't done anything wrong.

Tuesday, 4th March. Lunch with Lucy Salmon. I opted for a chicken kiev that proved on inspection to be empty. Instead of buttery garlic loveliness gushing out to glaze my chips when I cut into it, all that came out was a melancholy sigh. Also, one of my chips was a most unnatural green. Have I unwittingly done something to piss off the kitchen staff?

I'm still trying to get to the bottom of what precisely Barry Taylor would have to do to get Lucy interested in him. The short answer would seem to be getting her very drunk again. 'He's nice and everything,' Lucy said. 'He just doesn't seem to have many ambitions in life.' I assured her this isn't true, without going into specifics. 'I don't want to spend the rest of my days sitting in The Albion with Barry and Johnno McPhee trying to decide the precise difference in taste between Admiral's Folly, Old Reliable and Doughty Shirehorse.' Doughty Shirehorse has a musty quality and dense texture that tend to unsettle the uninitiated. Old Reliable is more storied, with an elegant almost citrussy aftertaste. Admiral's Folly is just flat-out horrible.

The next hurdle to overcome would be for Barry to learn to stop breathing through his mouth when he kisses. It's about as romantic as being breathalysed.

Lucy is still under the impression that there's some kind of future for her and Charlie. 'His wife doesn't understand him,' she told me, straight faced. The marriage is over in all but name (and a series of financial, emotional and legal entanglements going back almost twenty years). He wants to tell the world how much he loves Lucy, but things are so damn complicated. Where does Charlie get his material? *1000 Cheesy Chat-Up Lines for Adulterers?* I imagine him saying it all sitting in his

Y-fronts on the side of the bed in a Trusthouse Forte at three in the morning as Lucy threatens to call his wife. On the basis that Charlie keeps catching his wife going through his jacket pockets and checking his mobile phone bill, it sounds like she understands him all too well.

Lucy thinks she goes for unavailable men because her father wasn't always around when she was growing up. That sounds like it makes sense. She asked how old I was when I lost my father. I was thirteen, and I didn't lose him, he died. This clarification effectively if facetiously cut off that line of questioning. 'You don't really like talking about it, do you?' I guess not, Lucy.

Wednesday, 5th March. Went over to Miranda's after school to help her repaint her front room. Tom Downing was there as well, the proverbial third chopstick. What is that bloke's problem? 'I know what you're doing,' he told me on the way back to school. 'You've got to be the dog in the manger, haven't you?' I think the fumes must have got to him.

Caroline is coming down to Buxdon this weekend, which will be lovely. She asked me what I had planned: 'And don't say The Albion or the Buxdon Tea Shoppe.' Well, that rules out half Buxdon's potential attractions at one fell swoop. She sounded dubious about the local nightclub too. The fact it's called Hammers and you get in half-price on Saturday nights if you're wearing 70s fancy dress didn't do much to entice her. I'll probably try to keep us out of Miranda's way as well.

Thursday, 6th March. Barry Taylor and Johnno McPhee are signing up for The Albion pub quiz again, apparently not having humiliated themselves enough last time. They invited me to join them, but I can think of several things I'd rather spend tomorrow evening doing. They include kicking myself in the head.

'I reckon we're in with a chance of winning this time,' asserted Barry.

Especially if one of Pentangle has to do their homework that night, or slips and breaks a hip; or if Saxon or Whitesnake are playing in the vicinity.

Johnno McPhee claims to have a 'fool-proof scheme' that will ensure their victory. It'll need to be.

Friday, 7th March. Norrington came up after the tutorial meeting to ask my advice on something. It turned out to be a question about self-abuse. Why he came to me I don't know. He's worried that there's something unusual about the frequency with which he takes himself off and … takes himself off. 'If you see what I mean, Sir?' I said that I did, silently praying for a fire alarm. I said that his body was going through a lot of changes; that this was something all teenage boys do, although they tend not to talk about it. Especially not to their teachers, I thought. 'Did you used to, Sir?' No, no not me personally, but I'm told it's very common. 'Twenty times a day?' I agreed that did sound a little bit on the high side. I said he should probably try to find other ways of expending his energy, but that he should by no means feel a freak. I probably could have found a more sensitive form of words. Norrington said he'd found our chat very helpful, and stretched out a hand for me to shake. To my mild surprise it was a perfectly normal hand, rather than some kind of furrowed claw.

Twenty times a day? No wonder there's not much on his UCAS form. How does he find time to eat?

Barry Taylor and Johnno McPhee were a little disappointed to do so badly in the pub quiz last night. I think they were handicapped by the fact that the quiz master has changed his question book. 'That's hours of research down the khazi,' Johnno observed mournfully. He suspects Pentangle were tipped off about it in advance. However, the bottle of

Bulgarian Red they won won't go very far, since they had further weighed the odds in their favour by acquiring five new members. They're now calling themselves Tentacle.

Saturday, 8th March. Caroline and I tried the other pub in Buxdon last night, the Jolly Boatman. There was something of a stampede of Sixth Formers trying to hide when we came in, but I made it clear this wasn't a raid. As the name suggests, the Boatman has all the requisite display of oars and old photographs of boathouses, etc. It serves lager rather than obscure local brews, which was frankly a blessed relief.

I mentioned to Caroline that there's a school barn dance at the end of term. It was the Trotters' idea of a good way to raise money for the Auditorium and Drama Lab Fund and should be interesting, at least sociologically. Caroline said she'd make a note of it in her diary.

Caroline asked how plans for our holiday are coming along. Morgan and some of his mates are going skiing at the beginning of April, which sounds absolutely dreadful, but I said I'd think about it. We discussed Prague for a bit, and Caroline said it hadn't been as bad as all that. I conceded that there had been room for improvement in both the planning and the execution of the trip.

Sunday, 9th March. We watched a video with Barry Taylor last night. He lent me some of Brimscombe's diaries, and I spent the morning reading Caroline selected extracts. Brimscombe got two Valentine's cards in 1992, but thinks that at least one of them was a joke. The other he thinks was probably from his sister. I should have steered clear of the topic, actually, because Caroline started telling me about some dreadful card she got that she thinks is probably from Lulu or Toby.

Caroline picked up a copy of the *TES* on Friday and has found a teaching job in it that she thought I might be interested in. Unless, of course, I'm starting to settle in at Buxdon?

177

I reassured her that isn't the case. Interested? I'd chew my leg off to get a foot in the door. Although I can see how that might be counterproductive. It's a Girls' Grammar School in North East London, twenty-five minutes on the Central Line from Caroline's flat, progressive approach to education, London-adjusted pay, highest A-Level results in the borough. I suspect applications will be quite competitive.

As I was seeing Caroline off at the station two Japanese teenagers dressed as punk Ewoks came up and asked me for directions to Buxdon School. I must get to the bottom of this. When I got back to school they were standing outside the music block having their photograph taken with Mr Hallbrick. Long way to come just for that.

Monday, 10th March. I started filling in my application for that teaching job. It starts in September, and the deadline for applications is in early April. I'll get in touch with Professor Flicker right away to ask for a reference. Three weeks should be enough time for him to find a goose, pluck it, and put quill to parchment. I attached a CV to remind him he was my personal tutor for three years at uni and to let him know what I've been up to since the last time I asked him for a reference. I knew I should have sent him a Christmas card. I hope the letter wasn't too pushy. I hope he remembers who I am. Christ, knowing Old Flickery, I hope he remembers who he is.

Tuesday, 11th March. Got cogitating about the trip with Caroline. I've had an excellent idea. Term ends on Friday, 28 March, so if Caroline comes down for the barn dance we can head straight off somewhere. I think I know the perfect break for us. Peaceful, relaxing, and not too expensive. I collected some brochures at lunchtime from the Buxdon Travel Agency. While I was there I ran into Dr Cumnor, who was picking up an airline ticket for Tuscany. He's been invited to stay with at the Villa Tipton over the Easter holidays. Cumnor could at least have had the decency to look a bit shifty about it, as opposed to going on about needing to buy new swimming trunks and lots of suntan lotion.

Wednesday, 12th March. Mum rang to remind me it's Mothering Sunday this weekend and tell me how much she's looking forward to seeing us all. I've seen as much of Frank as I care to recently, if not more so, but I will be pumping Dom for info on how he managed to get someone to agree to publish his book. For all the response I've got from that agent I might as well have sent my sample chapters up the chimney.

From the staffroom window this lunch break I watched Hallbrick patrolling the school drive and attempting to make people pick up litter and threatening them with lines if they didn't comply. When I walked past to get to afternoon lessons he was refusing to let three First Years get to their class until they picked up a crisp packet none of them had dropped.

'Do you know what this tie means?'

The prefect's tie at Buxdon is an alarming combination of mauve, ochre and olivine.

'Does it means you're a prize suck?'

'Does it mean you're the king of the geeks?'

'Does it mean a colour-blind man is going around open-collared?'

I feel Hallbrick lacks the authority of some of the larger and more imposing prefects.

Thursday, 13th March. Booked the holiday. I've decided to make it a big surprise. Caroline asked if she should pack her dancing shoes. I suggested more like Wellington boots. Possibly also some footwear with a grippy sole.

Picked up a Mother's Day card in town. I went for the least nauseating message I could find, which was still pretty stomach upsetting:

A Mother is a precious gift,
Of which there's only one,
I hope this Mother's Day for you
Is full of Joy and Fun!

I guess anything is better than 'You are my mother HA HA
HA.'

Friday, 14th March. Home Sweet Home. I'm camping on the
downstairs couch while Dom and Karla get Dom's room and
Frank luxuriates in my bed. Frank turned up this morning
with what looked like several weeks' worth of washing, and
immediately started raiding the fridge. We've already had a
clash of wills. Frank wants to go into town tomorrow night
to meet an old mate, and is insisting on being driven. Why he
can't take the bus, I don't know. He's using the carrot and the
stick approach. The stick is that if I don't do it he's going to
make my life a misery. The carrot is I don't have to wear my
Goblin outfit. I suppose I should count myself lucky he hasn't
gone outside and fetched an actual stick. Yet.

I've already appealed to Mum, but she asks why we can't
just get along, is it so much to ask, etc., etc. Yes, sitting in a
pub with Frank and one of his mates all night, not drinking,
and then driving him home is a lot to ask, actually. I'm beginning to think it was very cunning of Dom never to learn how
to drive. He and Karla are staying in.

Saturday, 15th March. Frank has promised not to get too
drunk, and not to gang up on me with his mate. We're both
grown adults, he claims. We can go out for a pint and a bite
to eat, catch up with some old friends, and have a civilised
evening, can't we?

Sunday, 16th March. No, it turns out we can't. Frank was
almost friendly on the way to the pub. We reminisced about

the time we got sent to stay with Uncle Jeremy and Aunty Maureen, and agreed that for many reasons it's lucky they never had kids of their own. One good reason is Uncle Jeremy's belief that the Tale of Struwwelpeter would be just the right bedtime story for an eight-, a five- and a three-year-old. I don't believe when we asked for a story we specified one about a man with scissors for hands who chops off little kids' thumbs when they suck them. I think I'd already soiled myself before Uncle Jeremy took his moustache-trimming scissors out of his bathrobe pocket, held them up against the bedside lamp, and made us all look at the shadow on the wall. Dom didn't sleep for a week, even if Uncle Jeremy was only cutting his thumb off in silhouette. One thing's for sure: we never asked for a story again at Jeremy and Maureen's house. None of us ever sucked our thumbs, either.

As soon as we walked into the pub and I saw that the mate Frank was meeting was Dodgy Geoff, I knew we were in for trouble. We soon got onto all the fun we used to have together: the time they put me in a dinghy on the canal and took turns trying to sink it with an air-rifle; the time they persuaded me to shave my head; the time they both spent three weeks pretending not to be able to hear a word I said. It really is a wonder I'm as well adjusted as I am.

After that the evening went downhill. What can I say about Frank's best mate? The one purpose he seems to serve is that he makes Frank look like a high achiever. I thought at first that Dodgy Geoff had improved slightly. He was dressed fairly presentably, and asked how I was doing. Unlike in the old days when a half-nelson or a headlock would be the least I could expect in greeting. As befits a man whose teenage party trick was to grip onto a rope with his mouth and be swung around on it, Dodgy Geoff now lacks front teeth. Not that he would look particularly undodgy with them. He offered to sell me a telly. I turned him down. Then he asked me if I want to earn some 'ready', and launched into an incredibly complicated story involving a friend of a friend in Bristol who owes some money to another friend of a friend. It eventually became clear that Geoff doesn't want me to act as muscle – he's got three big lads ready to go down there and have a quiet word with this bloke – but none of them have transport. 'Have you seen the price of rail tickets, these days? It's criminal.' At that point I surreptitiously moved my car keys off the table and into my pocket. Dodgy Geoff spent the rest of the night trying to get me to drink, on the basis that if you suck a 10p coin before being breathalysed, the machine blows up and they can't charge you. I'm pretty sure that's not true.

The thing with Dodgy Geoff is that quite apart from his general dodginess, he's always telling you about 'crazy' things he's done. Not 'fun' crazy, though. He doesn't just do 'mad' things like stealing road furniture, drinking a lot and wearing wacky T-shirts, although he does do all those things. He's properly, pointlessly crazy, like a mentally ill person. A typical Dodgy Geoff anecdote involves talking his way into test-driving a BMW and parking it on the middle of a roundabout then running off, or getting stuck on the roof of a nightclub. Frank, of course, got completely smashed. I eventually got him into the car by bribing him with the promise of a kebab on the way home. As we drove off Dodgy Geoff was still insisting to the landlord that it wasn't him who knocked the condom machine off the wall of the gents.

We had to stop several times on the way back: Once to get Frank a kebab, and again for him to regurgitate it.

Frank was looking very sorry for himself this morning. We took Mum out for lunch and it all went quite well. I didn't get any closer to finding out his real feelings about Sig, or where he thinks that relationship is going, though. He claims the idea that relationships have to be going anywhere is a misleading metaphor, and instead compared his affair with Sig to a Merry-Go-Round. You don't necessarily get anywhere, but the ride is very pleasant. From his expression as he told me that he clearly thought he was being quite poetic and deep. He then saw fit to compare my relationship with Caroline to a Ghost Train. I demanded to know on what possible basis he could make that assertion. He initially claimed brotherly intuition, then reminded me he read my diary last time we were home.

If I had been expecting some kind of apology for last night I would have been disappointed. Despite having to be put in the car and then dragged to the front door, he suddenly recovered himself enough to get upstairs and ensconce himself in my bed. Sometimes I really hate Frank. I can't wait to see what Sig makes of Dodgy Geoff.

Karla is growing on me somewhat. She's obviously decided the best way to get through a weekend with the Bletches is to say as little as possible and get some reading done. More or less how Dom spent his adolescence, as I recall. Mum's thrilled that one of us has finally brought a girl home, although she does have a tendency to overestimate the cultural differences between Britain and the US: 'These are called "cranberries", have you had them before?' was one comment over Sunday lunch.

Dom had nothing very helpful to tell me about getting a book deal except that I should make full use of any contacts I had in the publishing world. I mentioned Kevin Williams and he pulled a face. Yeah right, Dom. Like being told by Margaret Drabble that you're going the wrong way around the buffet at the Oxford Food Symposium really makes you a literary player. I was going to point this out when Frank interrupted us:

'Are you a don, Dom?'

'No, they don't call us that at our university.'

'So you're not a don, Dom. You're not Don Dom Bletch.'

Dom gave a long deep sigh. 'No, Frank, I'm a lecturer.'

'You're a lecher?'

183

'No, a lecturer.'

'A Bletchurer?'

'Mum, can you please make him stop?'

I sometimes wish they'd had boarding at my school and I'd been a boarder – or that Frank and Dom had been.

As I was leaving I accidentally referred to returning to Buxdon as 'going home'. Mum was very upset.

Monday, 17th March. Got back to Buxdon late yesterday afternoon. Despite it being an exeat weekend, Marcus Lau was hanging around on the drive, looking as if he was deciding whether or not to make a break for freedom. I had a little chat with him and he told me that his parents had decided it was too long a trip for him to come home for just one weekend. I asked him where they live, and it turned out to be just the far side of Reading. Still, as I reassured him, home isn't all it's cracked up to be.

Tuesday, 18th March. Caroline has been on the internet and looked up the school in London where I'm going to apply for a job: The Lady Jane Grey Grammar School for Girls. It turns out I've got a man on the inside, Will Otway. He's somehow wangled himself a post there as Deputy Head of English. Caroline reminded me that she did suggest I look up some old mates and get in touch with them when I was hanging around in London the other week. It's going to look a bit fishy if I suddenly call him up out of the blue now. That's true, but in my defence there are a couple of things I'd like to raise. First, Will isn't my mate. He's the bloke who sat behind me in teacher training and relentlessly asked pointless questions. Second, I feel no compunction about getting in touch with Will out of the blue, since the only times he's ever contacted me over the past two years have been when he's got a stand-up comedy show he wants people to come to. I haven't ever been along to see him and I don't even think I ever let him know that I'm back from Japan. This hasn't stopped him e-mailing me every couple of months, I guess on the off-chance I want to hop on a plane and fly over to Highbury and Islington to catch him fifth on the bill upstairs in a pub. Third, he's not very funny. Having a drink with him is like being stuck in a lift with Robin Williams on a bad day. He does 'characters'. You can watch his little piggy eyes dart around the room for stuff to riff on. Also you never know if you're having a genuine conversation or if he's trying out new material. He's zany. Fourth, I don't like him. At all. I told Caroline I'd give him a ring this week and see if he wants to meet up for a pint.

Caroline's very keen to find out where we're going on holiday. I'm pretty sure now this is going to turn out to be a bad idea. I get the feeling Caroline is pretty sure of that too. It's too late to pull out now, though, because I've paid the deposit. And booked the life jackets.

Wednesday, 19th March. The Beast of Buxdon has struck again. The school awoke this morning to find an enormous phallus drawn in weed killer on the cricket pitch. That's going to make a great impression on the parents coming for the barn dance next week. It's definitely the work of the Beast, because they've signed it. The Head's having kittens.

No word from Professor Flicker yet about the reference letter. I'd use the computers in the library to send him a reminder, but it's a vain bloody hope the old soak ever checks his e-mail. I wonder if the school has any carrier pigeons. Or flying monkeys. Come on you bugger, reply to me. Perhaps he's trapped under a toppled pile of manuscripts. Perhaps he can't remember me. Perhaps he's just incredibly busy. I'd telephone, but I don't want to seem too pushy.

Thursday, 20th March. A surprise inspection of the school

lockers at lunchtime failed to uncover any clues as to who the Beast of Buxdon is. Although we didn't find any weed killer or other incriminating items the spot search did harvest two bottles of stolen Buxdon wine, three copies of *Razzle*, one bottle of poppers, one switchblade (which on closer inspection turned out to be a comb) and some of the least convincing fake ID I've ever seen. To my great relief there was no sign of that vanished starting pistol.

I rang Will Otway in the evening to see if he wanted to meet up at the weekend. He answered the phone in the voice of a very posh old lady, which immediately made me wish I hadn't bothered. When he found out it was me calling, he switched to a supposedly Japanese accent and asked if I missed the lice. It took me fifteen minutes to get off the line, by which time he'd also 'done': a drunk Scotsman, a simpering hairdresser, a Bangladeshi taxi driver and someone from Devon performing an exorcism in the style of an Evangelical preacher. I'd forgotten that if you don't laugh at something he then starts explaining it. No, I got it, Will.

The good news is that he's leaving Lady Jane Grey at the end of the year, and he'd love to meet up for a chat about it. The bad news is that he's performing on Saturday night and we're having a pint afterwards.

I called Dom after that, to discuss Frank and his problems. Karla thinks that we both need to have a heart-to-heart with Frank and confront the damaging nature of our relationships with him. I can imagine how that's going to go down with Frank.

Friday, 21st March. The headmaster cornered Dr Cumnor and me in the staffroom at break and observed that our department hasn't yet come up with any fundraising ideas for the Drama Auditorium and Theatre Lab, or whatever it's called. Dr Cumnor swiftly suggested a Home Clothes Day, which left me dangling. School Skimmington Ride? Victorian Clothes Day? Sponsored Skip? He asked me to come up with something proper by the start of next term. I'm not sure what the 'or else' is, but I have a nasty vision of myself sitting in a tub of baked beans having sponges thrown at me.

Chivers arrived at the tutorial meeting with his arm in plaster. Afterwards he asked if we could discuss a problem he's struggling with. 'I've been having these... feelings.' Oh God, not another one, I thought. Turns out he'd broken his arm playing football.

The main feeling that Chivers has been having is that he's a woman trapped in a man's body. I talked to him about gender roles and whether this was something he'd feel more comfortable discussing with matron or another healthcare professional. 'I somehow thought you'd be the one to understand,' he told me. I decided not to ask why. 'I think the other boys would understand too, if you had a talk to them,' he added. Perhaps, but I know one thing. The headmaster won't be too thrilled if one of the First XI is in the leaving photo wearing a frock.

Saturday, 22nd March. Caroline managed to weasel out of me where we're heading next weekend. She's coming down for the barn dance on Friday night, and staying at Buxdon for the weekend, then we're getting up early on Monday and heading for Norwich. 'Norwich?' She squealed excitedly. I've advised her to bring waterproofs – the forecast is dreadful. I rang up the travel agents yesterday and they confirmed that it's much too late to get my deposit back. 'We've had loads of people ringing up about that,' the woman chortled heartlessly.

Sunday, 23rd March. Caroline and I slogged up over East Finchley last night to see Will Otway's show. To Will's disappointment but not greatly to mine, the rest of the teacher-training gang failed to make it. Will was first on. He warned us before he started that he was trying out a new character tonight and that we should bear with him because he hadn't quite worked the kinks out yet. That got his biggest laugh of the night. The 'character' was a Bavarian tourist in London. This was signposted by the catchphrase 'Ve don't have ziss in Bavaria' and the fact Will was wearing lederhosen. The actual German tourists in the front row took it all in good spirits, and were the only people to respond to a fantastically obscure running joke about Die Toten Hosen.

We bought Will a pint afterwards ('Foster's? Ve don't have ziss in Bavaria') and tried to be encouraging. Caroline suggested that perhaps the audience wasn't really ready for observational material rather than straightforward jokes. It would also help if Will's observations were a bit less like the ramblings of a mental patient. 'Isn't it veird when you are walking through the park and all the ducks start asking you for a cigarette? Nein, nein, I have keine cigarettes. Stop following me.' This was met with a baffled silence, so Will came out of character to explain that when ducks quack it sounds a bit like someone saying 'Fag, fag.' Except it really doesn't.

We got onto schools and I told him some of the anxieties I'd had about teaching at Buxdon. Such as? Well, that people resent ex-public-schoolboys because the system is unfair and socially divisive and is seen as elitist. Will looked pensive. 'Do you think that's it? I'd always assumed people resent ex-public-schoolboys because they say stupid things in loud obnoxious voices.' There's that too. It came as little surprise to learn that Will is working on a character called Tarquin the Old Etonian.

Will did speak highly of Lady Jane Grey, though. He mentioned that he uses a lot of humour in the classroom. Without me even having to ask he said he'd be happy to put in a good word for me with the job application. I promised in return to give him a good review on Giggle.co.uk. He's leaving teaching to concentrate on his comedy full time. Will's someone else who should be heartily discouraged from following his dreams.

Apropos of which, I'm on my way back to Buxdon. Caroline claims to be very excited about our trip away. I hope she's not too excited. I have a horrible feeling about this trip; the feeling you get an instant before you slam your finger in a door. She was asking if there'll be fresh air and exercise. Oh yes, I can guarantee that.

Monday, 24th March. Chivers came to see me again after school. He was, to my relief, in his school uniform. I said I'd spent the weekend thinking carefully about what he'd told me and about what the best thing to do would be. This was something of an exaggeration but I had given the matter some thought on the train back to Buxdon. We discussed what it is that makes a man a man and a woman a woman, and talked about the norms and expectations of contemporary society.

It was only when Chivers mentioned that the specific woman's body he feels trapped in is a statuesque blonde called Nina that the penny finally dropped.

'You're winding me up, aren't you.'

'I'm afraid I am, Sir.'

'Thank God for that.'

'I'm winding you up. But Nina's deadly serious.'

'Oh run along, Chivers, you foolish boy.'

Tuesday, 25th March. Well, Caroline will be satisfied. The bust-up she predicted between Miranda and Lucy Salmon has come to pass. I went down to the kitchen to get a cup of tea a minute ago and Lucy Salmon was down there looking absolutely miserable, and with the kind of haircut usually associated with developmental difficulties or foolish teenage adventures in hairdressing. Barry Taylor and I have spent the last hour trying to reassure her it looks OK. It does not look

OK. Barry is still down there now with his tongue sticking out of the corner of his mouth, one eye closed, and a pair of scissors, trying to see if there's anything he can do. He'd have better luck with some glue.

Obviously it's Miranda's handiwork. 'I just said I wanted my fringe to look as nice as hers,' Lucy was sobbing. It seems 'From Hair to Eternity' was fully booked, and Miranda offered to have a go. Lucy's fringe currently resembles a coastline map of the south of England. Lucy's already been around all the hairdressers in Buxdon in a headscarf, but they're closed for the day.

'I'm sure it was an accident,' I said, but neither Barry nor Lucy looked at all convinced.

Wednesday, 26th March. Since it's the last week of term I decided to let the Third Years play hangman today. Not literally. I spoke to Marcus Lau after class, and he confirmed that he's not very happy at Buxdon. I said he must be looking forward to the end of the week, then. Not really, his parents are going skiing, so he's here for most of the holidays as well.

Thursday, 27th March. Still no word from Professor Flicker. I rang the school and told them my application might be a little late. They said that was OK, not least since I'm coming so highly recommended. I can only imagine what kind of wacky voice that recommendation was delivered in.

I've written two reminder letters to Flicker. I'm going to get Caroline's advice on which one I should send, although I'm pretty sure the second draft would be more politic. Not that Flicker seems to read his post anyway.

Friday, 28th March. Ellis took me aside after the tutor group meeting this morning. He's very worried about 'something peculiar' on a discreet portion of his anatomy. He was actually fiddling with his belt buckle to show me, when I told him that I got to the bottom of that joke on Monday. Once again, I could have chosen my words more wisely.

'What joke, Sir?'

I told him to take it to Matron if there's anything he's genuinely worried about.

I've got to get out of here.

Saw Lucy in town today. She was looking for a hat for tonight. She and Miranda aren't speaking. I fear there's going to be trouble at the barn dance. I managed to find not only hats for the barn dance for Caroline and me, but a captain's hat for our holiday. It rather suits me, I think.

Saturday, 29th March. Well, we got through the barn dance without a punch-up, although we came pretty close at times. Poor Lucy was smiling grimly under her straw bonnet and getting on with things. We all had a good dance, and people kept telling Lucy it didn't look that bad. Barry Taylor was doing his best to cheer her up by dancing like a fool. I hope he was dancing that way intentionally. Caroline was also being very supportive, although as she pointed out to me earlier, anyone who lets Miranda have a go with their fringe is looking for trouble. 'It's like asking a boa constrictor to baby-sit.'

Caroline and Lucy discussed Miranda at length while we were all getting ready:

Caroline: This is a woman who will never in her life have to call a plumber or get a cab, because there is always some mug who'll drop everything and do her bidding. And, weirder, who'll act like it's some great privilege that she's asked them.

Lucy: She's not even that pretty. If you ask me she looks like a scary little doll.

Caroline: And what about the way she has two different voices for talking to men and women?

Lucy: What about the way she's always tossing her hair. It looks like she has a neck problem.

Caroline: And her fake laugh?

Lucy: And the way she always has to borrow tampons.

Caroline: How annoying is *that*?

I kept my mouth very firmly shut throughout all this and attempted to exude sympathy if not empathy.

The Tiptons were at the dance, and politely ignored me. Whatever. Despite the large number of uncreditable and foolish actions I've performed since coming to Buxdon, at least I can hold my head up and say I'm the last uncorrupted man in the Buxdon English department. Dr Cumnor's off to Tuscany on Monday, and thinks it likely that Tipton's coursework folder will receive special commendation. I wonder if it's too late to change my mind.

About an hour into the dancing Miranda started crying and went out dramatically to sit on the steps outside weeping about how bad she felt and that she was sure everyone thought she was awful and hated her. Foolishly, she decided to say this to Caroline. I'm not sure what Caroline told her back, but that was the last we saw of Miranda all night. Caroline claimed to have poured a bucket of water over her and made her disappear in a puff of green smoke, but I think she was joking.

Sunday, 30th March. Caroline's having a shower now. I've warned her that washing conditions might be a bit primitive over the next week. She took the news fairly well. Although she did ask what on earth had made me think that what she had really been longing for was a week on a barge. I've confirmed to Caroline that this isn't going to turn out to be an April Fool. It's a unique way of seeing England, I paraphrased from the publicity brochure. She didn't look impressed. I haven't mentioned the chemical toilet yet. I doubt even letting Caroline wear the captain's hat is going to cheer her up. I've just checked the weather forecast again. A week of rain

Monday, 31 March. On the coach to Norwich now. I think we must be nearly there now, although the fog makes it hard to tell. I've shown Caroline the two drafts of my letter to Professor Flicker and she's suggested I send the second.

Caroline received some excellent news this morning. Rychard's got the job in Edinburgh. She told me it was lovely to see me taking pleasure in someone else's good fortune for once. It took me a moment to realise she meant Rychard's. Hell, I'll be there at the station with a hankie to wave him off.

I must find a post box before we set sail.

First Draft:

Matthew Bletch
Buxdon School
Buxdon

Professor Pointless Fucker
Department of English Literature
Faculty of Arse and Lettuce
University of *********

Dear Pootling Fart,

Where the fuck is my reference, you shrivelled old balloon? Have you written it? Did you send it already, to the wrong address? Did you roll it up in an empty port bottle and throw it in the river? Is someone carrying it to Buxdon in a cleft stick? Are you even now poised by the typewriter, searching for the *mot juste*? Have you misplaced my letter? Have you misplaced your mind? Are you peering rheumily at the computer the

department bought you and wondering whether it gets
Channel Five? Have you got so many nice things to say about
me you've run out of ink? Are you wandering around the
faculty in a shower cap and bathrobe, shouting obscenities?
Have you fallen and can't get up? Are you lost in the library?

Am I howling in a void, or do you bother to actually read
your correspondence? Are you stuck in a dumb-waiter? Tap
three times for 'yes'.

I hope all is well with you, and I'm very sorry to bother you
again about this, particularly at this busy time.

Best wishes,
Matthew

Second Draft:

Matthew Bletch
Mercer's Lodge
Buxdon School
Buxdon

Professor Peter Flicker
Department of English Literature
Faculty of Arts and Letters
University of *********

Dear Professor Flicker,

I'm so sorry to bother you again! I just wondered whether
you had had a chance to consider providing me with a
reference. Excuse this reminder, but the official deadline is
Friday, 4 April. Fortunately this is to a certain extent flexible.
I'm so sorry to badger you like this but I'm sure you will
understand that I'd like to know if I should contact another
referee. If you feel unable to provide a reference, for any
reason, it would be great if you could let me know. My e-mail
address is mbletch@buxdon.org.uk, if that would make things

easier. I've included my CV again, as well as the details of the position I'm applying for. I really appreciate your help with this, and I do understand that you must be extremely busy at the minute (as always!).

Hoping all is well with you,
Yours sincerely,
Matthew Bletch

Part Three:
Summer

April

Tuesday, 1st April. I'm beginning to wish this trip really had been an April Fool. Things started quite well yesterday. We passed a post box on the way from the coach station to the boatyard, and I sent the polite letter to Professor Flicker. Hopefully when I get back to Buxdon there'll be a reference waiting.

We got to the boatyard in plenty of time and were ushered onto the *Queen of the Fens.* The boatyard keeper gave us some helpful advice: Make sure you're moored securely at night; always keep to the left when you're passing other boats; don't smoke near the chemical toilet. I have to admit I didn't expect conditions inside the barge to be quite so intimate. It looked a lot bigger in the photo. 'You know how to handle a lock, don't you?' the boatyard keeper asked. I reassured him I didn't spend six months in the Sea Scouts for nothing.

What I hadn't anticipated was quite how many locks we were going to be encountering. I'd imagined us pootling along in the sunshine, waving at cows, pulling over at riverside inns for long balmy lunches and exchanging hearty greetings with all manner of picturesque river-folk, some of them in quaint rural costume. Everyone seemed to be having a great time in the brochure, which included some guff about the 'fellowship of the river' and 'the smell of the great outdoors'. The smell of the great outdoors turns out to be the lingering smell of engine fumes. Accompanied by the constant throbbing of the engine, except when it would suddenly belch out a cloud of smoke and shudder to a sullen halt. Bucolic interlude, my eye.

At least the noise of the engine, when it's running, tends

to obscure the hearty greetings of the other river users. It's hardly my fault that the *Queen of the Fens* has all the steering capability of a wonky-wheeled shopping trolley. This morning saw a typical exchange:

> *Caroline*: The *left*, Matt, the *left*. The man said to keep to the *left*.
>
> *Me*: I'm steering to the left. (Indicating wheel, which is full to port.)
>
> *Caroline*: Well, we're going to the right. Oh God.
>
> *The drizzle parts to reveal a two-storey riverboat crammed with pleasure-seekers, bearing down on us amidships. Some wave, others scatter in search of lifebelts, lifeboats, the captain, etc.*
>
> *Caroline*: Steer! Steer!
>
> *Me (as calmly as the situation allows)*: I *am* steering, Caroline; it's the boat that's not.
>
> *Captain of Pleasure Craft (through loudhailer, fortunately partly drowned out by the straining and sputtering of our engine)*: Where the ... do you think you're going, you ... Steer to the left.
>
> *Me (still remarkably calm)*: I *am* steering to the left.

By this point most of the people on the other craft had come to the side to shout at us, pass on helpful suggestions ('Nice hat, dickhead') and poke at us with boathooks. One woman kept screaming that we were all going to drown, which I thought was a bit dramatic. Eventually I managed to embed us in the bank, and the other boat passed us on the right. If you have to turn the wheel in the opposite direction to the one you want to go, I think a small notice on the steering column announcing this fact wouldn't have gone amiss. We got the hang of it eventually.

Caroline is in a mild but definite sulk. We moored up yesterday afternoon and I helped her unpack: 'Suntan lotion, won't need that. Sunglasses, won't need those. Shoes and dress for dancing, won't need those either. Raincoat, glad I brought that, eh?' We'd decided to moor up where we were rather than press on to Brundall for tea, because by this point the rain was hanging in heavy grey curtains and we kept losing sight of the bank. We agreed to skip dinner, because we were both feeling a bit queasy from the engine fumes.

I wish I'd brought something else to read than *Heart of Darkness*.

Wednesday, 2nd April. It kept raining for the rest of yesterday afternoon, into the evening, and all through the night. When we woke up this morning, it was raining. I've always assumed that a boat, of all things, would be waterproof.

Caroline obviously woke up this morning and decided to put a brave face on things, and we headed off once I'd got us untied and disentangled from the bank. I'd managed some pretty impressive rope-craft last night. When Matt Bletch ties a knot, it stays tied. I thought briefly we were going to have to gnaw through our moorings to escape. When we were finally on our way I let Caroline steer for a bit, and gave her the captain's hat. The brave face lasted until about noon, when she asked what we were having for lunch. Bear in mind that the only signs of civilisation we'd passed in the preceding forty-five minutes were some pylons, a motorway bridge, and a burned-out barn. None of which, I should add, were depicted in the brochure. I explained that we could stop and eat at the next place we passed.

Caroline: You mean you didn't bring any provisions?
Me: Yes, you saw the Sainsbury's bags.
Caroline (slowly): What's in the bags?
Me: Provisions. Dry provisions. For emergencies.
Caroline: I'm going down into the cabin now. If all there is in those bags is Peperamis, crisps, biscuits and lemon

sherbets I'm going to be very upset.

Me: We've got Tracker bars. And tea bags.

Caroline: Any milk?

Me: Jesus, we pass a cow every five minutes.

I'd assumed we'd also be passing a Sainsbury's Local or at least a service station of some kind.

Caroline: So what now, apart from the slow decline into cannibalism?

Me: You've got the captain's hat on. Besides, it's only two thumbnails on the map until we get to Reedham.

Two thumbnails and thirteen locks. For some reason Reedham was closed, but we managed to get a meal in a hotel. Caroline insisted on staying the night there, and I insisted on returning to the boat.

Thursday, 3rd April. Caroline reappeared this morning with some bags of shopping, and we set off again. She'd also managed to buy some jumpers and heavy-duty waterproofs in town. 'I think the sun's coming out,' I told her. I was wrong.

Friday, 4th April. Last night we cooked some of the stuff Caroline bought in Reedham. It's not often you can cook while actually sitting up in bed. We opened all the portholes but couldn't quite get rid of the frying smell. Caroline had also picked up some booze, which we got through very quickly and went to bed.

This morning we pressed on, with cracking hangovers not made better by the smells and noise of the engine. Fortunately it conked out about midday. I got it working again after a few hours and we moored up near Great Yarmouth. I think. The map doesn't seem to bear much resemblance to the route we've taken.

'A unique way to see England,' the brochure promised. What have we seen so far? We saw an otter yesterday. It was floating upside-down and had inflated to the size of a football.

Saturday, 5th April. We started our return journey. Caroline insisted on sleeping with the portholes shut last night because she thought she could hear voices in the woods. About two o'clock I woke up just in time to save us from being gassed by the chemical toilet.

It was a brilliant sunny day today and things actually improved for a bit. We had lunch at a riverside hostelry and Caroline cleaned herself up in the ladies. There was another boat moored up outside, and a whole grinning family sitting outside under an umbrella in matching spick-and-span uniforms. The paterfamilias had his compass on a string out and was examining the map with a magnifying glass, while his children danced an impromptu hornpipe to the claps of their Capri-trousered mother. I noted that their boat was considerably larger than ours. It even had a barbecue on deck. It was practically a ship. I wish our boat had a satellite dish.

Me: Maybe we could do that one day.
Caroline: If you think I'm ever setting foot on a barge again ...

The father was asking directions to the nearest campsite at the bar at the same time as I was getting drinks, and we exchanged a little river talk. He mentioned that his boat is officially an 'executive class river limousine', and asked about ours. I think the *Queen of the Fens* is a decommissioned coal barge. They have showers on theirs. I didn't mention that to Caroline. She discovered last night there's a crack in our bucket. Still, as I reassured Caroline, worse things happen at sea. Which interestingly enough Dom was insisting the other day is the underlying message of all Joseph Conrad's work.

About half an hour upriver I discovered I'd left my hat on the bar and we had to go back for it, which put us a little behind schedule. By the time it was getting dark we still hadn't reached the designated mooring spot. Caroline was getting a bit nervous, not least because a rather menacing gang of teenage boys had started following us along the bank. We made it to the right place eventually, and shared the last Tracker bar.

Caroline demanded to know how anyone can get lost on a canal. By 'anyone' she meant me. I assured her we're not lost and brought out the map to show her me the loop we've been doing: 'Look, we'll come out here, and then it's just a single thumbnail back to the boatyard up this blue line here.' Which will be fine if 'that blue line' is a waterway, rather than the A road Caroline believes it to be. By this point things were starting to get a little tense between us. Although I did get Caroline to admit that Prague hadn't been that bad after all.

Sunday, 6th April. I woke up in the night and discovered we'd started sinking. There was about three inches of muddy water on the floor and the barge has acquired a distinct lean. Caroline's upstairs 'driving', as she keeps calling it, and I'm down here trying to work out the instructions on the bilge pump. We must be nearly back at the dockyard now. We've passed the same power station an even number of times, so we must at least be going back the way we came. Unless it's a different power station.

Provisions and morale low. Caroline just went through my jacket pockets and accused me of secretly stockpiling sherbet lemons.

Monday, 7th April. We finally got back to the boatyard just after dusk. The boatyard keeper asked if we'd had a good time.

Returned to Buxdon by coach and arrived at two this morning to find letters from Professor Flicker and Aemelia Griffen the literary agent waiting for me. Professor Flicker's letter apologised for the slowness of his response, adding that he's been very busy with admin and marking. What a lovely man. I feel pretty guilty now. I'm glad I sent the second draft of the letter. He refers to my CV as 'strangely modest'. Perhaps I should have mentioned that I know how to play Pachinko and can use chopsticks.

Aemelia Griffin opens by congratulating me on the book. She says I write elegantly and she laughed 'several times'. She singled out for special praise the part when I'm in Tokyo and attempt to order a meal in a shop that only sells plastic food. Apparently my rising sense of bewilderment and frustration is very adroitly conveyed. Less pleasingly, she goes on to write that there's no shortage of books about Japan, and at times my approach (while amusing) seems a little gimmicky. She's afraid that they will be unable to represent your book at this time, but is sure it will find an agent who can respond more actively. Oh, and I should not hesitate to send them anything I write in the future. Gimmicky? This, from the agent who represents the authors of *Round Wales in a Milkfloat* and *Up the Amazon by Pedalo*?

It's just as well I've got a fallback plan. I'll pop Flicker's reference in with my application and get that off today. Good old Flickers, I always knew he'd come through in the end. I almost wish I'd bothered going to his *Paradise Lost* seminars now.

Tuesday, 8th April. That incredible old fool. I steamed open Flicker's reference before sending it yesterday, out of healthy curiosity. I'm bloody glad I did. He clearly has absolutely no idea who I am. The reference evidently describes an entirely different human being, possibly a composite of more than one person, if they've ever existed at all.

It's no wonder they never invite you on *Start the Week*, you lunatic. I spent the whole day altering my CV and application to match this imaginary 'Matthew Bletch' dredged from the lees of a port-soaked mind. As a result my personal statement now includes such extraordinary claims as: 'While at university I received special mention at the National Student Drama Festival for my nude production of the *Oresteia*. I still have a strong interest in drama, although obviously fully-clothed drama is more appropriate at Secondary School level.' Flicker also claims that I am an Olympic-level fencer, which I trust they won't put to the test in my interview. In the very unlikely event I get an interview. My middle name isn't actually Aloysius, either.

Wednesday, 9th April. Caroline points out that I could have e-mailed Flicker, explained the situation, and asked him to send a new reference directly. Yes, that might have been simpler. But I've grown rather fond of this other Matthew Bletch. I hope they don't ask me any questions about the year I spent digging wells in the Sudan or my time waitering at the River Café.

There aren't many people around at Buxdon. Dr Cumnor's in Tuscany, and Lucy Salmon has just got back from Tuscany and is spending a few days with her parents. Peter Wyndham is in France, the Headmaster is back in the Far East promoting the school again, and Tom Downing and Miranda have gone on the school ski trip. The groundwork is already laid out for the auditorium and drama lab, and the former Mercer's Field is fenced off.

Mum rang to see how the holiday went. It could have been worse, I suppose. We could have drowned or been robbed by pirates. Caroline thinks it's probably best if we don't see each other this weekend.

Thursday, 10th April. I made a strange discovery today, although after two terms at Buxdon it would be an exaggeration to say that this surprised me. I was in the English Department book annexe going through my set texts for next term. The Third Years are studying Keats and I was making sure there are enough copies to go around. The books were all in the annexe, but can there be an logical explanation why of thirty copies of Keats' *Selected Poems*, twenty-nine were signed 'Billy Green' and one 'The Beast of Buxdon'? In the same handwriting. I don't even teach a boy called Billy Green. Although the chances are pretty high I do teach the Beast of Buxdon.

Friday, 11th April. I must get my hair cut before the start of term. I'm starting to look like a mushroom. I definitely won't be asking Miranda to do it.

Barry Taylor and Johnno McPhee are planning a night at The Albion later, followed by a trip to Buxdon's sole nightclub, Hammers. I want to get up early tomorrow and send out some more sample chapters, so I've said I'll come for a pint but I'm not going to get Hammered. 'Every nites lady's night at Hammers,' claims the sign outside, unconvingingly and ungrammatically. I wonder who the lucky lady is. That's the kind of arch witticism that doesn't get a man very far in life, and gets him absolutely nowhere in Hammers.

Caroline reckons I should get in touch with Kevin Williams and see if he can fix me up with an agent. She's having dinner with Morgan then they may meet up with Rychard at his club. I asked her to pass on my congratulations regarding Edinburgh.

Saturday, 12th April. Ended up in Hammers last night with Barry Taylor and Johnno McPhee. The bouncers practically begged us to come in. There really is a collection of hammers, nailed to the wall behind the bar. We were among the few people in there apart from a gang of squaddies from Buxdon barracks. I definitely danced a lot, because there's half an inch of tarry black grime on my shoes. A man with no visible neck but very visible arms knocked my pint and stood on my foot. I didn't make a big deal of it. I was just hoping he'd get off my foot soon, rather than wondering why I was standing behind him so closely and pulling funny faces. It's something of a mystery how he even got into a white T-shirt that tight.

Hammers has mirrors around the dance floor, which doubles the horror. I remember staring into them at one point and seeing an endless shimmering parade of misery. The DJ insisted on inserting references to 'Buxdon' into every song he played, lest we manage to forget for one brief moment where we were: 'I spent the night in BUXDON, looking for a disco'; 'You were working as a waitress in THE BUXDON TEA SHOPPE when I met you'; 'Come on BUXDON, too-loo-rye-ay', etc. For some reason I felt that doing a Jarvis Cocker dance badly during every single song was some kind of ironical cultural comment on the idiots surrounding me, rather than marking me out as one of them. There was rather more sucking my cheeks in and pointing at myself in mirrors than is now entirely comfortable to recall. To be honest, once you've paid money to get into Hammers, the joke's on you whatever you do. Some of the squaddies didn't approve of Johnno's goatee, and we left.

Evidence suggests I had a kebab on the way home. I didn't get around to sending out any sample chapters this morning.

Sunday, 13th April. Really wish I hadn't been so hungover yesterday. I ran into the Headmaster on the drive, back from his travels in the Orient, and he asked me what fundraising ideas I'd come up with over the past two weeks. After a full minute of staring blankly into space I replied: 'How about a fundraising slave auction?' Even worse, he went for it. The only positive I can think of to come out of this is that I didn't promise to sign up for it. Barry Taylor loves the idea, not least since it gives him another opportunity to prance around in a toga. 'And it is for charity,' Barry asserted, incorrectly.

Monday, 14th April. Miranda and Tom Downing are back from the school ski trip. I walked in on them canoodling in the staffroom. I noisily collected my post and banged around with some mugs until they slowly climbed off each other. Miranda remembered something she had to post, which left me alone with a very smug Tom Downing. He was pointedly realigning his lycra shorts. 'No hard feelings, eh, mate?' he said, and insisted on shaking hands. 'The best man won in the end.' Whatever, mate. I wasn't aware there was even a competition. God knows what Miranda sees in him, but I suspect it's a cheap handyman. 'Are you signing up for this slave auction?' he asked me. No, of course I'm bloody not.

Tuesday, 15th April. Except that I see someone has signed me up for it. Someone with handwriting not dissimilar to Miranda's. I crossed myself off again immediately.

Caroline has spotted that Kevin Williams is giving a reading in London this weekend and suggested I go along and have a word with him about my sample chapters afterwards. 'It can't hurt to talk to him,' she said. No, but it could be really embarrassing, awkward and tedious.

Wednesday, 16th April. Lunch with Lucy Salmon. She's spending the weekend with Charlie. She wants to go somewhere special, because he's hinted that he has a big announcement to make. I advised her to avoid anything barge related.

Lucy described the slave auction as a terrible idea and wondered what idiot came up with it. She was unaware she's been signed up for it. I suspect I know by whom.

Lucy's fringe is growing back nicely, although her friendship with Miranda hasn't recovered quite so quickly. I must get my hair cut before I go up to London. I washed it this morning and it now looks like a loaf of bread.

*

Thursday, 17th April. Dr Cumnor's back from Tuscany, tanned and plump on free fruit. He says he and his wife had a wonderful time, and asked how my holiday was.

Cumnor wanted to talk to me about the set texts for this term. I failed to conceal my utter horror at his reminder I'm meant to be teaching *Sir Gawain and the Green Knight*. I may even have to read it again. At least it's short. I may not be able to enthuse the boys with a love of Middle English alliterative verse, but hopefully I can get it done in a term without provoking a mutiny. 'You think you've got it bad?' Cumnor said. 'I've got to do Thomas fucking Hardy again.' He's teaching *The Trumpet Major and Robert His Brother*, a novel which as I recall somehow manages to be almost as boring and dreary as its title.

Dr Cumnor has no idea who Billy Green is, or why his name appears on the flyleaf of every copy of Keats's *Selected Poems*. Of which, I discovered this morning, there are now only twenty-eight. Curiouser and curiouser.

Friday, 18th April. Big mistake getting my hair cut, and especially in deciding to get it done at 'Scissors' in the Market Square. I should have taken warning from the pictures in the window, which look like stills from *Miami Vice*. I don't even think the guy who did my hair was a qualified barber. I think I just wandered in during the middle of a hold-up, and he thought he could make a few extra quid. He lost his thinning scissors at one point, and managed to unplug the electric razor twice while he was doing the back. Which isn't blended in, as I specifically requested it to be.

The first thing Barry Taylor said when he saw me was: 'Been to "Scissors"?' I'm told that most people refer to it as 'Secateurs'.

At least it was only £4.50. I almost refused to pay. I definitely shouldn't have tipped.

*

Saturday, 19th April. Spent the best part of the evening trying to conceal my new haircut from Caroline with the aid of
some mellow lighting and my captain's hat. She eventually
insisted I take the hat off. 'What on earth have you done to
your head?' Well, I didn't do it myself, did I? If I had it would
probably look a lot better than it does. Does it really look as
bad as I think? 'It looks like you've been in a fire.' Caroline
then attempted to make me feel better by telling me that my
hair didn't look that good before. She's refusing to let me wear
the hat to Kevin Williams's reading tonight.

Sunday, 20th April. Kevin Williams looked surprised and
alarmed to see me at the reading. I can't really blame him
with this haircut. Is it my imagination or have people started
talking to me a lot more slowly?

The reading took place in a fishing goods shop off Oxford
Street, I suppose a tie-in with the theme of his latest opus, *A
Can of Worms*. I don't think he sold many books, but someone
did interrupt the Q&A session to ask him something about
tackle prices. The nicest thing I can honestly say about his
poetry is that it hasn't got any worse.

Williams claimed to have greatly enjoyed my sample chapters, and told me he's going to pass them on to an agent friend
of his this week. I said I'd see what I could do about getting
the school to order a few copies of *A Can of Worms*. I told him
it's definitely some of the best poetry about fishing I've ever
read. Apart from Ted Hughes. And Izaak Walton.

Caroline asked me later if Kevin Williams always seemed
that nervous and shifty. Well, he is a poet. On reflection he did
seem a bit jumpy, and not only because he was politely trying
to avoid staring at my hair. He asked after all at Buxdon, and
sent Iles his best wishes.

I think I've left my captain's hat at Caroline's. Luckily I've
still got the hat Mum gave me at Christmas. Although that has

the disadvantage of being the only item of head covering in the world that actually looks worse than this haircut.

Monday, 21st April. First day of term. Lucy Salmon's immediate response to my new haircut was to ask whether 'that was what I asked for?' Well, no, I didn't actually go in and demand 'a lot of scalp at the sides, an oddly-placed parallelogram of hair at the top, a step the thickness of a slice of bread at the back, and one sideburn half an inch higher than the other'. If I had, perhaps they would have fucked it up and accidentally given me a decent haircut. I thought she at least would be more sympathetic.

Lucy's weekend didn't go quite according to plan and she came back to Buxdon on Sunday morning. The 'big announcement' Charlie had for her was that he and his wife are having another child. 'Why?' Lucy demanded of me. 'He's got two already and they're rubbish.' Charlie wants to cut back how much they see each other, in order to wind things down. Lucy's told him where to stick it. It would be nice to say I didn't see that coming. I'm afraid I didn't have any particularly encouraging advice to give her. I avoided mentioning that Barry Taylor still likes her, because she seemed unhappy enough already. He'll be over the moon about this.

There was a special assembly to mark the start of the new term. I managed to avoid chapel last night by going to bed early. The headmaster reminded everyone about the Staff Slave Auction next Friday. Tom Downing and Miranda were sitting next to each other all through the start-of-term announcements, holding hands. Downing gave me a dismissive look. For some reason Downing seems to think that I'll think more of him now that he's going out with Miranda. In actuality I just think a little less of Miranda.

I saw the old man with the one-legged dog on my way into Buxdon this afternoon. The dog noticed the discarded remains of a kebab on the pavement, hopped over, took one sniff, and hopped away again. There's a significant warning there, I think.

Tuesday, 22nd April. If one more boy shouts 'Run, Forrest, Run!' at me, there's going to be detentions flying around.

As I was coming up the drive at lunchtime someone shouted out of one of the Old School windows: 'Who does your hair? Sweeney Todd?' It sounded liked Johnno McPhee. Even Dr Cumnor gave me a funny look this afternoon.

When I got back from dinner I found a note under my door, purportedly from Mrs O. Digby, saying that if I want to borrow the school lawnmower again I should ask in advance.

Wednesday, 23rd April. Helped Dr Cumnor unpack this term's set texts this afternoon. Not in the literary critical sense; in the sense of physically getting them out of a big box. Whoever decided on the cover for this schools edition of *Sir Gawain and the Green Knight* had a very funny idea of how to get boys reading. It looks like a Ladybird book. The Green Knight is laughing with his hands on his girdle, and looks more like the Jolly Green Giant. Still, you can't judge a book by its cover. On the back some liar claims *Gawain* is 'one of the most thrilling stories ever told'. Yeah, right. You can't fool the kids, man. In the interests of accuracy they should have added the clarificatory caveat that it's 'one of the most thrilling stories ever told in Middle English verse' and added 'apart from that bit that goes on and on about the design on Gawain's shield until you think you would literally die rather than check the glossary and notes one more time'. At least it's not *The Trumpet Major and Robert His Even More Annoying Brother.*

I wonder what they'll put on the cover of my book, if it's ever published. Hopefully not me dressed as a Samurai. Holding chopsticks. I wouldn't agree to that anyway, unless they really insist on it. Maybe something symbolic, like a bonsai tree and a little robot. Something along those lines, rather than specifically that, though, because that would be very rubbish.

I hope Kevin Williams' agent friend likes the sample chapters. Actually I don't care if they hate it as long as they offer to represent me and I can get out of here. Mrs O. Digby sent us all a note this morning reminding us that Mercers' Lodge is going to be demolished at the end of term to make way for the drama lab and theatre auditorium. Peter Wyndham was asking if I'd consider sharing a flat with him. I said I'd think about it. I believe that's what in the movie business they call a 'ticking clock'.

Thursday, 24th April. Barry mentioned earlier I've been signed up again for the Slave Auction. I'll deal with that first thing in the morning. I was walking back down the drive towards Mercer's Lodge just now when I heard someone telling me to hold it right there. The Head had mistaken me for one of the boys, but in any case he reminded me that a small pork pie hat isn't suitable apparel for a member of staff. This from a man who spent all last winter swanning around in a deerstalker. In any case, I agree with his aesthetic objections to this stupid hat. But it's a mild improvement on wandering about looking like I'm ready for my ECT.

Now I'm going to bed, perhaps to stay there until my hair's grown back.

Friday, 25th April. Went to cross my name off the board for the Slave Auction at mid-morning break only to find that the notice had been taken down. I hot-footed it over to the school office, where Mrs O. Digby was in the process of typing it up.

Me: I'm afraid there's been a mix-up.
Mrs O. Digby: The notice came down at 10:30. That was what was arranged.

Me: Yes, but there's been a mistake. I'm not meant to be on that list.

Mrs O. Digby: There we go. That's your name, isn't it?

Me: Yes, but that's not my handwriting. Look, it's clearly a woman's hand that's written that. I don't even own a green pen. And I know how many 'T's there are in Matthew.

Mrs O. Digby: I'm a school secretary, not a graphologist.

It was 10:36. Great. Just perfect. I really don't have the legs for a toga.

Saturday, 26th April. Caroline is highly amused by the news that I'm going to be sold off as a slave. She asked me to make sure someone gets some pictures. Caroline insists that she told me ages ago she has a work do on next Friday. As a result she'll be missing the auction. I must try and find out if they accept sealed bids.

Frank and Sig were in the living room, and Frank asked why anyone would possibly want me as a slave. I could paint a wall for them. I could put up some shelves. I could mow the lawn. I could make a shed. Frank expressed polite disbelief I could make a shed. 'You could navigate their boat, if they've got one,' Sig interjected helpfully.

Terrifyingly Frank and Sig are discussing getting tattoos. They asked if I had any suggestions. I suggested it was a really bad idea. Although it is the single most serious gesture of commitment to a relationship Frank has ever made.

Caroline says she doesn't know where my captain's hat is.

Sunday, 27th April. Oh the perfidy. Caroline and I were in bed this morning listening to *Desert Island Discs* when I noticed the songs they were playing were strangely familiar. Next I realised that I recognised the voice of the person being interviewed. I twigged who it was when they started telling the interviewer that inspiration can strike them at any time, so they always carry a notebook. Just this morning half a sonnet came to them in the taxi on the way to White City. That pointy-shoed freak. No wonder he looked so cagy when I was talking to him last weekend. He's stolen all our desert island discs. He even played 'Dreadlock Holiday', claiming to have first heard it on honeymoon and telling an amusing anecdote about how his wife thought it was by Bob Marley. What kind of person lies to Sue Lawley?

It's cheeky enough to borrow Barry's songs, but I was apoplectic when I realised he's stolen mine too. That really is low. Caroline said it might just be a coincidence. Yeah, right. 'Does it really matter?' There's a vote of confidence. It does matter, Caroline, if you're willing to accept that there's the slightest chance that I myself might achieve enough with my life to appear on *Desert Island Discs* myself. The amount of time I put into choosing those. I better hear from this agent friend of his or I'm going straight to the tabloids. Or at least ringing up the BBC to complain. I was going to call them up straight away but Caroline suggested there was the off-chance they'd mistake me for a nutter.

Monday, 28th April. There were two messages waiting for me when I got back to school. The first was from Selina Cowl, the literary agent. She mentions that Kevin Williams was extremely enthusiastic about my sample chapters. She liked them too – she writes that they made her 'laugh thoughtfully', which is the exact response I was hoping for. She's asked to see the rest of the book and would be keen to represent me and get some samples out to publishers and editors. In the circumstances it would be a bit churlish to report Kevin Williams to the BBC now. I imagine that's exactly the response he was counting on.

The other message, almost as exciting, is that I've got an interview for the job at Lady Jane Grey Grammar School for Girls in two weeks. I hope my hair's got back to normal before then. I can understand why they'd be keen to interview Matthew Aloysius Bletch. I wouldn't mind meeting him myself. I hope they don't ask about my time working on a Canadian rodeo. Bloody Professor Flicker. I didn't even know they had rodeos in Canada. Perhaps they don't. I should probably investigate that at some point in the next fortnight. It also might be an idea to find out how you pronounce 'Aloysius'.

Sig and Frank have booked to get their tattoos done on Friday afternoon. Frank is set on having 'Sig 4 Ever' on his arm, while Sig is planning on something rather more discreet on her ankle, perhaps a butterfly or a Chinese character. I asked to speak to Frank and asked if he'd thought this through. He wasn't to be dissuaded, even though I mentioned that I'm going to take great pleasure in saying 'I told you so' when he starts to regret it. He was, however, surprisingly receptive to the idea of getting 'Feed Me' tattooed on his tongue. Mum is very unhappy about it, but Frank has told her that if he decides he doesn't want it he can just get it removed.

Tuesday, 29th April. I handed out the Keats books in class today. There are now only twenty-seven of them. This suggests a hunger for poetry I have not hitherto suspected in the boys of Buxdon School. Or there's more going on here than meets the eye.

I'm going to hand out the copies of *Sir Gawain and the Green Knight* next week, so I rang Dom to see if he had any helpful advice about how to get the boys interested. I should have known he wouldn't be much help. I might as well have asked Frank. Dom said something about it being a fascinating exploration of codes of masculine behaviour and the codes of chivalry. I think I'll probably focus on the bloke who gets his head chopped off.

I let Barry have a tinker with my hair after lunch. It looks a bit better – not good, but certainly less attention attracting. There was a note pinned to my door when I got up this morning. It simply read 'Here hair here?'

I expect there's some boring lesson about vanity and judging people on appearances to be drawn from all this, but mostly the lesson I'm drawing is never get your hair cut at 'Scissors'.

Wednesday, 30th April. Two days left until the Staff Slave Auction. The boys are all discussing who they're going to be buying. Apart from Lucy and me, Barry Taylor, Tom Downing, and Emilia Browning are up for sale.

Iles asked me how much I think I'll raise for the school Auditorium and Drama Lab Fund. I don't care, but if I go for less than Tom Downing I'll be very annoyed.

May

Thursday, 1st May. The man from the *Sun* is back. I ran into him as I was walking back from town carrying the sheet that I'm planning to turn into a toga for the auction. When I suggested a staff slave auction I don't remember specifying an authentically-costumed slave auction. Of course strictly speaking only Roman citizens were allowed to wear togas, but I haven't brought this up for fear of being on stage tomorrow night bare but for my chains.

I told the man from the *Sun* I don't know anything about the stick-up at the tuck shop. Are there any suspects? Yes, one, but he goes only by the name 'The Beast' and I don't think the Head would appreciate that getting into the papers. Rumour has it they held up the tuck shop after school with a starting pistol. Do I have any idea where they might have got their hands on one of those? Nope, none at all. He seemed to buy that answer. I can only hope the Head does too.

The headmaster held an emergency assembly at lunchtime. 'What makes a pupil turn to gun crime?' he demanded. I don't think he expected people to shout out answers. 'The Devil', 'Boredom', 'Frustration' and 'Not being able to keep a goat' were not apparently the reasons he was thinking of. Instead we got told to be on our guard against a media that glorifies gangsterism and braggadocio. I was once told that certain sea-dwelling mammals are capable of sealing off their ear-holes with a special flap. It was never a skill I had much envied until the headmaster started reciting lyrics from *Regulate...G Funk Era*. He needs to work on his flow. I was tempted to suggest we get a few more gentle films for the school video collection.

Unfortunately I was distracted by catching Lucy's eye and collapsing in giggles as the headmaster announced that 'There is a nasty smell in this school; the smell of machismo.' So that's what it is. I had assumed it was the kitchens.

I was summoned to the headmaster's study after school for an interview. 'Dead-Eye' Dick Darling was coming out of the headmaster's office as I went in, and gave me a peculiar look. The Head wanted to know if anyone has shown any signs of disturbance in recent tutor group meetings. No, but of course that's only relatively speaking. They're looking into where the perpetrator got what the Head referred to as 'the weapon'. I pointed out that starting pistols are easily available at Army and Navy stores – a piece of information I realise in retrospect it's slightly suspicious that I know. I attempted to cover my tracks by adding that they also sometimes sell Nazi daggers, but I don't think I did myself any favours with that either. The Head wondered if I had any insight into why a boy would put his whole future at risk for £5 in loose change and forty Wham bars. Perhaps they were out of Highland Toffee?

Friday, 2nd May. The *Sun* went with the headline 'This is a Sticky-Up' and used the same picture of the school as last time. They managed to get the school fees wrong again. To everyone's relief there was no mention of the Beast of Buxdon. The cartoon was a drawing of a bunch of boys being told to turn out their pockets, and producing hand-grenades, pistols, and knives.

A subdued tutor group meeting today. No one took the opportunity to confess to any planned upcoming heists. Iles started to wonder out loud about where the robber got the starting pistol, and I sent him to check whether all the windows in my teaching room were closed. As it wasn't raining this was a bit suss.

Hallbrick was on duty in the tuck shop at the time of the

incident. The perpetrator had concealed their identity with a Buxdon School scarf, but he claims they had the cold eyes of a killer.

I put it to the Headmaster earlier that in light of this grave event it might be best to postpone or even cancel the staff slave auction tonight. He didn't go for it.

Oh, I got out and voted today too. I do trust that Phil Collins' promise at the last election to leave the country in the event of a Labour victory still holds, and that he can be legally held to it.

Saturday, 3rd May. I'm writing this in Caroline's flat. She's having a lie-in while I prepare breakfast. Since I'm her slave, she's drawn up a long list of task for me to do today. This includes a sink that wanted plunging and a set of drawers that needed realigning. I thought she was being saucy until she handed me the plunger.

I was the last of the slaves to be auctioned, and I had a lot to live up to. A cabal of Sixth Form boys (including Tipton, whose pocket money I suspect exceeds my annual wage) clubbed together to outbid Miranda and buy Tom Downing. He's worth £57 apparently. Bidding went high on Lucy Salmon as well, but Barry Taylor eventually faced down Mr Tipton to buy her for the weekend for £112. She looked rather nervous at the prospect. Barry himself was eventually bought by Mrs O. Digby for £2.50. I heard her afterwards telling the auctioneer that she'd just been scratching her head. Mrs Browning was bought by Mr Browning for £17.

Bidding on me started low. For a terrible instant I thought I was going to go to Bagley for 50p. But then someone at the back started bidding on me. I couldn't see who it was, but they were willing to stretch to 75p. Bagley countered with £1. The mystery bidder went up to £1.10 and Bagley shook his head slowly.

'Please come up to collect your slave,' announced the

221

auctioneer. 'They're all yours until Sunday evening at six, and please have them back safe and sound for school on Monday. Thank you all for coming and for your contributions to the Auditorium and Drama Lab Fund.'

I eventually persuaded Caroline to permit me to change out of my toga before we got the train to Paddington. I suppose the whole thing is kind of romantic, although Caroline says she decided to come in the end mainly to make sure Miranda didn't get me.

Frank and Sig were at the flat when we got to London. They've had their ink done. Sig was sitting there with her ankle in a plastic bag full of blood; Frank was lying on his front on the couch, shirtless and with a bandage around his shoulder. He has to go back next week because halfway through he was squirming and moaning so much they had to stop. I didn't say a word.

We stayed up to see Bloody Portillo lose his seat, although I was the only one of us who celebrated his losing his seat by punching the air and shouting 'Take that, Rychard.' I went to the shops this morning to get stuff for breakfast, but failed to spot mass jubilation, new era of hope, milkman whistling Oasis tunes, etc. So far Blair's Britain doesn't seem too different from Major's Britain. But after eighteen years of Tory misrule, you can't expect change overnight.

Sunday, 4th May. After I'd finished my tasks yesterday we went to Hampton Court Maze. We got lost, which I suppose is part of the point. But for three hours? A man on a ladder gave us directions out shortly before hypothermia set in. Still it gave us a chance to have some uninterrupted time together.

>*Me:* I'm pretty sure it's this way.
>*Caroline:* Are you sure we haven't been here before?
>*Me:* Sure I'm sure. Pretty sure. Probably.

Caroline: Well, I trust you. I'm putting myself in your hands. Just like on the boat, or when you said you were moving to Buxdon and it wouldn't affect our relationship.

Me (seeing as we've come to a dead end): Actually this may not be the right way.

Caroline: Do you think we should go back and retrace our steps?

Me: I think we may already be doing that.

I sometimes wish our relationship wasn't so relentlessly metaphorical.

On our way back from the tube to the flat the kids from the scary estate asked us if we wanted to buy a dog. I said we definitely didn't. For some reason, this makes me a puddlejumper. Whatever that is. I wonder if it's better or worse than being a munzie. Caroline pointed out that the kids didn't even have a dog with them. 'You give us the money and we'll bring you the dog,' the largest kid explained. 'Well, that sounds like an excellent deal,' I said loftily, apparently under the impression I was addressing a meeting of the Noel Coward Appreciation Society. As it happened, they weren't fans of arch irony, and informed me so. 'What kind of dog is it?' asked Caroline. 'Whatever kind you want.'

Frank's bandage has come off. He explained we have to bear in mind that it's a work in progress. At this stage Frank has 'Sig 4 Eve' written on one shoulder blade. HA HA HA.

Monday, 5th May. The police cars had gone by the time I got to Buxdon yesterday, and so had Ellis. I caught up with all the excitement from Barry Taylor. Someone had come forward over the weekend to tell the Headmaster that they saw Ellis fleeing the scene of the crime. Although his face and hair were hidden, Ellis had seemingly forgotten that his school scarf has a name-tag sown into it, which meant that his identity was written upside-down across the back of his head. Fortunately the police are not going to press charges, since he has agreed to restock the staffroom and reveal the location of his hidden cache of sweets. He is strenuously denying being the Beast of Buxdon. He is also refusing to reveal where he got the starting pistol, thank God.

Tom Downing is being predictably insufferable about having raised £57 at the Slave Auction. That's more than the collection at Brimscombe's funeral, he pointed out. He's downplaying the fact that the boys who bought him insisted on him running around and around the park while they shouted at with him with megaphones, before making him clean out the boathouse.

When I asked Barry Taylor how the last couple of days went, he merely smiled. When I added that spending one's weekend weatherproofing a shed for Mrs O. Digby wasn't everyone's idea of a good time, he merely smiled. 'Is that what she told you she bought me for? Well, if you want to believe that, you can.' He's right: I can and I do. He didn't find out what the O stands for.

Lucy has agreed to defer her period of slavery until next weekend, and she's given him a long list of terms and conditions regarding it. A very long list. I don't really blame her. Among other things, Lucy's flat-out refusing to wear a toga and feed him grapes all weekend.

Things would be very bleak indeed, except that I got a call from Selina Cowl saying she 'devoured' the rest of the book and can't wait to get it out to potential publishers. Let's hope they're hungry too! God, I wish I hadn't said that to Selina. I also wish people would stop walking behind me and whistling 'Who Will Buy?' as I make my way around the school.

Tuesday, 6th May. We had a special meeting for the Upper

Sixth before lessons, to set straight some of the rumours flying around the school. We were assured that Ellis had gone quietly, as opposed to holing up in the Lower School Common Room with a human shield of First Years. There is apparently also no truth in the rumours that he was the front-man for a larger cartel. Tipton was sent outside for asking if the Milky Bar Kid had a hand in the arrest. As the Upper Sixth are on revision leave from the beginning of half-term, Ellis will probably be suspended until then and allowed back to take exams. Although he won't be allowed to wear his school uniform. I don't know if he formally has to hand it back or whatever. His scarf at least will probably be kept as evidence.

The Beast of Buxdon was obviously a little riled at being upstaged. At about three o'clock today it was confirmed that the smell lingering around the geography block was neither machismo nor the school kitchens, but an attractively garnished crap sandwich someone had left on one of the desks. I hesitate to call him a poet, but the Beast does seem to have stumbled upon the perfect metaphor for geography A Level.

Wednesday, 7th May. The boys seemed about as thrilled as I'd expected to receive their copies of *Sir Gawain and the Green Knight*: 'Is this a kid's book?' 'You can tell us straight, Sir. Are we the remedial set?' 'It looks like *Dungeons and Dragons*.' 'There's no way I'm reading this on the bus.' 'Sir, it's not even in English.' 'I think they've bished the printing on this one.' 'This guy can't even spell. No wonder he wanted to stay anonymous.' I explained that it's in Middle English. 'Oh God, it's a poem.' 'But it doesn't even rhyme. I don't think.' That's because it's in alliterative verse. 'You mean it's from before they'd even invented rhyming?' More or less. Still, it's short and someone gets their head chopped off. 'Like *Highlander*?' A bit like that, yes. 'What's all this crap about the design on Sir Gawain's shield? It goes on for *pages*.' 'Why do we have to read this, Sir?' Because it's on the syllabus and because it's good for you. 'Who does your hair, Sir? Is it the council?' Right, books open and let's crack on.

Ellis was allowed back into school to collect some books this afternoon and he came to see me. We discussed revision schedules and exam technique, but before he left I couldn't resist asking why he'd done it. He looked at me sadly. 'I didn't want to be one of those kids from school that no one remembers.' I think we can safely say he's guaranteed that.

Caroline spoke to Morgan today, who mentioned that Alicia and Woggy's engagement is off. Woggy found Alicia on top of Peveril House. Who, it turns out, is definitely a person. Caroline hasn't heard all the details yet, but she's meeting up with Morgan for a drink tomorrow night.

Thursday, 8th May. Barry Taylor is very excited about the prospect of having Lucy as his slave for the weekend. He's taking her out to Chopstix on Friday; then on Saturday they're going to the Meadows to fly a kite. He's not sure what they'll be up to on Sunday. I don't think he's quite got the hang of the slave idea. I'm not sure Lucy is looking forward to the weekend quite so expectantly. Barry's been reminding her all week that she has to do whatever he wants. Lucy has been assiduous in clarifying that she doesn't and won't. Barry came over to show me the new suit he's bought to take her out in. 'I look pretty sharp, yeah?' He looks like the accused.

Barry let me borrow a couple of Brimscombe's diaries, since I keep reading them over at his. I do find them strangely soothing. Brimscombe records each time he starts a new toothbrush. It's a shame I know how it all ends.

Friday, 9th May. Dinner tonight with Caroline, Sig, Frank and Anya who makes curtains. Anya and Sig were having a disturbingly serious conversation about whether we wanted to show solidarity by having Tibetan flag curtains. She's making them herself and selling them at rallies and marches. I think the oppression of the Tibetan people is a tragedy and it's a scandal that the international political community hasn't done more to intervene. But I really don't see how Tibetan flag curtains will help. Her ambitions don't stop at curtains, though. Anya's a nice girl. And she's right, we've never experienced the horror of living under a tyrannical foreign regime and we have a global responsibility to stand up for those who do. I'll sign petitions, I'll write to my MP. But the idea that making a giant quilt in Trafalgar Square is going to have an impact on Chinese foreign policy seems to me a little bit naïve. Even if the Beastie Boys do help out. I raised this point, politely, and they all looked at me like I'd proposed knitting winter socks for the Chinese Army. Including Frank, who up until a few months ago thought wearing a T-shirt with a picture of Chairman Mao smoking a spliff on it was a genuine political intervention.

We started talking about the elections, and Anya told us she didn't vote. 'They're all as bad as each other, aren't they.' Yes, there are problems with our democratic process. But I'd still place more faith in an admittedly flawed system than in quilting for a brighter tomorrow.

I was reading Brimscombe's diaries on the train here. I'm up to 1989 now, and winds of change are blowing through the corridors of Buxdon. I just got to the bit where Brimscombe buys a birthday card for his sister and watches the fall of the Berlin Wall on TV.

Saturday, 10th May. It was a nice day, so Caroline and I went to the park. To my relief, we didn't bump into the scary kids on the way. Lovable little scamps. Probably out scrumping for alcopops or stealing someone's dog.

We got ice creams from a stall near the bandstand, and Caroline did that thing of jogging my arm so I got ice cream on my nose. Then we went rowing and I playfully splashed her with an oar. We wandered over to Round Pond and had the usual jokey disagreement about that misunderstanding on our first date. Caroline added that she was also a little surprised at the time that I'd brought three bottles of wine and no bottle opener.

As we were walking back Caroline gave me the full story on the Alicia/Woggy break-up. What I hadn't realised was that not only was Alicia having a thing with Peveril House, Woggy was having a thing with Miffy Spender, who I don't think I've met. Miffy is Tink Weevil's cousin, and was engaged to Jaques Gadzookis, but only for a bit, ages ago. It all came out when they turned out to be staying at adjacent ski lodges in Serre Chevalier. After that it all gets a bit complicated.

I also finally got to the bottom of why they call him Woggy. It's because when he was a child he couldn't pronounce Roger. It's like Chinky Hamilton, who's actually Charles Nicholas Hamilton, and not like Bunjy Yip, who's actually Benjamin. It doesn't explain Tink, Squiffy, Peveril, Bartlett, Miffy, Bohemond or Jaques, but then what does? Still, what's in a name? They'll all be up against the wall with Guy when the revolution comes. If it ever comes. On further considera-tion I'll probably be facing the brickwork too.

Sunday, 11th May. The big news of the day was that Caroline's brother Toby has got engaged. To simplify matters he's got engaged to his girlfriend Hannah, rather than to Alicia or Tink Weevil. There's an Appleby gathering next weekend to mark the announcement. I've already asked the headmaster for leave next Friday, to go up for the job interview in London. I'm going to pick up Caroline from work afterwards and we can go down to the Applebys' together. I told the headmaster I needed the time off for a doctor's appointment, obviously.

Sig and Frank spent the morning putting up the flat's new Tibetan flag curtains. It's showing solidarity all right, but I'm not sure how many oppressed Tibetan peasants are going to see them, or quite what their feelings on the matter would be if they did. There is no news yet of how Beijing has responded to Anya's savagely incisive political interior decorating. And Caroline owes Sig fifteen quid. For some reason they're actually paying above market price on the curtains.

Frank had his tattoo finished this week, and it actually looks quite good. Although since it's on his shoulder blade he can't see it. I spent a little while trying to convince him that the tattoo reads 'Kick Me', but he didn't go for it.

Monday, 12th May. The Brimscombe diaries have turned to hold the clue to two apparently unrelated mysteries that turn out to be linked. You'd have thought I've watched enough Miss Marples to see that coming. I turned in early with 1991 last night, and discovered that a band who all went to Buxdon about ten years ago have since become massive in Japan. I mean really massive. They have their own range of pocket tissues and there's a comic book about them. They also have a song about the Headmaster called 'Fool in a Cape'. Their lead singer? One Billy Green. The band as a whole are called The Billy Green Preservation Society, which perhaps explains why they haven't achieved greater recognition over here.

In September 1991, at the time of The Billy Green Preservation Society's one UK Top 40 hit (*The Coalescence* EP, which reached number 39 for a week after heavy rotation from John Peel), Billy Green wrote to thank Brimscombe for always supporting and encouraging him at school. So I guess some people do get to achieve their dreams, which is good to hear. Having said that, to record an EP that sounds like a meltier version of Slowdive and release it the same month as *Nevermind* has never been a particular dream of mine.

If you look them up online, as I did this morning, there are loads of websites in Japanese about them. One of them has a picture of me on it, standing in front of the school with two

Japanese teenagers and looking really uncomfortable. What remains a mystery is why Billy Green's name is written in all the school textbooks, and where those textbooks are vanishing to. I have my suspicions.

Barry Taylor seems pleased with how his weekend went. He helped Lucy with the gardening yesterday afternoon, which doesn't seem to me quite in fitting with the pair's supposed master-slave dialectic. I asked him what his next move will be. I don't imagine the Headmaster will go for a fundraising kissathon.

Tuesday, 13th May. Caroline pointed out on the phone that things are going to be a bit crowded at the Applebys' this weekend, what with us and Toby and Hannah and Lulu all there. I'm supposed to share a bed with Toby. Toby? The man's a trained killer. If I accidentally roll over and brush against him he'll probably strangle me without even waking up. He'll probably spend the whole night having a conversation in his sleep with 'Bad Toby' who speaks in a spooky deep voice. Caroline's sharing a bed with Lulu, which she's not too thrilled about either. God, what if Toby secretly sleepwalks nude as well? I might wake up and he's sitting by the side of the bed with nothing on but his regimental cap, field-stripping a rifle or prancing around with a sabre.

Apart from these admittedly unlikely possibilities, there is the more practical problem of sharing a bed with someone else when the person I'm used to shacking up with is my girlfriend. I might start nuzzling him in the night. I might mistake him for Caroline in a very bad light. I know Toby quite well, but not well enough to laugh off a spot of unconscious nocturnal grinding.

At least I'm not bedding down with the dogs. I hope Toby wears PJs. Old Sleepy does, and very stupid they look too.

*

Wednesday, 14th May. I had lunch with Lucy Salmon, and she filled me in on some of the details Barry left out in his account of their weekend. He failed to mention: using his chopsticks to make comedy fangs in Chopstix; almost flying his kite into an electricity pylon; getting in a shouting match with some ten-year-olds who called his kite 'gay', and then sulking about it for the rest of the day; repeatedly asking Lucy if she wanted to see his appendectomy scar (she didn't); and trying to impress her with a series of amazing facts of the kind that you find on beer mats. She wishes he would relax and just be himself. I didn't have the heart to tell her I'm afraid he is. Lunch itself was unremarkable, which was a marked improvement on the usual fare.

Thursday, 15th May. I reminded the boys in my tutor group to fill in their appointment cards for the Parent's Evening next week. My attempts to get a discussion about the election going didn't really get anywhere. Although Iles informed us that he feels betrayed and disappointed by Tony Blair.

I see from the appointment cards that I have fifteen minutes to report on the progress of each of my English students this year. One wonders, in the cases of Norrington and Monk, how I will possibly fill that amount of time. Except by going through their attendance record in great detail. Physically, Monk hasn't missed a single class. His only contributions to our discussions, however, have come out of his nose in bloody clots. I'm not looking forward to my chats with Ellis's parents or the Tiptons much either.

Friday, 16th May. I think the interview went well today. Will Otway was sitting in and although he raised an eyebrow at some of the claims on my CV, he didn't leap up and denounce me. I think he was preoccupied by my hair. Contrary to the usual laws of physics it's actually looking worse as it grows out. The main interviewer asked why I wanted to leave my current post and I said I felt ready for a change and a different challenge, rather than the fuller and more vitriolic answer I was capable of. And I had a host of things to say when they asked me to describe some unusual or unexpected situations that I've found myself in as a teacher. We had a tour of the school and they said they'd let me know their decision in due course.

Will Otway got eighty-six Valentine's cards this year.

Went up to Caroline's work to collect her and found her having what looked like a very serious talk with Rychard, in his office, with the door closed. He is her boss, I suppose. But she did seem a bit rattled when I turned up. I'm surprised they weren't overcome by the aftershave fumes. Thank God he's going to be out of here at the end of the month. He's invited me along to his leaving party and I said I'd be delighted to come. Oh yeah, I'll be celebrating all right. I'm on the train with Caroline now. She was reading one of the Brimscombe diaries, but I think she's fallen asleep. I should probably get some shut eye now as well so that I'm fully rested for tonight.

Saturday, 17th May. Pretty tired today, as I insisted on playing board games into the early hours of the morning. At about two a.m. I suggested a game of *Monopoly*. 'But that takes for ever,' Caroline said. Exactly.

In the end it was all right sharing a bed with Toby. Although he did steal all the covers and was snoring directly into the back of my head. So in reality it wasn't all right at all. I just bore in mind, all through a sleepless and seemingly endless night, that it could have been a lot worse. Just as dawn was creeping under the curtains, Toby asked me if I was awake. After some frantic consideration of my options, I confirmed I was.

Toby: Matt, I consider you a friend.

Me (mentally): Really? What on earth has led you to consider that, you freak? The fact that I'm boffing your sister?

Me (in actuality): Yeah, we're mates.

Toby: Do you think I'm doing the right thing getting married?

Oh God, that's a lot of responsibility to put on a person. I told myself to relax; he wouldn't want it in writing.

Me: Do you love her?

Toby: Yes, I think so. But what does that really mean? Does it mean I like Hannah a lot? Yes it does. Does it mean I want to have children with her? I think so ...

There was a lot more of this sort of stuff. By now I was more or less resigned to the inevitable hand on my thigh, but it never came. Toby was still talking, and I tuned back in.

Toby: So do you think I should marry her?

Me: Probably. Why not, eh?

I was quite relieved. I thought for a terrible moment he was going to ask me to be his best man.

This morning Caroline, Lulu and I were dispatched to the village for sausages. The butcher certainly seemed please to see us. He told Caroline he's building an extension to his house. Presumably to be known in future as the Appleby Wing. We bought sausages. A lot of sausages. If, perish the thought, the house had caught fire this afternoon and we had to escape from an attic window, we could quite easily have managed it on the string of Cumberlands we bought. Come to think of it, by the time we got to the bottom they probably would have been done. The butcher and Lulu had a professional conversation about whether ostrich sausages were a going concern. Neither seemed taken with the idea of 'Saustriches' as a brand name. The butcher wrapped the Cumberlands for us, into a package about the size of an infant. I'd been hoping he would just let me carry them home wrapped around me like a bandolier.

Lulu thinks that BSE is the best thing that has ever happened to the ostrich meat industry. There must be a mad cow joke in there somewhere.

Over lunch, Lulu opined that there's something very human about ostriches. She's wrong, so very wrong, but it kept the conversation going. I think she is confusing ostriches with Big Bird. I think I'm finally getting the hang of conversing with the Applebys. It turns out that it really doesn't matter what you say, as long as you say it with mad-eyed confidence and your mouth full.

Toby and Hannah are looking for places to live near Hannah's folks in Wiltshire. Mrs Appleby seems pleased at news of the engagement, although since Hannah will be living much further away she'll be gaining a daughter-in-law but losing a skivvy. They're getting married next year at the Applebys' local church, so I guess the vicar has forgiven Mrs Appleby for calling him a twat. Or maybe he's just afraid of her. Caroline once told me that when she was seven her ballet teacher told me her she had bandy legs, and she went home crying. I bet he still wonders who knocked his wing mirror off in the car park at Waitrose.

'Who will be next up the aisle, I wonder?' asked Mrs A, looking around the table. Although mostly at me and Caroline.

Sunday, 18th May. We all got up early and took the dogs for a walk by the river. Mr Sniffles seems to be recovering well from his operation. He disappeared off into the bushes briefly and returned with his jaws around a very angry swan. Lulu was delighted, until I pointed out that we could all be hanged for treason. Fortunately the swan escaped. I'm sure Lulu already had big plans for how to cook it.

When we got back to the house we sat around with the papers for a bit, but I found myself too full to read much. I did skim a very depressing article about something the French call 'deformation professionelle'. It's the phenomenon where you change your personality to fit your job, and explains why I spent the weekend using my teaching voice whenever I was asked a question as well as why I just told a room full of dogs to 'settle, now, settle' as I walked in. I really think they could afford to dumb the Young Telegraph down a bit.

Lulu has been reading the sample chapters I gave Toby, and she says she is enjoying it so far. Though she did seem surprised to learn it's set in Japan. In fact, I imagine the inside of Lulu's head as somewhat like Japan. It's full of little people running around talking in a language we can't understand. It's all very polite and well-regulated, but every so often you turn a corner and come across something that just flat out baffles you. Still, I'm glad Lulu likes the book. She also thinks my new haircut is an improvement.

Monday, 19th May. Close call today. The headmaster appeared out of nowhere in the Lower School corridor.

'Everything all right with you, Mr Bletch?'

'Fine [*nervous chuckle*]. Why wouldn't it be?'

'So things went well on Friday?'

My brain spent the next twenty seconds whirring in a frantic attempt to work out how the headmaster could possibly know about my interview. Of course, I thought, he probably knows the head at Lady Jane Grey from the Headmasters' Conference. They probably rang him up to find out more about my kayaking or interest in directing nudie theatre. Eventually the penny dropped.

'Oh, you mean at the doctor's. Yes, everything's fine. Just a check-up. All systems fully operational.'

'Very glad to hear it. Look forward to seeing you at the fundraising barbecue this weekend.'

The barbecue is Johnno McPhee's idea, obviously. I suppose it's too late now to suddenly fake a life-threatening illness. I'll have to hope for torrential rain instead.

Much discussion in the staffroom of what the best policy is for the Parents' Evening on Thursday. Mostly people have just been exchanging information about who the various names on their appointments cards that they don't recognise belong to. Lucy Salmon and I spent most of lunch break putting our heads together to try and think of anything remarkable about Norrington. We can't both tell his parents we think he has a tendency to hide his light under a bushel. (Translation: 'I don't know who the hell your son is, but I can't be absolutely certain he's as pointless as he appears'). The headmaster popped up again to remind us all to mention the Auditorium and Drama Lab Fund barbecue. I think they could have come up with a catchier title.

Lucy gave me some handy tips and pointers. She says I can use her old standby: 'First, let me ask *you* how you would describe your son's progress this term.' Even if the answer doesn't jog any memories, it gives you time to manoeuvre. If you're still struggling, the line 'What chiefly concerns me is the spiritual side of your son's development' usually works. Most parents can't get out of there quick enough.

Seen from this perspective, it puts my own old school reports in a whole different light. For all these years I thought the phrase 'We're all waiting expectantly for Matthew to show us what he can do' was a compliment. Turns out it just meant 'Matthew Bletch? Doesn't he have a sporty brother? Which of my sets is he in, again?' When it comes to Monk and Norrington's parents I'll avoid the phrase 'waiting to see what your son can do'. I've seen what they can do, the answers being 'shoot blood out of his nose' and 'sleep with his eyes open', respectively.

We've all chipped in for a bottle of sparkling wine, to be presented at the end of the evening to the member of staff who manages the slyest piece of honesty or most backhanded compliment.

Tuesday, 20 May. I didn't realise Toby was going to mention our discussion on Friday night to Caroline, Mrs Appleby and Hannah. None of whom are particularly impressed with me. Caroline asked if Toby had talked to me about getting married. I confirmed that he had. In fact I don't know why she asked me that, because she already knew the answer: 'You told him "Why not?" Was that genuinely the only thing you could think of to say?' Yes, yes it was actually. It seemed like a decent enough answer at the time.

Toby has asked Roland Rawlinson from school to be his best man. The same Roland Rawlinson, it turns out, who knows Miranda: he of the giant cycling legs. To my disgust, outrage and horror, Caroline actually used to fancy him. I wonder if Frank or Dom will ask me to be their best man. I somehow doubt it. But if Frank asks Dodgy Geoff instead of me, I'll be very hurt.

Wednesday, 21st May. Barry told me I look tired and stressed, and asked if I wanted an eye massage. A what? It all started when I came across him in the staffroom at lunch, rubbing his eyes. I thought at first he was crying, but he wasn't. When I say rubbing his eyes, I mean it literally. He had his fingers dug into his sockets and was massaging his eyeballs. He read about it on the internet and gives them to himself all the time. It's supposedly incredibly relaxing, but I decided to pass on the opportunity.

I've been feeling a bit anxious and paranoid ever since reading about '*deformation professionelle*' at the weekend. Has being at Buxdon changed me? Am I becoming teacherised? I reminded a class today that the bell is a signal to me that the lesson's over, not a sign for everyone to start making a hullabaloo. I even used the word 'hullabaloo'. Great, I'm not only becoming a teacher, I'm becoming a teacher from an Ealing Comedy. Next thing you know I'll be shaking my fist at people who cheek me and cycling around on a bike with a basket.

Thursday, 22nd May. Judging from the fact there was an ambulance outside the Old Building at mid-morning break, I guessed that Lucy had agreed to let Barry Taylor give her an eye massage. She turned up at the Parents' Evening wearing an eye patch. She didn't look particularly relaxed, either.

The Parents' Evening itself went off reasonably smoothly, although Norrington's mother demanded to know how according to her son's report card he's putting in 5/5 for effort, but only getting 1/5 for achievement. It's a mystery to me, too. Perhaps he's very thick. Norrington also seems to be on a one-boy mission to disprove the old fallacy that if you don't wash your hair for long enough it cleans itself.

I had a very long conversation with Chivers' parents about the number and variety of limbs he's managed to break this year. 'We don't believe in wrapping boys in cotton wool,' they told me. Perhaps they shouldn't dismiss that idea out of hand, because Chivers managed to fracture three fingers yesterday playing ping pong in one of the houserooms. The cast should be coming off by the start of exams. If he does well in his A levels they've promised him a mountain bike. I hope he's applied to universities with decent wheelchair access.

Awkward reunion with the Tiptons. Not least since I presented them with an invoice for thirty copies of the *Selected Poems* of John Keats. At the end of our English class today Tipton spotted some Japanese teenagers wandering down the drive looking for the site of the Billy Green Preservation

Society's first rehearsals, and got up to dash after them. As he did so he stumbled over Monk, tripped, dropped his bag, and scattered five copies of Keats over the classroom floor. All signed, allegedly, by Billy Green. 'I don't suppose you'd believe I'm just really into Romantic poetry at the moment, Sir?' No, I wouldn't. I spoke to Dr Cumnor about it this afternoon and he admitted that although they've had problem with graffiti before, this is the first time Buxdon has seen a black market trade in school textbooks. Mr and Mrs Tipton took it relatively gracefully. Mr Tipton has no problem replacing the books that have already been sold, but was initially reluctant to stump up for the rest, since their market value has been significantly increased. 'What's wrong with a bit of initiative?' I don't have a problem with initiative, but felt compelled to point out that as well as theft and defacement of school property, he's also technically been committing fraud.

I have an awful feeling that I got two of my Third Years mixed up.

No chance of not remembering who Ellis is, though. Both his parents came and spent the evening apologising to anyone who came within range. I made a valiant attempt to discuss their son's progress this year without mentioning his foray into armed robbery. It was a bit of an elephant in the room, though.

Mr Bagley and his son have reached a compromise. Bagley is off to college in September, but he's working at the stables near Little Chipping in the holidays. They've been discussing it for weeks and eventually Mr Bagley brought him round to see that was the most sensible thing to do. If he graduates he's getting a horse. What did I get when I graduated? A pair of Dad's old cufflinks.

Iles is having a gap year and reapplying to Oxbridge next year. His parents have excellent hair too.

There was no sign of Marcus Lau's parents.

Lucy Salmon was awarded the bottle of sparkling wine

for best comment of the evening. She has Monk for religious studies and told his parents that their son reminded her a little of God. One sometimes feels his presence, but no one can persuade him to speak.

Friday, 23rd May. Cooked dinner for Caroline last night, then Barry Taylor came over and we watched *World's Scariest Parasites* on Channel Five. Barry told us that the longest tapeworm ever found in a human being was 1.2 metres in length. If that's the kind of amazing fact he's been wooing Lucy Salmon with, I'm not surprised he still hasn't got anywhere. He offered Caroline an eye massage but I warned her against it.

I'm not in an entirely good mood with Barry at the moment. I asked the tutor group earlier today if they had any questions or anxieties about revision leave. Hallbrick produced the most amazing revision schedule I've ever seen. It was about two foot across and all the colours of the rainbow. I expect it took him about three days to finish. Then Tipton put his hand up.

Me: Yes, Sam, you have a question?
Tipton: Yes, Sir. I was just wondering if you could tell us all how you got the nickname Mister Goblin?
Me: OK, I said *revision-related* questions ...

Is there anyone left at Buxdon who doesn't know about that? I wish there was something equally embarrassing I could spread about Barry. I suppose I could tell people he secretly wants to punch a carp, but the downside to that would be that it's so weird people would assume I was making it up. And that I'm having a nervous breakdown.

Barry showed us a timetable of his own after the parasite programme was over, a school calendar on which he has marked the remaining opportunities this year for him to put the moves on Lucy Salmon. These include co-invigilating an exam, which seems a bit optimistic. Mildly more likely opportunities are Johnno McPhee's charity barbecue tomorrow, the Open Day and the June Ball. He asked for Caroline's advice, and she suggested coming in on her blind side.

Saturday, 24th May. The great Johnno McPhee Fundraising Barbecue was held today, despite the rain. Lucy offered to share her umbrella with us. Johnno was cooking under a suspended sheet of blue plastic, which I personally considered something of a fire risk. I was also a bit worried because due to the smoke, he was cooking wearing swimming goggles. Caroline was more worried about food poisoning. In retrospect I regret having watching that parasite documentary with her on Friday. Being under the umbrella meant that we were in a prime position to witness Barry Taylor's latest desperate attempts at seducing Lucy.

Lucy: Did you really think I'd fancy you because you can fit five frankfurters in your mouth at once?
Barry: Urrrgh ... Arrrgh
Caroline: Barry, are you choking? Do you need some help?

At least Lucy's eye patch has come off now.

The Trotters turned up as well, with baby Trotter in tow. It really does have eyes like angry Smarties. They offered it to Lucy to hold. 'Thanks, but I don't think I could eat a whole one. It isn't even cooked.' Later, Lucy mentioned to Caroline that Barry Taylor kisses like someone giving CPR. He also thinks that the singular of spaghetti is spaghetto. Barry is still optimistic about his chances with Lucy. He thinks she's starting to soften towards him. I hope so, but I'm not optimistic. Pandas have got together in less time than those two.

The barbecue raised about £12.50 and by the end of it

three Sixth Formers seemed to be coming down with pneumonia, the sheet of blue plastic had blown off across Upper Field and got stuck in a tree, and Barry said his stomach was feeling a bit gyppy. I'm so glad he no longer lives next door to me.

Sunday, 25th May. We went to the Buxdon Museum this afternoon. There was a special exhibition about eighteenth-century seed drills, some of which could once have been seen in the fields around Buxdon. There was also a scale model of Buxdon Mill, made with matchsticks by a homesick Buxdonian in a prisoner-of-war camp in the 1940s and smuggled out piece by piece. There was no mention of how. Astonishingly, we were practically the only people in there.

I suggested to Caroline that if I get the job in London we could move in together. She didn't respond with quite the gusto I'd hoped for: 'Why not, eh?' Then she changed the subject. Not very subtly either: 'Oh look! Waxworks.'

Caroline has had people ringing on the doorbell all week asking where they can get curtains like that. If those curtains really do free Tibet I'm going to have such egg on my face.

Monday, 26th May. I may have accidentally passed the information about Barry's kissing technique on to Peter Wyndham and Tom Downing over coffee. 'But that's in the strictest confidence, OK?' That should have reached the tattooed dinner lady by midweek at the latest.

The headmaster's warned us all to be on high alert this week. Traditionally, the last week before revision leave starts, the Upper Sixth pull pranks: filling the school fountain with bubble bath, cling-wrapping people's cars, putting hats and scarves on the Old Building gargoyles, that sort of thing. Obviously it would be out of character if the Beast misses this opportunity to strike.

Rychard's leaving party is on Friday at a shots and sushi

place on Dean Street called Bar Satori. According to Frank, a few years ago Bar Satori was briefly and tastelessly called Bar Kamikaze, and used to serve pitchers of sake until midnight. He thinks he's been there, but can't be one hundred per cent certain.

Tuesday, 27th May. I had a call from Selina Cowl, my literary agent. She's feeling positive about the feedback so far. At least, no one has actually said they hate it yet. She's not sure about the current title, though. I've made up a list of alternatives for her:

- *Waiter, This Fish is Raw*
- *Why Not Visit Japan?* (Question mark optional)
- *How Many Commuters Can You Fit on a Train?*
- *Sendai Bloody Sendai*
- *Gas Panic in Roppongi: Understanding Japanese Culture*
- *The Chrysanthemum and the Disposable Umbrella*
- *The Japanese: What Are They Like?*
- *How to be a Complete Barbarian*

I have to face it, none of those sounds like a bestseller, which are usually called things like *A Map of Heaven* or *The Blind Harpsichord Maker's Daughter*.

Peter Wyndham was asking whether I've had a chance to think about living with him next year. No, but I have spent a lot of time avoiding thinking about it. He wants an answer by Friday, because he's got an alternative offer from Rudolph Fane.

Wednesday, 28th May. Barry grabbed me in the staffroom earlier to ask if I was the one who's been telling everyone he kisses like someone attempting mouth-to-mouth resuscitation. More or less, I confirmed. Although the rumour seems to have gained something in transmission. I heard the tattooed dinner lady telling one of her mates this afternoon that kissing Barry is like getting your tongue stuck in a washing machine.

Caroline had lunch with Morgan today, who seemed rather low. He had an awful blind date with a mate of Alicia's last week. Apparently she fell asleep. I commiserated and told him it was probably just a boring movie. They were in Belgo's. Morgan thinks Alicia could at least have mentioned she was setting him up on a blind date with a narcoleptic. He would have brought a pillow.

I asked Caroline if she was looking forward to Rychard's leaving party but she was a little subdued about it. Personally I can't wait. Rychard asked her to see if I have any advice about what food to order. I've suggested he takes a gamble on the blowfish.

Thursday, 29th May. I got the job! Will Otway rang to tell me personally. Even the fact that he did so in a variety of voices couldn't quell my excitement. I'm out of here at the end of next month. Farewell Buxdon, don't forget to write. Ran over to Barry's to borrow *Rock Anthems* and spent lunch break jumping around my room. I passed my sincere regrets on to Peter Wyndham and wished him the best of luck living with Rudolph Fane. I'm going to surprise Caroline with the news tomorrow night. Which is shaping up to be the best night ever.

Friday, 30th May. As it was the last tutor group meeting before revision leave, I sent my tutees off with what I hope was a rousing speech. It concluded with the words 'Give 'em hell, boys, and don't forget to check both sides of the paper.' Since about half the group are currently suspended, this was rather less stirring than it could have been. Chivers and Bagley have been sent home early for an end-of-school prank that went too far. They cling-wrapped Hallbrick. They did give him a plastic straw to breathe through.

That pales into insignificance, however, in relation to the rest of the day's events. The Beast of Buxdon has been caught. The man who caught him? One Matthew Bletch. 'Now there's something to add to the CV,' Tom Downing observed sniffily. I think he's jealous that I'm the man of the hour. He also looks something of a fool for hinting strongly all term that the Beast was either me or Barry Taylor.

It went down like this. I'd 'accidentally' left the register for the *Gawain and the Green Night* class in Mercer's Lodge, and was idling over there when I spotted the front door wide open and a light on in the kitchen. I came into the kitchen to turn the light off, and arrived just in time to save Peter Wyndham's cafetière from a dreadful fate. Although I for one won't be drinking real coffee for a very long time. The Beast himself? None other than young Tipton. Let's see you charm and bribe your way out of this one, Sam. He's been in the headmaster's office all afternoon, and two of the Tiptons' cars are in the car park.

Up to London now for Rychard's leaving do. Could things get any better today? What's that taste in my mouth? I do believe it's unconditional victory.

It tasteth sweet.

Saturday, 31st May. It turns out things couldn't get any better. But they could and did turn with astonishing rapidity to total crap. Oh, are things going right for Matthew Bletch, just for once? Here's a giant spoonful of gall and wormwood. There must have been some mix-up and I'm stuck with Frank's karma.

Bar Satori itself was all right. I was sitting between Caroline and Ferris from Accounts, with Rychard at the head of the table. Over the starters I was talking to the guy opposite me, who knew Rychard from college. Charlie was the guy's name, and his wife was there too. It eventually dawned on me why some of the stuff he was telling me seemed so familiar when I mentioned that I teach at Buxdon and he looked panicked. His wife's ears pricked up as well, and she looked like she was going to be reducing him to sashimi later. I must admit I wouldn't have recognised him from Lucy's description. She had somehow failed to mention his tiny eyes, unevenly balanced shoulders and weird whinnying laugh. Lucy did say he looks like a Greek god. She just didn't specify Hephaestos. Sadly, Tom Downing is the only person I know who'd find that joke amusing.

I asked Charlie what he does, and he claimed to work in 'money'. I nodded as if I had the faintest clue what that meant. As he referred several times to his Ferrari, I don't think he meant an Exchange Bureau. His wife didn't look like she knew either. Fair enough – I've never been exactly sure what Caroline does, although I know her job title and I'm sure she's damn good at it.

I was planning to surprise Caroline with my big news when we got home, so that it wouldn't detract from Rychard's send-off. The others left, and Rychard, Caroline and I got into a sake-drinking contest, one of those contests in which no one really wins. I ended up doing my Toshiro Mifune impression, which no one got. Understandably, as it's pretty bad. Caroline guessed Sean Connery.

I was more or less coming around to the opinion that Rychard's OK really. I guess that's a tribute to the awesome power of sake.

We were the last ones left in the whole place by midnight, and we decided to have one last drink. Rychard proposed a toast to the future.

'So, I bet you're going to miss Caroline.'

This weirded me out, mostly because I wasn't the one saying it. It's understandable I was confused. For a bizarre drunken instant I wondered whether Rychard and I had magically swapped bodies. Then I wondered why, if Caroline was dying, why she would have told Rychard before she told me. Then I wondered exactly what the stricken expression on Caroline's face meant.

'When she moves to Edinburgh at the end of the month. I finally managed to persuade Head Office that we're such a great team it would be madness to split us up.'

My own surprise fell a bit flat after that. She says she's been waiting for the right opportunity to tell me. I think it's fair to say she missed it. Oh Caroline, no.

No, no, go not to Leith. Particularly not with Rychard.

June

Andy Bucket
Lamprey Books
Landsdowne Mews
London W10

Dear Selina,

Thank you so much for thinking of us here at Lamprey Books as a home for Matthew Bletch's *Here Comes the Angry Ice-Cream Van, Singing Songs of War*. I instantly loved the book and everyone I've showed it to here has agreed with me. It's funny, fresh and insightful. I particularly liked Matthew's description of his legs falling asleep at a formal dinner. It gave me pins and needles myself! It really was a joy to read and it is sure to find an appreciative audience.

Unfortunately, here at Lamprey we are currently restructuring our list and these are not the most promising times for young authors. As you know, this is an uncertain time in the publishing industry generally and we are all having to tighten our belts somewhat. As a result, I'm afraid we will have to pass on Matthew's book at this time. I hope Matthew will not be too downcast, as we are all great fans of his writing. We have several important and exciting books coming out shortly, which we have high hopes for. Next month we are bringing out *What's The (Real) Story?*, a warts'n'all account of life on the road with Oasis by Bruce Cooper, one of their former roadies; in March we publish *No Pantomimes in June*, the memoirs of Philip Highgate, one of Britain's most successful child actors of the 1940s; and in August we publish *Midnight in Kerala*, the long-awaited anthology of uncollected pieces by the late Dame Aurelia van Prink. The success we anticipate for these titles should put us on a much sounder basis for considering new work in around six or eight months' time. If Matthew's book is still doing the rounds then, we would be in a stronger position to reconsider our decision.

Please don't hesitate to send us whatever Matthew writes next.

Best,
Andy

Monday, 2nd June. A verbal warning, that's all Tipton got. This from a headmaster who suspended one of the boarders for a week for turning up after half-term with a pierced ear. I don't think any further comment's required on the matter. Wyndham's spitting feathers.

I got a parcel together for Caroline today: *Grave Robbers: The Grisly True Story of Burke and Hare, The Life and Times of Deacon Brodie* (both from the Grassmarket Press) and *Sunshine on Leith: The Greatest Hits of The Proclaimers.* If that doesn't put her off moving to Edinburgh, nothing will.

Caroline says it's a great town, and that the move will be good for her career. We haven't really discussed yet what this will mean for us. Let's face it, it's hardly going to give our relationship a boost. Caroline admits this wasn't the way she'd envisaged breaking the news to me. I'm not sure what was. A call from the airport? 'Hi Matt, it's Caroline. Guess where I am? I'll give you a clue, it's the capital of Scotland.' I'm refusing to acknowledge any parallel with my move to Buxdon. I was grudgingly prepared to concede that our relationship has been drifting for some time. Caroline tells me she carefully weighed up the pros and cons, and in the end just thought: 'Why not, eh?' I told her I appreciate her honesty.

Selina forwarded me a letter from Andy Bucket of Lamprey

Books, which arrived this morning. I'm beginning to wonder whether when people express an interest in what I write in the future they're merely being polite. I also think the title could do with another trip to the drawing board.

Tuesday, 3rd June. A boy walked past me in the corridor today in the usual state of fashionable Buxdon disarray, and I found myself bellowing at him to tuck his shirt in and do up his top button. I also called him a 'scruffy oik'. It was surprisingly satisfying. Can't wait for the next person to give me an excuse to throw a piece of chalk at them. There are some advantages to working in the private sector. I've so far withstood the temptation to start shouting 'Run! Run in the corridors.'

I told Lucy Salmon that Caroline might be moving to Edinburgh. Lucy reckons that perhaps some time apart will give Caroline and me a chance to learn and grow. It's a brilliant city, she told me. There's loads of great nightlife, lots of culture and a really energising atmosphere. Lucy had a boyfriend who moved there once. What happened? Oh, they broke up. I should have sent Caroline a copy of *Trainspotting*. Lucy has a maiden aunt with a spare room in Morningside, if Caroline needs somewhere to stay while she's looking for a place of her own. I said I'd pass that on.

The headmaster asked me over lunch how I know what it's like to kiss Barry Taylor. He's heard it's like having a filling redone.

Frank rang me out of the blue this evening. He didn't even want to borrow any money or need bailing out of somewhere. Much to my astonishment and mild alarm he wants to meet up for a pint and a serious conversation on Friday. 'So I guess you heard about Caroline moving to Edinburgh at the end of the month?' 'What? No. I haven't seen Sig or Mum this week. That's massive news.' 'Yeah, I'm pretty shaken up.' 'So does that mean her room's going to be available?' I'm bloody glad there's a silver lining in this for someone.

*

Wednesday, 4th June. I told Caroline about the room in Morningside. It turns out Lucy's aunt is not the only one with a spare room. As if to deliberately add insult to injury, Rychard has offered to let Lucy stay at his new place for the first couple of weeks. I'm so furious I could split an infinitive.

Now I'm torn, as far as leaving presents go, between giving Caroline a nice warm scarf and giving her a can of mace. Even though it gets cold up there I reminded her that's no reason to let Rychard snuggle up in her bed if he comes knocking in the small hours. Caroline says she resents the implication that Rychard wants her in Edinburgh for her body rather than her professional competence. I don't mean to imply that Rychard doesn't think she is an efficient and talented colleague and wants her to transfer with him for excellent work-based reasons. I just can't shake the suspicion that he would also not be averse to rubbing her all over, first with baby oil, then with himself.

Caroline thanked me for the parcel.

Thursday, 5th June. Barry Taylor came over to Mercer's Lodge this evening to try to be encouraging. 'Cheer up, mate. It's not as if she's moving to another country.' He brought me a year of Brimscombe's diaries to take my mind off things. Thanks, Barry. As if it wasn't depressing enough to have lived through 1993 once already.

After Barry had left, Dom rang to remind me it's his book launch next weekend and to see if I'm OK. I suspect Mum put him up to it. He seemed slightly disappointed to hear I can make it to the book launch. Dom wanted to know if Caroline and I are going to try to keep it together. I certainly hope so. I asked what he thought I should do. 'Sometimes it's better just to have a clean break,' Dom noted, 'rather than just making each other miserable and waiting for things to inevitably fizzle out.' Thanks for that, Dom. Next time I ask for advice, why don't you just hit me in the face with a shovel?

Dom was surprised to hear that I'm meeting up with Frank tomorrow night, although he thinks it's long overdue that we try to work out some of our differences. I can't shake the suspicion Sig has had a hand in all this. Frank and I are meeting at a pub called The Signalman and Ghost, round the corner from Paddington. I'm really looking forward to telling him what a total bastard he is for a few hours. If all goes according to plan, we'll meet up at seven fifteen, be in the pub by half past, have a pint and some scampi-flavoured snacks, catch up on each other's latest news, and by about eight he'll have broken down, started weeping, and admitted that Dad did use to call me 'El Tigre'.

Friday, 6th June. We'd literally just sat down with our pints in The Signalman and Ghost when Frank's phone went off. 'Yeah,' he said. 'Yeah. No, nothing important. Sure. Definitely.' He hung up and told me Dodgy Geoff was up in town and was on his way to meet us. Geoff particularly wanted to talk to me, because he's thinking of training to be a teacher. I made my excuses and left.

Why does Frank of all people have a mobile phone? I've been racking my brains ever since to think of any kind of emergency in which Frank might be the person I desperately need to call.

'That was quick,' Sig said when I arrived at the flat. 'So have you and Frank sorted everything out then?' No, not really. Still pretty much estranged.

Frank did have time to tell me he's read the sample chapters of my book that Dom left at Mum's. I asked what he thought, then wished I hadn't bothered. 'Do you know what it reminded me of?' Frank asked, 'Well you know how the *Police Academy* sequels are a bit funny and a bit shit at the same time? That's what your book is like. Except that the

Police Academy films are a bit funny.' On a more encouraging note, it is his third favourite book he's ever read, after *The Lion, the Witch and the Wardrobe* and *Little Ducky's Big Day*. He wants me to ask my agent if she's thought of printing it in a bath-proof edition.

Frank did, however, have a thought about a title that would move some copies. He suggests calling it *Stephen King* and having that written in big gold letters on the front and spine. Rather than a pseudonym, he proposed publishing it under the name of someone I don't like very much.

Saturday, 7th June. I'm doing my very best to make this a weekend so amazing that Caroline literally can't bear to go to Edinburgh.

We went for a long lunch in the pub round the corner. A grown man with a ninnyish haircut was sitting at the table next to us, showing everyone his Star Wars figures. He got very cross when someone tried to take one of them out of its box. I had a pint of white Belgian lager which cost £7.50 and tasted a bit like washing-up liquid. After that we decided to go for a coffee. On the way the bank machine swallowed my cash card, then a barista with scarily-plucked eyebrows brought us both the wrong drinks. On the walk back to the house a bunch of kids threw a sparkler at me. Why on earth would Caroline want to live anywhere but London?

She's going to lend me some money so I can take her out for a nice dinner tonight.

Sunday, 8th June. I asked Caroline over starters what would happen if I put my foot down and forbade her to move to Edinburgh. 'Nothing.' 'You mean you wouldn't go?' 'No, I mean I would go.' 'Would you be moved by the gesture?' 'To laughter, perhaps.' I'm glad I raised it hypothetically first, then, although it might have been a bit more forceful if I'd just said it. Caroline says maybe the move to Edinburgh will give us both a chance to learn and grow.

The restaurant described its menu as 'Fusion', without specifying of what. More insult with injury, perhaps. I had some kind of fish with slices of tangerine on it. The waiter did warn us that 'some of the combinations are quite challenging'. Caroline had lobster with chocolate sauce. She'd seen the restaurant reviewed the week before, and apparently the head chef is quite well known. He's been on the telly. Doing what? Turning up in disguise and playing practical jokes on the public?

We both skipped the calf's tongue jelly and stinging nettle sorbet and went straight for the bill. Caroline settled up by cheque and I promised to pay her back. After that I spent ten minutes in the gents splashing water on my face and wondering whether I had enough change in my pockets to get back to Buxdon today.

Monday, 9th June. I think I've worked out why Frank has a mobile phone: to wind me up. He's been ringing me all day and getting me to guess where he is. He just did it again. If he really is hiding in my cupboard in a clown wig and holding an axe, I'm going to be surprised and upset. I doubt he is, though. For one thing I could hear running water in the background. That's millennia of human ingenuity, effort and painstaking technological advancement for you. What do you get? What has all that heroic struggle resulted in? Frank phoning me for no reason from the bath.

He decided not to introduce Sig to Dodgy Geoff at the weekend. In fact, Frank had to give him the slip after they'd had a few drinks. Geoff had decided to come up for a weekend in London, despite having nowhere to stay, no money, and no friends in the city apart from Frank. If Geoff doesn't get accepted for teacher training (which I pray God he doesn't, and which he surely won't be) he's decided that he should be on the telly. As Frank commented, there's not a weekly episode of *Crimewatch* that goes out without him expecting to see Geoff on it, fleeing up the hard shoulder with a road sign under his arm, or ramraiding a Costcutter in a milk float. I asked Frank why he still hangs out with him. 'He's a mate, isn't he.'

I'm very curious as to how Frank can even afford a phone. I bet Mum's giving him pocket money. That really annoys me. He's not going to learn the value of things that way. I hope she's at least making him do the lawn or take the bins out.

Why Frank is suddenly so keen to talk about our relationship is another question entirely.

Tuesday, 10th June. Miranda and Tom Downing came up to me in the staffroom to say they'd heard about Caroline and me, and to offer their commiserations. That I really didn't need. Downing had various things to say along the lines of pain being a useful emotion and how we should always try to take a lesson from experience. If one more person tells me to use this as a chance to learn and grow, I'm going to start kicking people. I also used this opportunity to clarify to Tom and Miranda that Caroline and I aren't 'having problems'. We're merely facing logistical difficulties. Miranda nodded sympathetically. 'Is it the sex?'

I spent most of the evening trying to think of brilliant ways to convince Caroline not to go. The best I could come up with was a compilation tape of dog-related songs ('Dogs Run Free', 'Hounds of Love', 'Black Dog', 'I Wanna Be Your Dog', 'Diamond Dogs', 'Dog on Wheels', 'Martha My Dear'). It's either that or sending her an ear.

I didn't put anything by the Dogs D'Amour or Slaughter and the Dogs on the tape, for reasons I assume are obvious.

Wednesday, 11th June. The sun came out today and it was moderately warm, which seems to have sent the entire nation insane. There was the compulsory news footage of people splashing around in the fountain in Trafalgar Square and warnings about skin cancer. Barry Taylor was wandering around in shorts and sandals, which I could have done without. Johnno McPhee appeared at lunchtime entirely slathered in sun block, with luminous yellow stripes on each eyebrow. By that point it was starting to cloud over.

I'm a bit unclear why Tipton Construction have been given the contract for the new auditorium and drama lab. I discovered this morning why the windows in the Sixth Form Centre – a previous Tipton project – have stickers on saying 'Do Not Open.' I was supervising a revision session and it was getting a bit stuffy, so I had a fiddle with one of the rather attractive porthole windows to try to let some air in. It opened all right. Unfortunately it then dropped off its frame, bounced off the side of the building and went rolling off towards Upper Field. I decided not to bother trying to work the skylight.

Thursday, 12th June. Woke up with a sunburned nose. Johnno not that sympathetic.

I got the latest Appleby update from Caroline. Mrs Appleby is on the warpath. Toby and Hannah were staying, along with Roland Rawlinson and of course Lulu. At some point over the weekend someone flushed one or more condoms down the loo, and now the septic tank is overflowing into Margery's vegetable garden. Mrs Appleby didn't say condoms, of course. She said 'rubber articles'. Caroline was puzzled at first, picturing gardening gloves and wellies.

Caroline asked Hannah what she thought about her moving to Edinburgh. Hannah replied: 'Why not, eh?' She's presumably still cross with me about that, then.

Spoke to Mum, who's looking forward to Dom's book launch on Saturday. I wish I could muster the same enthusiasm. Mum asked how things are going with Caroline and I told her we're looking at this as a chance to learn and grow. Mum didn't seem convinced: 'Is it the sex?'

Friday, 13th June. Needless to say the tape didn't work. I knew I should have sent an ear. Although if Caroline doesn't think I'm much of an emotional investment with two ears, I doubt she'd go for me with one ear and a bloodied nubbin. I could send her someone else's ear.

Rychard's been showing Caroline pictures of his flat. Or 'their' flat as she referred to it once before seeing my reaction. It's got a split-floor living area, two double bedrooms, both with en suite bathrooms, study, recently refurbished kitchen, balcony, dining room that seats twelve, entrance hall with period features, secure parking, access to a private garden, and it's two minutes from the Royal Mile. Well I hope they both like bagpipers and mime artists, because come the summer they won't be able to step out their front door for them. The total rent is slightly less than Caroline and Sig are each paying at the moment. Caroline says the flat will be perfect if I come up to see her for Hogmanay. They'll have a great view of the fireworks from their balcony. I sincerely hope Rychard gets one in the eye. I said I'd rather been hoping to see her before then. I also thought living with Rychard was meant to be a temporary arrangement.

I reminded Caroline about Dom's book launch but she's made plans to meet up with Morgan. Unlike some people he's been really encouraging and understanding about her going. Yes, and come to think of it I bet he sent her that Valentine's card too.

Saturday, 14th June. Guess who turned up on *Top of the Pops* last night? The Billy Green Preservation Society. Caroline was considerably less excited about this than I was. I wouldn't have realised it was even them if I hadn't looked them up on the internet the other day. They've changed their name (to 'Pacino') and they've gone for a new sound and look too. Instead of baggy long-sleeve T-shirts, floppy fringes and

FX-laden guitar epics, they were jumping around onstage in charity-shop suits and performing a chirpy singalong about Michael Caine. I think it was called 'Get Carter'. From the fixed desperation in their faces, even they know they've missed the boat by about eighteen months. Britpop went thataway, lads.

I spoke to Caroline today about different options by which I could move to Edinburgh, but she wasn't especially encouraging. Even when I said I wouldn't find it a slur on my masculine dignity if I was the one who stayed at home and wrote while she supported me. I could sleep in the box room. I offered to do all the shopping and everything. She's asked me to stop referring to it as Rychard 'carrying her off'.

Sunday, 15th June. Caroline's sorting through some stuff, and I'm writing this in bed. She has accused me of being sulky. I can't think why. She's just reminded me it's Lulu's birthday next Saturday. Almost certainly our penultimate weekend together for months and we have to spend half of it with birdbrain.

Selected fragments of conversation from Dom's launch party (for *Masculinity in Crisis/Crisis in Masculinity*. 192pp. Parnassus Press. £27.95): 'His novels are very ordinary, but his interviews are brilliant' ... 'He has a problem with Thursdays' ... 'They're a very civilised couple. They argue a lot, but they do it in French' ... 'When I say North Oxford I don't mean Headington, do you know what I mean?' ... 'When I went into the viva they told me, "You should be examining us." So I did' ... 'It is from Hampstead Bazaar, since you ask' ...'I don't know what you mean, actually' ...

Expert comparison has concluded that the English Department's wine is slightly less tasty than Buxdon's. The red was like fermented Ribena, the white like paint stripper. Since we were next door to his office, Dom took the opportunity to formally return Frank's box of rubbish. Frank seem delighted to be reunited with his engraved tankard, and was wandering around for a while wearing a hat with the slogan 'Ski Instructors Do It With Their Feet Together' until Sig made him take it off.

Mum says I look tired and peaky. She's right. I have great blue saddlebags under my eyes. I've not been sleeping well. I got a few hours last night before I had a nightmare and my own pounding heart shook me awake. She did tell me my hair is looking good, which probably means it's time for another haircut.

Mum also asked me what I think of Frank and Sig's business plan. Am I always the last person to know anything? I assumed at first that Dodgy Geoff must be involved in some way. Apparently not. Mum saw his granny in Safeway this week and Geoff has unexpectedly left the country. I'm not sure the reason why, but I bet it's dodgy.

Anton was there, of all people. He's just got back together with his wife, although neither of them looked particularly thrilled about it. They spent the evening accusing each other of being drunk and complaining about the cost of babysitters. She went off to flirt with Dom, who looked terrified, and I asked Anton how things were going. It probably wasn't the most tactful of questions. 'I look like I'm just standing here, but inside I'm screaming,' he informed me. I chose a tactful moment to slip off for another drink.

Anton asked me when my book is coming out. That's a very good question. I discovered on Friday that it isn't always just politeness when publishers express an interest in seeing what you write in the future. Selina forwarded me a letter from Graham Henderson at Burdock Books, who has specifically asked not to be shown anything else by me, ever. He writes that 'In twenty years in the book trade I can't remember ever receiving a manuscript submission that has inspired such strong responses in our readers. Unfortunately, these responses were overwhelmingly negative. In fact, we were wondering if the whole thing is some kind of spoof. If so, we consider it to be in bad taste.' To illustrate the kind of thing Burdock Books are looking for he sent us a copy of one of their recent successes, William Further's 'charming and enchanting' *Gaijin Blues*. Thanks for passing that on, Selina.

Frank and Sig were hovering by the wine, and told me about their business plan. They're setting up an internet travel company, *Frank and Sig's Extreme Adventures*. Frank gave me a flyer for it. I imagine Sig helped him with the lay-out and design, but I would guess that he came up with the slogan 'Extreme Adventures: Because You Only Live Once' himself. I expect he also wrote the spiel. We are assured that Frank Bletch's Extreme Travel offers not just a holiday but 'a personalised travel experience', customised by a profes-sional 'with years of experience in overseas adventure, and close links to some of Europe's most exclusive ski resorts'. I couldn't find any mention of the hotel manager in Bielefeld who tried to shoot him with a crossbow. I'm not quite sure of the wisdom of mentioning that Frank held the 'Val D'Isere Pissed on the Piste' trophy three years running.

I mentioned to Frank that there may be moral and legal is-sues relating the 'Further Afield' section of the brochure, which shows 'Madame Minh Trinh, the friendly English-speaking hostess of the Traveller's Happy Time Hostel in Kathmandu, which offers full internet access and choice of European and Local Breakfasts'. Or rather, Sig in a tasselled veil standing in front of Mum's *Views of Snowdonia* calendar in the kitchen at home. 'That's a temporary photo,' Frank clarified.

Sig went over to say hello to Anton, and I asked Frank when he's got all this together. Frank enquired whether Dom and I really thought he had been lying around scratching his balls for the past six months. I thought the most tactful thing to do would be not to answer that question.

Frank wanted to know if I was interested in signing up. I don't think I'm exactly the target demographic: 'If, like Frank Bletch, you walk it like you talk it ... If you don't mind going off-piste once in a while ... If you don't fear fear ... If you've signed the disclaimer below ... Then you're ready for an Extreme Adventure.' I like the way the brochure explains that 'we call it an adventure rather than a holiday, because this isn't your run-of-the-mill blue-run and après-ski Sunday School excursion ... This is an experience ... a journey ... a fantastic voyage ... a Frank and Sig Extreme Adventure.' I'd just assumed it was an attempt to get around Trading Standards. 'Travelling with Frank Bletch doesn't just expand your mind. It blows it!' He said it. Anya's already signed up for one.

I can only hope that travelling with Frank Bletch doesn't begin with him packing the client in a large box and sending them somewhere with insufficient postage. Which would certainly be one way for me to give Caroline and Rychard a surprise in a few weeks time.

Things got even weirder after that. I was rooting through the canapés when Karla came over for a chat.

Karla: *(big smile)* Hi.
Me: *(slightly smaller smile)* Hi.
Awkward pause.
Me: I don't suppose you would happen to know what this is?
Karla: It's a stuffed Jalapeno pepper. They're good. Try one.

This was a bit unnecessary for her to suggest, since I was already holding one and I was hardly going to chuck it out the window. I sensed that this wasn't really what Karla came over for. Boy was I right. As I was chewing and smiling in a puzzled way, she got to the point.

Karla: I've noticed that you and Dom don't talk about your father much.

261

I mumbled something about the pepper being delicious.

Karla: I think you both have a lot of anger inside you.

Me: No we don't. (I said this in rather a grouchier voice than I'd intended. I may be imagining it, but I'm fairly sure at this point she touched my arm.)

Me: Mmmm, that really is an interesting combination. There's cheese actually inside the pepper.

Karla: It's OK to be angry.

Me: I bet these take ages to make. I wonder who thought of it first.

Karla: It's such a cruel disease. How old were you when …

Me: *(irritably)* Who says I'm angry about anything? I was thirteen, I think.

Karla: It must have been hard.

No shit, Karla.

Karla: Did you feel abandoned? Do you feel that the experience scarred you and your brothers in some way? Did you feel under pressure to be a man? To bottle things up?

How best to answer that question? Let's put it this way: Dom's hobby as a teenager was watching things rot. Potatoes, bits of bread, once a pork chop. Which some might say is not exactly the liveliest or best-adjusted way to spend your time. Frank, let's be honest, is an open psychic wound to this day.

Me: I can't speak for Dom or Frank but I think I've turned out OK.

Karla: But without a male role model in your life, at that key impressionable age …

Let's not exaggerate. I always had Frank and Dodgy Geoff. Fortunately at that point Dom called Karla over to have her picture taken. Sig was investigating the spread.

Sig: What was all that about?

Me: I think Karla is trying to get to the bottom of why the Bletch brothers are such a bunch of freaks.

Sig: If she finds out, tell her to let me know. Did you mention the time you accidentally called your driving instructor Dad?

Me: Frank told you about that, did he?

Sig: Oh, he tells me everything. The thing I've always wanted to ask about is Dom's hobby ...

Me: Try these peppers, they've got stuff in.

I managed to avoid Karla for the rest of the night. Dom caught up with me in the gents and asked what we'd been talking about. This and that, I told him. 'She can be pretty direct, can't she?' She certainly can.

When I came out, Mum and Sig were standing together, watching Frank across the room. I have to admit Frank scrubs up pretty well. He'd combed his hair and was even wearing a suit. Nor did he appear to be extorting money from people with threats or be about to cause any kind of unseemly ruckus.

Mum: I can't tell you what a transformation there's been in Frank since you two started going out. He's like a different person. You must tell me how you've managed it.

Sig looked modest and a little bit cagy at the same time, which is a tough trick to pull off.

Sig: I'm afraid I can't do that, Mrs Bletch. It's kind of a personal secret. All I can tell you is that the first step was cutting down his dairy intake.

Personally I suspect Sig of slipping something into Frank's food. I suppose it could also be the power of love.

As they were talking, one of the professors from Dom's department sidled up and nudged me. 'I don't suppose you know who that handsome woman is? I haven't been able to take my eyes off her all night.' Dude, that's my mum.

Monday, 16th June. Dr Cumnor asked me what I was planning to do for the Open Day this Saturday. *This* Saturday? Christ. The headmaster's already got me booked to show some parents around in the morning. I've got a long list of things the tour should take in, and a slightly shorter list of things to avoid. I see Mercers' Lodge isn't mentioned among the attractions.

Caroline rang to say that her father has booked us all in at a restaurant on Saturday evening, and I said I'd do my best to make it on time. I also better get Lulu a present. Henry's taking us to his favourite restaurant in town, so Caroline thinks we should probably dress up. I find it hard to imagine what Henry's favourite restaurant could be. It could either be fine dining at the Athenaeum, or we could find ourselves trooping into an Angus Steak House.

Wherever it is, I hope Henry's paying. I gave Caroline a cheque yesterday for our dinner the other weekend and had to warn her not to cash it until she gets to Edinburgh. I presume they accept English cheques up there.

Tuesday, 17th June. I've just practised the recommended route for prospective parents, and I think I can get around the school in about fifteen minutes on Saturday, if no one stops to gawp or ask questions. I'm afraid if anyone shows up in a wheelchair we'll have to leave them behind. Then I'll sit through one video in the English department, possibly on fast forward, grab a croque monsieur at the Language Lab café, and be on my way.

There's also the problem of what to get Lulu as a present. I popped into Woolies but they don't find they have that much demand for ostrich-related birthday gifts. I did, however, manage to find a card with two ostriches on it with their heads in the ground. All I had to do was to Tippex out the caption

'Happy Birthday, you Loony Bird!', which could easily have been misinterpreted. But then if Lulu or anyone else has already seen the card, and they see that I've Tippexed out the message, they'll think I think she really is a loony. Which I do, but if everyone else is just going to politely ignore it, I will too. So what I need now is either a really snappy caption, or an excuse why I've Tippexed out the original one. The only caption I have thought of so far is one ostrich saying to the other: 'Are you sure this is how Emu got the job?' And I don't honestly think that's much of an improvement.

Still more evidence of Tipton Construction's lackadaisical approach to health and safety has come to light. We had a fire alarm test this morning that revealed the fire exits on the top floor of the new science block all have their push-bars on the outside.

Wednesday, 18th June. Barry Taylor confronted me today and told me again to stop discussing how he kisses. The latest version doing the rounds is that kissing Barry is like being sucked down a plughole tongue first.

I'm afraid the whole thing's out of my hands now. After all, I wasn't the one who chalked it on the lunch board. He hadn't seen that, and dashed off looking upset.

The Headmaster has asked Barry if he can borrow the Brimscombe diaries. He's planning to write a history of the school and reckons they'll be an invaluable resource. I suspect he's going to be pretty disappointed. Barry and I had to borrow a wheelbarrow from the Groundskeeper after school to trolley them over.

I seem to have managed to lose one volume, though: 1993. I suppose we'll be forever denied Brimscombe's thoughts on the election of Bill Clinton or the Russian Constitutional Crisis now. Or perhaps just more stuff about Brimscombe's walking holidays and toothcare regime.

*

Thursday, 19th June. Frank rang. He wanted to know whether I could think of a good motto for his business. I proposed something from Horace: *'Caelum non animum mutant qui'*? He said it sounded cool, I suspect mostly because it has the word 'mutant' in. I didn't tell Frank that it means 'They change their skies but not their minds.' I offered to translate, but he claimed to know already. I also felt compelled to tell him that the phrase 'Frank Bletch accepts no responsibility' in the Extreme Adventures disclaimer may not be legally valid.

Frank noted that we still haven't had a proper chance to sit down and work through our problems. He suggested we do it on Sunday afternoon. Perfect timing, Frank. We've had twenty-seven years to find a suitable opportunity for this, and he wants to do it the least convenient possible time I can imagine. Which is absolutely typical Frank, as I shall take great pains to point out to him.

Had a search through my room for 1993. Brimscombe's diary for the year, that is. I checked behind the radiator, and found some lost A-level coursework from 1988. No sign of the diary, though. I think I may have left it at Caroline's.

Friday, 20th June. As it turns out, Sunday will be a good time for my talk with Frank, since Caroline is having a farewell lunch with Sig, Anya and Hannah to which neither of the Bletch brothers are invited. I somehow can't imagine any of those three advising Caroline to turn down the job in Edinburgh to stay in London with me. I can see their point.

I've managed to get an outfit together for the restaurant tomorrow night, from various sources. I borrowed proper shoes from Tom Downing, a suit jacket from Barry Taylor, a bow tie from Johnno McPhee, and suit trousers from Lost Property. For cufflinks I'm using Dad's old pair. The overall effect of the ensemble is more Charlie Chaplin than James Bond, but it'll have to do. I'll change on the train – I'm going to be hard pushed to get to Covent Garden at six, since the Open

Day officially finishes at four. I've still got to get a present for Lulu. And think of a caption for her card. Oh, and somehow persuade Caroline not to leave.

Sunday, 22nd June. I did eventually make it to the restaurant yesterday. The school tour was conducted at a snail's pace, because people kept asking questions I didn't know the answers to about when the school was built, who carved the gargoyles, what the school colours signify, and so forth. One old bastard insisted that he had carved his name into one of the tables in the library and we all fanned out and looked for it. Eventually I pretended to see it, and pointed out a bit of woodworm damage. He tried reading it through about fifteen different pairs of glasses, but didn't seem convinced. I assumed at the time he was an Old Buxdonian, although I suppose he might have carved it last Open Day. The crumbly sod was slowing down the whole tour. I almost managed to lose him when we were looking around the New Building. I'm sure he would have found his way out eventually.

Out on the drive we passed Tom Downing, demonstrating one of the rowing machines. I shouldn't have drawn attention to myself by quipping, 'I think you need to take it out of neutral, Tom, or you won't get anywhere.' He leaped off and insisted I have a try, and while I was muttering something about a weak back, leaving it to the experts, and being in a hurry, he got the parents on the tour to start chanting 'Row! Row! Row!' One old bloke shouted 'Grab him and strap him on it,' through saliva-speckled lips, which I thought was going a touch far.

Downing saddled me up on the device and put the handles in my hands, then fiddled around with something on the side. 'You're making it easier for me, aren't you?' I asked, nervously eyeing the various hulking Sixth Formers who made up the demonstration team. 'Don't worry,' he assured me. 'It's only a five-minute erg. That's just a warm-up.'

The rest of the tour was curtailed, although the two parents who helped carry me at least got to see the school sanatorium. Matron was rather brusque. 'Keep your back straight,' she told me. Well I would have if I could have. 'Did Mr Downing not show you how to loosen up beforehand?' she demanded. No the bastard didn't. The remainder of my tour group seemed quite happy to go off and watch him effortlessly gliding back and forth, the rowing machine humming happily. He even waved at me as I hobbled over to the English department, my spine tinkling like a xylophone. I think it was Johnno McPhee shouting 'Esmerelda! Esmerelda!' at me from the rugby pitch.

I decided to skip the video and croque monsieur and just try to get to the train station. I'd already packed a change of clothes into a bag and Miranda saw me struggling up the drive and offered me a lift to the station. That was really very sweet of her. She even let me choose the music. This proved more difficult than expected. All she had in the box in the glove compartment were compilation tapes labelled things like 'Back to Goa 2' and 'Into the Valley of Dub'. She actually owns a compilation called 'Ambient Shit #4'. She also has *The Best of The Farm*. I thought for a ghastly moment I was going to have to put The Boo Radleys on.

Miranda tells me things are going well with Tom, although she did mention something about some rather peculiar pants he has a special attachment to.

I managed to catch the train, and got changed in some discomfort in one of the toilet cubicles. There was a terrifying moment when I found myself with both arms stuck awkwardly over my head and my shirt halfway on, and wondered whether I would manage to escape or if they'd have to feed me my dinner by rolling potatoes down my sleeves and pour my wine into my collar-hole. While I was worrying about that I should have been worrying about the automated door, rather than unlocking it with my arse. Fortunately, but painfully, I wriggled myself loose before I asphyxiated. In the process I managed to punch myself in my own chin and bite my tongue, but otherwise I emerged from the experience unscathed. Bloody idiot for thinking I'd be saving time by not undoing the buttons, really.

The rest of the operation went smoothly, except when I rested one shoe in the sink, having forgotten that the tap and soap dispenser both operate using motion detectors.

When I eventually got out, there was an eight-year-old girl waiting outside in tears and a small puddle. Her mum gave me a really nasty look. I decided they wouldn't be the best people to ask for help tying my shoelaces. By this point my back was really killing me, but as opening lines go, 'You're probably wondering why my shoe is dripping' isn't one of the most reassuring.

I missed the starters, but the Applebys had kindly ordered me a main, which turned out to be the smallest bird I have ever seen. Lulu took this opportunity to tell me a story she had been saving for me. She claims that when she was out looking at a potential ostrich field the other day, she saw 'a tiny little bird, with orange and black stripes'. How odd. Yes, she said, it was exactly the size of a bee. Around this time I started to wish I was still stuck in the train toilet. Could it in fact have been, I ventured, a bee? She reluctantly conceded that it might have been.

Henry had booked us into what must surely be the gloomiest restaurant in London, and between courses managed to nearly brain himself on a low-hanging stag's head on the way to the gents. I gave a very much truncated account of my adventures on the train, which got decent laughs but not very much sympathy. Henry enquired whether Caroline hadn't mentioned on the phone that the restaurant is really very casual. No, surprisingly, she hadn't. Otherwise I don't think I would have spent forty-five minutes brutalising myself in a small metal room, would I? And I wouldn't have punched myself in the chin and bitten my tongue. And, when it came to dessert and I tried to swallow the first spoonful of lemon sorbet, it wouldn't have felt like I had just taken a mouthful of citrus-flavoured broken glass.

Caroline said the whole episode was absurd. Well, I never claimed it wasn't. I did manage three-and-a-half minutes on the rowing machine, though. They stopped the clock at the point when I came off the seat and went sliding along the crossbar, cushioned only by myself.

Lulu seemed pleased with her present, and didn't mind that it wasn't wrapped. I hadn't really had much of a chance to look at it, and when I lurched into Waterstone's and demanded a book about ostriches for a birthday present, they not unnaturally directed me to the children's section. I wish I'd checked it more carefully, as the main scene involves a family of ostriches being torn apart by some lions. Lulu was a little upset. The cover does advise parents to exercise caution before giving it to more impressionable children, so I guess I should have run it past with Margery and Henry first.

I wrote the card on the train, and the caption is clearly the work of a man in the last stages of pain and desperation. One ostrich is saying to the other: 'I think we're wearing the same hat.' Lulu found that hilarious. I had to explain it to Toby for some time, which kind of took the freshness out of the joke. 'I see,' he said, finally and without any trace of a smile. Thank God at that point Lulu's gâteau arrived, because she was still worried about how two ostriches could talk to each other if their heads were underground, and how they could see each other's hats. That they could talk at all would, I think, be the most important issue to address.

Frank and I had our long-deferred serious conversation at lunchtime. Frank started the ball rolling: 'You know it's never easy being the oldest child ...' Essentially, Frank claims that he still remembers being the only kid in the family, a time when he was always the centre of attention, when he didn't have any responsibilities, and when he could gratify whatever intake/output desires flickered across his forebrain without any thought of the consequences. I avoided the obvious gag. According to Frank he has always at some level thought of me as a threat. I suspect Frank had been carefully coached in what to say by Sig, but this did at least confirm what I have long suspected. Although I'm not sure why I'm a threat, since of the two of us, I'm not the pummelling, girlfriend-stealing, bed-annexing one. He even admitted that once or twice he may have heard Dad refer to me as 'El Tigre', although he still maintains that Dad did it with a mocking tone in his voice.

By the time we'd worked everything through I had to dash for the train. I felt a lot better about things, and was glad we'd finally found the chance for a proper talk. Then Frank asked me whether I'd be interested in investing any of my savings in Frank and Sig's Extreme Adventures.

'Was all this just a hollow charade to get your hands on my money?'

'On your mummy?'

I said 'money'. I definitely said 'money'.

I spoke to Caroline this evening and she asked after my back. It's much better except when I'm sitting, lying or standing. I'm going to spend the evening immersed in a barrel of deep heat. After dinner last night we had a long walk along the river. It occurs to me that if Caroline is going to suddenly decide she loves me too much to go, or I'm going to declare that I'm chucking it all in and coming with her, we're both cutting it very fine indeed. For one thing there's only about twelve pages left in this journal.

Monday, 23rd June. Dom rang to ask me when he and I were going to work through our issues. Thank God he turned out to be joking.

I missed a lot of excitement here by skipping the end of the Open Day. Marcus Lau did a bunk, and managed to row halfway to Abingdon in one of the Lower School sculls. He was hotly pursued by the Kayaking Club, but managed to lose them just past Farmoor weir. They found the boat tied up outside a country pub and called the police, but he turned up safe and sound at home on Saturday night. He's back at Buxdon now, because his parents hadn't mentioned to him that they'd be away for the week. Tom Downing, who was meant to be keeping an eye on things, is in big trouble. The Headmaster is extremely angry, partly I suspect at the thought of all the money we could have raised if we'd arranged sponsorship for Marcus in advance.

I get the feeling Selina Cowl and I are really scraping the barrel now when it comes to publishers. She forwarded the following on to me this morning, from Merlin Quarrell at the Lyonesse Press: 'Dear Selina,' he writes. 'Thank you for sending us Matthew Bletch's *The Road is Narrow, The Deep North is Far, and Other Good Reasons Not to Follow in the Footsteps of Basho*. As you know we are keen to build on and diversify our reputation as one of the leading homes for Cornish-themed non-fiction.' So far so good, you might think.

He then goes on to write that they don't see how they would fit my work into their current list. He does have a point, which he goes on to spell out at length: 'Our "cash cow" publication over the next few months will be H.A. Symons' *An Invitation to Cornish Grammar, 15th edition*; but we also have a fascinating study of gay motifs in Arthurian Literature, Charles Peake's *From Ralph's Cupboard to Tregagle's Hole,* coming out in August. In fiction, we are proud to be publishing T.U. Trewhalla's *The Lady of Zennor*, the second volume of his "alternative historical" series *The Chronicles of the Last Wolf*. Further afield, our autumn publications also include Lady Maureen Wist's *County Families of Devon: A Geneology*

1500–1756 and Fred Halpin's *Screaming Skulls of South West England: A Visitor's Companion.*'

He expresses an interest in anything I write in the future, particularly if it's about Cornwall or the South West more generally. Maybe it's my titles that are putting people off. Or, let's face it, maybe it's the book itself.

My back is still agony. I shifted around carefully for hours last night trying to find a comfortable position, eventually concluding that there wasn't one. I had to get up at one point to open the window, because I was worried about gassing myself to death with Deep Heat fumes. Matters weren't helped by having to lug back on the train a big box of my stuff that Caroline doesn't feel the need to take to Edinburgh with her. I wonder if she'll be more or less likely to stay when I tell her I may never stand up fully straight again.

Tuesday, 24th June. I'm slowly beginning to recover from my ordeal by ergo, although I don't remember my arms being this long before. Perhaps it's just that my body has been compressed. My legs seem a lot bandier than usual as well. Tom Downing has been removed from Rowing Club duties until the end of term. Unfortunately this has given him a lot more spare time to spend mooning about in the staffroom with Miranda. Talk about the sublime and the ridiculous. Downing's mostly in trouble for losing a boy and a boat, but letting a seventy-year-old man have a go on the rowing machine wasn't one of his better plans either.

I found the missing Brimscombe diary in the box of my things Caroline gave me at the weekend. At the moment he can't decide whether to spend Easter with his sister again, or to stay at school and catch up with some marking. It's certainly a cliffhanger.

I mentioned to Caroline that it's the Buxdon June Ball this Saturday, and that she's very much invited. Frustratingly this turns out to be compulsory for the staff. She doesn't think she's going to be able to make it. Rychard's driving down on Sunday to give her a lift. That's kind of him. The wanker. The stuff that doesn't fit in the car she's getting Sig and Frank to send on. I advised her to leave sufficient postage behind, and to make sure Sig oversees the operation.

Music at the Ball will be provided by reunited old boys Equinox, who promise to provide 'progressive jazz rock' as purveyed by a group of middle-aged investment brokers. The Billy Green Preservation Society are presumably otherwise engaged. Mercifully after dinner there's a disco. If that's no good there's always Hammers. I can see why Caroline might want to give it a miss. I know I do. I think my chances of persuading Caroline to stay are presently oscillating between none and ludicrously slight. I've been looking up flights to Edinburgh and I can probably get up there the weekend after next.

Wednesday, 25th June. Woke up to find that the whole of the Old Building has been cordoned off. Health and Safety people were going in and out in chemical-proof clothing and all my lessons for the day are cancelled.

The headmaster's in a fine old mood. No one seems to know what's going on with the inspectors. They were meant to come in and check the roof for pigeons, but I doubt that's why they've sealed the area. Unless they found some seriously scary pigeons.

I spoke to Mum and asked her if I could move home for the summer. I'm trying hard not to see that as a defeat. My room will be free, since Frank is moving in with Sig as soon as he gets back from overseeing the first Extreme Adventures holiday. Mum wasn't discouraging about it, but I did get the impression she'd been looking forward to having the house to herself for a bit. Frank and Sig fly out to Budapest tonight.

I discussed with Caroline when would be the best time to call and meet up once she's settled in Edinburgh. She says we'll have to see how it works out, because 'we're both starting new lives and we'll be meeting lots of new people'. Yes, and what's exciting is that we'll be going through that process together. Or at least at the same time.

Thursday, 26th June. The plot thickens. The Old Building is still sealed off, so I spent the morning finishing off Brimscombe's diary. Which sheds light on a few things. No wonder the Head was keen to get his hands on these. In his entry for 19 October 1993 Brimscombe records that:

> Mr Tipton and his team examined the Old Building attics today, and confirmed that the substance found is indeed asbestos. After discussion with the headmaster and myself, it was decided to seal the attic until further notice. The headmaster promised me that further action will be taken on this matter once funds become available.

I saw Mr Tipton arriving for a meeting with the Headmaster earlier, and he's just left, looking most unhappy. I'm glad that's cleared that mystery up, although I had quite been looking forward to the June Ball being disrupted by an attack of giant killer pigeons.

I went through the rest of the box of stuff Caroline returned to me and found the diary I gave her for Christmas. She hasn't written in it once. She's also given me my sample chapters back. And my Captain's hat.

Friday, 27th June. The headmaster called us all in for a meeting first thing and explained that the Old Building will be out of bounds until further notice, due to 'extensive restructuring work'. If any gentlemen of the press come around asking questions we have been instructed not to say anything. Because of the specialist nature of the work involved, Tipton Construction will not be overseeing the project. The headmaster couldn't predict the size of the budget involved, but he could confirm that the Auditorium and Drama Lab project will be on hold for the foreseeable future. As a result, for the present Mercer's Lodge is saved. All teachers who wish to remain there over the summer should talk to Mrs O. Digby. So the good news is that I don't have to move back home next week. I expect Mum will be relieved too. It's amazing what small mercies are starting to look like triumphs. If I'd made up a list of my goals for this year I wouldn't have even thought to put 'Not be homeless.'

After lunch I supervised the last exam of the year, the Cambridge STEP paper. Iles handed it in after an hour and then announced he was off to Glastonbury. 'Bet you're glad to be getting out of this place, Sir. I know I am.' I've got the strong suspicion that Iles is going to be one of those people who go through life compensating for having gone to public school by pre-emptively telling you how much they hated it. Yeah mate, the whole system's unfair and exclusive and you didn't get to meet enough girls when you were a teenager. I should have asked him to take some flyers for Frank and Sig's Extreme Adventures.

Saturday, 28th June. Barry Taylor dragged me down to The Albion yesterday afternoon to sample their new range of summer ciders, which was a bad idea. As we walked in we ignored the catcalls and hoots from various people who recognised us from the pub quiz.

After we'd worked through the various ciders on offer at the bar, the landlord offered us his special scrumpy. This usually lives in a back room in a large plastic drum with withered apples still bobbing in it. He warned us to 'look out for wasps when you're drinking that'. I thought he meant it attracted wasps, until he flicked a floating one out of Barry's glass. That's how you tell it's good scrumpy, he claimed. I somehow doubt that that's the method that EU inspectors use.

Barry observed that tonight is his last chance of the year to get together with Lucy Salmon. You just don't get it, do you? She doesn't fancy you. Accept it. She's not interested. Lucy Salmon is never going to go out with Barry Taylor. That's a fact. Barry asked if I was saying he should play harder to get. I'm saying he should give up. Forget it. She's never going to snog him again, I'm never going to get my book published, Caroline is going to go out with Rychard, we're all going to do jobs we don't really like for the rest of our lives, and then we're going to die. Probably of alcoholism; possibly just of boredom and slow decay. That's life. Barry reckons Lucy might be won over when she sees him in evening dress.

I spoke to Caroline briefly today. She says we need to have a proper talk once she's arrived about when we'll next be seeing each other. I mentioned I was thinking about next weekend but she sounded ambivalent. She's going through her suitcase now to make sure she's taking everything she'll need.

Sunday, 29th June. Of all the ways I imagined spending my final Saturday night of the Buxdon school year, I didn't think it would be cutting some rug with Mrs Tipton while a sweating man in a jaunty cummerbund played slap bass. I don't have that many prog-jazz-rock moves, so I sort of swayed and clicked my fingers while being frugged at by Mrs Tipton. Interesting style of dancing she has. It's like watching the latter-day Stevie Nicks trying to disentangle herself from some Laura Ashley curtains.

It was pretty bold of the Tiptons to show up at all, considering the circumstances. Tipton Construction is being investigated for several building projects that have failed to meet safety standards, as well as for some highly suspicious accounting. The Tiptons were sitting on the headmaster's table, and he looked exquisitely uncomfortable all night. During the main course I thought he was going to take the honourable way out and fall on his fish knife.

Equinox had managed to get all their original members together, with the exception of the keyboard player. Apparently he isn't in the midst of a vast public midlife crisis yet. Instead, they'd dragged up someone's son to vamp his way through a particularly painful 'calypso' version of 'Smoke on the Water'. He didn't much look like he wanted to be there, and I could certainly sympathise. I think they'd stapled him to his stool. 'Who's got the funk?' the guitarist asked at one point. It sounded like a genuine question. They ended by doing 'Rock the Casbah', except they changed the word 'Casbah' to 'Marquee'...

I discovered there's another Tipton starting at Buxdon in September. This one just aced the Scholarship exam, allegedly, so I imagine Mrs Frattini will be airing out the guest bedroom at the villa before too long. Sam Tipton still isn't sure whether he's going to spend his gap year portering at Sotheby's or waitering at Brown's, so I suggested an Extreme Adventure and gave them the web address. 'It would be good for Sam to try something unpredictable,' Mrs Tipton said. I can certainly guarantee that.

After Equinox and the dinner, the disco came as a very welcome relief. Even the least appropriate choice of music ever didn't dampen the mood: Pulp's 'Common People', followed with 'Eton Rifles' by The Jam. The sight of Mr Tipton pogoing was pretty memorable. He sat down for a bit after that. I can't recall if we ever found his shoe. Someone went up and had a word with the DJ after that, and he started taking requests. What is it with these people and Reggae? I wonder if Bob Marley sat back after a hard day's recording and thought to himself, 'Someday this song is really going to speak to some posh English cats.' Both Mrs Tipton and Barry Taylor are under the impression that 'Redemption Song' includes the lines 'Pirates oh they row by,' perhaps describing an exciting incident at Henley Regatta.

Miranda brought Tom Downing over to apologise for the rowing-machine incident. They're planning a holiday together this summer, and I heartily recommended an Extreme Adventure. I still can't work out what Miranda sees in that bloke. It's certainly not his dancing. He looked like someone trying to do the Safety Dance on a bouncy castle.

Lucy and I sat out the next couple of songs on the lawn, in order to let the Buxdon wine and ostrich steak settle. The ostrich was surprisingly nice. It tasted like chicken. Lucy was having about as good a time as me. She'd had stern words with Miranda, who was in charge of booking the entertainment. There was a last minute change of plan, because one of the Fat Cats' Blues Band had suffered a coronary.

After a while Barry came out to find us, and made it quite clear that my presence wasn't necessary. I located Mrs O. Digby swaying with her husband to 'Lady in Red'. I waited for them to finish then went over to say hello and ask a question that has been tormenting me all year: what the 'O' in O. Digby stands for. It's a doozy. I'm not surprised she just uses the initial. She made me promise not to tell anyone, and it's a promise I intend to keep.

I went back out to tell Barry and Lucy, but they'd disappeared. As the last people were clearing out, Mr Tipton demonstrated that he still hasn't learned to do the tablecloth trick.

Barry and Lucy reappeared, arm in arm, at the after-party at Mercer's Lodge. We all went out on the lawn to watch the speed cameras catch the last of the leaving parents, and we stayed there until the sun started coming up over the bulldozers. Barry remembered something he'd brought me from home, and went back to his room to fetch it.

Me: What made you change your mind, after all that?
Lucy: About what?

Me: About Barry ...

Lucy: What makes you think I've changed my mind? The thing is, Matt, I'm drunk.

Me: So do you think when you sober up you guys are going to give it a chance?

Lucy: Give me one good reason for thinking that it would work out.

Me: ...

Lucy: I have to admit his kissing has improved a little.

When Barry reappeared he was carrying a tape-deck which he plugged in to the socket in the kitchen and propped in the window. I have confirmed one thing to my own satisfaction if still not to Barry's: 'You Don't Pull No Punches, But You Don't Push The River' by Van Morrison is definitely not about walloping a carp. God only knows what it is about, though

So, Caroline's gone. The falcon hath borne my maid away.

Monday, 30th June. Caroline doesn't think I should come up to see her this weekend. 'It might be a bit weird for Rychard.' Yes, Caroline, that's precisely the point.

It slowly dawned on me, as we were talking, that Caroline didn't seem keen for me to come up any weekend in the near future. I asked her if this was in fact the case. She conceded that it was, and then added that she thinks we should also talk less on the phone. We're both starting a new chapter in our lives and for the moment perhaps we should focus on the future rather than the past. One day in Edinburgh and Rychard's already worked his insidious magic. Actually, Caroline says this is something she's been thinking about for a while. You'd think she'd have given me some kind of hint or clue.

I pointed out that all this sounds almost as if we're breaking up. Caroline wanted it put on record that she wasn't the one who first suggested that. I'm not suggesting anything, I insisted. 'Yes, but since you've raised it,' Caroline said, 'maybe it would be better if we do have a break.' I didn't mean that, I countered. I didn't even imply it. I was just observing that it's not going to be much of a relationship if we don't see each other and we don't talk. 'Then perhaps we should call it a day.' At this point I tried desperately to rewind the conversation, and said I'd be very happy in a relationship that consisted mainly of occasional letters and text messages. 'That wouldn't be fair on you,' she told me. What a perfect end to the year. I think I've somehow just managed to break up with myself.

I apologised to Caroline; she said I had nothing to apologise for. I apologised for apologising. She started crying because I was apologising. I started apologising because she was crying. I told her I want my dog tape back, she told me she had to go because Rychard was making lunch. I told her I'd ring her back to talk about it some more later, and she said she was going to be out. We're going to speak later in the week. So now we're still talking on the phone, but we're no longer going out. I suppose that's a compromise inasmuch as it's not what either of us wanted. The great news is that we'll always be friends. Another awkward friendship being exactly what I need in my life. Although now we've broken up, it's cool if I come up to Edinburgh one weekend.

Not having anything better to do, and sitting in your bedroom throwing playing cards into a hat being much less fun than the movies make it look, I went over to the staffroom to pick up my post. On the way I passed Lucy Salmon and Barry Taylor holding hands. They quickly separated when they saw me. So at last they've got together. I suppose that's some kind of happy ending. 'You see?' Barry crowed. 'I told you sometimes life works out the way you want.' I didn't get Lucy's thoughts on the matter.

There were six letters waiting for me. The first was a very nice letter from Marcus Lau, thanking me for teaching him, saying how much I'd done to help him settle in, and asking once and for all whether Nelly Dean is a reliable narrator.

There was also rather a sweet letter from Ellis, attached to a wrapped-up bottle. He just wanted to let me know how much he has enjoyed the class and how he will never forget my lessons. And he can be sure I'll never forget him. I made a valiant effort to picture his face, but it's still something of a blur. The bottle turned out to be Buxdon white.

The third letter was from someone at Padfoot Press, saying that they like the book and want to publish it. I was going to ring Caroline and tell her, then remembered.

The other three letters were all requests for references.

As I was heading back to Mercer's Lodge, I ran into the headmaster.

'So Matthew, you'll be leaving us next term.'

I confirmed this, and assured him that it has been a year I shall long remember and treasure.

'I'm glad I've caught you, because I wanted to talk to you about your living arrangements over the next few months. Obviously we'd love to have you here, but since you're strictly speaking no longer a member of staff, I'm afraid ...'

He seemed so sincere, saying this, that he almost managed to persuade at least one of us that his regret was genuine. As opposed to his final fussily bureaucratic poke at someone soon to be moving outside his reach for ever.

'Well, I'm glad I've caught you too, Headmaster. The thing is I've finally managed to track down that missing Brimscombe diary.'

I've read before about people blanching, but I'd never seen the phenomenon in action.

'I see. Interesting?'

'Very interesting, Ed. If you like I'd be happy to pass it on to you when I've finished with it. Perhaps at the end of the summer?'

He thinks we may be able to come to some arrangement

about accommodation. Indeed, I may be in line for an upgrade. I'll be sure to leave a note for my successor.

There's something I've been wondering all year, and I finally got around to asking about it. The headmaster looked at me for a long time before intoning his reply:

'One thing in life is certain, Mr Bletch. If you have to ask what *it* is, then you may be sure that you do not possess it.'

Thank God for that.

July

Hi Matt, it's Caroline.

Well, here I am. If you're still reading this, how are you? I haven't heard from you for a while, so I hope all is well. I guess Sig or Frank have probably told you that I've moved out of Rychard's flat. It got a bit intense living with Rychard and working with him. I also came to the realisation in the end that he's an utter prat. I know, I can't say I wasn't warned.

He's a much queerer fish than he initially appears. I had sort of assumed that he would annoy me in certain ways, for example by being a bit of a slimy Sloaney fool. I had also braced myself to put up with him having a crowd of awful mates. Actually, Rychard doesn't have awful friends. Or any friends at all, from what I can gather. He isn't even called Rychard. It's his middle name, and his real name is Tony. The fact that he swapped them around when he went to uni tells you quite a lot.

Matters came to a head over the cooking arrangements. It was nice of him to put me up and all, but ... Rychard's the most passive-aggressive cook I've ever encountered. You're trying to cook something, and he drifts through the kitchen, looks over your shoulder, and makes suggestions. Suggestions in the form of casual questions. He asks you things like, 'Oh, you're not peeling those first?' and 'Are you going to add all that salt?' and 'I've got some courgettes that would go brilliantly with that. Would you like me to get them out?' Then, without asking, he turns the hob up or down. It's very, very creepy. And then he sits and watches you eat it, and asks whether those courgettes weren't a good idea, or tells you how

284

he would have made that salad. He reminisces about great meals he has made for people in the past, especially girlfriends. Which is like boasting about your sex life, except weirder. I suspect that this is a taster of what he would actually be like in bed, and made me very much more determined never to find out.

Also, no one needs to wear that much aftershave.

I moved a week ago, and Rychard's already invited me back for dinner twice. I'm living with Fran from production now, and I can't tell you what a relief it's been that neither of us have been tempted to enter the kitchen once. We've got enough silver trays in the living room to build a Cyberman.

I've been thinking about you a lot recently, often with affection. I even started wondering about what it would have been like if we had ended up living together, although Christ knows you have some pretty annoying habits too. As do we all, I suppose. But taking a book to read on the loo is very weird. Weird and unhygienic. And writing your diary in there is just bizarre. Yes, your *diary*. I've never understood why you insist on calling it a 'journal'.

Let's be honest, Matt, I regard you with tremendous fondness but you are one hell of an oddbod. I don't mean that as a dig. A case in point: Why did you never invite me to stay at your mum's? I took you to meet my parents loads of times, and for goodness' sakes they're embarrassing enough. We won't even get into the way you have always taken a mildly prurient interest in Lulu. But you never once invited me down to yours. Even at Christmas when Dom took his girlfriend. I even asked Frank about it on New Year's Eve, and he said you were probably afraid that he would steal me off you. Is that true? Or were you just concerned that if I was there for Christmas there would be fewer satsumas to go around? I could have brought some, you know.

Some other stuff, just to get it off my chest. What kind of person hates The Beatles and reggae? Why do you always sniff the spines of books? What do you think you're going to find, a truffle? Have you noticed that you never, ever, like the place that you're living in? You hated Japan when you were living there, you made it perfectly clear that you despise London, and you certainly weren't a big fan of Buxdon. In fact, you don't seem to like anything. You don't even seem to like your friends much. And if you do like them why do you spend so much time scribbling mean nonsense about them? In your *diary*. Above all, why do you have such a problem with emotion? It's as if by constantly writing and talking about things you can escape from ever having to properly confront them. I don't mean to be hurtful, Matt, but sometimes going out with you is like dating a tin of Alphabetti Spaghetti. No offence. Not that there's even any point telling you all this, since all you'll do with it is put it in a book someday.

I'm sorry, I didn't mean to write a long, complainy letter. I come across in your diary as a right moaning Minnie, and I don't think that's quite fair. Yes, I read your diary. And goodness knows you've tried to read mine enough times. Did you really think I was going to fall for that Christmas present trick? The question is what you really wanted to find there. It's not like I'm the astonishingly secretive one out of the pair of us. If you don't actually like pheasant, I'm sure my parents wouldn't have been so terribly upset. I can't believe you'd lie about your height, though. Did you really think you'd get away with it?

Frank and Sig tell me you've got a book deal. That's excellent news, congratulations. As you know I'm not the biggest fan of travel writing, but I am genuinely pleased for you. Most people realise quite quickly that no one cares that much about what you did on a gap year. And as for all those smug little photos of the author up a mountain with some tribes people, or dressed as a Bedouin ... But yours was OK. I particularly like the way that, whereas most travel books emphasise the mind-broadening effects of being away from

home, yours seems designed to illustrate the exact opposite.
I hope that was intentional. Just a hint, but at some point it
might be worth trying to write about a subject other than stuff
that's just happened to you. Although I notice it doesn't have a
dedication yet.

I think that's more or less all I wanted to say. I don't want to
get into another long discussion of our sex life. And I think you
place an undue importance on the whole thing in your diary. I
didn't go on about the time you fell out of bed and landed on
your own erection. Even though I was the one who had to ring
NHS Direct. But generally things were usually OK. Although
you may not want that recommendation added to the bottom
of you CV. Everyone's different, and there may be people
who are really into your acutely self-conscious love-making
technique. I suppose in some ways it's quite flattering to be
constantly asked if things are all right. Generally, if you have
to ask if someone is having a good time ... Anyway, it's not
the be-all and end-all, is it? For future reference, though, I will
add this suggestion: it's really not necessary to say 'Thank you
very much' afterwards. To tell the truth, it comes across as a bit
strange. Right, that's it: I've put it out there and I'm just going
to leave it hanging.

This has turned into a very long letter, so I'll leave it there.
It looks like I'll be in Edinburgh for another eighteen months
or so, but I'll probably be down south for Christmas, if you're
around. It would be nice to catch up if you are. I'll meet you at
the corner of Round Pond.

Take good care of yourself. I'm not going to write 'love'.

Fond regards,
Caroline

Epilogue

Ten Years On...

Barry Taylor and **Lucy Salmon** were married in Buxdon Chapel in 1999. **Miranda Bell** did not attend the ceremony.

Having graduated from Oxford with a 2:2 in Classics and Ancient History, **Bagley** currently works full-time at the Little Chipping Riding School. His graduation thesis examined the cavalry tactics of the Roman civil wars and received special commendation from his examiners.

Billy Green last appeared on UK television in 2002, on a pop music quiz show in which a panel of celebrities were asked to pick the real Billy Green out of a line-up of five people. They failed to do so. He is currently playing live and working on new material.

The remainder of the Billy Green Preservation Society reunited without Billy for a one-off gig at the London Astoria in 2006. It surprised promoters and critics by selling out in record time. They are now touring with Echobelly and Thurman.

Caroline Appleby spent two years in Edinburgh, before being promoted to a position in London. She began dating **Morgan Hartley** in 2000. She was surprised to learn that he had been in love with her since they were children, and had sent her a Valentine's Card every year since 1989.

Since 2005 **Chivers** has been living as a woman.

Dodgy Geoff qualified as a teacher in 1999.

Dominic Bletch and **Karla** were married in Massachusetts in 2000. Matt and Frank discovered accidentally at the wedding that there had been a stag party to which neither were invited. Dom and Karla moved to the United States permanently in 2002, where both lecture at UCSD.

Dom's *Masculinity in Crisis/Crisis in Masculinity* has established itself as a minor classic in the field of Masculinity Studies. In 2004 Dom received a letter from a prospective graduate student asking if he would be prepared to supervise a PhD on the career of his brother Frank Bletch in its cultural and sociological context. He refused.

In 2003 Karla received a Fulbright grant of $280,000 to head a research team investigating elements of post-traumatic stress disorder in former pupils of British public schools.

Edmund Josephus Perse MA (Oxon) retired in 2001, to work on a history of Buxdon School, from its origins as a charity school for poor scholars of the parish to the present day. He is an active figure in the Old Buxdonian Society.

Edmund Trotter, now ten, is looking forward to starting at Buxdon in the autumn. Both his parents still teach at the School.

Ellis has not returned to visit Buxdon since leaving, nor does the O.B. society have his current address. He lives in Fulham with his partner.

Frank Bletch and **Sig** married on a beach in Goa in 1998. In the same year they sold their shares in Extreme Adventures to a major travel company. They own a large house in Strawberry

Hills, Jamaica, and spend six months of each year travelling. Their joint show, 'How to be an Extreme Traveller', received mixed reviews at the 2006 Edinburgh Festival.

Hallbrick writes for the *Guardian*.

Hannah and **Toby** married in 1998. Their first child, Horatio, was born later that year. They have a house outside Winchester, and Hannah works three days a week in a local art gallery. In 2007 Toby was posted to Basra.

Henry and Margery Appleby still live in the country. Henry has for several years been a key figure in the Countryside Alliance. He appeared on the Channel 4 News in 2004 after being truncheoned during a peaceful demonstration. His letters on a range of subjects have been published in the *Daily Telegraph* and *The Times*. He is currently involved in litigation with the Ramblers' Association.

Iles was named as one of 2004's most promising poets under thirty in *The Times*. His work has appeared in various small journals (*Equinox, the small journal, Take This* and *Dissentia*), and he is currently completing his first full-length collection. He decided not to reapply to Oxbridge in the end and attended Bristol University from 1998-2001, where he had a bloody good time and came out with a First.

Johnno McPhee was bitten by an orangutan on an Extreme Adventures holiday in Borneo in 2003. He has since appeared in programmes about animal attacks on Channel Five and is a well-known spokesperson on conservation issues in his native New Zealand.

Kevin Williams received the OBE in 2002. He is working on a children's opera.

The **Lionel Brimscombe Memorial Library** (formerly Buxdon School Library) was completed in 1998, with the considerable financial aid from the Tipton family.

Lucy Salmon continues to teach at Buxdon. She became housemistress of Salmon's Boarding House last year.

Lulu Appleby is one of the South East's most prominent producers of organic ostrich meat. Her farms have won several awards, and she is frequently asked to appear on Radio 4 to discuss agricultural issues. She is currently negotiating an exclusive contract with a supermarket chain. Her recipes have appeared in *Country Living*, *Sainsbury's Magazine* and *Vogue*.

Marcus Lau is now a property developer based in Hong Kong. He currently owns property in Kowloon Bay, Victoria Peak, and on the mainland. His son, Matthew Lau, was born in 2006. Despite spending part of the year at his house in Wimbledon, Marcus has no plans to send his son to Buxdon.

Matthew Bletch is in a relationship. His book, eventually titled *The Wandering Barbarian*, was published by the Padfoot Press in 1998. Against his better instincts, he agreed to appear in a kimono on the cover.

Matt taught at Lady Jane Grey Grammar School for Girls until the summer of 2006. He is currently working on a range of projects, including an account of his adventures in Japanese television and a radio drama about teaching in a public school.

Matt's **Aunt Maureen** and **Uncle Jeremy** are undergoing a trial separation. Maureen claims to feel happier than she has for decades. **Uncle Jeremy** is making great strides with his cooking and housekeeping, and is considering losing the moustache.

Miranda Bell and **Tom Downing** dated for a year before breaking up acrimoniously on Open Day 1998. Downing still teaches at Buxdon, and coached the First VIII to their victory at Henley in 1999.

Since 2004 **Monk** has been teaching in the Physics Department of Buxdon School. His nosebleeds have considerably improved. In September 2006 he, Lucy Salmon and Barry Taylor were victorious in The Albion pub quiz. They won £17 and a bottle of Albanian red.

Morgan Hartley and **Caroline Appleby** were married in 2004. A painful ear infection the following year led to Morgan's discovery that for many years he had been operating at a lower-than-usual level of hearing capacity. He has since been fitted with grommets.

The best man at the wedding was **Peveril House**.

Norrington is a highly successful IT consultant. He is also a key figure in the O.B. Society, and has over 400 friends on Facebook.

Roland Rawlinson and Lulu were married in 1999. Roland proposed on a cycling holiday in the Netherlands.

In 2005 **Rychard** left his job and put his savings into setting up a restaurant in a remote corner of Devon. Despite the failure of the restaurant, the success of the reality TV series based on his experiment and sales of the accompanying book have kept him from bankruptcy. He is currently in negotiations for a second series, set in the South of France

Since his father's retirement in 2005, **Sam Tipton** has been MD of Tipton Enterprises. The firm continues to flourish, and in 2006 Sam Tipton was cleared by a jury of his peers from all involvement in a nasty case of bid-rigging involving the shareholders of a rival firm receiving some disgusting but biodegradable material in the post.

Sig returned to and completed her PhD in 1999, as a part-time student at the University of the West Indies. **Anton** acted as her external examiner.

Tibet is still not free. To protest and learn more, please visit www.freetibet.org.

Tink Weevil was a bridesmaid at Caroline's wedding, which is where she first met Matthew Bletch. They have been dating for six months. Caroline approves of the relationship, although she did take Tink aside early on and give her various pieces of advice that have since proved extremely helpful. Tink has not yet met either of Matt's brothers, but they will both be in England for Christmas, and she has been invited to join the Bletches for the celebration.

Will Otway is a presenter on E4.